BETWEEN TWO FIRES

Historical Fiction Published by McBooks Press

BY ALEXANDER KENT
Midshipman Bolitho
Stand into Danger
In Gallant Company
Sloop of War
To Glory We Steer
Command a King's Ship
Passage to Mutiny
With All Despatch
Form Line of Battle!
Enemy in Sight!
The Flag Captain
Signal–Close Action!
The Inshore Squadron
A Tradition of Victory
Success to the Brave
Colours Aloft!
Honour this Day
The Only Victor
Beyond the Reef
The Darkening Sea
For My Country's Freedom
Cross of St George
Sword of Honour
Second to None
Relentless Pursuit

BY DUDLEY POPE
Ramage
Ramage & The Drumbeat
Ramage & The Freebooters
Governor Ramage R.N.
Ramage's Prize
Ramage & The Guillotine
Ramage's Diamond
Ramage's Mutiny
Ramage & The Rebels
The Ramage Touch
Ramage's Signal
Ramage & The Renegades
Ramage's Devil
Ramage's Trial
Ramage's Challenge
Ramage at Trafalgar
Ramage & The Saracens
Ramage & The Dido

BY DAVID DONACHIE
The Devil's Own Luck
The Dying Trade
A Hanging Matter
An Element of Chance
The Scent of Betrayal
A Game of Bones

BY DEWEY LAMBDIN
The French Admiral
Jester's Fortune

BY DOUGLAS REEMAN
Badge of Glory
First to Land
The Horizon
Dust on the Sea

BY V.A. STUART
Victors and Lords
The Sepoy Mutiny
Massacre at Cawnpore
The Cannons of Lucknow
The Heroic Garrison

BY C. NORTHCOTE PARKINSON
The Guernseyman
Devil to Pay
The Fireship
Touch and Go

BY CAPTAIN FREDERICK MARRYAT
Frank Mildmay OR *The Naval Officer*
The King's Own
Mr Midshipman Easy
Newton Forster OR
The Merchant Service
Snarleyyow OR *The Dog Fiend*
The Privateersman
The Phantom Ship

BY JAN NEEDLE
A Fine Boy for Killing
The Wicked Trade

BY IRV C. ROGERS
Motoo Eetee

BY NICHOLAS NICASTRO
The Eighteenth Captain
Between Two Fires

BY W. CLARK RUSSELL
Wreck of the Grosvenor
Yarn of Old Harbour Town

BY RAFAEL SABATINI
Captain Blood

BY MICHAEL SCOTT
Tom Cringle's Log

BY A.D. HOWDEN SMITH
Porto Bello Gold

BY R.F. DELDERFIELD
Too Few for Drums
Seven Men of Gascony

BETWEEN TWO FIRES

NICHOLAS NICASTRO

THE JOHN PAUL JONES TRILOGY
2

MCBOOKS PRESS
ITHACA, NEW YORK

Cover painting: *Engagement Between the "Bonhomme Richard" and
the "Serapis" off Flamborough Head, 1779,* by Richard Willis.
Courtesy of The Bridgeman Art Library
Sketchbook illustrations by William M. Benson

Library of Congress Cataloging-in-Publication Data

Nicastro, Nicholas.
   Between two fires / by Nicholas Nicastro.
      p. cm. — (The John Paul Jones trilogy ; v. 2)
   ISBN 1-59013-033-2 (alk. paper)
   1. Jones, John Paul, 1747-1792--Fiction. 2. United
States—History—Revolution, 1775-1783—Naval operations—
Fiction. 3.Admirals—Fiction. I. Title.
   PS3564.I193 B48 2002
   813'.54—dc21
                                        2002010211

Distributed to the trade by National Book Network, Inc.,
15200 NBN Way, Blue Ridge Summit, PA 17214
800-462-6420

Additional copies of this book may be ordered from any
bookstore or directly from McBooks Press, Inc., ID Booth
Building, 520 North Meadow St., Ithaca, NY 14850.
Please include $4.00 postage and handling with mail orders.
New York State residents must add sales tax. All McBooks Press
publications can also be ordered by calling toll-free
1-888-BOOKS11 (1-888-266-5711).

Please call to request a free catalog.

Visit the McBooks Press website at www.mcbooks.com.

Printed in the United States of America

10 9 8 7 6 5 4 3 2 1

This book is dedicated to

my mother and father,

to whom I owe so much.

I.

THE COMPANY lay napping on the shore in parti-colored heaps of taffeta, muslin, and silk. Around them, the carcasses of Muscovy ducks and larded turkeys were similarly heaped on silver picnic services. The bones, like the mouths of the smeared, sleeping picnickers, were still dressed with remnants of braised onion and spinach and croutons. Neither heap moved much under the early August sun. Only the odd protuberant belly rose and fell in a slow, indolent rhythm.

Meanwhile, out on the water, two vessels closed on one another. The first was commanded by the ninth Comte de la Rochejaquelein, future lord of the Loire estate of the eighth Comte, Minister of Royal Fishponds and Warden of Lepidoptery. A boy most resplendent in his gilded and piped admiral's uniform, he waved a tasseled sword above his head, shouting insults at his opponent in whatever English words came to him.

"You cellar of salt! Feckless puppy! Son of a mountainous continent! Come now to taste my metal!"

His opponent was the American captain, John Paul Jones, late of the storied action against HMS *Drake* near Belfast, now plowing a deep furrow in the water as he calmly directed his vessel athwart the comte's. Already he had gained the positional advantage, coming about on the other's bow as its crew struggled helplessly to turn their broadside toward the enemy. Jones, sensing a rout, did his opponent the courtesy of offering quarter.

"You have fought most well, Mister Count, and have done your king's navy much credit. But may I prevail upon you now to forego the needless suffering of yourself and your crew?"

The boy spat in the water and fixed a contemptuous eye on Jones.

"*Mon cher le Capitaine,* my disadvantage is but temporal. Do yourself upon me and suffer thereafter!"

Jones swung his craft around into the wind and presented his broadside to Monsieur le Comte's bow. The latter stood with most evident courage on his deck, one leg cocked forward, as if prepared personally to receive the captain's fire. Jones obliged. Digging his oar deep under the surface of the pond, he flicked it deftly upward to produce a sharp swell that set the other rowboat to violent rocking. This maneuver cost the boy his footing, pitching him into the outstretched arms of his sisters. Jones then brought his blade down in a series of abrupt chopping motions, striking off arcing sheets of water, deluging the enemy and spoiling the ostrich plume on Monsieur le Comte's hat. The girls squealed and kicked; the deeply moistened comte took a spray of pond water full in the face and was momentarily speechless. Jones rowed away, and was far out of range when the children finally managed to get their hands in the water to answer his barrage with a random burst of meager splashes.

"A baptism by fire!" Jones taunted them, sitting back as his boat glided. "Be but thankful I did not board you outright!"

"*After him!*" the young comte screamed. His sisters leaned dutifully on their oars. Indeed, Jones was impressed with the latters' fighting spirit—they compared favorably to the lowborn male clodhoppers and pressed pub crawlers who blighted most of France's warships.

Jones did not bother to row. Instead, he let his adversary close in behind him. And when he began to take watery "fire" from the cupped hands of the comte, he suddenly slapped the pond with both oars, again sending a devastating salvo directly behind him. While the others were momentarily disarrayed by this counterpunch, Jones's oars bit the water in opposing directions and spun his boat around as if on a pivot (suggesting something of the unique joy of commanding a Roman galley, he mused). Then he surged forward again, passing the enemy on his port side.

Another wave of water broke over the comte's gunwales. This time, however, Monsieur le Comte's larboard oarsman, his cousin Delphine, managed a slice at the water herself. Jones's white linen blouse was wet to his skin.

"A creditable shot!" he praised her. "Perhaps it is you who should be in command, instead of Mister Comte!"

"She knows her place *subalterne*. As will you!" the boy sneered, attempting several more ineffectual swipes with his sword.

Jones commenced another turn.

"Captain Jones! If you please!"

Someone, a periwigged servant, was calling to him from the shore.

"Yes?" he answered, squinting through the raking sunlight at the figure on the grass.

"Monsieur, it is your coach to L'Orient. They wait in the court-yard."

They were early. Jones put his head down, all humor gone.

"Yes. I will be there," he said.

He pulled for the shore with long, easy strokes. His many weeks of waiting, of pining and pleading for an opportunity to repeat his success with the *Ranger,* albeit on a grander scale, were finally at an end. The many days of staring at himself in mirrors, won-dering if his valor was spent, his career prematurely nipped, his character destined never to be well and publicly established, were over. Except for a slight paunch born of too many well-sauced French meals, he believed himself the same man who departed Portsmouth eighteen months before. Indeed, the same man who captained his first ship more than ten years before. The same man, except for a few more creases now lining his parlor-pale face.

But a new anxiety dogged him now: the worry that his success had been not only a matter of good luck (of course it was), but a matter of inspiration—of the kind of grace that comes to boy post

captains and heartsick poets who amuse Fate with their preten-
sions. This next cruise would not be inspiring. Its success would
be the fruit of long and tedious labor and, more precisely, of pol-
iticking, which to him was the very opposite of poesy. Would he
fail now, without the excuse of inexperience?

The comte's boat was now close behind him.

"You flee in fear!" the boy was saying. "Strike your flag, I say!"

"If I had a flag, I would strike. I am defeated!"

"Patronizer. You break off to take a coach."

"Alas, the *Bon Homme Richard* is waiting for me. Pray excuse
my surrender."

"But I have not yet begun to fight!" the boy wailed. He tossed
himself in the well of the rowboat, initiating a tantrum: "No! No!
No! No! No! Cowards! Cheaters! I claim my destiny! Fight with
me!"

His plumed hat had come off in the course of this performance. While he was thus engaged, Delphine seized it and, fluffing
the damp comb, set the hat on her own head.

"The Admiralty salutes you, *le Capitaine* Paul Jones!" she
shouted to him. "Now go forth and tame the Lion!"

This amused Jones. On shore, he bowed deeply to her, and
then to the rest of the guests. The latter were red-eyed and uncom-
prehending, freshly awoken by the messenger's arrival.

When he had mounted the stairs up to the Hotel Valentinois,
one of the picnickers, a minor chevalier whose only battles were
with tough cuts of meat at the dinner table, turned to his wife.

"Remind me, who is that man?"

"The American captain, Paul Jones. You met him this morning at quoits."

"Oh yes, the short, earnest one. I remember. His French is terrible." And he fell back to resume his nap.

II.

"Every Brave man Show himself Now hereafter for we will find many Dangerous times during the action of the war, for we will see a many Brave men amongst the American Soldiers which we Shall meet, with their sharp edge tools. I therefore Say you must Stand like good Soldier against your own white Brother because just as soon as he find you out that you are against him he then will Show you no mercy . . ."

—Cornplanter, Senecah sachem, 1777

LET THE GODS of my fathers and yours warrant the truth of my story. Let Shagodyoweh, the foul giant of the edge of the world, make my people's windows break and their plows shiver in the ground if I lie. Let nightmares trouble us, and our women give birth from under their armpits like Daughter gave birth to Tawiskaron, the evil twin, who is also called Bad Mind and made all crooked streams and biting flies. Let no false face cure us and the Roman Papa and Jesus Christ and Allah together cast us into the pit. And lastly, let my bones of a liar never rest in the earth, and my spirit never find peace, until the Mud-turtle is recalled by the Great Spirit and this world-on-his-back ends.

I am talking to you because I am dead. There are things I have seen that you have not. I can speak because, unlike dead white people, the throats of our dead are not stopped up with soil. Instead, we sit together on wooden scaffolds our relatives build for us in the forest. We are facing west, dressed in our finest suits of clothes, our guns left cradled in our stiff and bony grips. We have all been here for years, old warriors talking together, though many of us died young. One of the things they talk about behind my back (for they are all behind me, and I can't turn around) is the fact that I was put up here not by my parents, or by my children, but by a white man. A white soldier, in fact.

What I want to tell you is how this happened. I could tell you quickly, but being dead, I have nothing but time. So I will tell you at my own pace. If you don't like it, go ask another corpse.

My name is Two Fires. Among whites, I add the first name Joseph. I am of the Bear clan of the Gweugwehono, which in our language means People-Who-Live-in-the-Muddy-Land. We are also known by the French as "Oiogoua" and by the English as "Cayuga," but I will use the proper name as I talk to you. My childhood is not important, but I will tell you how I got my name. I was born of the white woman Sarah Whitcombe during the Midwinter ceremonies 32 years ago. My mother was a captive from a raid on a column of Long Knives near Tioga. She was adopted by our family.

My father Mantinoah was once a fine hunter. When he first saw my mother, though, he became poisoned with love and a fool to the animals in the forest. From that day on, deer miles away could hear the crooked rhythm of my father's frustrated heart and refused to be taken. Women in town began to call him "Stone Foot," because they thought his steps betrayed him in the hunt, and this nickname stuck with him for the rest of his years.

My father did all the things a hunter does to satisfy his prey. He burned tobacco to the spirit of Little Deer, promising always to honor her with a third part of the meat he took. He fasted, shaved himself, and put off wearing all buckskin. He did all this, but nothing worked. In his despair, he went into his house and didn't come out until the false faces visited him.

The cornhusk maskers came first, banging on Mantinoah's door and his windows and his roof, poking and teasing and pulling his hair, rolling about like dogs on his floor. Then the true face entered. This was a very sad face, with wide, red eyes and great streams of tears etched on it. Stone Foot looked upon him, a face as miserable as his, and embarrassed himself by exposing his sadness further, wailing "Oh, Shagodyoweh, I am weak with the curse of feeling. What shall I do?" To which the face replied, "How should I know? I am as weak as you."

´ With that, my father knew he, like Shagodyoweh himself, could not be cured from this kind of illness. The face then gave Mantinoah the Three Rare Words of Requickening, saying "eyes" and wiping away his tears with a fawn skin, and saying "ears" and blowing into his ears, and then saying "throat" and blowing hot ashes into his open mouth with a pipe, to let him breathe again. And like Aionwatha, the great warrior who had lost seven daughters and received the Three Words from the sage called Peacemaker, my father did these same things to the sad face in his turn. This was how Mantinoah got over his sadness.

Soon after Sarah Whitcombe was led to the house of my grandmother. The old woman had not spoken or moved her right arm in six years, so she used her left hand to accept the gift of corn flour cake from the bride. Mantinoah came forward then to give Sarah the flank of a doe, and with that the couple was married.

Not long after, Mantinoah had a son. How this involved the Midwinter Festival I will tell you. My mother had become plump when she joined our people, and because of this, and because she was ignorant of our custom, she successfully hid her pregnancy until it had gone far. Now, on the first day of the Festival, all the newborns of the village were named in a ceremony called Boiling-of-the-Babies. Though you whites want to go on thinking of us as savages, this ritual did not call for cooking any babies. Instead, we went to the old-style longhouse we had for ceremonies and just gave the babies names. Then we ate a meal of boiled corn and bean soup, which my mother was honored to help prepare.

At the time in the ceremony when everyone was happy and relaxed and looking forward to the feast to come, my mother felt the changes coming over her. It happened so quickly, they say, that the women did not have time to take her to her own bed. I was born right there, in the longhouse, between the two big cast iron soup pots we had traded the Quebecois for and which we still used when I attended the very last Midwinter at my town, only a few years ago. Even as I was coming out, they tell me, the women of the longhouse were weeping and gnashing their teeth all around my mother because she was polluting the place with her blood. The second I was born, three of them took my mother by the legs and dragged her like a sack to just outside the east door. The afterbirth was not saved and lodged the right way in the cleft of a maple, but was snatched and eaten by a dog. Tobacco was burned right away in the place between the two boiling pots. On account of all the commotion my arrival caused, and the place where I chose to appear, I was called Two Fires.

We lived at the center of the world, in that land of great long lakes in the shape of the Creator's hand as He pressed it down upon the earth. Our town was near the lake named after our people, in the land that later was stolen and became the State of New York. It was called Chonodote, "Peach Town," because we had orchards a couple miles up from shore. Though you whites say you brought the cultivation of crops to us, we had long grown corn, kidney beans, squash, pumpkins, apples, peaches, and pears in our fields. And here are more things we grew: cranberries, tobacco, gourds, blueberries, rice.

I won't lie and say our lives were perfect. All I can say is that if you're a white man, living in your dreary, suffocating white town with your tight white hard clothes and your bland white mush food, then, well, we lived better than you do. We had warm, dry wooden houses with shuttered glass windows and lofts full of supplies. Our women had calico and flannel dresses and shoes of soft fawn skin and mink pelts. They had silver jewelry and steel needles from New England, fine things of copper from the Great

Lakes, obsidian from Mexico, serpent's teeth from the ocean, and shell from the islands. In the summer, when we were home from hunting or fishing trips, we could get up late on warm mornings and get some cider or berry juice and walk on the palisade wall around the town, looking out on our fields of corn twenty feet high. On the other side we could look down to the lake glimmering white and blue in the sun, or the woods hugging the land straight from valley to hilltop. We could look at these things and be secure without a piece of paper that told us we owned it, or gave it temporarily in trust, or had use-rights, or any of the other ways people pretend they own their Mother.

We all traded with the whites, but we did it on our terms, and we didn't need money to keep ourselves. All around, for free, we had wild fruits in their seasons—fox grapes, cherries, strawberries, raspberries, partridgeberry, wintergreen, elderberry, blackberry, dewberry, huckleberry, whortleberry, gooseberry. There was maple syrup and wild mushrooms, wild leeks and onions, artichoke root, wild hops, walnuts, hickory nuts, butternuts, acorns, hazelnuts, chestnuts, and beechnuts. We collected and used sassafras, snakeroot, spikenard. Before the last war and the treaty that followed it, before most of the game was shot out by dumb whites and Indians working for the fur companies, the forest had deer and moose and elk and bear and mink and turkeys and muskrat, and beaver bigger than dogs, and the streams were full of fish and ducks and geese. From the air we could pick off passenger pigeons as easily as berries from the bush. In the spring, when the new grass grew out on the ranges beyond the Western door, we could even go out and take our pick of the bison there.

So don't listen to the liars who say how hard things were for us, on our own. Before the war we never starved. We were never so desperate for food that we needed to hang around the British forts. That was the Americans' doing, by the command of the Destroyer of Towns, the criminal George Washington.

I was old enough to remember when Sarah gave my father a daughter, whom he picked up. When she was old enough to have a name, she was called Fallen Leaf, because she was born in the time when the land around the shores were scattered with yellow and red and brown leaves. My mother would take us both along the trail to a stream where she would wash her last garment from her days at Tioga: a long, heavy woolen skirt in the style of the white women. This washing took a long time, and she would put my sister in a pile of fresh fallen leaves, which was as soft as the finest swaddling clothes of cloth. As she lay there, and I was nearby throwing rocks in the stream, our mother would talk to us in English, and that's how we learned that language.

"Who made the world?" she would ask me as she pounded away with the washing stone.

"The Good Spirit made the world," I answered her.

"You mean God made it, you little heathen."

"God is not the Good Spirit?"

"Of course not. God isn't always good. He has his own plan."

"Then I don't like God."

"That's all right. He doesn't like your kind of people either."

She liked to talk to me this way, showing contempt for the family that had adopted her. But she never left our town, even after our father died.

Once Mantinoah came along the path from the lands of the Onundagaono, with a bark barrel on his shoulder full of elk meat he had caught and cured by himself in the woods. This success had put him in a good mood, and though he rarely smiled publicly, he did that morning as he saw us there at the washing, and his daughter in the pile of leaves. Even as an infant she was beautiful, smiling back at him. So he said, "She looks happy there, so that will be her name." And our mother said, "Okay." And that's how she was named Fallen Leaf.

These were the last years of the old way for our people, but many of us did not see the trouble coming. The Gweugwehono guarded the southern door of the longhouse nation the French misnamed "Iroquois" or the British just lumped as "Senecah." We, along with the Ganeagaono, the Nundawaono, the Onundagaono, the Onayotekaono, and later, the Dusgaowhono, lived on the land between the Great Lakes on the west, the North River ("Hudson's River") to the east, and Quebec to the north. We held the power amongst most of the people living to the south and to the east of the Mississippi. We had this power, but we only called ourselves "nations" because that's how the whites understood such things. To them, agreements were made between "nations" or, perhaps, with "tribes." But we didn't think of ourselves as nations like Britain or America, or as "tribes" either. We were just "the people" or "the whole people" or, sometimes, "the people of the big longhouse."

During the second-to-last war between the whites, the British whipped the French. This worried some of us, because we had become used to playing one nation of whites against the other, and using promises of trade by one to undercut their enemy's negotiating position. Who would the British hate, if they couldn't hate the French anymore? Fortunately, the Americans soon had a quarrel with their king in England, and they stood in for the French very well. So things were okay as long as the British and Americans competed for favors from us.

This story begins when I was eighteen. By then I had been leaving town and going into the woods like a man for a few years. In the spring we trapped and shot the birds returning from the south; in the summer we chased the deer and the bear. Sometimes we also harassed American settlers, but not very seriously. We just mooned their daughters or put oblong fruits down the crotches of their scarecrows, which truly enraged them.

Once, I found a rifle that had been left hanging on a tree by a white farmer who was busy filling woodchuck holes in a field. The gun had a maple stock, brass fittings, and was nearly as long as I was. The caliber, I learned later, was .57. Since the farmer wasn't using it, I took that rifle, and used it whenever I had ammunition. I was happy to have it, of course, but thinking back on it now I guess the gun possessed me more than I possessed it. I took many foolish chances stealing things—farming implements, snowshoes, game from other men's traps—to trade for shot and powder. Perhaps if I'd never taken it I never would have ended up being away so long or so far, when Sullivan's army came.

When the last war started, some of us welcomed it. The American settlers had been encroaching on our homelands and needed a lesson. We were reminded of this many times by agents of the British, who came around making grand promises and firing up the more ambitious youths with dreams of glory in war. But the sachems were cautious. They told the young men that neither the British nor the Americans were trustworthy, and that our fighters should stay out of this latest quarrel.

There were a lot of hotheads among the young men of the Gweugwehono who didn't want to listen to the words of old men. Each had his reasons. Some argued that the elders had had their chance to become great captains in the war between Britain and France and feared their deeds would be surpassed by their sons. Others suspected that some sachems were too jealous of their power to put aside their official names and take up the ax as common warriors, as tradition provided. Still others said that the British and Americans had very short memories and needed to be reminded how the edge of the tomahawk feels every few years. More than a few had personal grudges to settle—men who had lost brothers and wives and friends to white soldiers who liked to shoot at us for sport.

But the whites weren't to blame for Mantinoah's death. That came in the late spring of my last year at home. He had gone down the southern path toward the lands of the Shawnee, to a fishing camp on the west branch of the river. On his way, he crossed paths with a Shawnee war party coming in the other direction. Skilled as he was in forest fighting, he managed to avoid them, though they came so close that he could hear them whispering to each other. That was when Stone Foot stepped into a deadfall set for deer, just off the path. It was just a shallow one—poorly made, he said. But one of the stakes at the bottom stabbed into and out of his right foot, then back into his knee again. Even with this pain he made no sound to give himself away to the Shawnee. And when they were gone, he pulled himself off the trap, and walked, bleeding and hobbled, the forty miles back to town. It took two days.

I was not there when he came back or when he died. But I've been told of how he came out of the woods with a look of excitement on his face, as if he had caught some rare piece of game. My mother tried to force him to rest, but instead he limped around the place showing off his triple injury, explaining how the stake had found its way through the small bones of his foot, and pointing out the odd white discharge that had begun to flow thick and stinking from the unclosed wound.

The usual treatments did not help him because he had been too long on the trail coming home. On the second night back he had a dream that required the attention of two medicine men. First, he explained it to them, saying that he had been floating on the water, perhaps the Susquehanna, where it was very wide and he could not see the shore. There he met a beaver, swimming out in the middle of the stream. Mantinoah asked him, "Hey, Beaver, why are you out here, so far from your lodge?"

To which the beaver answered, "To kill the bear."

And Mantinoah said, "You will not kill the bear; it will kill you."

And the beaver replied, "Then help me and let's die together."

So my father said, "Okay," and he grabbed the beaver's tail and was suddenly pulled along the surface of the water so fast he left a wake. And that's when the dream ended.

Fallen Leaf was there, and she told me how the medicine men sat for a long time, just stroking their chins, wondering about this dream. They wondered so long, though, that Mantinoah died before they could agree on what it meant and what to do about it. This was very bad, because that meant the dream would be frustrated and the dreamer's spirit unsettled. And unsettled spirits were the reason things went wrong in our town.

Anyway, they dressed his body up in his leggings and cap and put his gun in his hands and sat him up on the scaffold. His body was left like this, facing west, for three months. Then they made a hole in the ground for him, scorched the soil around it, and finished burying him.

Though she had lived with us for many years by then, Sarah Whitcombe didn't know how to mourn correctly. She did it like the whites, becoming, if anything, more quiet and alone, and courteous to everyone, as if her pain was some kind of private business of hers. She spent most her time in the little cabin my father built for her near the Bear longhouse.

But Fallen Leaf mourned very well. She gathered ashes from Mantinoah's grave and rubbed them into her face until she was black with them. She found patches of thicket in the woods and rolled in them, moaning, until she rose with her hair a tangle of dead weeds and burrs. She stopped cleaning her clothes. She answered her elders with insults, and kicked puppies and children when they were in her way. And everyone knew why she did these things and understood just how good a daughter she was. She was better than good—like many of the adopted whites and half-breeds, she always had to be the most serious, the most Indian of the Indians. Beautiful as she was, all the young men found her just too frightening to marry.

Now these were the times when the missionary in our town, the Father Du Lac, thought it was best for him to strike. He'd arrived in Chonodote two years before, carrying only a walking stick and the gray woolen robes on his back. We'd seen such robes before—they'd been coming up the warrior's path from the British colonies or down the Genesee River from the French for generations. And though they never found more than three people from among us to wear the cross and serve Jesus Christ, they kept coming, kept up the steady dripping of water on the rock.

This gray robe was long and tall, with a head of red hair. Everyone came to his first sermon to look at this remarkable hair. And Du Lac, believing his audience was hanging on his every word, started his sermon with the Lord's Creed, which we had all heard before. After all that, he very slowly and vividly sketched the story of Adam and Eve, of the serpent and the apple, of the fall and the Christian God's curse on humanity. He also went on about the stain on all people that never washed off, and how Jesus Christ made it all go away, and that our stain would still be there if we didn't accept Him. When he was done, he was happy to see an elder nodding at him.

"Yes, we have often felt it is so," a sachem told him. This sachem was Deawateho, whose name in English means, "Having a Glimpse."

"The Almighty be praised. Bless this village, where the Holy Spirit hath preceded me into the hearts of these children!" said Du Lac.

"Yes, we agree it is bad to eat raw apples. It is much better to press them into cider. Thank you for telling us this."

"And it is good to wash," a woman suggested. "If a stain is not put into water quickly, it is hard to wash away later."

"And beware talking snakes," suggested another.

"Yes, all of this is true," said Deawateho. "When you see him, thank Roman Papa for sending us word of these things."

And the congregation broke up fast. The only effect of this meeting was that Du Lac was never served apples when he came to "minister" to people in their houses. Instead, they gave him soup or corn porridge. Few showed up for his services either, because we had all heard this story before and, besides, all the Christians disagreed with each other anyway, and what kind of god would let his children argue with each other when he should have peace in his family? Du Lac got bigger crowds, though, when the white traders were in the area and he got glass beads to give the women as gifts. These beads were prized much above the usual porcupine quills for jewelry. But even then, all the women would just sit quietly for all the time it took, accept their two or three beads, and then run back to their houses to sew them on their dresses.

When Fallen Leaf was mourning our father, Du Lac came out of the hut he'd built for himself against a corner of the palisade and found her in her bunk. And, as usual, he went on and on about his God and his saints and his martyrs, and the strange way the Christian God showed his stewardship of the world, until her patience wore out and she knelt before him.

"Yes, let us pray . . ."

He knelt, facing her, and put his hands together. But her hands stayed on her thighs, and her eyes stared unblinking at him, until he heard the sound of her urine pooling in the dirt. And then she got up and left him there on the floor, kneeling before the round, still mirror of her contempt.

My mourning began the minute I came home and learned the news. It ended ten days later, when I was ready to go back out and work my vengeance against the Shawnee. Fallen Leaf, you see, was not content with the customary ten days, but gave every sign that she would not be the same until our father's place in our family was taken by an adopted hostage. Now I understand that you don't understand this, that among "civilized" nations, people don't replace other people when they die. But of course this is a lie. You do it all the time, after what you call a "decent interval." We're just more honest about it.

I left before the dawn on the eleventh day. Fallen Leaf came out to give me food for my journey: cornmeal and blackberries in a slab of maple sugar, wrapped in a pouch of white fawn skin. In the gloom and under so many layers of ashes I could barely make out her face. Instead, I saw her eyes shining from beneath the weight of her grief. She didn't need to say anything to me, and I didn't speak to her. As we hugged, I could smell the earth and dog dung in her hair—that fine hair she got from the fur of the bear of her mother's clan, which was black like all Gweugwehono but also hard blue, like the last light in the sky before a winter night. I gave her the last kiss I ever did that morning.

So I put the bear fat and paint on my face, stripped off all clothes but a breech-cloth, and struck out down the warrior's path my father had used, toward the Susquehanna. I left the gun behind, because now I was hunting men. I covered thirty miles in the first day and set no fire that night.

The next morning I was standing on the banks of the west fork—as good a place as any to begin my search. The first people I saw was a trio of Shawnee going upriver, probably toward a fishing camp. These were too many to kill at once, so I let them go. A few miles farther on I sat in some bushes and watched six women collect puffballs. They seemed healthy and capable of lots of good labor for us, but they were women and we already had too many of those. So I let them go too.

Then I met two Shawnee hunters—a father and son. We all saw each other at the same moment. I was beating my way through a marsh to avoid being seen on the path, and they were collecting turtles in a burlap sack with the Dutch name "Dreienbeeck" burnt on its side. The broad red stripe of paint on my face and the ax in my hand could leave no doubt what I wanted, so they put the sack down and took out their knives.

"Warrior, who are you here for? Me or my son?"

"Either is okay," I told him. "Or I could kill you both, to ease my father's spirit."

He put down his knife. "Then honor me by taking me, and let my son go."

"Father, together we can kill him," said the boy.

I found this boast a little bit annoying, and it drove all thought of compromise from my mind. "No," I said. "I will first kill your son, then return with you to Chonodote."

"Let's fight, then," said the old man.

So he took up his knife and, with a cry, ran at me. His plan was perhaps to sacrifice himself and wound me enough for his son to finish me. Anyway, I avoided his first swipe with the knife and spun toward the boy, who was not far behind him. The son was not well trained in fighting, because he didn't have his guard up. My ax found its way into the middle of his face, and he fell, exhaling brains from his split-open nose. When I pulled the blade out and turned quickly to face an attack from the father, he was just sitting on the ground.

"Warrior, that was my only son. Tell me for whom you mourn, as I do now."

So I told him the story of my father's death. And when I got to the end, he nodded, saying, "I see. But you should know, before I leave this place as your captive, that I do it to show you what kind of man a Shawnee father is, and that my heart is greater than yours. Do you understand?"

"I understand that you come with me on my terms, not yours," I replied. For I was young and haughty, and I believed my ax showed my worth better than his words showed his.

He kept his word and made no trouble on the two-day march

back home. When we were close to town, I made a few whoops to tell everybody I was coming. They were all waiting for me inside the palisade as I led the Shawnee inside—the women gathering to jeer and throw dog excrement at him, the children running up and counting coup. The warriors—the ones who were not out hunting or fishing—watched from way off, pretending, like they always do, not to care so much about the triumph of another man.

Deawateho stepped forward, saying "Young man, I see your hunt went well. Tell us the story of how you took this Shawnee."

So I told them, taking care to tell the story plainly so as not to seem like I was bragging. Bragging brought on jealousy, and jealousy, bad witchcraft. And when that was done, I did the wardance like I was supposed to, and Deawateho seemed pleased with how I handled myself.

Fallen Leaf came out at last. She had left off rubbing her face with ashes, but still had not gone back to wearing normal clothes or washing herself. She was barebreasted, with her eyes very bright and unblinking and her hair a thick and tangled nest. The Shawnee had not reacted at all when he'd been pelted with shit or struck by little boys with sticks. But when he saw this woman with burning eyes, he gave a little gasp and seemed to straighten up on his feet. For all over Turtle Island, women did not go to war or hunt, but made up for this in the depth of cruelty allowed them in their grief. And it was well-known that no kind of woman was more cruel than a young one, suffering her first loss.

"Who have you brought to me now, brother?" she asked. She picked up the shaft of a broken hoe lying there nearby and used this to poke at him, as if he were unworthy to touch. "But you must be joking, bringing this dog of a Shawnee here."

"He watched his own son die and didn't flinch."

She regarded him with disgust. "I don't believe he is worthy of taking my father's place. But let's test him."

"Okay."

So we led him to the center of the town, where a large oak tree had been left with its lower branches sawn off. It had an iron pulley attached to it, and we tied the Shawnee's arms to one side and yanked him off his feet with the other. So he was hanging there, swaying slowly, as the crowd looked up at him. His eyes were closed, and he had stopped breathing hard. He was doing very well so far.

Some of the other women brought some sticks and small logs to fill the shallow pit under the Shawnee's feet. The kindling was burning right away, with small flames going, smoke rising up around the Shawnee's buckskin leggings. A young warrior came up casually and, measuring the leggings by sight, decided he liked them and pulled them off the Shawnee's legs.

"What a small cock," Fallen Leaf pointed. "It's a baby's cock, that one!" And everyone else laughed, except me, because I knew nobody showed a warrior's cock when he was hanging over the fire, unless he were crazy or stupid.

"The fire is low, brother."

I got down on my knees and blew on the flames, and soon they made a fine, fast campfire. The Shawnee was sweating hard then, starting to roll his head on his shoulders, but still not crying out. Father Du Lac came out, going right up to him and putting a hand on his leg because the Shawnee's head was too high up to reach. He said a blessing in Latin, out loud, then washed his hands of it and went back right away to his little house. His shoulders were rounded with a fatigue that puzzled us, because he never did anything but pray and mind everyone else's business.

The flames came close enough to the Shawnee's feet that the first blisters rose, broke, and began to flow. Nobody made jokes now, because this was a man's death. The blackening began to show, and Fallen Leaf watched him closely. "He will cry out," she told us. "I can see it in his face."

And the Shawnee did cry out, in a way. He opened his eyes to the sky and sang in a wavering but strong voice: "Great Spirit, hear my deathsong. Great Spirit, see that my house is empty because I have kept nothing. Great Spirit, see that my heart is full because I come to the Hunting Ground. Great Spirit, see that I have done no witchery. Great Spirit, before I die, let me show these mud people that I am worthy of this death. Great Spirit, let them weep for the man they let go. Great Spirit, hear my deathsong . . ."

"Good. Very good," Deawateho judged, nodding his head.

The first parts to go were the fingernails, which we pulled off one by one. This was easy to do and painful for a prisoner, so if he was going to cry out, he could do it then and save us the trouble of going on to removing the nose, the tip of the tongue, one of the eyes. We preferred to take only one eye because it was fair that a man see who's doing all this to him. With this Shawnee, we got all the way to popping out his left eyeball with a charred stick, to which he said, "Thank you, brother," as if I was scratching his itchy back.

With every passing minute the mood in the crowd became more serious, and more and more men drifted in from the woods to watch. For as the Shawnee went longer with a brave face, everyone began to feel in love with him. As his feet and legs were now as charred as the logs beneath them, and the odor of cooking flesh rose up, the children stopped flitting around, and people stood with unthrown excrement in their hands, wondering.

Fallen Leaf pointed at the Shawnee's legs. "Brother, those logs are all burned. They will suffocate the fire if they aren't moved."

Everyone looked to me. Their eyes showed disgust and pity, but also anticipation. They were all waiting to see if the Great Spirit would actually hear the Shawnee, and come among us to make something more of this pain.

Grasping my ax, I knelt close enough to the fire to smell my own hair beginning to singe. The bear fat on my face melted and ran into my eyes and mouth. With three swings, I had the

Shawnee's right leg separated from the rest of him, at the knee. Much blood fell into the flames, where it hissed and boiled in the loose ashes. Three more swings, and I had both legs free, and stacked them neatly with the split logs in the fire, making sure to leave a little airway for the flames to breathe. Then I stepped back.

At some point, while I was busy tending the fire, the Shawnee finally broke and began to scream. His cry pierced the heart like an infant's or a rabbit being slaughtered. It filled him so much it seemed to come from nowhere exactly on his body. It was as if the stumps of his legs had sprouted screaming mouths and tongues.

Fallen Leaf turned to the crowd. "See, I told you he'd break."

And yes, there was a sense of relief among everyone, because though it was fairly rare to see sacred things happen, sacred things weren't always welcome, since they could be very upsetting. All of the men turned away right then; most of the women went back to their chores. The fate of the Shawnee had become a matter for our family to settle.

"Brother, this man is unworthy to take our father's place. Let's find someone else."

And that was the end. I cut the Shawnee's throat. Later, his body was taken down and left, as usual, for three days in the open air before it was finally buried. All he had of his personal things was an old chipped shark's tooth on a leather strap around his neck. We put that into his grave with him.

That wasn't the end of the story. Later, when Sarah Whitcombe learned what had happened to the Shawnee, she came out of her cabin and started to yell at Fallen Leaf and me. She said a lot of ignorant things, calling us animals, calling us dogs, insects, and worms. She said (and I remember this very well) that she didn't care what we "monkeys" did to torment each other, but that she wouldn't have it done in the name of her husband, who was a wise and gentle man.

At this, Fallen Leaf picked up a stick and began to beat our mother. And all the men just stood around and watched her, too surprised to do anything. "Go back to your hole, Yangeese!" my sister was yelling as the other covered her head and cried in fear. "What kind of wife are you? You don't even know how to mourn! Who's the dog now, as I beat you?"

That was when I got hold of her arms. Our mother was running then, running back to her little cabin where she cried. It took a while for Fallen Leaf to calm down enough for me to let her go. Then she took her stick and whipped me across my face, saying "And you . . . !" She didn't finish what she wanted to say, but blazed at me. Then she walked away as everyone watched her—a child so good, so perfect in her rage, so hard like a stone, no one wished for a daughter like her.

So, you whites ask why we do these things, if we say we aren't savages. But you are hypocrites to ask this. I have with my own eyes seen how the British and the French work tortures on their war captives. The lucky ones are shot or cut down with bayonets right away, because your commanding officers don't like to slow down their columns with gangs of prisoners. The unlucky ones are tossed in earthen holes or in the bellies of prison boats, where they slowly starve or dry up. In the dark, they rot from filth and die of diseases that are not worthy of men—not even white men— to die from. When these captives give themselves up to the instincts of animals, your soldier guards, who mostly stand around bored by the suffering they see, either encourage them and wager on who will be beaten or infected or buggered, or, in their Christian charity, they decide to beat some or all of the prisoners with truncheons, lead pipes, or whips.

I've seen the columns of bag-skinned skeletons forced out into the open air for their "exercise." I've also seen the open pits stacked with pale, naked corpses, laid to rest with nothing more than a gob of spit and a scattering of lime. I've seen these things and you haven't, if you accuse the Gweugwehono of savagery. Our savagery provides that the captive dies with a face and with a chance for honor. Your civilization does its murdering hidden away, so you can stand to live with yourselves. About the only thing that's honest about you is that you worship a torture idol—that cross—in your churches.

I have said enough about this and have nothing more to add.

The next time, I struck north-east, into the Ganeagaonoga, or what you would call the lands of the Mohawks. This trip was a little longer. It took almost five days for me to go through the mountains and down to the shores of Oneadalote ("Champlain"). There, I was pleased and entertained to see that a navy battle had been laid for me to watch. As the red glow of the sunset warmed the back of my neck, I sat down on a rocky beach with a corn cake and watched two fleets of boats, one Yangeese and one British, have a very funny fight with each other.

I say very funny because there was a lot of firing and yelling, and much maneuvering with sails and oars, but nobody was hitting anybody. The Yangeese were on the left in a bunch of little boats with just one cannon in the front of each. It looked like they had been waiting there to spring a trap, hidden from the rest of the lake by a low island to the east. When the British came by in their bigger boats, the Americans popped out like the wolverine and surprised them. Or that was their plan. The British did come by like they planned, and the Yangeese did spring their ambush. But their trouble was they couldn't hit the British with their guns. Their aim was so bad, one of their shots flew over my head and split a tree behind me, and I was watching from way off in the west!

The British were always pretty good soldiers. Now they were coming up to fire back at the little Yangeese boats, although they were having trouble fighting the wind. One big ship got towed into range by a few rowboats, and it fired all its guns at once.

There were one, two, three plumes of water thrown up all around a Yangeese boat, then a shot that cut it in half. This seemed to enrage the Americans, who swarmed closer to the big boat and hit it a few times. After that, the big boat seemed to get blown off by the wind and couldn't hit the little ones at all because its guns were all pointing off to shore.

More big British sailboats came up. The Yangeese were being slowly beaten, but I must say they fought hard and took their losses with a brave face. This surprised me, because among our people the Americans are famous for showing their rumps the first moment things don't go their way. By the time the sun was down, two of their boats were burning and one was heading for the rocks of the island. They must have thought this was a safe place to land, but they were wrong: my brothers the Ganeagaono were waiting there for them when they came off. These Ganeagaono war parties must have been well paid by the British, because they just killed the Americans quickly, like little birds in a sack, and didn't bother to strip the bodies for booty. I could see the shoreline fill up with bobbing Yangeese corpses, their heads or butts lit up by the flaming wrecks of their boats. The Americans must have seen it too, because the ones flailing in the water just turned around in the middle of the channel and flailed toward me instead. That's when I wiped the crumbs off my fingers, took out my ax, and stood up to welcome them.

"Hey there, brave soldier. Over here," I called out to the first one, in English.

"Oh, thank God," the Yangeese groaned, and he turned over to float the last few yards to shore on his back. I waded in to help him onto the flat but slippery rocks around there. When I got him out of the water and onto his shaky legs, I had a look at him: tall, almost six feet, stripped to the waist and muscular, with powder stains on his forearms and on his face. A good catch.

"Didn't know we had Indian allies around here," he was saying to me as he got his breath back, "but I thank ye just the same."

"*Help!*"

There was another man struggling to my bit of shore. I waded in again, this time a little farther out, and had a look at him. This fellow was injured. He had one eye put out and a bone sticking out around his elbow.

"Help me," he demanded.

"Okay," I answered, and pushed him under the surface. He was exhausted from the swim and didn't struggle much—just a weak hand on my shoulder, some noisy bubbles at the surface.

"Hey there. What are you doing?" the first white guy was asking me.

The injured one had stopped moving. I gave him a little shove out to the deeper water and waded back.

"He was hurt. He would never have made the trip. And if the Ganeagaono had caught him, he would be much worse off than he is now."

"Who?"

"The Mohawks."

"And who are you?"

"Joseph. C'mon."

I hit the guy on the side of his head with the blunt end of my ax. He fell, and I tied his hands together and made a little leather lead to hold in my hands. This wouldn't have been necessary with a Shawnee or a Delaware, but an American probably would run off if given the chance.

It took him a good hour to wake up again. So I sat and waited as night fell on the battle and the firing stopped. The day hadn't gone well for the Americans; a bunch more of their boats were either sunk or burning on the shore, and the rest were gathered together in the center. The big British boats were much closer now—the one the Americans had damaged was safely far away, to the south.

Somewhere to my left, from the forest, there was pistol fire. Then somebody far away was screaming. Some of the Yangeese sailors were probably fighting the Ganeagaono, trying to get back to their forts below the lake. The ones who were caught were being done the honor of proving themselves in a warrior's death. The ones who ran or cowered were probably just shot or hit with a war club or rock. And the noises from these fights in the woods went on for some time, long after things had gone quiet on the water.

By the time the sun came up the next day we were ten miles from the lake, heading west. My new captive was able to walk, but he wasn't really awake on his feet until the sunshine hit his face. Then he spoke.

"Hey, there . . . what's yer name again?"

"Joseph."

"Joseph. Where we going?"

"Chonodote."

"That's where you live?"

"Uh-huh."

"Do you want to know my name?"

"No."

Every once in a while he would ask more questions, and I would answer with a word or two. There really wasn't much point in conversing with him like a man until he had a real name and became my brother. Before that, it made as much sense to befriend him as to befriend a snake that might bite me, or a coyote that might steal from my traps.

We were only two days into the trip back when he began to complain of fatigue. This was a bad sign, because a man who couldn't suffer tired legs would probably not show a brave face with no legs at all.

As we neared home, the Yangeese was stumbling and complaining that his soft feet were blistered from the walking. I gave the usual warning as we approached, and everyone was out to greet us in the finest clothes as we passed through the palisade. The Yangeese's face seemed to brighten as he saw all our women standing there in their jewelry and embroidered cloaks and cloth dresses—like proper white women, he probably thought. He stood there, as if amused, when I did the war dance for everyone, and even smiled when Fallen Leaf came out, naked and magnificently painted, and stood there unashamed among the glad young ladies.

But he didn't seem to like it at all when the crowd parted and he saw the nice big fire roaring under the hanging shackles. He fell down right away and started to cry, refusing to move his feet as we dragged him toward the fire. He squirmed like an infant going into the cradleboard when he was trussed up, and then he pissed himself. Fallen Leaf just stood there, looking at me with disapproval.

"Brother, is *this* how you honor our father?"

"This man is a brave soldier. I caught him fighting with the British."

The Yangeese whimpered as he hung there, trying and failing to kick the flaming logs away.

"I'm disappointed in you," was all she said, and she turned away to return to her house. And as the Yangeese did more and more to embarrass himself, the crowd steadily trickled away. There's not much interest in killing cowards, after all. It just becomes something to do, like picking up the dog shit from around your house.

So I took him down and led him outside the walls. He was weeping and pleading for his life the whole way, and I became so disgusted with him I untied his hands.

"Go. Get out of my sight. And may your cowardice infect all the whites," I told him.

He looked at me as if he couldn't believe his good luck. So I gave him a hard kick in the ass to start him going.

"I said go!"

And off he went. I don't know if he ever reached any of his people. The closest settlements were at Tioga, but he was heading in the wrong direction when he ran off. Then again, nobody ever found his body in the woods, so he might have made it.

So low was the quality of the candidates I had brought to her, Fallen Leaf was no longer talking to me. She didn't bring me food for the trail when I left for the third time, either. I had to eat what I could hunt on the way. Fortunately I brought the .57 this time. The first day out I shot a doe, and after I dressed her up and smoked her, I had more meat than I could carry on such a long trip. I wrapped the rest tightly in the deer's own skin along with a heavy rock, tied a string to the bundle, and threw the whole thing into a pond. If I was lucky and the trip was not too long, I thought I might be able to retrieve some of the cache later.

I headed more directly north this time, into New France. After following the St. Lawrence River for a few days, I stood opposite the stone walls of Quebec City, sitting proud on its bluff. Now, our people never really understood why anybody would be stupid enough to build permanent towns behind walls made of rock. Sure, the walls are strong and resist cannon fire better than wood. But people in towns will always log all the firewood out of the land around them, and exhaust the soil with their crops and wash it all down into the streams until there's nothing left. Garbage and human and animal filth always rise. The game disappears for miles around. Instead of relying on permanent towns, it's better to build ones you can leave without tears. That way, your enemy doesn't have an easy target, so you won't have to face cannon fire in the first place. Our war chiefs think the French lost Canada because they depended too much on the walls and guns of Quebec.

I passed a good number of Quebecois farms on my way. Many of them were raising a strange kind of corn that didn't grow very high and kept European breeds of ox and pig and sheep in neat wooden barns with stone silos and tin roofs that gleamed in the sun. The more I walked, the more I began to see that the hills around there were covered with these farms, but there were no towns anymore, other than the white ones.

There were plenty of Quebecois fishermen and carters and woodcutters around the city and the Orleans island nearby, all for the picking. But I wasn't looking for another white captive. So I went on downstream, where I might find a nice, strong Innu or an Abenaki or a Cree. Nobody had brought a prisoner back from this far away in a long time, and Fallen Leaf might have been impressed enough by this feat to give up her mourning.

As I headed east and the river got wider, I began to see big English boats out there. I'd heard about these really big vessels back home—about their wide gray sails and the whole villages of men who worked on them. Though we didn't envy life in your white towns, the idea of sailing around Turtle Island, taking captives and glory amongst distant people, appealed to quite a few of our young men. Maybe in that we weren't so different from the whites.

Anyway, the really sad part of my story begins when I went down to the river bank to drink some water and have a closer look at one of these boats. This was taking a chance right away, because it was common for whites with guns to just shoot at people for no reason, just for showing their faces at the wrong time. But I'd never heard of anybody getting shot at from a big boat, so I went down and stood on the shore, shading my eyes with my hands and looking.

This boat had half-a-dozen triangle-shaped sails hanging on it, and ten or twelve of the little doors along one side that I knew hid the cannon. I could also see that the sails weren't in one piece, but that seams and patches showed as the sun shined through them. This made sense, because I figured it would probably take the captain's wife many years to weave a big-boat sail all at once.

Had I known then what I know now, I also would have noticed the boat was not flying a flag, which would have warned me.

There was a commotion. Some sailors were standing together on the boat, talking to each other and looking at me. Others were untying the ropes around a rowboat on the deck. Soon, four men were on the river, rowing in my direction. I have to say this made me a little nervous, because who knew what they were up to. I had my .57 with me, so I made a clear show of shotting and powdering it, to show them that I wasn't just your average savage they were coming toward, and that I was ready for them.

"*Pace,* young sir!" one of them was calling to me from the rowboat, through a speaking-horn. "We come in trade!" He was standing up, with a blue coat and one of those queer sharp-cornered hats white officers wear.

I stood my ground, and they landed. Only the officer got out of the boat, the others just sitting with the ends of their oars sticking up in the air. The guy came toward me with a cloth bag in his hand. When he got closer, I could see his uniform was in better shape than he was—he was missing teeth, and his face was scarred from the pox.

"*Pace,*" the spotted officer said again. "You speakee? You know language?"

"Joseph Two Fires, sir. And to whom do I have the pleasure of speaking?" I replied. I liked to talk this way when I met assholes who ask if I "speakee."

"Eh, just as well, then," he said. "We're bound upriver to Trois Rivieres. Can you tell me where we might find a pilot? I have goods to trade for information. . . ." And he opened his bag and showed me his goods: a tangle of rusty iron needles, thimbles, tweezers, hooks. I eyed them, and then him. It was easy to see he was lying. Everyone knew you found upstream pilots at Quebec.

"What do you really want?" I asked him.

He stood there, still looking and smiling at me, not moving his

eyes until it was too late. I felt the end of a gun in the small of
my back.

"Disarm, nigger," a voice said behind me.

I didn't disarm. Instead, I pulled the trigger on my .57. As it
was, I had a misfire, and the pox-faced officer didn't die right there
and then. Instead, six other soldiers were suddenly piling on me.
While I was watching the first rowboat, another must have
launched and come around the far side of the big vessel.

"Get on top of him! Beat him! Kick him, right there!" the officer was yelling. His men obeyed orders, kicking me in the stomach,
kidneys, balls, kidneys again, face. While I was taking this, I had
one of those odd times when, in the middle of trouble, I noticed
something very particular: I noticed that one of the guys kicking
me was barefoot, and that he had very ugly feet. They were knobby,
they stank, and his toes were bent and the nails needed cutting.

I would have told him so, except that's when I passed out.

III.

Woman is like a book which, be it good or bad, must begin to please with its title page; if that is not interesting, it does not rouse a desire to read, and that desire is equal in force to the interest the title page inspires.

—Giacomo Girolamo Casanova, *Memoirs,* 1789

THEY ALWAYS took their walks near the wharves of Ceres Street at a particular time. Around four, the roustabouts and the inspectors and the supercargoes all lit off to their dining tables, leaving the wharves littered with jobs half-done. In the milder months, the little leg of the Picataqua that found its way along that part of Portsmouth was as still and somnolent as the suppertime streets. Everything seemed suspended, or at least realistically arranged for their perusal, until an hour later when the boardinghouses and bars and ship galleys would simultaneously disgorge their sated, jabbering, and freshly liquored customers. Freshly fortified, they would render all the half-jobs fully done, all the stores stacked and loads stowed and ropes coiled, tarred, or tied off in neat, professional knots—before everyone retired for good in the evening.

But by that time John and Rebeccah's walk would be long over, and she would be disrobed and unfurled before her writing table, describing to herself the evening's progress in her peculiar, self-taught script. Though she was alone, she made certain she looked pretty sitting there, one coil of blonde hair arranged over her shoulder like *this,* legs crossed at the knee like *that,* dressing gown open at the throat only down to *there,* showing perhaps the soft cleft of a throat with just the most suggestive sheen of perspiration (never "sweat") raised by the humid airs of the season. Like every young girl with a new lover, she tried out her prospective name in several variations, writing:

Mrs. John Wickes Severence
Mrs. Rebeccah Severence
Mrs. Captain J. W. Severence

The first version would, of course, be her legal name should a marriage be commenced. Yet, in a way, just the act of repeatedly writing those names together—"Rebeccah" and "Severence"—lent a reality to the prospect which was, at first, deeply intriguing and curiously thrilling. It faded quickly, of course, which moved her to try even more fantastical forms to stir up the feeling again, such as:

Mrs. Rebeccah Shays John Wickes Severence
Mrs. Captain Rebeccah Shays John Wickes Severence Esq.

But then, unlike most young girls, she felt she must also laboriously scratch the experiments out. Her father begrudged her candles, writing paper, and ink, and looked not kindly on such frivolities. Instead of "versifying," he would tell her, she should be thinking about how to finally get herself off the family dole. Her younger sister was already married, he often reminded her. She was spoiling her looks, staying up late and squinting at dimly lit papers. He would regularly examine her eyes, hoving in close with a magnifier and a lantern, shaking his head sadly at the first damning creases. He told her laughing too much produced crow's feet, so she rationed her smiles.

There were more pleasant places to walk than on Ceres Street. A stroll along one of the mill ponds would have been quieter. They would have been alone, except perhaps for the bees and dragonflies veering over the water lilies, and for the small boys who hid on the banks to see if her suitor would steal a kiss. It would even be dark enough there, in the evenings, for her to kiss him back.

But Severence preferred the wharves. Though he was commissioned as an army officer, he had once gone to sea himself. There were, apparently, certain memories attached to that experience that were precious to him. The spectacle of ships fitting out or off-loading pleased him, for some reason. She didn't question it, but instead kept one of her rationed smiles on her face and succeeded in being pleasant.

Most of the time they talked about nothing much. The season: whether or not this summer or spring or autumn was a "good" summer or spring or autumn. Her father: whether he was well, whether his business was well. Her health: whether her medicine helped her nerves, or whether the weather or her father worsened them. But sometimes he would surprise her with some comment, some question that demanded a deeper sympathy between them, and an acknowledgment that she was not as simple as she was trying to pretend. Maybe it was the ink stains on her fingers, which she tried to wash off—but not too diligently. Maybe it was the way she allowed herself a raised eyebrow when he quoted someone, such as Johnson or Thomas Gray, and he would intentionally mangle it to see if she would notice. Or maybe it was the way she let him grasp her hand so high on her wrist that it wasn't like holding hands at all, but more like she was letting herself be led away.

He turned and looked at her, and she would let him stare at her profile for a while, until she turned to look back.

"What?" she asked.

"When will you be honest?"

She blinked—with perhaps too much show of incomprehension.

"Honest? I'm always honest," she replied, outrageously.

"I've seen lying women. You're not that good a liar."

"I'm sorry."

He laughed. "You're sorry! You're diabolical, that's what you are!"

He laughed and led her briefly onto Market Street, then quickly to Deer Street, which was not the one she lived on.

"Where are we going?"

"I have something to tell you," he said. "And I don't want to rush."

Something to *tell* her, not to *ask* her, she noted. They walked several blocks in silence, until they paused under an elm that cast a deep shadow in the twilight. He was facing her now, and holding her hand straight down against him. Her bright sleeve stood out easily against his gabardine coat, as did the skin of her hand. He was brazenly but matter-of-factly pressing it against the front of his pants.

"Is this what you wanted to tell me?" she asked him coolly, but without moving her hand.

"Just as I thought," he answered. "A strumpet, beneath it all."

"Not in the least. But that would be more than you deserve, *dénaturer.*"

And he laughed at her again—mobilizing that cleft of a scar on his left cheek, that implausibly chiseled jawline and permanent hint of stubble that made him seem more a caricature of manhood compared to the ghastly, ghostly insurers' sons and lawyers' apprentices who had courted her before. She was ordinarily immune to such Adonic exaggeration; such qualities seemed too clear a kind of statement, like neat scotch or cherry pie without the crust. She was immune to it, that is, in principle. Confronted with it, she merely kept her eyes down, and her hand unresisting.

His eyes were his redeeming quality, though. They were a very bright blue and seemed very used to frequent, even girlish laughing. They were laughing at her now, as they often did, though clearly not in ridicule but in delight. He seemed to enjoy both her scruples and the way they had of falling away in inverse proportion to his outrageousness. Once, he had moved to kiss the inside of her wrist in public, and she instantly froze over and terminated their afternoon together, and a week of afternoons after that. Another time, not long after they had met, he very firmly grasped her left buttock through her skirt as they kissed, and she had impulsively cocked her hip to present the cheek to his hand. In short, his seduction of her was not a war with a well-defined front that moved steadily, inevitably to her south. Instead, it was guerrilla war, with no clear measure of progress and unpredictability the only rule. This ambiguity seemed to keep his perverse interest and, in turn, her options, alive.

"We've been seeing each other for some time," he was saying to her, stepping his cane along the walk with his right hand as she held his left. "And I feel you deserve to be asked what I'd like to ask you."

She kept her eyes staring ahead. Was this going to be the Proposal after all? . . .

"We only owe each other a friendship, of which I am more than confident."

"I assumed we're well beyond that," he replied. "And I think you know that, too."

He led them in a vaguely dance like 180-degree turn, back toward Ceres Street. It was all she could do to remain moving, languid. She was light on her tiny feet like good prospective brides always are, floating right from the courtship down the aisle, across the threshold and into the nuptial bed. Keep light! Keep light! she ordered herself.

"As you know, I've been thinking some time on what I might do next," he told her. "All I've known for sure is that I'm not going back out to sea. That life is finished for me."

"Yes," she concurred, of course wondering why he then insisted on promenading with her along the waterfront.

"It's '79 already, and this war can't go on much longer. Some

arrangement is bound to be made. Some accommodation. A settlement on the taxes. Perhaps they'll let someone sit in Parliament
for the colonies. . . ."

"Or someone for each of the thirteen. Thirteen MPs," she
impulsively suggested. "Or perhaps one for each of the major
counties or boroughs. How many would that make? Dozens, at
least."

"I've thought seriously of resigning my commission," he
resumed as if she'd said nothing. "Thanks, of course, to my happily departed father, my income is more than enough for me to
turn my energies to anything I might fancy, practical or otherwise."

"Yes," she agreed.

"But I don't imagine myself settling back in New-York. There's
not much to hold me there—or in Philadelphia or Boston, even
less so."

"Nor I."

"And thinking more along those lines, how there is little to
interest me in the trades or in government, I began to understand
I had other . . . priorities . . . that must be addressed."

She didn't answer this time, but instead looked down at the
ground to hide her rising anxiety. She was becoming very conscious of how her hand was perspiring into his, and how un-
attractive that must seem to him. She didn't answer but kept light.

"There are many opportunities elsewhere. There are places
where the Severence name won't precede me. In the West."

So that was the plan, she thought. He would marry her, and
then he would make of her a frontier wife, out in some remote
streamside fastness in Pennsylvania. Yes, she supposed it could be
done. She imagined herself hoeing squash and shooting and raising sons who would grow up never seeing the steepled skylines of
Christian civilization. It was not what she imagined, of course, but
it would be possible.

"When the arrangements for peace are made, there are going to be business opportunities. There can be a dozen more massacres like the one at Cherry Valley, and settlement will still go on. And all of those settlers are going to need supplies."

"It stands to reason," she replied. She was relegating herself to the role of counterpoint in a Socratic dialogue, but she dared not presume where he was going with this proposal.

"And there are the Indians, too. After the peace, the Iroquois nations will prosper with the rest of us. They'll want manufactures. Do you follow me?"

She didn't quite follow him. "I follow you," she said.

"Sullivan is fitting out an expedition against the Senecah at Easton. I might manage to attach myself to his staff. I can't think of a better way to survey future prospects in the north woods. Can you?"

"No."

"Now, I know what you're thinking. You're thinking, 'How can he believe he can cultivate business contacts with the savages when he'll be part of an army attacking them?' But the Iroquois have faced invasions like this many times before, from the French and from us. They've never been more than slightly inconvenienced by them. They simply disappear into the woods and come back when it's safe. The wars always end, but trade goes on."

"Yes, trade goes on," she said, and then allowed herself to stare directly at him, in his eyes, for just a few seconds. And then she knew, with a peculiar combination of disappointment and relief, that he would have nothing more to propose that day.

"So what do you think of my plan?"

"I *adore* your plan," she said. "A survey of business opportunities in Iroquois country—how ingenious. And the army will pay your travelling expenses, no less. Very clever."

He blushed at her flattery and seemed, by his silence, to require more.

"Your plan has a pleasing flexibility as well. No matter which side prevails, there will be trade. Or do you have particular interests in that regard? . . ."

"In earnest, no," he replied, a furrow creasing his fine, oblivious forehead. "My fighting in this conflict will be purely *pro forma*. I assume the same is true of Sullivan himself. A better lawyer than general, they say. Got his flank turned at Brooklyn. Mark this: instead of a moot court, Sullivan will run a moot war!"

With that they proceeded, without much more discussion, back toward her father's house on Court Street. The twilight had faded by then, and they found the oil lamp already filled and lit for them in the parlor. Rebeccah's long career as prospective betrothed had taught her to read her father's assessment of her affairs in the condition of the lamp: the more oil he put into it, the more time he was prepared to allow an acquaintanceship to proceed. This time it was filled right up to the brim. He had recently made inquiries into the connections of Severence's family in the assurance trades in New-York, and was evidently pleased by what he had learned.

They also found one glass of porter on the table, for Severence. There was also a twist of tobacco and a mostly unused clay pipe. He took up the pipe but wouldn't drink the porter without sharing it with her, which of course would not be appropriate for an unmarried female to touch in the sole company of a man. Instead, she took up her proper role as hostess and seated herself in front of the spinet to play for him. She did this competently, her voice assiduously in tune but somewhat thin, singing verses he heard but did not listen to because his mind was elsewhere.

The thought that he was actually *afraid* to put aside his uniform occurred to him as he broke off the used end of the pipe and stuffed it absently into his watch pocket. He had, after all, gone directly from his father's house to the army, with no independent career in between. For the prospect of a prosperous, civilian John Severence, he simply had no frame of reference.

In fact, though the military sciences bored him, business held the distinction of boring him even more. This prospecting trip with Sullivan was a stopgap, a way *not* to think, because he really had no plan, except, possibly, to get married. And, much to his surprise, Rebeccah had not saved him from the journey by objecting to it. He had rehearsed to himself exactly how far he would insist on the plan without actually winning his argument. An autumn service in the little church on Bow Street would have been pleasant. But, apparently, she didn't want him, and had raced for the easy exit he had provided for her.

It was just as well, of course; though he knew he looked superficially pleasing to women, none who had actually gotten to know him had cared much to go forward. There was something about him, or something not about him, that chilled them all. His common venality, for one thing. His persistent mopiness, for another. There comes a time in the life of the intelligent gentleman when he realizes he's not the complex, irresistible creature he once believed he was. Women would not necessarily find him fascinating, if only they got to know him. He learns his lovemaking is unremarkable. He is not splendidly misunderstood after all.

His mood was alternately anxious and resigned, as he sat there with the pipe in his lips but not inhaling, wondering, "Whither Severence? Whither he?" The last note of Rebeccah's song had died on its string, and she'd been looking at him for some time.

"Wonderful, my dear," he said at last, as he belatedly recalled her presence in the room. "Wonderful, as always."

"You weren't listening."

"Of course I was."

"Then you are either a liar or have a very poor ear!"

At that they laughed together, as they usually did, and passed the rest of the hour talking about the usual things—the weather, her father, her health—until the grandfather clock on the landing struck nine and he rose to leave.

"Will you be leaving us very soon?" she asked, standing up.

"There are some details to see to. My army uniform is eaten through by moths, and I can't very well wear marine colors on the trails."

"So you will need a whole new uniform?"

"I'm afraid."

"How unfortunate."

Silence, broken only by an offhand "Well, then . . ." from him, and deepened by a weak but clearly miserable smile from her. Severence was emboldened by this, taking her in his arms and placing a kiss on the peak of her forehead. Her skin smelled of a combination of cosmetic wax, rose water, and the tobacco he had been smoking.

"I will write to you. May I write to you?" he asked.

She simultaneously burst out with a laugh and with tears. "You'd better, you stupid fool!"

This last exchange disconcerted her more than any of his oafish gropings or innuendoes. Later, she rehearsed it and re-rehearsed it in her mind, and found herself less and less ready for sleep. Tears? Were there reservoirs of feeling for him within her that she hadn't considered? Something deeper, beneath the uneven rind of their friendship or the dry flesh of her loneliness or, within that, the tart juice of erotic curiosity? She rushed her spell at her toilette—the question shivered her calm. Her hair would go only half-brushed. Nor would she have patience for writing long letters to herself tonight.

Instead, she fingered the cap of the half-empty laudanum bottle as the drug descended in a spreading wave down her chest. When it reached her stomach, the heat turned to a tingling weightlessness that rushed to her limbs, her head, her sex. She dropped the cap and fell back into her bedclothes, letting her worries sink beneath a spreading drift of languor, wishing in some vague way that she could die without knowing Heaven or Hell, but just nothing. So she slept.

Severence's head was too full of plans and prospects to go back to his rooms right away. Walking almost at random, he found his way onto the quayside at Strawberry Bank, where the old channel ran some distance into town. Proceeding east, he reached the Piscataqua and found a young quarter moon riding high above the shipyard at Rising Castle, across the river. There, in the faint light, he could just make out the keel and unfinished ribs in the hull of a large vessel, the American 74, reclining in her slipway like a skeleton in a cradle. Indeed, it had lain there, apparently unchanged, for all the months he had spent in Portsmouth.

He wondered what the Continental Navy would accomplish with such a big warship. Once free of the British blockade, which would not be too difficult to escape, an errant 74 could fall in with all manner of convoys. It could brush aside the Royal Navy frigates dispatched to protect them and carry enough men for dozens of prize-crews. Exactly how many British ships of the line would have to be pulled from service along the Atlantic coast to neutralize such a threat? How much better would the odds therefore be for the long-promised French fleets in breaking the British hammer-lock on American ports? And how many Continental warships and privateers could therefore operate with impunity, with the Royal Navy stretched thin everywhere?

Severence smiled; these were the kinds of speculations Jones delighted in. The thoughts that helped him lull himself to sleep at night. Damn the man's soul, he thought. What was the little hero, the little prig, the little pain in the ass doing right then?

IV.

JONES WAS HAVING the line of his nose inspected. His inspector was Mademoiselle Henriette d'Barlejou, a barely noble but inquisitive Frenchwoman. Henriette was an artist of a very unique, scholarly kind. It was her belief that the Divine Creator was not entirely remote from the profane world, but incorporated into His design subtle aspects of His perfection that might be uncovered by suitably trained persons. In her case, her training was in the survey, appreciation, and reproduction of human physiognomies. It was her project, she had once declared to Jones, to achieve nothing less than the fully scientific reconstitution of the face of Christ.

He had met her two months before, in the Chaumont salon at Passy. She had swam toward him through a watery miasma of social tedium and miraculously saved his evening with her particular theories. Over china cups of chocolate and cream, she explained how the idea for her project had occurred to her several years before, while she was still living at the convent school of the Abbaie de Panthemont in Paris. There, she had stumbled across the works of one Tadeusz Bór Kazimierz, a little-recalled Polish theologian who had, two hundred years earlier, held against orthodoxy by arguing that aspects of the secular world commonly held to be "imperfect" were in fact only so in light of incomplete or flawed knowledge.

Henriette's skill with a sketching pencil had always been a matter of pride to her, but also of puzzlement. For what reason had the Almighty placed such brilliance in a respectable young woman, for whom a manual talent could never be more than a diverting hobby? For what decent purpose could her flair for portraiture ever be consecrated? Reading Kazimierz, she suddenly saw her

Quelles contradictions !
Ce que je puisse employer d'ici
est comment l'œil est furieux et
doux en même temps.

Il n'y a pas de calme en lui que j
le puisse dessiner de la vie.
Il faut que je poursuive toute la journée
et puis reconstruire tout de mémoire.
On j'ai pris le nez, j'ai perdu l'œil!

there to lose? Three days after their first meeting, she received an invitation to join his squadron. Her response was immediate and enthusiastic.

"Yes, *yes*," she was telling him as she examined his profile from a slightly low angle. "There is no doubt a hint of majesty about your nostrils. It is most evident in the light at sea."

"What rot and nonsense!" he cried, meanwhile blushing strenuously under his blue peaked cap. He was, in fact, feeling, if not majestic then at least magisterial in the new blue-on-white uniform he had had made for this cruise. Indeed, this was the first occasion where he had allowed himself the indulgence of wearing gold epaulets on both shoulders. At that point, just six days out from Groix, the uniform still had that land-bound freshness, the fabric crisp and cool, the blue vivid and unspotted, the white glaringly bright. That would rapidly fade after several weeks of desultory washing in used water.

For her part, Henriette had, on astonishingly short notice, pulled together quite a varied collection of outfits for her maritime research. She was wearing wool trousers, trimmed with fleece, which she presumed would protect her from the cool winds that characterized the northern route. Over that, she could choose from cotton dresses, cinched with a seal-skin belt at the waist, in an assortment of practical colors, including "oceanic blue," "bowhead gray," or, for battles, "incarnadine." Her uniform was completed by a straw sun hat that was secured on her head by a blue silk ribbon. At Jones's suggestion, she had also packed a beaver fur bonnet for especially cold evenings. The total effect, she hoped, would be to make her appear more serious, more rigorous, than normal female *couture* would suggest. She counted as evidence of success that none of the men or officers, with the exception of Jones, would even look at her.

"Ah, how pretty *Le Cerf* looks coming about," she pointed beyond the rail.

Jones turned. "That is a frigate—*Pallas*," he said patiently. "*Le Cerf* is a smaller vessel, a cutter. You can tell the difference because a frigate is square rigged with three masts. The cutter has two masts, with square sails on both—except for *Vengeance*, which has a hermaphrodite rig."

"Hermaphrodite?"

"She has a combined rig, with square sails on the fore and fore-and-aft triangular sails on the mainmast, secured by a boom."

"I see. But why so many different kinds of sails and rigs? And why must they always be so confusable?"

"They're not," he stated and then, in an instantaneously deafening voice, shouted, "Mr. *Lunt!*"

"Sir?" responded his second lieutenant.

"Heave the chip."

"Again, sir?"

Jones answered with a freezing stare. Lunt, who should have known better after serving under Jones on the sloop *Providence*, made no more comment but passed the order to the sailing-master. This was his own elder cousin, Cutting Lunt. Henriette had immediately noted the broad family resemblance when she came on board. The angle of declivity of the upper cheekbones was the main clue.

From Cutting, the order passed to the boatswain, Mr. Turner, and from there to the boatswain's mate, whose name even Jones did not know at that point

The "chip"—a triangular piece of wood with a long, knotted cord attached to it—was thrown over the stern. After the cord ran out behind the ship for exactly 28 seconds, Turner read off the vessel's speed.

"Two and one-half knots," he said.

Jones winced. This was painfully slow progress before a light but steady wind. It was no wonder *Pallas*, in the nautical equivalent of pacing impatiently, had to wear back and forth to keep from outstripping the flagship. The smaller and even faster vessels in the squadron, the corvette *Le Vengeance* and the cutter *Le Cerf*, were running so far ahead they were barely hull-up to the northwest. Of the other frigate in the force, *Alliance*, he had neither seen nor heard for 24 hours.

"Alert me the second *Alliance* is sighted," he told Lunt. And then, with a slight bow of his head to the *mademoiselle*, he retired below to write angry letters.

Seated there at the little desk in his cabin, he stared absently out the windows of his stern gallery, the quill and knife poised in his hands. His circumstances now were not ideal, but nor were they completely hopeless. This new vessel was, in fact, by far the largest and best armed he had commanded to date. She was an old East Indiaman, seasoned and tough, bearing twenty-eight long 12-pounders, most of them new, and a battery of six old 18's he longed to try on the hide of an enemy frigate. She wasn't pretty, though. While his *Ranger* skipped like a blue porpoise over the water, the Indiaman hunkered down deep, stolid and entirely black, like a broad, foul-tempered whale. She sailed well in foul weather, but in good, she moved as if dragging an anchor. His only chance of catching fast prey, he expected, would be to send her smaller consorts to harass and slow them down, until the flagship could lumber up and deliver the *coup de grace*.

For a crew, he collected the best he could. The L'Orient docks were thick with men looking for a short cruise and a fast fortune, but few with a taste for military discipline and hard fighting. His recruiters had luck mostly with those who had some personal reason to sail against England—black Irish, down-at-heels Scots, Continental Navy veterans of Forten Prison or the Old Mill with scores to settle against the Royal Navy. There were Swedes and Portuguese and Hindoos, who may not have understood what they'd signed on for. And there were Frenchmen: near 150 of them in marines' uniforms of red and white. His vessel was, in fact, a floating cacophony of languages, customs, and purposes that would, nevertheless, have to fight as a single, solid extension of his own will.

"On board the *Bon Homme Richard,* at sea, August 17, 1779. To the Venerable Minister of Marine M. de Sartine," he began. "In the letter of the third day of the month instant, I reminded you that I have always professed a preference for a fast vessel, and that the *Bon Homme Richard,* nee *Le Duc de Duras,* would be entirely inadequate in this respect."

Jones paused again and wondered what, exactly, he wanted to say to Sartine. This was a man who, largely through an astonishing capacity for inactivity, had humiliated him by keeping him bottled up in Brest and Passy for the greater part of a year. A man who had scarcely moved a bejeweled finger to assure Jones acquired command on *L'Indien,* a truly fast ship. A man he was sure was entirely tired of Jones's observations, requests, and demands, no matter how genteelly penned. What would he possibly say to Sartine that would make the least difference?

The circumstances were not ideal.

Someone knocked.

"Yes?"

"Begging your pardon, Commodore, but the *Alliance* is sighted," a voice, that of Midshipman Mayrant, said through the door.

"Already? Where?"

"Uh . . . three points on the starboard beam. Closing fast."

"That idiot Landais!"

"Sir?"

"Nothing. Thank you, Mr. Mayrant. I'll be up presently."

He then tore up the letter to Sartine and began another:

"On board the *Bon Homme Richard,* at sea, August 17, 1779. To the Venerable Benjamin Franklin, Minister Plenipotentiary of the Continental Congress to His Most Christian Majesty Louis XVI,

Hotel Valentinois, Passy," he began. "Most heartfelt greetings to you. In the letter of the third day of the month instant, I reported to you my unease with the instrument of a concordat between the captains of this squadron. Whereas I am mindful of the particular concerns of Monsieur de Chaumont, I trust you may recall I advised you that any such legal agreement, signed by all captains *as if coequals,* would work only to undermine the authority of the present commodore, and to promote insubordination of both the gross and subtle kinds . . ."

With a sudden pitch of the hull, Jones's pen point skidded disastrously across the page.

"What the devil is it now?" he shouted, rising. The lurch suggested that the *Richard* had run aground, though in their present location, many miles west of Ushant, that would be impossible. There was a riot of yelling above his head, and the sound of bare feet and boots charging around the deck.

Springing up the companion-way, he finally found the *Alliance.* Her bow was nestled heavily against *Richard*'s starboard beam, her bowsprit having ripped straight through the foremast shrouds. There was a dull creaking as the two vessels ground against each other in the slow swell, the bare and ample breasts of *Alliance*'s Minerva figurehead thumping rhythmically up and down on *Richard*'s fiferail.

Immediately, even before white-hot rage, Jones felt embarrassment at the accident. If anyone in the British or French navies had been on hand to see it, they would hardly have had grounds to believe that the Navy of Congress, and Jones's squadron in particular, was a professional operation. D'Orvilliers's vessels did not go blundering into each other in foul weather, much less fair. Nor did Keppel's nor Hardy's nor Rodney's. Such things only happened in Spanish fleets. Fortunately, they were too far from land for any fishermen or beachcombers to witness it.

It was bad enough, however, that Henriette was there. She,

fortunately, was acute enough not to ask any questions of him at that point, saying merely, "Oh dear."

Jones bit his lip and sarcastically addressed the gathering crowd on the other deck. "Good morrow! Is Captain Landais about?"

"I am here," came the reply, laced with a thick French accent.

"Captain, would you be *so kind* as to trim your forecourse and haul off?"

"Nay, *sir,* I find I must decline. But I invite you to trim a course and haul yourself off."

"Captain, need I remind you who is in command here?"

"Sir, I know you have in your possession a piece of paper that represents to that effect."

Most of *Richard*'s deck hands had gathered behind their commander. Rather than dispute uselessly with a fool, Jones turned to them.

"Well, are you all *statues?* Lieutenant Dale!"

Dale, the first lieutenant, stepped forward. The accident had caught him off-watch, so he wore only his breeches and a loose ribbon in his hair. The way the latter spread over the nape of his long neck and thin shoulders immediately attracted Henriette's professional attention. So did the deep, pink furrow that began at his left temple and coursed, hairless, across half his skull. This was a wound, she was given to understand, that he had sustained while fighting on the Loyalist side in the waters off Virginia. He was converted to freedom's cause as a prisoner of John Barry on the *Lexington,* and, as with most converts, his zeal exceeded that of many career patriots. More to the point, in Henriette's view, was the dark and feminine softness of his eyes. Could those eyes, with proper anthropictographic treatment, represent our Savior's?

"Here, sir," the lieutenant said.

"Dale," Jones growled, "see to this mess. When I come back on this deck in two hours, I don't want to see any reminder of it whatsoever. Do you understand?"

"I do."

Even without Landais's active help, the differing rigs of the two frigates assured they behaved differently in the wind. They inevitably began to draw apart. Under the close supervision of the sailing-master's mates, the landsmen all got axes and commenced hacking off what was unsalvageable. Landais, meanwhile, was prevailed upon to pay a courtesy visit to his commodore. Henriette had a close look at him as he passed on his way to Jones's cabin: a stocky, round-shouldered man, face soft and windburn-red, eyes blazing simultaneously with pride and unspecific terror. His uniform was even more encrusted with gold piping than Jones's, but without the latter's flair for martial style. He would be of no use to her project, though he might do well as a model for Pilate. She also recognized, of course, that she was already partial to Jones's point of view in this travelling clash of personalities.

An hour later the carpenter was painting the replacement rail. Landais mounted the companion-way with his expression set in the same obstinate sneer, with Jones close behind.

"Lieutenant Dale," the latter began, "Captain Landais and I have clarified our respective responsibilities in this operation. *Alliance* is to remain not more than five cables off our port quarter, unless he receives orders directing him otherwise."

Landais then produced a hearty wad of sputum and deposited it on Jones's immaculate deck. "Lieute-nahnt," he said, "The 'commodore' appears to forget the terms of the concordat he has signed, which does not dispose him to issue such orders to a gentleman and an equal—"

"Sir, I will see you in irons for this!" Jones thundered.

"And he has once again mistaken me for a Lieute-nahnt Simpson or a Mungu-Maxwell," Landais went on to the embarrassed Dale. "Unlike them, I have been warned about him. His arrogance precedes him in this mission, so you see. And thus I honor his plan . . ."

He stepped over the rail and began his descent to the *Alliance*'s gig.

"Landais, you will be tried and broken if you disobey me again. Do you hear?"

The gig pulled away from the *Richard*.

"Landais! Not more than five cables!"

Jones got his answer fifteen minutes later when the *Alliance*, her bowsprit unrepaired, turned hard to port and bisected *Richard*'s wake. It seemed almost as if Landais was taking up the station Jones had commanded—until it became clear that the *Alliance* was not stopping. In less than a half hour she was hull-down on the western horizon. Palpably humiliated by this defiance, Jones looked for someone else to dress down. He settled on Henry Lunt, who had been senior officer on deck when the *Alliance* had rammed the flagship.

"Mister Dale, if you please . . . ," Henriette entreated the lieutenant as her host raged at Lunt.

"Madame?" Dale answered, though he still did not look at her.

"This enmity between our captains seems very deep. Why were they made to serve together, if they so hated each other?"

"Madame, Captains Jones and Landais never met each other before this expedition."

"But he wears an American officer's uniform, no?"

"Well, yes. But he only recently came to America, to find a ship to command. And not everybody in America knows each other . . ."

She smiled. "But, of course not. What I meant was, they are so much alike—both of them foreign captains in a young navy. Both ambitious."

He met her eyes for the first time. "Then I'd say you have your answer," he said.

All this unpleasantness was not permitted to affect the routine of shipboard social life. Jones still took dinner in his cabin at

precisely four bells on the dogwatch—or 6 PM, to the rest of Chris-
tendom—and Henriette was still seated at his left, as usual. She
was not certain, but she suspected the captain believed his cabin
was the only proper place for a woman to take a meal at sea. This
evidently had something to do with the fact that the cramped eat-
ing quarters of the petty officers and midshipmen guaranteed that
a diner's elbows and thighs were likely to become intimately
acquainted with the less public bodily regions of his or her neighbors, and vice versa. At Jones's table, by contrast, there were no
more than six, and more typically four, guests. This company,
along with her, ranged from the ship's surgeon Lawrence Brooke,
Lieutenant Dale and one of the Lunts, to a midshipman or two
who received invitations on a rotating basis.

The food at sea remained good as long as the stores of fresh
vegetables and livestock and wine held out. On most warships, this
wasn't long. On this, just the sixth night out, the last capon was
slaughtered and served on a bed of vigorously boiled cabbage. Jones
was quiet, his appetite still recuperating from his latest taste of
Landais. Surgeon Brooke filled the gap handily, though, holding
forth on the general inadvisability of surgery in medical practice.

"So you frown on use of the scalpel under any circumstances?"
Dale asked.

"No, not all circumstances. But the empirical man will say, will
know, that cutting men open with a knife is barely ever an effective means of treatment."

"Why?"

"Because the body, you see, has a natural tendency toward
equilibrium of its diverse liquid and gaseous humors. This balance clearly depends upon isolation from the chaos of the
extra-somatic world. Do you know, for instance, what the largest
organ in the body is?"

Dale fidgeted with his chicken bones as he thought. Henriette,
meanwhile, was considering that Surgeon Brooke's forehead had

two very definite lobes, and that this lobular shape was not useful to her. As for his eyes and the bridge of his nose, these were partially covered by the wire reading spectacles he wore even when he was not with a book.

"The lungs?" Dale suggested.

"The liver," guessed Jones.

"No, it's the skin," Henriette said.

"The lady is quite correct," Brooke smiled. "The largest and most complex organ of the body is the skin, because it is the skin's responsibility to maintain the integrity of the body's essences. This is a matter of physical integument, of temperature, of cleanliness, as well as of encapsulation of the spiritual fluids. These latter are the most important, because as all know, they show the least specific gravity of all organic constituents. They will, upon rending of the protective membrane, immediately rush to fill the next most expansive container, which would be a surgical theatre, in most cases, or the whole world, if the procedure is held out of doors."

Brooke was having difficulty separating his chicken leg from its thigh. The location of the joint appeared to be concealed under a protective membrane of poultry gravy. Soon he switched from gently probing with his knife tip to hacking at his food.

"Do I take it that you have a similar view of amputations?" Jones asked, eyeing this struggle.

"Ah, amputations. But of course they are a different thing. I would hesitate to call them *surgery,* no? The élan vital naturally tends to flow away from wounds, so there is reduced danger. Amputations are therefore more akin to cutting hair or fingernails."

"I'm confused," said Dale. "Didn't you say the . . . *élan* . . . rushes through breaks in the skin?"

"Yes. But it depends on the quality of the break, of course. Wounds are violent events visited upon both the body and the spirit, from which the latter tends to retract."

The thought occurred to Henriette that, according to Brooke's reasoning, a surgeon would do better to run his patients through with a boarding pike than to risk incisions with a scalpel. But she also knew that her position in the ship's company was still tentative, and that making an enemy of the doctor would hardly be to her advantage. Instead, she nodded agreeably with all the others, except for Jones, who seemed to be listening to something else.

"Excuse me," he said, rising. "Something appears about to happen . . ."

With that, he was through the door. And sure enough, the lookout cried out immediately that a sail was sighted to the northeast. With somewhat less haste than Jones, they all retired to the topdeck. Brooke kept his wineglass with him. With Henriette on his arm, dressed now in a more conventional lavender touring dress, they looked like a typical bourgeois couple out for an evening at the Palais Royal.

The strange sail closed rapidly on the Indiaman, causing no small amount of indefinite anxiety among the officers and men as Dale and Jones examined it in their spyglasses. They were heard to murmur to each other, but with no verdict until Jones finally lowered his telescope.

"She flies no flag, but by her line and rig we believe she is from a colonial port—probably a northern one."

"A letter of marque? A privateer?" asked Lunt.

"The distinction hardly signifies. She spotted us and decided to investigate, hoping we were a British merchantman. Presently, she will note that we also fly no flag and see the lower gun ports for our 18s, and decide she has no chance against us."

At that, the intruder trimmed her course to run parallel with *Richard*. She was a two-master, a good deal smaller than the Indiaman, with just eight gun ports visible. The rest of the crew saw this, most of them breaking their vigil and returning to their duties.

"We'll see no more of her in a few minutes," Jones turned to

Henriette, suddenly conversational. "Privateers are vessels outfitted by civilians, authorized by a government to raid upon enemy commerce. They are profit-taking ventures, so they very rarely will attack a vessel of equal strength, much less one exceeding theirs."

"A legitimate form of piracy, then?" she asked.

"They have their uses . . . especially for nations without a proper navy."

Jones's attention was diverted by something—a splash off the intruder's starboard beam. He and Dale resorted to their spyglasses again.

"Now what is this?" the lieutenant muttered.

"Mr. Lunt, please back the mains," Jones said quietly. "Mr. Lunt-the-other-one, launch the dinghy with four men. Our friends appear to have a man overboard."

Brooke and Henriette stepped forward to the rail, trying to improve their view. Indeed, she could see a speck of something, a speck with limbs, breaststroking away from the intruder and toward the *Richard*. But why would a man finding himself accidentally overboard swim away from the closest help?

The mainsails were turned away from the wind, slowing the *Richard*'s progress. Very quickly, it seemed to Henriette, one of the Indiaman's small boats was in the water with Cutting Lunt in the bow, pulling hard for the victim. Meanwhile, the intruder had also backed her sails, but because she was much faster than the *Richard*, her momentum had carried her several hundred yards beyond. The privateer lowered her own boat, which seemed to have an equal chance of reaching the victim first. A number of idlers and sailors off-watch gathered again at the *Richard*'s rail, cheering their boat onward. And because it was a fair day, Henriette could hear a faint answering chorus from the privateer.

"Remarkable how sound carries over water," she said to Brooke.

"There are very good physical reasons for that," he replied. "Very good reasons."

But the race was over quickly. Whether due to some aspect of the current or the quality of the oarsmen, Lunt and his crew reached the swimmer first, with their rivals still a hundred yards short. Lunt and an oarsman each took an arm to pull the victim to safety. The latter seemed to be mostly naked, with just a breech-cloth and some sort of strap around his upper arm. He was lying against the legs of the other oarsmen, drenched and wheezing, his lips moving.

"What are they conversing about?" Jones demanded. "What could they have to bloody *discuss?*"

The privateer's boat was now in the vicinity, and the mid-oceanic palaver widened. Lunt was now seated again, addressing himself to the party in the other boat and doing much shrugging. *Richard*'s launch came about, and the discussion continued as both boats pulled back to the Indiaman. At length they could hear bits of the running argument and the privateer's coxswain con-cluding with ". . . a *most* unacceptable decision for a ship's master, if he be a man of laws . . ."

"Good morrow, Mr. Lunt!" Jones called out. "What might the issue be, pray?"

"We appear to have a volunteer, sir. But this gentleman does-n't seem to appreciate his man's zeal to serve in the Navy of Congress."

"I have no doubt you simply misheard the gentleman, Lunt. I scarcely can imagine an American holding such an opinion."

"Silas Hagland, of the ship *Desdemona*, Captain," the other coxswain identified himself. "Your man here does not seem to understand that ships of the Navy of Congress do not *kidnap* duly enlisted volunteers from a vessel bearing a commission from the very same congress."

"You seem to suggest, if I gather your meaning, that we are on the same side in the present conflict?"

"Precisely!"

Je ne suis pas à
la hauteur de la tâche.

Je les ferai cruels.

"Then you will understand when I tell you, Mister Haglan, that I have often shipped light of crew because of vessels bearing your kind of commission. What do you say to that?"

"I hardly know, sir."

"Nor do I, except that the Navy of Congress will do well to survive such allies. And so I bid you good afternoon, sir."

"Captain, I feel confident in remarking that the *Desdemona*'s master will not endorse your reasoning."

"Then I invite your master to make his complaint to the nearest appropriate authorities, with my compliments. Good-bye."

With that, Jones nodded to Dale, who ordered hands to the braces. The *Richard* did not exactly *leap* forward, but she did open up blue water between herself and the privateer's boat. Soon the coxswain's protests were lost in the sibilant rustle of her wake, and Henriette noted a very definite air of self-satisfaction wreathed around the captain. He evidently did not like privateers, either.

Lunt reappeared on deck, with the ship's newest volunteer dragging himself behind. Considering the exertion of his sudden swim, his condition could have been far worse.

"So what sort of fish have we dragged for ourselves today?" asked the captain.

"He looks to be a Hindoo," said Cutting Lunt, standing aside for the senior officers to have a closer look.

Henriette knew enough of the world's savage races to know this was not a Hindu. The superior aspect of his features showed too much dishlike broadness, the proportions of his limbs were too short relative to his generously muscled trunk for him to be a native of Asia. His skin also appeared to have an incongruous whiteness—except for the long, red welts that snaked around his arms and torso.

"Your back seems to be well acquainted with the cat," Jones addressed him. "Tell us, what crimes did you commit?"

"None. And which have *you* committed?" the savage parried.

"Careful, nigger. You're talking to the captain," Dale said.

The eyes of the "Hindoo" rose off the deck and shot directly at Jones.

"Are you a great war captain?"

"Of all the impertinence!" Dale cast about for something to hit the man with, but could find nothing immediately to hand.

"Steady, Dale. Your English appears to be quite good, friend. Are you Mahican? Senecah?"

No answer.

"It is not as if it matters to me in the least what tribe of heathen you hail from. But at least tell us your name."

"My name is Joseph . . . to you."

Jones laughed. "Joseph to me, eh! Well, all right, then, I will be 'war captain' to you! Is there anything you can do on board a ship?"

"I can fight—if you are worthy to lead."

The newcomer was every bit as insolent with the captain as Landais was, Henriette noted, but Jones's reaction was far different. Each tart response only seemed to delight the captain more.

"I will endeavor to be so worthy. In return, you will observe our discipline, yes? Do what is asked of you?"

Joseph frowned gravely. "Of course."

"Fair enough."

"Captain, the *Desdemona* . . . ," Henry Lunt interrupted.

The privateer had brought herself on a course oblique to *Richard*. She was now only a few hundred yards to port, and her gun ports were open.

"Quarters, sir?" asked Dale.

Jones made a quick appraisal: he saw no fighting sails, no anti-boarding nets set, no preparation for deck action. It was a bluff.

"Of course not. Ignore them. Put Mr. Joseph-to-you to work with the landsmen. I'll be below for now."

Il a des rainures
profondes au dos.

And with that, Jones shot the privateer a parting glance and, with a wide turn that was certainly visible from the other deck, moved toward the ladderway.

Just then the crack of a fired gun froze everyone—including Jones. As it echoed, all ears listened for the hiss of the ball in flight. But it never came. Instead, a puff of powder smoke appeared on the side of the privateer opposite to the *Richard.*

Jones continued below. Having made her protest, the privateer put her helm up and slunk away toward the north-west.

Joseph looked at Henriette, whom he caught with her eyes fixed on the fresh scars arcing around his chest. "Something else you want to see, lady?"

She turned away with a blush.

"Never mind her, nigger!" Lunt shoved him. "Now that you're staying with us, come meet your new friends."

V.

*Men are wicked. Care must be taken especially not to suffer
surprise, because surprises intimidate and terrify. This never
happens when preparations are made, however vexatious the
event anticipated.*

—Frederick the Great, *Anti-Machiavelli,* 1740

JULY 31

My dear Rebeccah:

This morning we started north from Wyoming. At that point
where logistical matters end and military tactics begin, educated
officers always pause for an important task: to decide on a proper
classical precedent. Of course, the popularity of Caesar's histories
among Latin tutors guaranteed that his campaigns in Gaul come
to mind first. Due in no small part to the fact that these campaigns ended in victory for the modern, civilizing army, they were
pleasing prototypes of military operations deep in savage country.

But it scarcely demands remark that, for better and for worse,
the congress has yet to commission a Caesar. This oversight recalls
the virtual undoing of the latter's conquests when, in 9 AD, three
legions under Publius Quintilius Varus were surprised and anni-
hilated in the Teutoburg forest by a horde of barbarian pikemen.
Fifteen thousand legionaries, the cream of the best under Roman
arms, were trapped between a forest and a swamp and flailed for
their lives for the better part of three days. Their enemy seemed to
sprout from the oak trunks and congeal full-armed direct from the
mud. Hardly anyone escaped. The magnitude of the defeat shook
the most powerful man in the world, the Emperor Augustus, so

deeply that for years after, he was given to impotent despair, crying, "Publius Quintilius Varus, give me back my legions!"

Fret not, my love. This is the eighteenth century, and savages never again will defeat modern armies. The force under Sullivan is not a gang of flighty, fidgeting militia, but hardened Continentals all. Where Varus's legions wielded arms hardly better than the bludgeons and blades of their enemies, ours is amply equipped with more firearms than the Senecah have probably seen, let alone procured, in 150 years. We also have eleven artillery pieces, from long sixes to grasshoppers, which have no parallel at all in the savage's world.

Perhaps most important, we have an officers' corps that is, in my experience, unique in its quiet fury. None of them have been insensate to the predations of the Senecah along our frontiers in recent years, while many of our militia have been off east, settling accounts with the lobsterbacks. After the events at Wyoming, at Cherry Valley, Cobleskill, and Minisink, it would not be an exaggeration to say that there is a general taste for slow, complete, and conclusive vengeance on them all. Of the usual lust for simple adventure, for the sort of action imagined by immature minds, there is very little taste. Instead of saucy novels and letters from sweethearts, our officers spend hours in diligent study of Frederick the Great's operational instructions or Lloyd's *History of the Late War in Germany*. Drinking is discreet. For lack of fodder, cavalrymen readily give up their mounts, just for an opportunity to kill Indians anywhere, any time, in any manner feasible.

But it would be inaccurate to attribute our motives only to moral outrage. In fact, the campaign has always been intended to make the enemy harvest the just fruits of their own policy of economic war against the colonies. His Majesty's Criminals, along with their half-naked red allies and Tories, know very well that it does not take many massacres of white women and children or many indiscriminate burnings of houses and slaughterings of livestock to induce a scattered and vulnerable population of settlers to flee their farms. The last two years of their campaign of terror has depopulated a wide swath of territory across the northern frontier, from the Mohawk River in New York through the lower reaches of the Susquehanna and the Chesapeake. Men who are not farming are likewise not producing provisions, either for use by the Continental Army or by the body of civilians. It would serve our adversaries very well, in fact, to make us choose between abject servitude and feeding our children. Having seen what I have seen over these years of fighting, and known the inside of one of their prisons, I am well acquainted with the political uses they make of hunger.

But we colonials also know a few things. We know, first, that the Six Nations are vulnerable to this very same sort of warfare-against-economies. They are likewise thinly spread across the land and can hardly muster two thousand warriors among them. And though we know that the lone Senecah or Mohawk brave is a stout and formidable fighter, and that Butler and his lackeys have supplied many of them with firearms and powder, the brave's individual skills are useless against massed fire. Indeed, he *flees* before it. We know that the Iroquois have exercised imperial ambitions of their own in the past, and have earned for themselves many enemies among the tribes of Virginia, Ohio, and New England. Thus, with the help of our Indians, our Mahicans and Cherokees and Shawnees, we can and will invade the heartland of *their* Indians and, inevitably, force them to heel.

We also know that the sachems of the Six Nations are not stupid men. They must understand that if they cannot face our force openly, and cannot defend their villages and fields, that they must resign themselves to a realistic and mutually profitable policy of neutrality, proper to their relative weakness and inevitable decline in the face of historical necessity. Their other choices—outright defeat or outright despoliation of their lands and dependence on the British for all their food and supplies—would be a fate too terrible, too unnecessary, even for these savages to suffer.

The butchers of Wyoming and Cherry Valley will no doubt have their influence on the ultimate consequence of our campaign. Their names are already notorious throughout the colonies: Colonel John Butler was the Tory commander at Wyoming, and his son Lieutenant Walter Butler led at Cherry Valley. The latter had the support of Joseph Brant, a Mohawk war chief and Christian convert who is well connected among the royal authorities in the north. The elder Butler is a wilderness commander of some skill, and a fine recruiter—by collecting and training Loyalist Rangers from his base in Niagara, and leading them on raids from Mohawk country to deep in Pennsylvania, he has contrived to make himself a considerable nuisance. His son Walter, on the other hand, has not covered his family name with glory. After suffering capture as a spy near Fort Clayton in '77, he was sentenced to death by Arnold, but gained the sympathy of his captors with a fine simulation of illness. Once transferred to a hospital, he made his escape, but left with no tender feelings for the rebels who had taken pity on him. Instead, he plotted his revenge and secured it with the lives of 45 settlers at Cherry Valley. No one knows if those acts were sufficient to restore his peevish pride.

That Brant took an active role in the butchery is claimed by some but not proven. He is something of a celebrity among those in higher social circles who had cast their eyes down upon the Indian yet pronounced him salvageable. Having converted to the Church of England and translated Scripture from English to the Mohawk tongue, he is at least as educated as many of the white officers he has scalped. There is a story, well known along the Continental line, that Brant once spared the life of a lieutenant the Mohawks had tied to a tree for the purpose of scoring with hot irons. The man, an officer of the Connecticut levy, had learned that Brant had been inducted into the Free and Accepted Order of Freemasons and had the presence of mind, before his scoring, to display the secret gesture of that brotherhood. Of the shape of this gesture I must confess my ignorance, but the performance had its proper effect on Brother Brant, who instantly ordered the officer's release. This testament to Brant's noble sensibility is not generally disputed by anyone in or out of the order, but has earned him precious little credit since the massacre. Indeed, tales of the savage's handsome manner and keen mind have earned him a great deal of jealous enmity. He will do well to stay clear of us.

I have joined this drama *in medias res*. The main army left Easton more than a month ago, marching the 65 miles up to Fort Wyoming via a road cut for their purpose. Apparently, General Sullivan believed this work of engineering was necessary because use of the Indian trails would alert the enemy to our intentions. Of course, I am not entirely sure what our enemies would have thought of the obvious din of axes on trees and shovels on rock for the better part of the summer, but there is no doubt the general grasps such matters better than I do.

There is a saying that military amateurs dwell on strategy, but professionals on logistics. The month of July, I understand, was spent in collecting a mountain of supplies—shoes, blankets, leggings and shirts, hats, musket and artillery shot and powder and canisters to carry them, flints, tents, camp stools and furniture for the officers, canteens, haversacks, tools for erecting fortifications and digging entrenchments, instruments of music, cooking and dining equipage, salthorse, hardbread, blacksmith's and surgeon's supplies, horse fodder, shoals of shoats, gaggles of geese, firkins of flour, rundlets of rum, and no less than 700 standing head of cattle. Altogether this trove—the portion that couldn't walk on its own legs, that is—was enough to burden 120 boats and 1,200 packhorses.

Again, this appeared to me excessive. The collection of such an enormity of stores delayed the expedition until late in the

summer, and save for the timely arrival of certain boats and wagons filled with necessaries, might have resulted in its outright
cancellation. Against such worries, the general posed the fact that
once his force was north of Tioga, he could not to allow his troops
to hunt for game, lest their gunfire give away our position to the
enemy.

But there is a more fundamental reason, I think. No one, possibly least of all Washington's French and Spanish advisors, had
any real knowledge of what is required for a modern army to
enter, survive in, and prevail in a wilderness utterly innocent of
roads, farms, or substantial towns. If one mounts the heights over
the Wyoming Valley and looks about, one gathers two predomi-
nant impressions: First, there is the unrelenting richness of the
land—the close and choking verdure of the woods, the blooming
meadows innocent of hoof and plow, the wild streams that seem
to pour from the beating heart of the world. Second, one is confronted with the stupefying way this richness extends on and on,
beyond hill after hill, mile after green mile, over topography that
grants no credit to the scale of human endeavors. An army ten
times the size of ours would be swallowed up by it. Any officer
with a modicum of experience, aware of the many ways men can
sicken, become injured, dispirited, or afraid, can only look at the
task of possessing such an immensity, and shudder.

Our task is complicated further by a lack of good maps or
intelligence about the land we are poised to invade. We have native
guides, to be sure, but even they concede that the state of their
knowledge may well be out of date. The lands of the Six Nations
are known to be crossed by diverse foot trails, but only the most
significant are known to our guides or discovered by our scouts.
The Senecah and their allies have settlements of sorts, we understand, but of their location and extent we can only surmise. Our
ignorance stems most particularly from the Iroquois' skill in

excluding all surveyors and foreign spies from their lands, with a mind toward discouraging exactly the sort of operation upon which we embark.

Our commander does not content himself with worry, however. I have met with him only twice so far: once for a brief introduction and review of my orders, once over dinner in his tent. Physically, he is unimpressive, of average height and build, dark and quick features, his manner one of evident discomfort and impatience. His most distinctive feature is a certain curl at the edges of his lips—a curl that appears supercilious when he is in repose, but in fact reflects something more fundamental. Rather, it is an emotional barometer, becoming more and more arched as his mood sours. For John Sullivan is, if anything, embodied activity, with hands and eyes moving all of the time, his casual conversation often interrupted by sudden orders to his orderlies or lieutenants. He is deeply reluctant to leave any matter to luck on this journey. I believe he is determined to grasp every detail but the middle names of all of his troops.

Luck, alas, has been a fickle friend to him. Though his career had a fair beginning in the New Hampshire delegation to congress, his record as general has been marked by more zeal than talent. He anchored Washington's right during many of the late battles in New York and New Jersey, and acquitted himself serviceably at Trenton and Princeton. On several occasions, though, he has found himself outmaneuvered. At Long Island, he was flanked by Howe, particularly because he failed to monitor the Jamaica Road approaches to Brooklyn adequately. At Brandywine Creek, his right was turned again, also by Howe, because no one among Washington's general staff seemed to know exactly how many fording places there were on the stream. Both defeats, that is, were the result of gross failures of survey and intelligence. This is exactly the deficiency he means to make up in the present campaign, notwithstanding the fact that we have a much worse picture of the lands of the Six Nations than we do of Brooklyn or Pennsylvania.

Fairly or unfairly, Sullivan has become a favorite whipping boy in congress, especially amongst those who would attack George Washington but lack the stones to do so directly. When the decision to chasten the Six Nations was first announced, many cheered. When the leadership fell to Sullivan, many groaned. None of this was lost on Sullivan, who has responded first by developing a torturous peptic ulcer, and second by trading in his youthful fire for a plodding circumspection. While there is still the prospect that he might conquer brilliantly against the Iroquois, he seems more determined not to gratify his critics by losing. Instead of a dagger thrust into the heart of the Indian Confederacy, Sullivan has imagined this campaign as a boulder on the savages' backs, grinding them down to a sure but unspectacular death.

I did tell you he was a lawyer in private life, did I not? I have it on good authority, from an old colonel of Virginia here called Enoch Poor, that an acquaintance of his in Durham has had extensive legal dealings with Sullivan. Poor was slow to unbutton his lips at first, but a bottle of porter in my tent set him off. He told me that our commander is renowned in that colony for his malicious litigations against property. His method, I understand, was to take upon himself the responsibility of guaranteeing the town taxes. If funds owed him were not forthcoming, he was practiced at exacting interim charges and "service fees." Extended tardiness commonly resulted in Sullivan himself winning deed to the taxpayer's property at court. These maneuvers he accomplished with a sureness that has lately escaped him on the battlefield. Indeed, he is so fine a lawyer that a mob of angry defendants once had occasion to surround his house. None of the petitions against his conduct harmed his interests, said Poor, because Sullivan counted both the colonial governor and the attorney general amongst his associates. Thus it seems that the current operations against the property of the Indians are entirely within his dubious sort of expertise.

Or so say the detractors. Paul Jones had legions of wagging venomous tongues behind him as well, but I found both his strengths and weaknesses of character to be far more peculiar than either his critics or his champions imagined. So it is likely to be with Sullivan. Of his devotion to the cause, there can be no dispute: Sullivan was an eloquent voice for the rights of the colonies in New Hampshire, and among the first to wager his position and fortune on the struggle. He has shown no concern with finance or personal enrichment since his veritably religious conversion to the cause of liberty. Washington must think highly of him, because he keeps sending him assignments. There is more than a bit of Jones in the way he tends to remind those who have forgotten that he has sacrificed much for freedom, of the way (as he says) he "exchanged domestic ease for the dusty field of Mars."

My estimation of him, in short, is not complete.

Our first meeting was in his private marquee, some time after sunset the day I arrived in camp. His tent was set close by the water, well placed for the river breezes to cut through the August heat. It was a glad affair, orthogonal with two side bays, and gold tassels fluttering from the poles. His valet, a wretch named Unger, was his manservant in private life, for whom he had procured a lieutenant's commission. He seemed to consider himself the sole arbiter of a very precious resource in the general's time, warning me, "We have scheduled you for ten minutes, Captain. Do you understand? Ten minutes, very strictly timed." And he held up a pocket watch to prove his capability at "strict timing."

"Of course," I replied, feeling a perverse temptation to antagonize him. "The matter of my orders shan't take long. No longer than ten or fifteen minutes."

"*Ten* minutes, sir."

"As I said," I jibed, ducking inside.

Sullivan's private quarters did not mirror the celebrated orderliness of his mind. Rather, it evoked the image of a beach where books, loose papers, writing implements, and drinking glasses washed indiscriminately ashore. I did not see him at first because he was bent behind his desk, apparently searching for some particular piece of detritus. When he straightened, I was looking at a face of dark complexion and black eyes. The latter were almost the sort one sees on the faces of fancy dolls—except that his moved, quickly and all the time.

"Captain Severence, I expect," he said at once, rising to shake my hand. He was only slightly my inferior in height.

"At your disposal," I replied, presenting him the packet containing my orders. He merely glanced at this and put it aside.

"This is from Mr. Jay?"

"I am fortunate to have entered his acquaintance through the good offices of Mr. Franklin."

"Indeed. Franklin, Jay, John Paul Jones. You are well connected, sir."

"I have yet to introduce myself to George Washington, as I understand you have done."

He smiled. "My sole advantage, but I will own it. Drink?"

He produced two glasses—mine clean, his used.

"Unfortunately, I have not been able to get my own wine stores up from Easton, so you have my apologies," he said.

"I am far from the epicure my connections might suggest, sir."

"Then we shall get along fine together in the woods. So you were on the lakes with Arnold?"

"I was."

"A very creditable action. Congratulations. So what do your orders say?"

"In essence, I am to accompany you, assisting you in any fashion you see fit. As a field officer of some little experience,

I flatter myself that I might be useful in that regard."

"I see. Go on."

"To confer and advise with you on matters diplomatic with the Senecah and any other tribes, and to aid the commanding officer in the administration of all prisoners."

Sullivan clucked his tongue. "I can promise you little to do in that regard. Diplomacy and prisoners do not figure prominently in *my* orders. What else?"

I hesitated just long enough to signal the appropriate discomfort with the rest.

"I am also to file an independent report on the conduct of the operation."

He frowned into his glass. "Was that Jay's idea?"

"I could not say."

Sullivan settled back onto his leather camp stool, regarding me through lowered eyelids. I could only assume he was deciding whether I was an agent sent by his enemies in congress. In truth, I had not anticipated the possibility that my presence would trigger such a suspicion.

"I can only say, sir, that the idea that I might be placed at your disposal originated from me, not Mr. Jay or anyone else. Allow me to confess that I have a certain, if you please, interest in this part of the continent. Of course, it is entirely within your prerogative to delegate me to operations that might be fairly remote from your flag. Among the garrisons along your supply lines, for instance . . ."

Sullivan's face brightened. That is, it brightened as much as his dusky features allowed.

"An interest, eh? Tell me, would you say it is speculative or intellectual?"

Not knowing where he was bound, I played the safe card and answered, "Both."

He nodded and turned to poke amongst the strewn reams for

something. Very quickly, he came forth holding a book with a red morocco cover and corners battered from frequent use.

"Take this. Study it. Come back to me in three days with your arguments for why the author's arguments are wrong."

I glanced at the spine. The title was *Christianity as Old as the Creation, or the Gospel a Republication of the Religion of Nature*, by Matthew Tindal.

"Er, the general may have a misimpression of my use of the word 'intellectual.' My grasp of theology is but slight."

"Mr. Severence, these matters have nothing to do with theology. Tell me: do you live among the rest of us within this terrestrial orb?"

"It would seem so."

"Is your existence but at the pleasure of the one and true Creator, omniscient and all powerful, who rules over this world and the next?"

"I would not dispute it."

"Then your stake in these matters, as a servant of our Lord Jesus Christ, is as urgent as any theologian's. Come back in three days. Consider this my first order."

Much puzzled but without grounds to dispute him further, I bowed and turned to leave. I did this not a moment too soon, as Unger was standing behind me, pointing at the omniscient and all-powerful face of his pocket watch.

Thus proceeded our first meeting, in the full oddity it is within my power to relate.

Yours ever in love,
JOHN

P.S. Perhaps too late, I am aware that the previous account is not the usual matter of love letters home. I trust in your intrinsic patience to indulge my compulsion to share all of my thoughts and impressions. As you were the first to lay your gentle blessing

upon my project here, I can conceive of no other manner to conduct this correspondence than in complete candor. Please know,
however, that behind every excrescence of my poor prose lies a
deep and abiding desire to be done with the ordeal of a life without you. Do not doubt, my love, that it will be so, soon enough.

P.P.S. Before sealing this letter to you, I am likewise compelled to
despair of the fact that our correspondence must necessarily be
one way only. Posted letters may reach as far as Wyoming, I am
told, and personal letters may be carried with our official
dispatches south. But once we are at Tioga and beyond, the opportunities for provisioning will be over until we return. Reply to me,
of course, but please do so with a mind that I will not receive your
letters until the end of the campaign, September at the earliest. I
also trust I need not make plain that your circumspection must
match my candor line-for-line. Though your noble natural
impulses might suggest to you that your closest intimates might
be safe with our confidences, I must prevail upon you in the
strongest terms that espionage is as great a danger to this project
as cannon and musket-fire. In this, I enlist you as my own sweet
soldier.

VI.

SOME DREAMS only make sense when they're ready. I told you that when my father was dying, he had a dream about the beaver swimming on a river so wide the land was out of sight. It was only when I woke up on the *Desdemona* that I understood he was not dreaming of the Susquehanna or the Delaware at all. Instead, the beaver was on the St. Lawrence River, on the stretch of it where you traveled east and the banks marched away to the north-west and south-east and the sweet water ran to salt. I stood up when I realized this, up from my work scrubbing the deck with a flat stone, and said to my father, "Yes, I know where you were now. I understand it all." I was only partly telling the truth to him, though, because I still didn't know what the beaver meant or who the bear was he would fight. But I figured I would find out soon.

So when the press-gang was finished beating me, they took me back to their ship and threw me into its cellar. Ship cellars aren't like the ones under houses—it was damp, yes, but there was no smell of earth or dust. Instead, I was lying on blocks of stone that stunk worse than the most rancid heap of meat. I was down there for a long time, maybe days, wondering what kind of cargo the foolish whites thought they were carrying, this load of rotten stones. I heard the water flowing around below me and, sometimes, live things moving around in the water.

The dark was so thick it was easy to confuse when I was awake and when I was asleep. For fun, I would watch the bright lights that you see in the dark, floating in front of your eyes. You know these lights swimming around in the jelly of your eyeballs because they hardly move when you flick your gaze here and there. After a while, I got good at making these spots form any shape I wanted. The curve of Fallen Leaf's cheek glowing like old embers. A False

Face of flashing blue cheeks and purple tears. Whole constellations of red spinning sunflowers and trembling curtains of thin, cold green, like the lights that shine in the night sky in winter. At the same time, I noticed my cell was beginning to rock gently up and down and side to side. Not so much at first, but more as time passed. At that time I hadn't seen the ocean yet, though I had walked the shores of Neahga Tecarneodi ("Lake Ontario") and knew about waves. Lying there and thinking about it for a while, I realized that the ship was nothing but a big canoe, and like a canoe you could tell when the ship was turning when it hit the waves at different angles.

After a while they let me out. They seemed disappointed when I came up without looking like I'd suffered too much. One of them had a ladle of water in his hand, grinning and holding it there as if he expected me to jump at it. But I just yawned and gave myself a nice stretch and scratched my balls. The guy spat at me, saying, "Too dumb t'drink, bilge monkey? My, yer ugly. Get up 'ere wi' ye."

They shoved me up the ladder, into the sun for the first time in days. And while my eyes screamed in my skull, the voice of that same prick, the officer I almost shot on the riverbank, was talking to me, saying, "What a lucky red ape you are, Mr. Joseph Two Fires! We're going to give you a taste of civilization on this trip— make you an honest dollar, maybe even show you Europe. Do you know what that is? *Eur*-up. Tell me now, won't that make you the most well-traveled little Mongol?"

"Would that be England, France, or the Netherlands to which we are bound?" I asked, meaning to rile him. And he answered by planting the point of his shoe into the pit of my stomach.

"Fetch him a holystone! Don't let me hear him speak again!" he shouted to someone, then to me, "Some bodies don't know how to be grateful!" And then he stomped off.

I didn't spend much time on the *Desdemona,* so I don't have much to tell you about the tribe I found there. The manner in which they took me and the way I became well acquainted with the wrong ends of the officers' boots was not worthy of a warrior's loyalty. They told me I was there to fight with the rest of them against the English father's ships, but I didn't see how standing on a deck shooting at other guys standing on decks really amounts to fighting. That was more like what the little boys in Chonodote did, throwing rocks at each other from behind trees. The only way a man could get any killing done on the ocean, I figured, was to put his ship next to his enemy's and jump over on him. But that's not how they fought on the *Desdemona*. I'll say more on that later.

What struck me most about that ship was the crowding. There were hundreds of bodies on the deck, and while it seemed like a big ship when I saw it from the riverbank, it didn't seem nearly big enough to hold so many men. You couldn't stand up or turn around without running into somebody. It seemed white people didn't need so much air and sunlight and space as normal folks. That struck me. That, and the smell of tar, tar everywhere, on everything. It was as if I was hostage to a tribe of men who sweated and pissed tar.

I never did learn anybody's name. I only saw the captain three times. He was squat and softly fleshy like a pregnant woman, and had small piggy eyes with yellow edges. He made a pretty contrast to the crew, which looked and acted like a gang of lean, sick, permanently hungry coyotes, constantly squabbling and stealing from each other because they were all miserable for money and women and had no respect for themselves. When they weren't loafing through their watches, they were gambling, complaining about the food, or lying in their bunks with their hands down their pants, yanking. Most of all, though, they gossiped: about the grog such-and-so had hidden away, and what somebody else had heard one of the officers say about something the captain said, or about something just as foolish. They liked to share these secrets in front of me as if I didn't "speakee," even though I never hid the fact that I spoke English better than most of them.

The only name I did learn was by accident, when they hauled me up from my swabbing on the third or fourth afternoon of my "cruise," in front of these two guys sitting at a desk. One was a lieutenant in a black suit, who was busy shining his nails with a neat little chamois cloth but never raising an eye to look at me. The other was the ship's clerk—a young man, no more than twenty, with half his face marked by an old burn. He was writing my name at the bottom of a column on the last page of a big book lying open in front of him.

"Tell us whether you can write, Mr. Two Fires," the clerk said.

"Have savages ever been known to write?" I answered.

The clerk smiled. This expression made his burn break into a web of scarry lines.

"We need your agreement to the division of shares," he said. "By act of congress, able seamen, ordinaries, landsmen, and boys may divide 17/40th's of all prize-money. There are 82 hands in your class, and 17/40ths divided by 82 gives a 1/193rd personal share, collectible upon auction of said prizes, if any. Understand? Good. Make your mark here."

He dipped the pen and held it out to me.

"I think our Hindu deserves a better lay than that, Stephen," the lieutenant suddenly suggested. "Wouldn't you like a bigger number than that, boy? How about a 1/386th share instead?"

He was talking to me, but winking at the clerk. The latter, Stephen, entered into the spirit of the joke fast, saying, "Nay, to look at him, he's a doughty fighter. How about 1/772nd, my friend?" And the two of them had a good laugh together.

I took the pen and made my mark: *Mr. Joseph Two Fires.* I left out the number in the share column. It didn't matter—this "savage" wouldn't be around long enough to get paid.

Every story about a guy who goes out on the ocean for the first time mentions getting seasick. And I won't disappoint you: I did get sick, though only when they finally let me out of the cellar. Getting kicked in the stomach a lot didn't help much. While I was bent over scrubbing the deck, I had occasion to let fly with whatever poor salted meat or plaster-hard biscuit I was able to temporarily keep down. Making such a mess often meant I earned another kick or a nip on the back with the cat o' nine tails.

I did learn one thing from the crew, though. Many of them were raw "landsmen," too. The old sailor's treatment for seasickness, I saw, was to tie a string around a small fish, like a chub, and then swallow the fish while somebody else held the string. Once it was all the way down, they would slowly haul the fish back up the guy's throat. You might imagine this set off some hard heaving, which also had the effect of making the seasickness seem not so bad by comparison. I tried this on myself and it worked, but only for the nausea. It did nothing for the headaches. At home this would have been treated with a tea brewed from yarrow, but the remedy was unknown to the whites.

So as the ship went east and the shore fled farther away, I did my job and pretended to accept my fate. I also spoke as little as possible, because everybody already assumed I was at best childlike and at worst just dumb, and I wanted them to continue to think of me that way. As time passed, there were fewer eyes on me, and I managed to become almost invisible to them. This would be useful to me when I saw my opening later.

When being invisible got boring, I amused myself by playing on their fears of having a full-fruited savage in their mess. Once, I sat down in front of my watch-mates and very slowly began to lick one of my feet up and down, from heel to ball to between the toes. After they all watched for a bit, one of them finally spoke up, asking, "Hey there, Eskimo . . . what's yer madness now? 'At some sort o' custom?"

He and his friends laughed, though a little nervously. But nobody was laughing when I answered, saying, "Me miss-e man-meat. Man-skin tastem yum-yum. You want-e?" And I held out my foot for them to share a taste.

"Bugger the devil, he's a *cannibal* . . . ," one of them breathed.

To complete the picture, I picked some dry skin off my heel and ate it. After this, none of the whites asked about my "customs" anymore. The show did have an effect on their sleeping customs, though. Where many of them used to pass the night with their feet sticking out of their bunks, the threat of cannibalism made them keep their extremities tucked neatly and tightly under their blankets.

But there wasn't much else to laugh at on that sad ship. What was hard to understand about that time was not that they took me by force and put to me a test of character. That was something my people did to enemies all the time. What was hard to figure is that the whites didn't take somebody and try to find the extent of his manhood. Instead, they just made him busy at the kind of work that made him the opposite of a man. Work that was monotonous, pointless, demeaning. Why go to the trouble of capturing a man if a woman or a machine or an animal would have done just as well? Why make the effort?

Anyway, within a week there was no sign of land at all around us. I understood we were beyond Turtle Island entirely. Now our people were not so ignorant of the world as many would have you believe. We had long been dealing with French, English, Dutch, Italians, Irish, Portuguese, Spanish, and even the occasional lost, crazy Russian. Many of these trappers and traders were only too happy to describe their understandings of geography to us, often in exchange for our knowledge of rivers, hunting grounds, and lakes. These swaps more often than not happened under well-liquored circumstances, using crude maps scratched with charred sticks in the dirt. But they were enough to give us a good idea of where Europe was and how far away. We knew that England was an island, and that she and the Dutch, unlike the French and Spanish, were against the authority of the Papa in Rome. We also knew that the Russians and the Mohammedan lived even farther east, and that the whites thought they could keep sailing that way and reach the western shores of Turtle Island again. But opinion was divided on whether this was really true or if the whites were just confused about how their compasses worked at the ends of the earth.

So I understood fine when I overheard that we were near the coast of Ireland, and we began to see many ships again because we were close to many ports. The *Desdemona* examined all of these, approaching with her guns covered until we could tell if the prey was enemy, ally, or neutral. Each time, the officers decided either the prey was not from a hostile kingdom or was too big to attack or escorted by too many of her friends or just "suspicious looking." Their cowardice was more sickening than the motion of the ship. So the joke was on that idiot clerk, Stephen, and the lieutenant: they were so cautious, nobody looked like they'd collect any prize-money, never mind the official size of my share.

By then, barely anyone was keeping watch on me. It would have been easy to slip away, except that I wasn't so sure how far I could get in such sick, weakened shape. It's also hard to make out accurate distances on the sea, with no trees or hills to relieve the eye. I'm telling you this because I don't want you to think I was broken by them, staying on that ship for so long.

My hand was finally forced one day when I overheard the officers talking about turning around, back out to sea, the next day or the one after. I figured that would mean we would run across fewer ships and have no chance of seeing land at all. There weren't too many decent opportunities left.

Less than an hour later, the sails of another ship broke the water. The *Desdemona* edged closer for her usual look, closing in enough to make out the stranger's hull, because ships of every size looked pretty much the same from the feet of the sails upward. I was coiling a rope at the time, doing my best to look like a piece of the woodwork. But if you'd put your hand to me then, you would have figured my heart was burrowing her way out of my chest.

"She's frigate-sized, possibly an Indiaman," the stout little captain said, as he held his puckered little eyes to his telescope. "I don't see a flag."

"Then she's French or Dutch, if she's running this close to the Scillies without colors," said the lieutenant.

"Alas, she's too heavy a catch for us to weigh." And the captain put his telescope away.

And with that, I placed the rope carefully on the deck. In three running steps, I was flying over the side and falling down, down almost forever. When I finally hit the water, it didn't feel like I expected: it was much colder and the salt burned at my throat. I had no experience with it; to the Gweugwehono, all water was either sweet or swamp, and only subservient tribes had to live down by the ocean.

Now while you're picturing this, with me swimming up and down those big swells and the *Desdemona*'s boat coming after me, you might also ask why I was working so hard to trade one master for another. What difference could it make, this choice? The answer is, probably nothing. No difference, except that it was *my* choice. This was a little thing, I admit, but it kept me ahead of the oars splashing behind me, and the lieutenant's voice rising over the water, like this:

"After him, boys, that soaken little rat! Pull, my lovelies, and we'll share a piece of 'im together, that's my promise to you! We'll roast 'im and eat 'im, red meat first, with 'is blood as dressing! Look at 'im there, sweet for the picking. Pull, now . . ."

With this encouragement, I kicked and churned with strength

I did not suspect, breathing as much foam and water as air, until I heard another voice. This one was insisting, "Larboard, I said, larboard so I might have him! . . ." Lifting my head to see, I saw a bald man just ahead of me, leaning over a bow with his arms spread. And between his short hanging sleeves, I saw an enormous black ship, turning on the waves like a man on a trail pausing to answer a question.

"Hey, Beaver, why are you out here, so far from your lodge?" the bald man held me, asked me.

"To kill the bear," I said to him, though he was frowning at me, as if he didn't understand. "To kill the bear."

VII.

A battle has a long tail.

—Henry IV

AUGUST 30

My dear Rebeccah:

Yesterday we met the Senecah. As I am writing to you now, you can well guess that I was not honored to be counted among the casualties. My deepest agony, indeed, is that engendered by our long separation and my guilt at not having written to you since the last day of the month ultimate. However, it appears to be in the nature of this odd expedition that nothing much happens at all—until something does. The intermittent pattern of this correspondence should, at least, give you the quality of my experience here.

The sixty-mile march from Wyoming to Tioga Point took eleven days. In that time, Sullivan experimented with and perfected the marching order best suited to our purposes. As everyone knows, the Indian fights best with the advantage of surprise. It should follow, then, that the prudent commander frustrates this tactic by sending out as many pickets and scouts as can be spared from the main force. This Sullivan has done, employing our division of frontier riflemen for this purpose. Our eyes and ears are therefore spread out over miles in every direction, with specific instructions to study every crag and defile, to sweep every shoreline, to scrutinize and certify the solitude of every hilltop. Our advance knowledge of the disposition of the land and the enemy ahead is therefore very good so good, in fact, that a repetition of the intelligence failures that wrecked certain of Sullivan's other endeavors is all but impossible.

But the enemy is not obliged to defeat us outright. Rather, a successful assault on our supply train, which is frankly enormous, would serve just as well to compel the general to withdraw. While a smaller, faster force might have subsisted off the land or off stores raided from the Indians themselves, the necessity of a decisive strike has assured that we are too many for such improvisation. A large army, deep in the wilderness without adequate supplies, is particularly vulnerable because it is slower and harder to coordinate. With our stores, we constitute a colossus bestriding the Indian nations; without them, we are a stranded leviathan beset by wolves.

To assure their safety, our packhorses and artillery march in the center of a hollow square formed by four Continental brigades. This is a secure order, but presents a wide profile, obliging us to spread over a front far broader than the poor Indian trails and riverbanks we are obliged to use. There are, therefore, also many obstacles for us to flow over, around, and through, making necessary many turns and adjustments. Brigades of men are assigned solely to cutting down trees, filling in mud holes, and grading ramps for the great guns—all tasks that consume significant time. And, unavoidably, mistakes and miscommunications also delay our progress. So there are good reasons why commanders operating in the woods, like our adversaries Butler and Brant, prefer the speed of running just a few men abreast. But Sullivan makes an obsession of security, and for that reason we adopt not only the form, but the speed of the turtle.

There is another factor that one might expect to delay us further, but which, in fact, does not. I refer to the legion of females —some 500 in all—who have accompanied us on this march. A good number of them are the wives and sisters of men in the line, who occupy themselves with tasks of cooking, fetching of firewood, and they will (in due course) minister to the wounded. These women are often more experienced in the rigors of camp life than the green recruits they come to serve. The column has never been slowed in the least by them, even though they tend to scatter themselves over a wide area behind and beside the troops. Like most commanders I have known, Sullivan seems content to perceive them as part of the landscape.

The deliberateness of our march is cast aside when it becomes necessary for us to ford a river. The marching order must break formation to do so, with substantial numbers of men wet to their necks and their weapons and powder lofted dry but useless over their heads. Just a few enemy riflemen, situated on some convenient height above our fording place, could pick off whole columns in just a few minutes. Or a concerted attack could be mounted against half of the army while the other half is standing on the far side of the river, helpless to intervene. Fortunately for us, the rivers here run gently and low in late summer. The general also causes river crossings to proceed very quickly, with not more than an hour of vulnerability risked to cross all three thousand officers and men. Stragglers are dealt with in a manner it would not befit your feminine sensibility to read.

Sullivan's precautions have made the marches uneventful, even dull. The enemy must be observing us, but keeps himself out of sight. One of our advance parties discovered a fresh fire pit fifteen miles from Fort Wyoming, so recently abandoned they could rekindle the flame with a few puffs of breath. But there was only one pit, and, as Sullivan argued, a Senecah scout party would not be so reckless as to give away their presence with a fire. The pit was probably used by trappers.

Moving into the Indian lands, the soldier naturally is beset by staring eyes, real or imagined. Yet, marching in such serene security, he also has time to linger on less malignant prospects. The country, that is, is exceedingly rich, with unbroken woodland and streams larded with fish spread to infinity in all directions. The land's profile seems arranged into the perfect curves beloved of landscape painters, with valleys deep but not sunken, hills that frame but do not belittle, and streams clear and cool and livened with sunlight. Natural amphitheatres abound, all fit for the setting of some rustic drama or as beds for indolent giants. The skies in late August complete this peace, either by presenting a face of mild, unblemished blue or scattered banks of cloud to cast sprays of soft shadow on the nodding hillsides.

With every step, the soldier sets his foot on pillowy topsoil that seems never to have borne the weight of a man before. With every pause in the march, he hears insects singing in the grass beside him that may never have been heard by a civilized ear. With every canteen of water from a deep and unsounded lake, he shares a draught with Adam. These notions have worked on the minds of all the men, until they all go through this land in a state of continual astonishment, and perhaps whatever degree of envy it is possible to feel for the savages.

Tioga Point lies at the confluence of the Susquehanna and Chemung rivers. Geography would dictate a thriving community there, but politics and war have delayed settlement. Incursions by the Senecah have despoiled the place of everything but overgrown fields and empty, scorched barns. This was a truly distressing sight, particularly for the large number of our men who were once farmers and farmhands.

Tioga was also the point where our force was to meet with that under General James Clinton of New-York, who was leading some 1,600 officers and men from Canajoharie down the east branch of the Susquehanna. This was a much-anticipated event, signifying the final assembly of our force, and in a multitude (some 4,500 troops) that should easily crush whatever meager numbers the Indians may collect. It would also comprise an army, Sullivan would proudly note, that represented fully a quarter of all Revolutionary forces under arms on the continent. Whether it was truly advisable for a substantial portion of the Continental Army to be marched into a remote corner of the country, away from the main theatres of war, was a question that surely occurred to all, but was (of course) voiced by none. That decision was made months before, by Washington, in all his profound and worshipful wisdom.

While we waited for Clinton, Sullivan directed the construction of a stockade for the protection of his precious stores. This task was executed in great part by womanly labor: where a good number of the men were engaged in sitting, gently rubbing their feet, or beating the bushes for nuts and berries, there were many female hands to be seen hauling wood and fetching tools for the carpenters. One of these, a young woman with striking dark eyes and a new wedding ring on a chain around her neck, tottered right past me as I sat on my horse, a wood beam slung precariously across her narrow shoulders. She smiled pleasantly at me as she passed.

"Good morrow, Captain," she said.

"Er, good morrow," I replied, well embarrassed. Indeed, though Sullivan has a talent for ignoring such spectacles, this girl caused me much guilt as I sat and watched her and her sisters toiling away as many of we men took repose on our tender flanks.

Our rest ended when Sullivan ordered us up the Chemung to destroy an Indian village said to lie some twelve miles away. We left after sunset, arranged in the usual order, with 250 left behind to guard the stockade. The going was predictably gradual in the dark, and I warrant even a deaf Indian could probably have heard our tumbling approach through the underbrush. When I arrived in the village at dawn with the forward column under Edward Hand, I saw our riflemen milling from cabin to cabin, sweeping the Indians' kitchen gardens for edibles, or else leaning lazily against their weapons, gnawing contentedly on ears of fresh Indian corn. All told, there were about twenty buildings scattered along the bank, all clad in bark but quite well built. The village was deserted, our diners reported, probably within a matter of minutes or hours before our forces arrived. Then Sullivan himself finally came up, clearly much vexed by failing to catch the savages.

"Mr. Hand, will you see to the torches?" he hissed through that prominently curled lip.

"Certainly," said the other, who was equally notable for a tanned face, so dark it appeared almost orange in the morning light. In fact, I have not exchanged three words with General Hand in all our weeks together. This most certainly is because he is infected with the same suspicion our commander entertained about me— that I am a spy sent by John Jay. But he does appear to be a competent and loyal field officer.

Just before the torches were set, gunfire sounded from some distance to the west. Sullivan and I immediately rode in that direction together, with two hundred reinforcing troops forming up and following us as best they could. The firing continued as we picked our way around the swamps and mudflats and dodged low-hanging branches along the riverbank. It stopped just before we broke into a clearing and saw a firing line of Major Parr's rifles arranged perpendicular to the stream. We could also hear but not see other figures—our adversaries or our men pursuing them— crashing through the brush away from us.

"What is your report, Major?" Sullivan asked Parr, who was dismounted and standing at the end of his firing line.

"A dozen of them laid fire on us from the slope," he said. "We formed up and . . ." He motioned toward two clothed lumps on the ground among the trees.

We dismounted to view the bodies. They were lying twisted where they fell, their attitudes exactly as if pressed into the earth in midstride by some carelessly stepping giant. Their faces and chests were trimmed with red and black stripes. One of them still clutched a musket as gladly etched and painted as himself.

Physically, they were not quite what I had supposed, based per-haps on exaggerated accounts of their prowess. One of them appeared quite plump, in fact. The haze of black powder, at once acrid and faintly sweet, still lingered above them.

"Are there no more?" asked the clearly unimpressed Sullivan, scanning the forest about him.

"The savages are expert at removing their casualties," Parr remarked.

"A pity. Now, please follow procedure."

The major nodded at Sullivan, then at a lieutenant standing by with two pistols.

"Processing!" cried the latter.

Two men put aside their rifles and approached the bodies with small iron hand hatchets. As we watched, they each bent over a corpse and scraped off a length of the scalp. They did the deed with a tentative sawing motion, holding the head by the hair. This act did not draw much blood—what flow I saw was in the nature of a slow, moist seeping, as if they were slicing melons.

"Leave the rest for the crows," Sullivan said as he mounted his horse and swung it around. He moved away without saying any-thing more to me, pausing only to gaze with studied compassion on our casualties—some half-dozen Pennsylvania farm boys in all states of bodily disassembly. What was remarkable, indeed, was that each wound was both gruesome and mortal, as if the Senecah had studied their targets for some time and nominated each man for a different sort of horrid death. Noting that one boy was still alive, though thrashing desperately and thoroughly disemboweled, the general hastened to lend his canteen. Two intermediaries of successively lower rank passed the boon gradually down the chain of command to the wounded hero's lips. The latter interrupted his agony to writhe to a sort of recumbent attention.

"Thank you," he finally said, though the act of swallowing appeared to torment him.

"You depart this life well, my boy," Sullivan told him. "Mark me, your sons will grow up free on this land."

"Then I'd better get a wife first," came the weak reply.

Sullivan sat back in his saddle and crossed his arms conversationally. "Tell me, have you ever read any of that Deist falderal? Matthew Tindal, perhaps? Or Morgan? I ask because it is most material to the disposition of the soul."

"No."

"How unfortunate. My brief is thus: never accept the proposition of a natural law anterior to the Revelation. In my opinion, it is an abomination even to suggest the possibility. It is worse than popery. There is no moral law superfluous to the revealed Word of our Savior, for if it were not superfluous, He would have revealed it. *Ceteris paribus,* any truth not divinely asserted is no truth but error. This is most important for the learned man to remember, particularly in places like this. Do you understand? My boy? Hallo?"

Sullivan's peroration on the revealed Word was the last utterance the boy heard. The highly unequal symposium having ended abruptly, the general dutifully bowed his head and offered up several rare seconds of his silence. Then he retrieved his canteen and rode off.

"*Ceteris paribus,*" Parr muttered, though not necessarily to me. We glanced sharply at each other and, in a painfully awkward pass, were momentarily surprised by each other's presence.

The party in the clearing was growing in size as more of our men drifted back through the forest, rifles slung heavily over their shoulders. Having tried and failed to catch up with the savages, they wore faces glazed with disappointment and the sheen of fatigue. A few held souvenirs from this first encounter: knapsacks, beadwork, bits of clothing or personal items either shot off or dropped by the fleeing enemy. Small knots of riflemen soon gathered listlessly to examine and trade these curios. The prospect of profit instantly revived a number of them, and the tableau began to take on something of the quality of a market. If our enemy had thought to double back on us at that moment, he could easily have exacted his own kind of profit.

I preferred not to imagine it. Instead, my eye was drawn to something rising above the trees to the east: it was the smoke of the Indian village on the Chemung, burning at last. The fumes rose in torpid stages, as if reluctant to smudge that sky, that land. The men around me then interrupted their negotiations to heave up a listless impression of a cheer.

Thus, it began.

Our force united with those of General Clinton six days later. The arrival of the latter, escorted by one thousand of our men sent upriver to meet them, was naturally an occasion for much genuine, if nervous, celebration. Genuine, because the consolidation rendered us numerically invulnerable. Nervous, because the rejoicing necessarily implied the fundamental gravity of our situation deep in the wilderness, where the appearance of any friendly white face had to be savored as a rare event.

In any case, the leavened mood lasted longer among the officers than among the men, who managed several hearty rounds of "huzzah" before the practicalities of camp existence reabsorbed their energies. The former, including Sullivan, the Generals Hand and Poor, Major Parr, and myself, turned our own attentions to a number of rich dinners in honor of Clinton's successful passage from the Mohawk to Tioga. Over a very fortifying series of suckling pigs, stewed rabbits, compoted pigeons, and legs of mutton and veal, supplemented each time by corn, squash, and beans harvested from the red villages we had so far "processed," we skillfully exercised the prerogatives of command in the general's marquee. These, Sullivan assured us over sweet wine and ices, would be the last of such luxuries we would see before our successful return to Wyoming, or our defeat. We therefore ate with a certain degree of resignation that singularly focused the mind. These were, indeed, among the finest meals I have ever enjoyed, outside of France.

True to his word, Sullivan placed the entire expedition on half-rations just as we left Tioga. Our daily board was thereafter reduced to the following, except for the occasional additions due to officers:

1/2 pound bread

1/2 pound beef and 1/2 pound fresh fish; if no fish were available on a particular day, 1/2 pound of mutton or pork

1/2 pint of milk or 1/2 gill of rice

1/2 quart beer

1/2 gill peas or beans

These victuals are in addition to the 3 ounces of butter and 1/2 pint of vinegar per week doled to each man. Altogether, they are perhaps sufficient to keep body and soul together during an endless, exhausting march through swamp, range, and stream. But the ration is not nearly enough to stave off constant pangs of hunger. Sullivan is, again, properly aware of the sacrifice made by his men and promises safe passage back to Tioga for any man who cannot "belly up to the bar of privation." The pride of the young men has so far constrained any of them from taking him up on this offer.

Perhaps by virtue of his late arrival, General Clinton has shown none of the coolness that has limited my intercourse with Generals Hand and Poor. Rather, he has treated me with all the sincere companionability of a lifelong colleague. His uncommonly pale green eyes, gleaming out from beneath a wild upswerving thicket of eyebrows, fall lightly and attentively on everyone. To my jokes, he laughs; to my strategical interjections, he grants due weight. For a man of 45 or 46, he seems almost too readily flushed with good, honest cheer, raising the perhaps ungracious suspicion that he is simpleminded.

But a simple man would hardly have led his men over hundreds of miles of hostile territory without loss of a single man.

This feat was, by itself, more encouraging to our prospects than the unopposed burning of a dozen villages: it suggested that the Tory Butler and his Mohawk lackey Joseph Brant were caught utterly unprepared for our incursion, and would be capable of mounting only limited resistance.

"In two months, between the Mohawk and here, we saw nothing of them," Clinton spoke as plumes of pipe smoke wreathed the tent. "Against settlers, women, and children, they show no quarter, hmm? But against men, they will not stand. Curious, is it not?"

"Perhaps not, if one takes note of how they fight their own wars," interjected Parr. "In their battles it is customary for one of the antagonists to flee before there are very many casualties."

Clinton snorted. "One would hardly dignify such conduct as the waging of war, yes? Battle without casualties? Perhaps for the men in my line, but the devil take me if the enemy escapes without his blood decorating the field!"

"I believe the major means only to suggest how the savage understands war," I said. "But it is also true that certain Europeans take a similar view. At sea, our French allies most often decline to try conclusions with a force of equal strength. They prefer to cripple the enemy's rigging and escape. Yet, we would not maintain that the Frenchman knows nothing of war-making, would we?"

There was a momentary silence—one that gave me sudden cause to regret having indulged a contrarian point of view. Sullivan took up the challenge.

"Our Captain Severence shows an admirable sympathy for the Indian way of thinking. One would almost say he believes their mores have a certain dignity."

"I would say so, yes."

"Really? I would say not dignity, but a kind of consistency, perhaps. Dignity implies viability, which the Indian's way of life certainly does not possess. Rather, it is a relic. Wouldn't you agree?"

I was not sure I agreed at all. Instead, I shrugged.

Sullivan laughed. "Come now, Mister Severence! These are not the plains of Europe we are fighting upon! It is we who are here, on *their* land, poised to take *them* within the bosom of civilized nations. Surely that is a truth you cannot dispute!"

"So held Thrasymachus," I replied.

Sullivan frowned. "Thrasymachus argued only for the justice of the strong. It is hardly an argument at all, but a surrender to mere political necessity. I suggest not that our superiority rests on our strength, but the exact reverse: that we are strong because we are right. That is, because we act in accord with the wisdom of the Creator. Tell me, have you found an opportunity to read Mr. Tindal yet?"

"I confess I have not . . . as yet."

"Then I look forward to our discussions when you have," he said, tipping his glass.

With that, the discussion devolved into pleasantries, and the guests melted away. For my part, I returned to my tent and, cursing my imprudence, set a light and took up the inevitable Mr. Tindal. As I read, I found the aridity of the text did not keep my attention from wandering, first to the gentle tinkling of plate and glassware some yards away, as Sullivan's orderlies cleaned and stored the general's dinner service. These sounds, so redolent of civilized, city pleasures, were curiously juxtaposed with the sounds of the forest all around us—the whisper of the late-summer river, the clatter of the insects, the owl in mourning. All around us, beyond the circle of our little lamps, stood a gloom that seemed, at that moment, to be as profoundly deep and inscrutable as a darkest blight of frozen shadow in the deepest crater on the far side of the Moon. Unlike Sullivan, I do not find it self-evident that there is any wisdom, divine or otherwise, in our presence here. Thinking such thoughts and indulging such doubts, I fell asleep with both the baying of wolves and the pleading drone of Tindal's prose chorusing discordantly in my ears.

The next day had the air of a fresh start for the expedition. From that day onward, there would be no more resupply or reinforcement or letters from home. There would be no further white settlements, sacked or otherwise, for us to defend or avenge. From there, we could trust only in the genius of our commander and the rightness of our cause to bring us across the chasm.

Sullivan decreed festivities before we departed. All hat brims were decorated with sprigs of fresh sumac. In an odd use of army provender, sacks of flour were set out so the men might whiten their hair. This gave our host the appearance of an army of nobles and judges. And judges we are, in a particular sense. Our charge is to execute a certain sentence, handed down from the highest of all benches.

The band was enjoined to play for the men one last time before their instruments were stored in the stockade. As the fifes piped and the drums pounded forth an insipidly chipper military air, the men's faces appeared pensive and grim under their artificially wizened heads. The scarcely less cloying ring of Chaplain Rogers' voice quickly followed the roll of the drums across the verdant wastes, describing the heaven that awaits us, we instruments of divine affliction. The program concluded with a thirteen-gun salute, conducted under the close scrutiny of Sullivan himself, who interrupted his conversation with General Hand like a pure denizen of the opera pausing to hear the aria. But I'd warrant there were not a few who wondered, after Sullivan placed us all on half-rations, why shooting at wild game would give away our progress to the enemy but the roll of drums and the voices of the great guns would not.

At last, with the general's sword raised on high and the fifes happily left behind, our host surged forward along the right-hand shore. Beside us ran our fleet of some 25 bateaux, bearing additional supplies, and two gunboats armed with a coehorn each, which Sullivan assigned to protect the boats and to pour grenadoes on any opposition by land.

Though he intended the forces by land and the forces by water to combine their advantages, the bateaux quickly moved ahead of us as the army marched into vales of green but sodden ground. All were then obliged to stop as the artillery were collectively coaxed and cursed and pushed and hauled through soft banks which, under the punishment of many hundreds of hooves and feet that swarmed about the stuck carriages, were rendered into great wallows of mud. Just gaining a foothold in the morass presented a challenge to the men, many of whom lacked shoes. As one bootless private leaned with all his weight into the task, he slipped and shattered a jaw against the transom. Sullivan had him led back to Tioga.

The general sentiment about the great guns changed quickly after the third or fourth of these ordeals. Instead of tokens of Christian genius and industry, they came to be the leaden encumbrances of our wasting and doom. The artillerymen, like nannies of a class of unruly but privileged brats, smile and make light of the seriousness of the delays. Suffice it to say that their assurances did little to lighten the gathering gloom that settled over the expedition that day. Moving the guns was exacting a cost, both in time and casualties.

Yet there was, and continues to be, a deep reluctance to rid ourselves of them. The guns have become, in fact, both the emblems of our inevitability and tests of our own worth to bear them. As if the small metallic gods of our own tribe, we bear them around the forest as they crush us, and in return they sweep away our enemies. And, indeed, they did cast the decisive bolts of thunder in the coming battle, as I will relate. But in this wilderness, under these conditions, we have come to fear these guns, with all the reverence and dread the word "fear" implies in the simpler races.

The daily march on the 29th instant began in typical fashion, with much of our number pressed into the razing of stumps and the leveling of land before our guns and wagons. The Chemung River was on our left, a cohort of hillocks crowding in upon us on our right, and much bog and swamp in our path. The drudgery was broken at last by a dispatch from our scouts some miles ahead, who reported sighting the smoke of many campfires in the dawn light, the number being equal to half the number set by our force. This intelligence moved us all to much anxiousness and excitement, not having been sure until that moment that our march would be opposed at all, or when, or where.

The general ordered our pace redoubled. Not long after, a second dispatch arrived: a fortification was sighted, arranged perpendicular to the riverbank, and some one half-mile in length. The breastworks were said to be camouflaged with the green boughs of trees, as if to deceive our approach. Their ambuscade might have worked, in fact, if one exuberant brave had not accidentally shown himself crouching there, painted in his gay fashion, in plain sight to our scouts. There was some thought given to killing him with a rifle shot, but to Sullivan's relief, our advantage was not squandered by this foolish act.

It was not until midday before we in the main force, including the brigades under Poor, Clinton, and Maxwell, arrived in the vicinity. Ragged fighting had already developed between the Indians and General Hand. The latter had gathered Parr's riflemen in his center, strung along in a line parallel to the breastworks at a range of 150 yards. From that position they poured accurate fire onto the fortification. Their ambush foiled, the Senecah broke cover and entertained the riflemen with a series of berserk charges and equally berserk retreats, leaping and whooping, with the evident purpose of drawing Parr's men into pursuing them. As the main army had not even been engaged, Parr and Hand wisely held their men back.

When Sullivan finally arrived, he appeared to begrudge every moment of conflict unsupervised by himself. Though Hand and Parr had done very well, he barely acknowledged them. Instead, he unfurled his master plan: a multiple envelopment that called for Poor and Clinton to proceed beneath the high ground to the right, Odgen's New Jerseyites to circle around the breastworks from the river side, and Hand to press forward under the cover of Proctor's artillery. The latter would be quickly placed on a low hill—a mere bump, really—400 yards from the ambuscade. At this, the collected officers either sighed or laughed, depending upon whether they were assigned to move or to depend upon the protection of the great guns. After all the tears, sweat, and blood expended in moving the gun carriages, there was little faith they could be placed in time.

"And what might be so amusing, eh?" Sullivan demanded, looking to me, although I had been careful to be one of the few not to sigh or laugh.

"Nothing, sir. It is a singular plan," I replied.

"It is not singular. It is not Alexander's prosecution of Porus. But it will conquer."

Sullivan, who was not a stranger to bending ears before the bar, could persuade men when he required it. This statement, "It will conquer," had its good effect; his staff sat about on their horses, nodding gravely and granting, yes, it will conquer. So we did it.

For lack of explicit orders, and supposing that mounting the high ground would give me a superior view of the action, I attached myself to Poor's force. This brigade, numbering less than five hundred men, was hastily arranged in loose ranks and propelled to the right under strict orders of silence. Moving forward with the center, I proceeded with sword drawn several paces to Poor's right.

The apprehension on the faces around us was distinct and rampant. Men who had appeared jocular and unconcerned the moment before the charge were suddenly heavy limbed, their mouths dry of spit, eyes turned toward their commander as if to assure his ongoing participation. A few others, to be sure, showed the opposite transformation, and were bright eyed and fairly grinning now at the immediate prospect of resolution. How I might have appeared to the others, I cannot say.

Orders notwithstanding, it is impossible to make silent the march of one thousand feet on a floor of dry leaves. On the slope before us, toting tomahawks and muskets feathered like exotic birds, the painted Senecah were intermittently visible, darting confidently, almost recklessly, from cover to cover. As we pressed forward, terrifying whoops would suddenly ring out from ahead and from either flank. Frequently, the threats resolved themselves into English, as in (if you will forgive me) "Yangeese women, come taste our cocks!" Or when a voice would pick out some individual man from the ranks and make a personalized threat, as in "Hey, red-haired boy, I have a long fingernail here to scoop out your heart!" The men, though hardened Continentals all, did not encounter such taunts facing British regulars on open fields. With each cry, many of them would simultaneously give a start. Some would shoulder and aim their firepieces in the direction of some voice, though they were forbidden to waste powder in this way.

What was perhaps most worrying of all was that, despite the assurances of our Oneida scouts, we still had no definite idea of the size of the force opposing us. It might have been no more than twenty pickets, or it might have been an equal force of hardened, red-faced renegades and Tory Rangers. Even so, and despite the distractions of the Senecah scouts, we pressed forward, gods and victims all.

We pressed on, that is, until the men ahead began to sink to their knees into another bog. A groan went up then from every throat, irrespective of rank. Once again, Sullivan's plans appeared to suffer from a lack of proper knowledge of the field. As Ogden and Hand were supposed to be enveloping the enemy from the left and the center, the right arm of our army's embrace was held back by the increasingly impossible terrain. "Hey, Yangeese soldiers, don't go that way!" some hidden brave suggested with mocking regret. But his warning was too late for us. As the soft mud swallowed my legs up to my boot tops, I despaired over my choice to join Poor. Far from a panorama of the field, I now would be consigned to see nothing of the action at all.

Pops of musket fire began to sound from the woods. Many emanated from the direction of Hand's brigade; other isolated reports echoed from the hill before us. Upon one flash and puff from a firing pan, one Continental, bent over to sniff the scent of a floating blossom, had a ball shear off the whole of his lower jaw. The appendage skidded across the water toward Poor. He regarded the jaw sternly as it presented itself there, tongue still quivering, and then sank. "Tarnation swamp!" he cried, slapping the water with his hand like Croesus castigating the Hellespont.

Then, thankfully, we heard our cannon speak for the first time, voices deep and resonant as a curse from Jehovah. There was a hiss as the ball arced over the line of the treetops and fell with a crack against what must have been the substance of the breastworks. All at once, a spontaneous cheer went up from among us.

"That's Proctor givin' 'em one for!" Poor cried out, waving his hat over his head. "Shall we get a taste of what's glory, boys?"

"Here, here!" shouted some. Others responded with whoops not unlike the savages'.

"Then fix bayonets!"

The blades were torn from their scabbards and twisted home on each muzzle. These were not the fey French bayonets, mind, but ones close to British issue, a full 17 inches long. The Senecah suddenly broke off their taunting.

"Forward! On the double!"

Thus we charged. At first, only our arms and knees sped as the men flailed through the mud, putting the most perfectly ferocious face on our immobility. But the footing soon improved; the tops of boots reappeared at last, and with our sudden freedom we began to accelerate, gathering momentum like a great, soggy, woolen wave.

The wave crashed at the foot of the hill as the savages were flushed one by one. They outpaced us easily up the slope, but that didn't seem to matter very much as we swept up after them. The liberation of our feet from the muck made all of us, shod in all our various ways, feel we were no longer marching but flying over the dry earth. We were too exhilarated to perceive fully our own exhaustion.

There were no nervous glances backward then, no twitching recoils from imagined threats. In some metamorphosis instantly attained, we had become a single body, achieving that unity of martial spirit that field commanders pray for but can never truly count upon. It is the fruit of circumstances—or, in this case, the savages' fear of the bayonet—that filled us with an ill humor contemptuous of all opposition yet precisely balanced with the demands of our discipline. Wisely, Poor issued no further orders, saying nothing more that might upset the sudden equilibrium. Rather, he ran before me waving his sword, injuring more low-hanging branches than adversaries.

The pace of Proctor's fire, meanwhile, kept pace with our charge, spurring us upward as the reports followed each other more closely. The detonations shifted, indeed, from the cracking thud of solid balls to the metallic precipitation of canister shot, and thence to the hollow eruption of incendiary bombs. The artillery crews had evidently found their mark against the enemy breastworks.

But then, just as suddenly, the vanguard at the top of the hill was halting, falling, crawling toward what poor cover it could find. Our perfect coordination had vanished. The men behind and below noted the flagging momentum and slowed themselves, conscious at last of their fatigue. Instead of a triumphal wave crashing and washing the crest clean of opposition, we were a sputtering stream pooling feebly at the top, facing an imminent prospect of being swept off ourselves.

Once at the summit myself, I saw the reason: some unknown numbers of braves had positioned themselves behind trees and were pouring steady fire on whomever showed a head above the crown of the hill. Their fire, in fact, was so admirably disciplined that it seemed we were facing a force of drilled riflemen.

"The Senakee," Poor turned to me, "are learning how to fight properly." This statement surprised me not because of what he said, but because it was the first time he had addressed me directly in the weeks I had known him. Yet the only reply I could hit upon was the tactically astute exclamation, "Hmmm, yes."

Peeking through screens of fallen trunks and knotted roots, we could all see one reason for the enemies' good order. There were a few, no more than a handful, of white faces with regular uniforms—green coats with red facings—among the savages. These were members of Colonel Butler's Loyalist Rangers. As we were set fairly close together, this intelligence spread quickly along our line. Yet it had the opposite effect than one might think: instead of intimidating the men with the prospect of facing professionals, the Rangers' presence seemed to render the enemy's face more familiar, and therefore defeatable.

The brigade launched its final advance with bayonet. Amid the steady pelting of balls on the trees and rocks around us, we all managed a hearty shout and orderly charge that had a highly favorable result. The savages, faced with the immediate prospect of disembowelment, broke and ran. The Loyalists, cursing their allies, broke after them. At that moment, I saw that we had opposed no more than forty men, not including Butler's gang. The fleetness of the enemy, moreover, was truly astonishing: a few were able to outrun our skirmishers even with wounded comrades clinging to their backs. Perhaps for this reason, we found no dead Indian bodies on the hill. In fact, we found much spilled blood, but could claim no scalps. My own sword had not come within forty yards of an enemy throat, white or red.

And so we gained possession of the hill commanding the entire field of action that afternoon. Our losses, miraculously, were limited to twenty wounded and just three dead—the wretch hit in the jaw in the swamp, a private struck in the forehead as he peered over the crest of the hill, and an unknown body found later on the slope, stripped, beheaded, and left in a stand of laurel bushes. By then, sadly, we had become accustomed to such grisly discoveries, given the savages' skill at picking off solitary victims at the extremities of camps and formations.

Poor, having called back our piecemeal pursuit and collected the brigade on the hilltop, sent word down to Sullivan of our victory. The general's standing orders, of course, were to press onward to complete the envelopment. But commanding that height at last, we could plainly see that the plan was in profound disarray. The breastworks were already smoldering, undefended and overswarmed by Hand's men. Clinton was on a lower piece of ground to our south, forming up to launch a rout. Ogden was far away, near the river, but we could see evidence of him pushing far to the right, very close to an Indian village of a dozen buildings huddled on the near bank. Considering how rapidly the enemy was able to maneuver before us, it seemed unlikely they would be enveloped from either flank.

Nevertheless, the brigade was thrown in motion again and proceeded thence down the far side of the slope toward the river.

When we reached the village some hours later it was found, as usual, abandoned. No serious thought was given to a chase beyond the Chemung.

Sullivan arrived not long after we did. Despite the fact that we had overwhelmingly prevailed that day, his tongue was sharp and his mood was sour. He gathered the brigade commanders and polled them all about the confirmed casualties—mostly the enemy's. The total did not please him.

"Twelve? Can no one find me more than twelve of the rascals?"

"There were many more, but they were carried off," Hand observed.

"Then I will hear no more complaints of troops with no boots, as an Indian without shoes appears to bear the advantage!"

"They are not barefoot, sir. There are leather leggings on them, moccasins. They are light and waterproof. Properly oiled, they are better than boots, perhaps . . . ," Parr interjected. At this, Sullivan shifted in his camp stool and delivered a withering stare that reduced the young man to blushing silence.

Just at that moment Clinton, whose absence had scarcely been noticed, approached with a handful of guards and two prisoners. They were Senecah—the first tall, clad in a loincloth and those celebrated leggings, his left eye put out. The second was shorter by almost half, anomalously attired in a fine linen blouse and pantaloons and a complete array of war paint. They both fixed their gazes on us with a contempt so pure it might have been practiced before a mirror.

"They gave us a merry chase, but we got 'em before they went to ground," Clinton was boasting. "We saw their backs in this fight more than their fronts."

Sullivan was standing, regarding the prisoners as if he'd arrived at a particularly untidy carriage accident.

"Have you gotten anything out of them? Spoken to them?" he asked.

"My lieutenant got a faceful of spit from the little one," said Clinton.

Sullivan smiled. And then, after a very lawyerly pause, he pronounced "It doesn't matter. We know their predicament. We know they lack the resources to stop us. The fight today was their best attempt. It failed."

"Oh, I wouldn't say this was their only chance," Clinton went on, failing to perceive that Sullivan was not talking to him.

"There's nothing between us and their homelands. Their victuals. Their wives and children," Sullivan continued. "I've heard that their women have extra sets of teats, like bitches. I've never believed it. But perhaps we will find out tomorrow . . . "

Neither prisoner reacted to the threat. Instead, the tall one yawned.

"One might also note that there is nothing between this army and the longhouse at Senecah Castle. We have a boot upon their vitals. Wouldn't it be ironic, Mr. Severence, to see the longhouse devoured by flames gathered from the council fire itself?"

This last threat drew a small response from the short one. For just an instant, his contempt was converted to incredulousness. The change was quickly reversed, but Sullivan had noted it. He was satisfied.

"Process the prisoners," he said, turning away.

Since the skirmish outside Tioga earlier that week, I had learned what "processing" of Indians meant. I rose.

"General, if I might beg a brief word?"

Sullivan halted, wheeled. I approached closely and whispered to him.

"Sir, as I might humbly presume to remind you, I have been enjoined by congress to undertake the administration of all native prisoners."

He stood without replying, his eyes set hard like gleaming black pearls. With an apprehension that was, perhaps, all too obvious, I nonetheless continued in jabbering fashion, "And understanding as I do what your last order is taken to mean, I, again most respectfully, must suggest that this might not be widely understood to conform to any standard of treatment of captives . . . "

"I recall your very *first* order, Mr. Severence," he interjected in a voice one might use calling across a crowded street, "was to 'assist me in any fashion I see fit.' Would that be an accurate representation?"

I glanced after the prisoners as they were led off into the woods.

"That would be accurate, indeed, but the one order does not supersede the other, in my estimation."

"Oh, in your estimation, it does not supersede, eh? Tell me why."

"Sir, I am hardly as expert as yourself in these matters. I can only hazard the notion that congress would not have added the subsequent order if it did not intend for its execution, notwithstanding the content of the first order."

The prisoners were being spun around and backed against a single large tree. One of Parr's lieutenants was loading two pistols as the Senecah watched with mild curiosity.

"An interesting interpretation of military law, Mr. Severence," Sullivan was musing. "If I am to take your meaning, you would take a series of orders to comprise a set of coequal injunctions. But tell me, then, why the orders are numbered in your commission, if congress did not intend for one order to manifest eminence over any of the others?"

The pistols were loaded and being cocked.

"Eh . . . I cannot tell you why they are numbered . . . except, perhaps, for convenience of organization . . . yet I must entreat you to belay your order that we may treat of this matter . . ."

The executioner raised the first pistol and straightaway, without blindfolding him, shot the tall captive in the face. No one spoke as the report echoed in the forest around us.

"General Sullivan," I finally said, scarcely able to drive the edge of disgust from my voice, "I really must protest."

"Yes, I see you must," he replied.

The second pistol rang out. The second prisoner fell on the first in an embrace that seemed oddly protective.

"Severence, you say you have seen the face of war, but I see you have not profited from your experience. Would you have me make a collection of these creatures? Put them on display, perhaps?"

"*General,* if you please," said I, returning to a whisper. "Allow me to point out that it is the strategic goal of this expedition, as it has been explained to me, to pacify this wilderness. If it please the general, this task would prove more tractable with the savages holding us in *respect,* not in contempt because we execute prisoners . . ."

"You presume to lecture me, *sir,* regarding the strategic goal of this expedition?"

". . . and allow me to suggest further, if it be the general's pleasure, that he will find his tactical goals more attainable if he practices clemency . . ."

"It is *not* the general's pleasure, I may assure you."

". . . and that any prospective attack on Fort Niagara, which must be regarded as the ultimate goal if we are to secure this area of the frontier for congress permanently, will be far more likely to succeed with a chastened but allied nation of Senecah at our backs. . . ."

"The reduction of Fort Niagara is *not* the purpose of this operation, Severence! I am at a loss to ascertain where you might have gained that impression."

"Sir, it is obvious."

"What is obvious, Captain, is your insubordination. I have half a mind to see you run the gauntlet."

"Sir, I truly do not intend the remotest disrespect, but . . ."

The lieutenant in charge of the "processing" appeared suddenly at the general's side as we argued. He was no more than a youth, his face pocked. He saluted in gangling fashion.

"What is it, Lieutenant?" Sullivan asked.

"General, I regret to report that the head wound on the short one has rendered him unsuitable to scalp. Sir."

Sullivan sucked his teeth in a wan show of regret.

"That is unfortunate, Lieutenant. Carry on." Turning back, he said, "A shame," pursing his lips as he looked at me. "It's the little things that can change it all. The whole tenor of the affair. The little things. Do you follow me, Severence?"

I looked at the ground. "I confess, I cannot, sir."

Have you had enough of such tales of war, my dear? I suspect it may be so, and as my hand wearies, so shall I kiss you good night for now.

With all my love,
JOHN

VIII.

"WHAT SAYS your Mr. Severence?" Rebeccah's father quizzed her as she appeared at breakfast. He apparently well knew that the second letter from Iroquois country had arrived the day before and that she'd opened it instantly. He had somehow even come to know the exact contents of the first letter, she perceived. This was very likely with the cooperation of Amie, the fifteen-year-old Bajan girl who cleaned her room on Tuesdays and Fridays.

Very little of what occurred in Portsmouth escaped the notice of Elijah Shays. Installed in his office in the front right parlor of his house, he let the tendrils of his awareness sweep searchingly in all directions. His eyes, set narrowly atop the long, thin Shays nose, barely left the papers and the faces that constituted his affairs. They rarely needed to. After many years spent steadily refining the mechanisms of his intelligence, he could now remain there behind his desk, dressed in one of his three fine black worsted suits, and read the condition of the world from the state of his clients.

The war and the ongoing blockade of colonial ports had made many losers among Shays's peers. It had also made a few winners, especially among those with enough capital to afford a few losses to Royal Navy action. If one out of five of his vessels were confiscated, Shays more than made up for it with windfalls brought in by the other four. Despite the war, his neighbors still demanded their West Indian sugar, their molasses and coffee and spices and rubber. Outbound, the world still paid for the colonies' tobacco, timber, corn, copper, and animal skins—all at wartime premiums.

The burnishing of his fortune gave Shays the opportunity

to acquire other sorts of collectibles, such as the political kind. As his connections matured in Boston, New-York, and Philadelphia, he experienced something he could only describe as a sort of ecstatic self-satisfaction. Not even the misfortunes of an empire could slow his rise. Though he knew it to be a conceit, he seemed destined to own everything, and to know everyone and everything of consequence around him. He didn't know how to put a foot wrong.

It was so much more puzzling, then, that his bowels were in such disorder. The problem had been so prolonged, so recalcitrant, that he had lately come to be obsessed with matters *a posteriori.* He was regular, to be sure, and prized his normalcy with respect to quantity. But the quality, alas! In his youth his turds were something close to sculptures, and so fragrant he welcomed each day by lingering over his exertions. In consistency, they were as pleasant as warm buttered scones. In Boston, he once amused himself by purchasing a porcelain chamber pot with George III's face at the bottom, and the words *Pro iustitia sedeo* ("I sit for justice") emblazoned under the king's sneering visage. How he had always enjoyed covering that face! What convenient pleasure was available to him every morning!

But now he was cursed with softness, shapelessness, indeterminacy. With his best effort, the king was never more than slightly soiled. Every time that chubby face reappeared at the bottom of the pot, proclaiming Shays's failure. The horror! The horror! He hired and fired dozens of doctors. He struggled to remain philosophical about the whole thing.

His daughter was in equal but different agony. She had awoken with a headache before first light and lain awake for three hours. Similar symptoms had greeted her the morning before that, aggravated by a bout of vomiting. She'd eaten nothing since, which inevitably contributed to the faintness that came and went throughout the day. Lately, she was useless for both her primary occupations: reading and embroidery. Even the sight of her father's usual breakfast—a glass of warm water infused with bouillon and half a lemon—nauseated her.

"He writes of good progress," she told him, "and sends his kind regards to you."

"As one would expect, from such a well-turned-out young man," said Shays, in a tone that implied she had somehow questioned Severences's personal quality. Or that was how it sounded to her, in her current foul mood.

"He finds good prospects among the Senecah, once all is settled. The country is abundantly blessed."

"Any fighting?"

"Some. It did not touch him, though."

"Splendid. For all of us."

And he went back to sawing his lemon patiently in half with his steak knife, using short strokes that grated against the surface of his china plate. He was wondering how a man's bowels should perform on campaign. Only a madman can insulate his rectum from his fear. But what of all the clean water and open air of the frontier lands? Would those conditions correct this, the only blemish on his horizon? He thought and chewed and thought some more until he believed, with the thrill of suspense, that he might make a movement again soon.

Rebeccah excused herself after a sip of tea and the smallest crumb of bread. It was puzzling how bloated her abdomen felt when she had barely eaten anything in 48 hours. This had nothing to do with the obvious womanly reason: she was in midcycle. The cause, she decided, could only be the alarming condition of her laudanum bottle. Which is to say, it was empty.

So she returned to her room to put on a street dress, shoes, and her wool mantelet. Her inward disarray was reflected, it seemed, in her inability to find a matched pair of stockings. After a fruitless search, she gave up, pulling on a mismatched pair and muttering to herself, "I am falling apart."

She picked out a hat. She found and donned her gloves. She took a sunshade for her head, not because the light was particularly strong, but because she looked forward to shedding her excess nervous energy by wringing the handle. And then, with a speed unusual for a stately young girl, she was down on Market Street the moment the shops opened.

She proceeded first to the apothecary on the corner of Ceres Street. At the door she met the raw, windburned face of Mrs. Sparshot, the midwife who had delivered both Rebeccah herself and her sister.

"Becky, my little dearie! But how very grown-up you look! Step back and let me drink you in!"

She had, in fact, encountered Mrs. Sparshot at least half-a-dozen times since she had been introduced to society. Each time the old woman had expressed the very same wonderment at how "grown-up" she looked. Still, Rebeccah took half a step back in order to be fully drunk in.

"What a lovely you've become. Yes, as soft and hale as a fresh peach."

And Mrs. Sparshot took the liberty to lay her gloveless hand on Rebeccah's cheek, stroking her with a vaguely worrisome relish that Rebeccah recalled from their many hours sitting beside each other at the tea table. Years before, Rebeccah's ripeness had likewise been tested on her arm, her bare knee, and the side of her chest beside the budding peach pits of her adolescent breasts.

The woman insisted on chatting for some moments. Rebeccah obliged, though growing more anxious and impatient as she struggled both to follow her inanities and to avoid gazing at the sturdy shafts of the woman's fine mustache. At the same time, Rebeccah also struggled to keep her mind off the way her own body was rebelling against her. She became conscious of a strange weariness in her arms and legs, as if she'd run all the way from her house. Nausea flitted in, teasing her from the edge of her awareness.

"I really must press on, then," Mrs. Sparshot announced. "You really are quite the distraction, you little flirt!"

The conversation finally ended with hand squeezes and cheek pecks and promises of invitations to tea-and-cakes. To say the least, Rebeccah was already deeply annoyed when she got inside and learned the bad news: the shop was out of the laudanum she demanded. The tincture's present popularity, as the druggist informed her, was completely unanticipated.

"You may have trouble finding it anywhere in town, at least until the week next," he warned her.

Despite herself, she felt her face flush and her chest tighten. She thanked him kindly, rationing him a smile, and walked quickly on to the next shop, on Bow Street, not far from the wharves. She walked there with her head down and her hand pressing her hat down on her head, though there was no wind that day. That trip, too, was in vain. It seemed the product was particularly popular in recent weeks. She was about to perform the same polite retreat as followed her first failure when she reconsidered. She turned back toward the clerk as his eyes flicked up at her through half-spectacles perched on the end of his knobby nose.

"If you please . . . waiting until next week would not be . . . not be acceptable at the moment. Might I prevail on you to think of some other outlet . . . if only for a limited supply . . . somewhere?"

He regarded her for a long moment, seeing, she feared, straight into the heart of her desperation. With dread wafting over her, she understood perfectly that she did not appear pretty at that moment. She did not seem well schooled or mild mannered. Her face flushed.

"I'm sorry, Miss. I cannot help you, though I would."

This did not surprise her. What consideration should she have expected, given her lamentable state? Her head swimming, her stomach as heavy and tightly knotted as a tree root, she nodded and turned to leave.

"But . . . if you go to the end of Market Street, to the northern end, you will see a house," the clerk continued.

"A house . . ."

"A black-shingled house. There will be a boy standing in front of it. He will be wearing short pantaloons and a cap with a fish hawk's feather in it. If you approach him and mention my name, he may help you."

At those words, "he may help you," she felt as if she might burst into tears. "What name shall I mention?" she asked.

"Ezekiel."

It was fortunate that it was impossible for her to run in her skirts. That would have been all too obvious a demonstration of her abjectness. As it was, she reached Market Street and saw the boy, oil-smeared sailor's cap on his head, loitering in front of a shingled house in exactly the manner the shopkeep had described.

"Excuse me, young man," she approached him, clinging to a shadow of adult dignity in the pitiless face of her lack. "I am told by *Ezekiel* that you may be able to help me."

The boy stared at her narrowly. "Help you?" he asked.

"Yes," she said, resisting the urge to make her requirements more explicit. Instead, she squarely returned his gaze, inspecting him. He looked no more than ten years old, but affected the manner of a twenty-year-old dandy. The fish hawk remnant in his cap, however, barely qualified as a feather. Instead, it was a mere quill with a half-a-dozen poor twisted tendrils projecting from it.

"All right, then," he relented. "If it's 'Zekiel, as you say. Not offen we see the young ones. Sometimes. But not offen. You wantin' the drops?"

She nodded.

"Got a crown?"

The cost was ridiculous, criminal. But by this point there was no sense in dickering over price. She nodded again.

"Best you lose it over there, on the ground . . . " he said, tossing his soft, whiskerless chin at a patch of dandelions under the front window of the house. She inclined her head in that direction, and the boy crossed his arms as if preparing for a long wait.

"You mean—I must drop your money over there?" she asked him. "Why? Is all this somehow illegal?"

"Nah. It's *fun*."

The boy was serious in this assertion of fun. Rebeccah strolled toward the dandelions with a deliberate nonchalance unworthy of the most wooden of actresses. But as the street around them was utterly deserted, there was no one to fool. Her crown now in her hand, she made a wide lazy turn, her skirts swaying, and looked away as she dropped the coin in the weeds. Then she proceeded back to where the boy was waiting for her.

"Well, lookee, will ya?" the boy exclaimed, plucking forth the gold coin and pocketing it. "Wait 'ere, Miss," he then said, adding a preposterously wry wink.

He disappeared into the house. She thought she saw something move—a puff of breath on the curtain in the front window, a vibration of the glass as someone trod the floorboards of the room within—but decided that inquisitiveness would not serve her in this case.

Instead, she gazed out onto the river and watched a shifting shoal of shadow cast on the water by a bank of low, dismal clouds. She was pondering now, quite suddenly, the meaning of the letters Severence had written to her. Certainly, his account would qualify in anyone's judgment as vivid material. It was, by turns, fascinating, educational, and repulsive. What it was not, she believed, was the sort of thing one wrote to a fiancée or sweetheart. Did that mean, therefore, that he did not wish to think of her in that fashion? And if he didn't, did that betoken his high estimation of her intellect? Or did it suggest that, at a sobering physical distance, he had decided to withdraw his romantic stake in her and treat her as some standard intimate, like a steadfast, sympathetic but chaste friend?

Still more puzzling, she could not say which alternative she herself preferred. She didn't know whether to feel complimented or abandoned by his frankness. This, she thought, was what she was reduced to: the luxury of a choice of disappointments.

The front door slammed and the boy bounded down the steps. He was holding a thin flask of brown glass with an India rubber stopper. He was no longer winking but grinning complacently, as if well aware of the magnitude of her need.

"You must mix this," he held it out to her.

"I know."

Their business concluded, the boy then lowered the brim of his cap down over his eyes and leaned back in exactly the same attitude she had first seen him.

Rebeccah, with a perverse impulse, merely slipped the bottle into an inside pocket of her mantelet. No, she would not run home to indulge. She would not return to the shops to face a world of Mrs. Sparshots. Instead, she would circle the collect pond and work to somehow construct a vessel for her tumbling, unavailing thoughts. Perhaps, with some effort, she would even imagine her John out there, many hundreds of miles to the west, suffering experiences she might, weeks hence, read about. Or imagine the prospect of him returned to her, taking their usual rounds of the town at dusk. She found herself smiling at the prospect. Her stomach steadied; her head, for the moment, ceased to pound, when she was thinking such thoughts and feeling the smooth surface of the bottle in her pocket, cool beneath her fingertips.

IX.

THE *BON HOMME RICHARD* squadron lurked around the back door of Britain through the summer. The time, place, and manner in which Jones would land was a matter that preoccupied him deeply, like an actor contemplating his return to the stage after a great triumph. Would he tread the quay-side boards of lowland Scotland again, daring to finish the engagement he had started at Whitehaven? Or would he make his area debut in an Irish venue, beating in close and unleashing incendiaries to burn out British coasters at Belfast? Or perhaps he would swing south from the Orkneys and descend on the exposed eastern flanks of Scotland and England. The possibilities seemed as varied and complex as the coasts of the home islands themselves.

Ireland became less attractive after the element of surprise was decidedly lost there. Late in August *Richard* found herself driven uncomfortably close to the rocks north of Mizen Head. Unwilling to gamble with his flagship, Jones ordered the *Richard*'s barge launched to tow the ship clear of danger. No sooner had the boat's Irish crew set their oars to water than they broke for the coast and for freedom. This desertion necessarily vexed Jones, but not as much as it did the sailing master Cutting Lunt. Almost before Jones could open his mouth, Lunt had taken a handful of men and another boat and made out after them. Not long after a deep fog swallowed up the coast, the *Richard*, and the boats. Despite two days of painstaking search, with lights put out and signal guns fired every fifteen minutes, nothing was heard of the Irish or of Lunt again.

With two boats lost and the master almost certainly captured ashore, there was no chance the squadron could surprise anyone in the entire west of Ireland. So Jones stood out to sea again, hoping to outrun the news of his own reappearance on the enemy coast. Striking north-east, the hunting began to improve: in the Minch just east of the Butt of Lewis, the very British appearance of the Indiaman and her officers fooled the captain of the enemy privateer *Union* into straying too close under the *Richard*'s guns. Opening his ports, Jones demanded and immediately received their surrender. In the *Union*'s hold, Lieutenant Dale found a consignment of infantry uniforms— the second cargo of clothing for the Canada army he had intercepted in his career (the first with the capture of the *Mellish* off Nova Scotia in '76). With the two prizes together, Jones could have outfitted a large army of lobsterbacks all by himself.

Alliance made a capture of her own, the cargo vessel *Betsey*, which Landais clung to with the jealous tenacity of a starving raptor. After the two prizes were manned and sent on their way to a friendly port, the squadron rounded the Orkneys and proceeded southeast, standing well off the coast. At that point, Jones finally settled in his mind where he would strike on land. He signaled a conference of commanders in his cabin. Cottineau of *Pallas* and Ricot of *Vengeance* assented; Landais, for his part, took the occasion to show his wake and vanish again over the eastern horizon.

Henriette was not invited to this conference. Instead, she placed herself in a good position to appreciate the Frenchmen as they boarded. The *Pallas*'s Capitaine de Brulôt Denis-Nicolas Cottineau de Kerloguen was a mere apostrophe of a man—thin and perpetually buoyant, as if his enthusiasm rarely obligated him to touch the ground. This, clearly, was Landais's polar opposite, a man very much pleased to serve under a commodore of Jones's quality. His features, unfortunately, were too dark and quick for her use, although she believed he might serve as a model for one of the Apostles. Lieutenant de Vaisseau Philip Ricot of *Vengeance*, by contrast, looked the worse for having been prematurely awakened from a late afternoon nap. He mounted the topdeck from his barge only with difficulty and ambled on his thick, stockinged legs as if he was unused to rising to his feet. The way his eyeballs seemed to settle heavily into bags beneath his lower lids suggested, vaguely, that Ricot would be skeptical about anything Jones had to suggest.

The meeting of captains started with kisses all around—a particularly French custom that Jones had only recently mastered. The trick, he'd learned, was not to apply lip to the proffered cheek, but merely to smack near it with a kissing sound. He learned this lesson quickly after he once applied a wet, loose smooch to the face of the Marquis de Lafayette, at which the priggish dandy blushed like a flattered schoolgirl.

"If you will not object, we will conduct this meeting in English," began Jones.

"Please," said Cottineau, looking too agitated to seat himself. Ricot, in contrast, settled in a chair beside the stern gallery and stared out at the horizon. Autumn came to Scottish waters depressingly early, he'd found. For a week, the sky had been an unrelieved gray, the seas ominously churning, the winds shifting absurdly around the compass. He, personally, had not felt warmth in his limbs since the end of August.

Jones directed his comments to Cottineau's eager face. He began, "There can be no doubt that this squadron has accomplished a number of significant captures these last weeks. But as you will no doubt agree, our primary . . . our *strategic* purpose has not yet been met. We have not diverted significant resources away from the Channel coast."

"When was the Admiral d'Orvilliers scheduled to make his landing?" asked Cottineau.

"That is not a matter of scheduling. It is a matter, first, of bringing Hardy's fleet to conclusions. And as you must grant, the ships of the Spanish line are likely to be miserably handled, it would seem the initiative would belong to Hardy. . . ."

Jones broke off as he stared at Ricot, who was sitting with his face turned away, absently rubbing his thighs. Jones's impatience begged to mature into a strapping fury—he was, after all, addressing Cottineau and Ricot as coequals, though the latter officially held the inferior rank in the French service. But it would not be in Jones's interest to make an enemy of Ricot, yet. He opted instead for measured sarcasm.

"Are we boring you, Mister Ricot?"

Ricot gifted him with his attention again.

"Certainly," he said, matching the commodore's rhetorical mode. "I am *entranced* by every word."

"Good. We must therefore proceed under the assumption that d'Orvilliers has not yet disposed of Hardy and has not yet landed his troops. It would also follow, then, that we bear the responsibility to take the initiative here, in this theatre. Correct?"

"*Mais oui,*" Cottineau exclaimed. "Let us proceed to action boldly! My honor stands as pledged!"

Ricot shifted heavily on his keel. "Yes, I agree. Except that we also bear the responsibility, implicitly, not to render ourselves *destroyed.* Correct?"

"Yes, of course," Jones replied evenly, governing himself. "It would certainly not be my intent to take undue risks, as I presumed would be obvious."

"Good. So what do you suggest?"

Jones gestured toward the chart open on his desk. Cottineau moved forward to regard it, but Ricot didn't budge.

"We now stand just a few days from the mouth of the Firth. I propose that we proceed through it to the roadstead at Leith and present the authorities there with a proposition."

He paused, but neither of the others thought to interject.

"This would be a demand for ransom," he continued, "presented against the threat that the town would be put to the torch."

Ricot frowned. "I am stunned, Commodore. Such an operation does not seem to me the fit occupation of gentlemen under arms. A raid, yes. The dealing of damage, certainly. But ransom? It seems unworthy of you . . . more the work of corsairs and ruffians . . . *la merde.*"

"I would not disagree with you," Jones parried. "Except that I could name for you half-a-dozen occasions where British *gentlemen* have engaged in far more reproachable work in the colonies. It would seem, therefore, that the Admiralty has proven itself innocent of the most fundamental of moral verities—the protection of noncombatants."

"And so we teach them a lesson. Certainly!" added Cottineau. "Except for one single matter, perhaps: if we are sailed up the Firth, what is to preserve us from being trapped in it, should a superior enemy force take up position behind us?"

Cottineau had presented his objection delicately, apologetically.

Ricot, meanwhile, had planted his gaze on the deck. "I am here to kill British, not to teach them," he said. "Nor does our concordat provide for such precipitous operations."

Again, that damnable concordat! thought Jones. To Ricot's bleat, he would say nothing. He turned to Cottineau instead.

"A most correct question to pose. My answer is not half so good: there is no guarantee, save d'Orvilliers' fleet in the Channel. Between the French and the Spanish he has . . . how many? At least sixty ships in his line? That compares favorably with the very Armada of Phillip II, does it not?"

"In terms of guns mounted, yes. But in terms of vessels and men, no."

"My point is that there should be no significant enemy force anywhere near the Firth. Nowhere north of the Wash, I would venture."

Cottineau, who had still not taken a seat, paced up and down with his hair grazing the timbers above him. "Yes, yes. It is an impossible situation for our British friends. We must be virtually unopposed."

Ricot did not interject, but shifted his boots to assert his continued opposition.

"As for the ransom itself . . . I have not thought much on it," Jones continued. "Except that it would likely be subject to the same share formula as for a prize vessel . . ."

Ricot stopped moving his feet and looked up.

" . . . and that we might easily demand a sum such as, say, two hundred thousand pounds? More or less."

There was a pause as Jones watched each man inwardly calculate his share.

"I think, perhaps, that the commodore is correct about the likelihood of opposition," Ricot remarked, a thoughtful frown breaking over his face.

"Even so, the Firth is easily wide enough at her mouth to afford us an escape by stealth," Cottineau concurred.

"And our orders—to raise a diversion—cannot be made more clear . . ."

"So what would our commodore have us do?"

By that point Jones merely listened, clearly gratified by the tide of unanimity but exactly aware of what had inspired it.

Only details remained to be discussed—including how the plan might be altered should Landais appear again—until, at Jones's signal, the steward delivered three glasses of porter and the meeting was closed.

On the quarterdeck, Cottineau and Ricot found the sea had

gotten up a bit while they were below. There were long, steep swells riding in from the east, with caps of peppery foam blowing across the troughs to the waves ahead. Both barges were riding nearby, prepared to return the captains to their commands, but the ships themselves were gone. Both *Pallas* and *Vengeance* had apparently put their helms down and disappeared over the east horizon.

"None of us could see why they flew away," the remaining Lunt, Henry, explained to the captains. "Though it must have been the possibility of a prize, hull down for us."

"That was the command I left with them to pursue vigorously in my absence," Cottineau testified.

"As did I," answered Ricot.

And with that they stood awkwardly on Jones's quarterdeck, hands tightly clasped behind them, caps plastered to the windward sides of their heads by the North Sea breeze, dry-docked by circumstances. It was the moment Henriette had been waiting for.

"If you please, gentlemen—might you indulge me in this brief moment?" she begged the orphans, holding up her sketching tablet and pencils.

Cottineau scrutinized her, standing before him in her ruffled green smock and white leggings striped with tiny waveforms, and tossed his head in surrender.

"Oh, thank you, my dear captain! Now if you will be so good as to turn your eyes to the light, your shoulders oblique to the rail? Yes, that is just so. . ."

The French commanders were guests on the *Richard* for another six hours, during which time Henriette collected an abundance of views of their noses and of the puffy sacks suspended below Ricot's rheumy eyes. The ordeal was not rewarded by additional captures, however: *Pallas* and *Vengeance* chased a merchant brig for ten leagues before resolving her to be Swedish, and therefore not legitimately seizable.

Comme si Pilate avait vogué
a bord d'un navire!

Un Apôtre, peut-être?

The mouth of the Firth was still several days off. The time was invested in drills firing the great guns, upon which Jones was puzzled to discover that the aggregate firing rate on the larboard side was a full ten seconds faster per three discharges than that on the starboard side. The commodore dropped everything, including his own meals, in order to trace the reason for this difference. But there seemed no accounting for it. He tried using identical gun crews in drills on both sides; he warned them to use precisely the same techniques for worming, priming, shotting, and firing the guns, though no such reminder should have been necessary. He tried threats, rewards, and elegant tantrums such as he had seen in Italian operas in Paris, including appeals to heaven and hurling his hat to the deck and kicking it. Dale, for his part, cursed at them with English, French, and a few Swedish and Gaelic words he'd picked up in Mill Prison. For the benefit of the Portuguese among the crews, Jones found that the boatswain, Turner, had spent some time in the merchant trades at Madeira and Lisbon, and enlisted him especially to curse the men in their own mother tongue.

For all these efforts, the only compensation was a drop in the interval between the first and second shot on the larboard side of eight seconds, and the starboard seven. The amount of powder and shot they were working through just in practice, however, was immense. It was Dale who finally spoke up to assert the interests of providing for actual battle.

Joseph Two Fires was busy filing the rust off the vessel's sizable collection of boarding pikes and sabers. Looking up from his work, he saw an enormous cleft appear between the Scottish headlands. This gave the country a passing resemblance to that around the St. Lawrence. Like that river so close to his home, the Firth of Forth was fringed with alternating stripes of cultivation and wilderness; like the "mouth of the bottle" near Quebec, the Firth dramatically shrank in breadth as the squadron beat up it to the

westward. He expected to see the tin roofs of the Quebecois shining in the daylight, but saw only the dull stony piles of Scottish
farmhouses and henges.

He had learned enough about navigation during his months
at sea to know he was nowhere near Turtle Island. But he was so
moved by the illusion that he paused, sadly, to regard the caking
of the rust dislodged onto his hands by the file. The feeling of the
powder between his fingers reminded him of the grit of ochre
when, in a former life, he painted himself for a trip down the warrior's path. Mixing the rust with some spit, he covered his face
with it. The pigment stung his eyes and the broken sores around
his wind-chapped lips, and he found himself weeping with long-
ing for Chonodote. The tears cleared pale, spreading rays from his
lower eyelids down the rusty surface of his cheeks, rendering him
so frightful in the eyes of a young midshipman that the boy shuddered and ran from Two Fires' presence.

As often happened, a warrior's act of decorating himself for
battle somehow made a fight inevitable. Two Fires was among
more than a hundred men mustered in ranks on the *Richard*'s
decks that day as they proceeded up the Firth. The party was composed of those most superfluous to the working of the ship—Irish
landsmen and French marines and criminals and unclassifiables
like himself. Their job would be to man the landing force that
would occupy parts of the town ahead and collect the first half of
the ransom. Jones stood before them and explained this with a
grin that suggested he envied their errand. For a gentleman of
such determined grace, he was good at flattering roughnecks:

"How the world will marvel at you, bringing humility to the
haughty Briton! Tomorrow, you will accomplish what kingdoms
could not—what monarchs could not. For you proceed forth as
free men, enfolded in the wise wings of Liberty. May the instruments of tyranny fly before you!"

Jones was mixing his metaphors hard, but the men cheered,

raising on high their freshly disrusted pikes and sabers.

"But mark this," he continued in a voice so quiet and measured it exacted their attention as fully as a gunshot. "The genius of Liberty is not the sister to Chaos. Any man who fails to follow our directions will be triced up and flogged. For theft, there will be flogging. For pointless vandalism, flogging. For disobedience or hardness of hearing, flogging. If any man shows discourtesy toward females, I will have him hauled back here and flog him myself. We will not have it said we conducted ourselves in accord with the lies they tell about us. I want the word of all of you upon this matter—your promise as men, to me as a man. Tell me, can you give me that promise, fellows?"

His request, following so closely upon vivid promises of tricing up and flogging, drew only a vague murmur.

"I am not reassured," he rumbled.

There was a somewhat louder, confused mass of affirmation, with some shouting "Aye!", some "Oui!", a few "Ja," some just grunting, some pounding their feet on the deck.

"I trust you, then," Jones replied. "Mr. Dale, dismiss them."

"Now get out of our sights, you lot of rank jackasses!" Dale dismissed them, adding, "And remember that you plight what remains of your honor tomorrow!"

The muster dissolved, leaving Jones standing before Two Fires, who remained at attention before him.

"Well, Mr. Joseph-to-me, you will have your chance soon. But mark this: you will act strictly under the rules of civilized warfare."

Two Fires smiled. "I will follow my war captain."

Jones was pleased with the words, but not entirely with the smile.

The little squadron did not proceed toward Leith unnoticed. Since the mouth of the Firth widens from west to east, it was difficult to see anything to landward at first. But as the stony beaches marched inevitably closer, Henriette could begin to count the men on horseback shadowing them on both the north and south. Frequently, the wind went over to the west and the vessels were forced to tack. On these occasions, all parties got an even closer look. She could make out the clothes on the figures ashore, from the brick red uniforms of the scouts to the long, greasy coats and beards of the shepherds staring from fields. Early one evening Henriette thought she smelled a pig roasting and, looking over the rail, saw not a whole house, but the brick crown of a chimney standing just clear of a hill, wreathed by a curl of cooking smoke. Such precious domesticity filled her with a warmth that was surprisingly rueful; though she considered herself too exceptional, too devoted to her projects to miss such conventional pleasures, it would be long indeed before she was back in the world of women again.

Mists and sudden suffocating fogs were endemic in this season and in this place. Fear of collisions and groundings began to wear on the nerves of the captains and sailing-masters, none of whom had any particular experience in those waters. Their troubles unexpectedly ended when a skiff appeared one morning to their windward, carrying five Scotsmen. Jones was on his quarterdeck as the boat approached.

"Good morrow, friends!" the commodore called.

"Good mahrow!" came the thickly accented reply. "Mae we come alongside ye?"

"Nay, I insist upon it!"

The skiff approached and tied up alongside. One man, dressed well but in the clean and slightly outmoded fashion of a servant, came aboard.

"Andrew Patton," he introduced himself, "'o the estate of Sir John Anstruther . . . o'er there . . ." And he jabbed a finger behind him, toward the north shore.

"How do you do, Mr. Patton? And how might I help you?"

"I just thank th' Laird we found a navy ship s'close, whun we wair resigned to a lang hale, out to the frigates nair the Isle o' May."

"Heavens!"

"And wi' the pirate Joones about! But that's the matter to hand: himself has need of po'der, if ye can spare it. A cannon 'na plenty 'o shot, he's got. But the lot's 'nathin wi'out po'der. The hale Toon's prostate wi'out it."

"Prostrate, you mean?"

"Exactly! I tell ye, the lang country's up 'n it over the pirate. Only the Laird kens whut the bloody basturd wull do! The navy canna abandon us! So if ye can spare the po'der in the name o' amity, ye will find himself most obliged. Ye might even come up fer a taste o' stag, once th' business is done. He told me to invite ye."

"How splendid that sounds! You must tell Sir Anstruther I have every intention of attending his grace upon the appropriate opportunity. But for now, will a small cask do?"

"Since 'e's got but one ball—cannonball, I mean—a small one should do."

"Certainly."

The crew, which did nothing to spoil Jones's little joke on the servant, nevertheless prepared quietly to capture the skiff. A gun port was opened on the starboard side, and a slow match smoked behind a gunner's back.

But Jones stayed in character. He frowned at the sight of the open gun port, motioning with forefinger and thumb that it be closed. A small cask of powder was hauled up from the magazine, and the skiff even loaded down with a dozen extra balls for the local eminence's little signal cannon. Patton was delighted and only too gracious when Jones presented a request of his own.

"Might ye—might *you* spare a pilot for the king's squadron? I shanna—*shall not* need him for long. Our work should be done in a couple of days." Exposed to the example of Patton's hopeless brogue, Jones had to work hard to keep his own accent in check.

"Wi' our thanks, take 'im," said the other. And the skiff's pilot, a cadaverous, gristled joint of a man with waist-length growth of beard from his chin, surrendered his place at the tiller and climbed up to the deck of the *Richard*.

"May Joones taste yer metal!" cried Patton as he cast off.

"May the bloody bastard show his true cowardice at your broadside!" replied Jones.

With that, the skiff melted back into the mist. Jones then turned to the pilot. "You can get us athwart the town of Leith, inside the Inchkeith, can you not?"

"O' course. But the villain won't be there," the other answered, his voice freighted with all the self-assurance of a local confronting an ignorant outsider.

"I shan't na'worry about that."

"Really? An' why not?"

"Because I am your villain."

The man frowned, shaking his head as if he hadn't taken Jones's meaning.

"I am Paul Jones," the commodore explained gently.

The old man, who suddenly became short of spit, began to swallow rapidly. His eyes fluttering, his lower body shook, and he struggled to make his voice function. "This is not His Majesty's ship *Romney?*" he asked.

"We call her *Bon Homme Richard*. But we hope to meet your *Romney*, presently."

"Then I'm dead for sure," the pilot finally said, looking as if he would collapse.

But Jones would never be so indelicate a host as to execute his guests. Laughing out loud at this display of dread, he stood on tiptoe to put his arm around the taller man's bony shoulders.

"Hardly! You are my prisoner, it is true. And you will conduct us as I have directed. But no harm will come to you—upon my honor as an officer of the Navy of Congress."

At this news the pilot just nodded, a bovine daze breaking over his face, as if his neck had just slipped the knot on the scaffold. Such fear struck Henriette as unreasoned: the commodore had, after all, asked specifically for a pilot, and he could reasonably be expected to employ his services, even if he were a wanton marauder. Not even pirates strove to run onto sandbars or break themselves on the rocks. The thought occurred to her that the Scottish race would provide much material for her conception of Peter—the thick-skulled fisherman—but not for the lively figure of the Prince of Peace.

The invasion of Britain was set for the next day. In the morning, with their new guest installed behind the binnacle, the miniature Armada proceeded confidently toward the south shore of the Firth. The quays and steeples of Leith formed out of the mist, the sounds of the town drifting out to the straining ears and itchy fingers of the landing force. Jones and Dale stood above, eyes pressed against their spyglasses, watching the accumulating commotion ashore.

"They know we are here," said Dale.

"They know the enemy is in the Firth," replied Jones. "Today we are, instead, HMS *Romney* and consorts."

Above them, and from the masts of *Pallas* and *Vengeance*, Jones had installed the Blue ensign of the Royal Navy. This was the first time he had impersonated a member of that squadron; previously, he had preferred the Red. Such were his only compensations on this cruise. Like a proper commodore, he could not take command of a boat himself, as he did at Whitehaven. This time, he would remain confidently and sternly and superfluously *behind*. One consequence of success, it appeared, was to make a man too valuable a figure to ever have an opportunity to repeat it. In fact, amid the distractions of daily command, the idea of his own redundancy had never occurred to him before. The thought had a surprisingly unsettling effect on him.

Dale, meanwhile, was watching the mist above the town vanish. It did not depart with a teasing, subtle rise. Instead, it disappeared suddenly, like a curtain ripped open. Where the city had been concealed behind a dark, undifferentiated cloud, they could now plainly see the rising mass of Edinburgh Castle.

The water between the ship and the shore was rapidly changing its mood. A front of gray darkness was sweeping the width of the Firth. Though the waves were the same, the pattern of the ripples atop the waves suddenly deepened and changed their direction, pointing now directly to the south, toward the Pentland Hills.

"Sir, I . . ." Dale began.

The gale broke on the *Richard* with a force that staggered her. Sails that were tightly trimmed a moment before were now shivering and screaming, daylight flashing through tears in their cheap patchwork. Where a moment before the Indiaman had been on a broad reach on the starboard beam, the instant shift of wind had placed her yards in the position exactly best for throwing her backward.

"Fall off! Fall off, damn you, before she makes sternway!" barked Jones.

The master's mate, who seemed equally startled by the wind coming from the commodore's mouth as from the Scottish hills, grappled with the wheel, hand over hand. His idea was to turn the *Richard*'s heading all the way around, so she might run before the wind.

"No! Let her turn into the teeth of it! Luff through it!" Jones roared.

But it was too late. As the ship lumbered around, the crew was slow getting to the braces, and she stalled. The wind was now pouring over the beam, the hull heeling over precipitously because the *Richard* was carrying too much canvas. Jones and Dale calmly hooked their elbows through the rail as the angle of the deck passed fifty degrees and the yardarms bent to wet their tips in the Firth. The landing boats inclined absurdly in their stays; the mob of would-be invaders broke in a tangled mass of arms and legs struggling for purchase. Two Fires drove the point of his boarding pike into the deck and used it to steady himself. Henriette, who was braced firmly with one arm snaked through the ratlines, modestly gathered the hems of her skirts together with her other hand as she ascended above the male eyes below. Jones could hear a sickening rout of crashes from below—the china plate from his own service disintegrating, he suspected. He could also detect a softer sound: the steady, hollow torturing of wood. It could only be the rudder out of the water, suffering as the gale-driven swells drove against it.

The able seamen had already launched themselves aloft to furl the courses. As a frothy soup began to churn through the woodwork of the opposite rail, the *Richard* at last seemed to settle on her keel and, with a chunky sort of grace, to push her masts slowly back to vertical.

"*Mon dieu,*" Henriette breathed as gravity befriended her again.

"She's a fine lady in a scrap," Dale finally said to Jones as they regained their feet.

"If only she sailed so well in light air as in foul."

"Captain, the corvette!" cried Lunt.

Jones slid down to the other rail and peered through the rain of salt water dripping from the larboard shrouds. To the north, he saw the *Vengeance* from a startling vantage. She was completely knocked on her side, her keel high and dry before him.

"Bloody . . . bloody . . . ," he began, feeling the impulse to curse his foul luck in even less seemly terms. But the same impulse that always backed his mental sails did so again. Instead, he chewed the inside of his larboard cheek until it bled onto his tongue.

"We all said she was crank," Dale was saying. "She flies like a lark in the sun, but give her some hard blow . . ."

There was the same kind of crashing on *Vengeance* as they heard on *Richard,* only worse. On the corvette's mid deck, crewmen could look up and see twelve-hundred-pound long guns suspended above them, straining against their tackle. Rock ballast and livestock and casks of gunpowder not profoundly secured were falling from their places. Meanwhile, as the corvette's sails settled into the water, they grew heavier, making it still more difficult for the ship to right herself.

"Ricot will have to dismast her, if he's not a fool," said Lunt.

"She will right," replied Dale.

"Not in this bitch of a breeze," swore the other, stopping himself to glance apologetically at Henriette.

She winked at him, and he momentarily forgot the point he'd wanted to make.

"The devil take it, what's going on? Are we in battle and no one told me?" Brooke shouted from the companion-way. The front of his surgeon's smock was stained with a liquid that was too blue to be either blood or rum.

"Not now, Mr. Brooke," warned Jones.

Pallas, at least, seemed to have weathered the surprise with some degree of professionalism. She was then about a mile to the north west, luffing up nicely, her crew no doubt looking with equal astonishment at *Vengeance*'s predicament.

"Wear her around, Mr. Carswell," Jones told the master's mate. "And make toward the *Vengeance.* Carefully, if you please."

But Carswell, who had almost planted the ship's beam-ends in the Firth, was shaking too violently now to put his hands on the wheel. Instead, the old pilot from Sir John's yacht took over.

The gale seemed to weaken. This lifted some of the lateral pressure on the corvette's hull, and her masts finally began to rise. As the *Richard* came around to her larboard side, *Vengeance* righted herself, a cloud of loose spray flying from her rig the way drops come off a dog shaking itself off after a swim. Ricot had also had the good sense to cut his courses free while they were in the water. They dangled there, like laundry, but still catching enough breeze to bring the corvette's bow safely upwind.

Jones brought out his speaking-trumpet. "Have you need of any assistance, Mr. Ricot?" he asked. He could see Ricot on his deck, the lower half of his uniform dark with wet. He merely stared up at Jones passing by, his only reply the fury in his eyes.

"Oh dear, is he all right?" asked Henriette.

"He's *relieved*, can't you see?" Dale told her. "He lost no men, and his guns were not unshipped."

"Mr. Dale, when the squadron is ready . . . signal a north-easterly heading. When we are to leeward of the Isle of May, inform me."

The lieutenant watched him speak, with puzzlement. Jones's teeth and tongue were bloody, as if he had suffered a wound inside his mouth. "Commodore, what of the landing?"

The landing corps had shakily reassembled at the boats. But to Jones, the question was unwelcome as the gale. He could, after all, live with defeat in combat. He could live with reversals of fortune related to weather, to chance, even to cowardice. Those things were to be expected in mounting any complex military enterprise.

What he could not live with was the suspicion that he was being *mocked*. And he could not believe the good citizens of Leith, watching his squadron collectively prone on its beam-ends, bowed and bent before the gale like a line of knock-kneed ballerinas, were not laughing at him. How could such miserable sailing compel respect, much less the terror that would civilize the enemy?

"Just . . . do as I ask," he finally answered, his tone verging on a plea.

"We'll get 'em next time, boys," Dale said as he turned to the men. They were scattering to their usual duties, but heavily, as if each dragged a truck of disappointments. "You can count on it. *Count on it.*"

X.

What was to be done? Here was the army starved and naked, and there their country sitting still and expecting the army to do notable things while fainting from sheer starvation. All things considered, the army was not to be blamed. Reader, suffer what we did and you will say so, too.

—Joseph Plumb Martin, *A Narrative of Some of the Adventures, Dangers and Sufferings of a Revolutionary Soldier,*

1830

SEPTEMBER 4

My dear Rebeccah:

It is a matter of perennial puzzlement among armchair moralists that the twin demons of rapine and atrocity often attend invading armies. Why is it, they wonder, that some bodies of men but not others, or some individuals but not others, commend themselves to habits of conduct that would fill them with indignant horror if the same such crimes were committed upon their familiars? We have all heard, *ad nauseam,* of homes and churches torched, of wanton massacre of innocents, irrespective of age, of tortures committed upon duly rendered and defenseless prisoners. In the progress of this war (if its manifestation may be called such), it seems no one spares the knife an extra twist in the back of the enemy. I speak of both sides.

The commonest explanation lies in that most soothing of sanctimonies: the casting of righteous blame. Some men, it is thought, are simple but frustrated moral defectives. The promise of rapine attracts them to enlist, and in uniform they gain license to perform acts, in distant places, that they dare not elsewhere. Atrocity, in this view, is the direct consequence of personal evil.

Yet, having served these last years among thousands of common soldiers, both of the Continental and state levies, both on land and at sea, I may say with confidence that, while such men do exist, they are exceedingly rare. Far more common than the unredeemable brute is the tender father who, in the morning, empties the contents of an infant's skull against the trunk of a tree and in the evening wrings tears of regret from the depths of his soul. The compassionate neighbor who comforts him, moreover, is one as prone as any to perpetrate some like horror the very next day, and then bitterly regret it.

The next most common way to account for this, then, is to cast blame not on the men, but on the institution of war itself. Some, inspired in no small part by the views of Monsieur Rousseau, hold the great majority of men to be good in their essence. Under just circumstances, they are incapable of malefaction. Warfare, however, is the opposite of just circumstance: at its core, it is predicated upon the doing of repugnant acts to the persons of other men. The institution is rooted, it is argued, in the demands of monstrous artifices—the faction, the state—that may only be slaked by the sacrifice of all that is most precious. Such unnatural appetites can only lead to larger, more jealous states, to deeper demands for sacrifice, and inevitably to greater, more deeply dreadful wars.

Although I recognize an element of truth in such a view, it seems to me altogether too easy to disavow mankind's deep requirement for warfare. War, it should be recalled, is not the prerogative of states only, but of any body of men in social intercourse with one another. Our General Sullivan, for example, would scarcely grant the Senecah the status of civilized nation, yet even he would be compelled to admit the Senecah do wage war. Warfare itself may be understood to be a consequence of deeper motives, such as the need for land or supplies of whatever sort.

Why, then, should one stop at condemning war, but not instead go on to denounce the Creator who devised the unequal provision of resources that lies at its root?

If the institution of war promotes atrocity, why do so many soldiers never stoop to it? The question goes to the heart of the experience of warfare, which is rather different from what some might suppose. Far from an orgy of violence and blood, war is overwhelmingly a matter of procedure, labor, and boredom. The soldier's career, at whichever rank he attains, is made up of a thousand modest plans to overcome a thousand petty obstacles. This is so much more the case when the army is a poor one, as is the Continental.

To my mind, rapacious acts are not the consequence of total moral collapse, but instead of a myriad of small frustrations. The soldier wakes up from a sleepless night huddled on the wet or frozen ground, his body wrapped around his cold musket to keep the pan dry. Aching and exhausted, he may look forward (as on this campaign) to only a half-ration of belly timber—a gill of wheat or flour, a few ounces of lean meat with no bread, or of bread with no meat. If he is lucky, he may forage for walnuts or some root vegetables from some scorched house garden. Unsatisfied, his head buzzing from want, he may then be forced to march, very often without shoes, for miles on maneuvers whose point he cannot see, against an enemy he cannot defeat. On the way, he derives no inspiration from arrogant but green officers, who owe their commissions to the cronies of their fathers and who look down upon him imperiously from horseback. Moreover, he is not cheered but despised by his own countrymen, who see him as an agent of an occupying army from the empire of Philadelphia, bent on commandeering what it can and looting the rest. Where a word or a smile from a pretty face might make up for a week of light rations, American women scatter at first sight of a column of their country's soldiers. And why should they not, when a good number of the men have barely the slops to cover their modesty? The soldier's experience, in short, is one of chronic denial of his basic human requirements for sustenance and for respect. In exchange for this, this *nothing*, the Continental is expected to face down and win battles against a force of fed, rested, and experienced professionals. Defeat, of course, renders him only more fit for his countrymen's contempt.

Upon these discomforts, which may stretch on for months before the relief of a decent meal or a pair of boots or leave to go home, we might also heap the daily horror of campaign in enemy lands. The soldier who indulges some pretension to privacy and strays too far into the forest—just a few yards, in most cases—risks mutilation and death by a skulking, tireless foe. Though the soldier is endlessly tasked with protecting and removing a mountain of stores, he benefits little from this bounty and must function in a constant state of hunger. The roads here, in Iroquois country, are no more than trails, doubly increasing the effort that must be expended to operate a modern army.

Imagine, then, the disposition of a typical soldier upon entering an enemy village. Imagine the particular discomfort of his headache that morning, the gnawing pain of a bad back slung for the night on a bed of rocks. Imagine some small but insistent malady that plagues and saps his patience—a bad tooth, a hemorrhoid, a toenail ripped off on a ragged log. Imagine how these might darken his mood, blighting his intercourse with his equally short-tempered messmates, reducing all civility to snaps, snarls, and threats. Imagine further that one of these messmates, perhaps a friend or acquaintance of long standing from his own small town, was discovered in the woods hours before, stripped and beheaded and skinned. Imagine, then, what that soldier, in that state, might be capable of.

To Sullivan's credit, he has consistently sought to lighten the burden on the men. As the army has marched farther and farther beyond the limits of settlement, he has taken extra measures to assure that they do not also exceed the frontiers of civility. Where, in the interest of saving fodder for the pack animals, the cavalry had given up their mounts at Wyoming, many of the officers kept their horses up to the battle on the Chemung River. The attitudes of the common men had been clear about these privileged lads: anyone who forded a river on his horse, for instance, was scorned behind his back, while anyone who dismounted and waded ahead was thought a stout fellow. None of this was obvious, of course; such judgments were ubiquitous, buzzing, yet strictly implicit. I perceived it three crossings before the battle, and got accustomed to wearing a uniform that seemed permanently wet up to my breast.

All this has ended as we have struck north on the creek that leads to Senecah Lake. A suggestion, very much like an order, came down that all mounts be surrendered for transport back to Tioga. Sullivan, leading now by example, walks beside his columns as they tramp northward. Anyone seated high above the commander himself is now truly obvious. As this is as likely true for enemy snipers as for our own troops, there are no more mounted officers among us. The campaign has truly become a march of republican equals (more or less) against barbarism (more or less).

After the victory at the Chemung, the army paused for a day to burn the nearby houses and fields. Special attention was paid to the fields of corn stretching away through the laps of the valleys toward the hills. These were burnt, the ashes overturned, and then, in a dramatic gesture, sown with salt in the fashion of Scipio Africanus reducing the city of Carthage. Would that Sullivan had had a real city to raze and sow with salt! The desperate wish showed in his eyes as the men went about the elaborate destruction of those scanty remains.

Our next target before Senecah Lake was the place called Catherine's Town. Of its shape and extent our Oneida informants could say nothing. We did know that it was named for Catherine Montour, a mongrel half-French, half-Huron woman taken prisoner by the Senecah more than seventy years previous.

Montour grew up speaking English, French, Huron, and Senecah with equal facility and, in her capacity as interpreter between the settlements and the tribes, made regular visits for both diplomacy and shopping to New-York and Philadelphia. Alas, she also had a daughter who, we were told, played an infamous part in the Wyoming massacre of '78. This daughter, who was known as "Queen" Esther, had demanded a body of live prisoners for her satisfaction and received sixteen of them from Butler. All of the prisoners were settlers and included men, women, and boys. Upon their arrangement in a line before her, the "Queen," who had stripped herself naked except for a crucifix and a belt of seashells around her waist, took a cudgel and staved in the skulls of fourteen miserable souls. When she turned to the last two, her face and breasts were lathered in blood and brain. The survivors ran for their lives through the assembled Senecah warriors, who laughed and kicked at them as they fled.

Sullivan heard this tale third- or fourth-hand from the quartermasters at Easton, and decided to take seriously the prospect of exacting vengeance upon this woman. Orders were distributed to all scouts and pickets to secure her person at whatever cost. As the town ahead was named after her mother, he reasonably expected to find some hint of her presence there. I would not put it beyond the general's imaginings that he would capture this "queen" and parade her through the streets of Philadelphia, while he followed behind in a silver chariot festooned with laurels.

Before making this glorious capture, we were obliged to wade through another swamp, this one more than eight miles long and composed mainly of sheets of tea-colored water laid up under groves of pine trees. We were, by that time, much practiced at moving the guns over soft ground and negotiated this obstacle in little more than twelve hours. Yet even before the last man in Clinton's rearguard had quit the swamp, we could see the glow of Catherine's Town alight ahead of us. Yet again, we arrived (albeit on foot this time) with our vanguard haunting a landscape of scorched desolation, all thirty houses destroyed, all animals dead or scattered to the woods. And yet again, the Senecah left intact their fields and orchards, leaving that laborious task to our enthusiastic execution.

The town was not as deserted as it first seemed, however. Just an hour after our arrival a knot of Hand's men approached the general staff, holding something between them. As they came closer, I could see they had a short plank of wood, with a vaguely human shape seated upon it. She was a woman of greatly advanced age, hunched with rounded back on her makeshift seat, her two leathery claws curled around the men's shoulders.

"Beggin' the gen'ral's pardon," began one of her discoverers, a corporal, "we found 'er lying in the leaves, there . . ." And he pointed to a spot some distance out of town.

The crone wore a long, finely embroidered cotton dress with bits of rounded iridescent shell sewn on the breast. One of her eyes was rendered dull and milky by a cataract. The other fixed us with a deep, baleful stare.

Sullivan crouched a bit to speak to her.

"Are you Queen Esther? Hallo?"

No answer. Sullivan summoned one of our Indian scouts to interpret. Upon hearing her own language, she spoke without hesitation.

"Her name is She-Places-Two-Bets," the Oneida told us. "She is one hundred and fifty years old."

A gasp was audible from the small crowd of officers and regulars gathered around us. Sullivan shook his head.

"Nonsense. She is likely no older than myself. Ask her why she is here, why did she not leave with the others?"

The old women then spoke for some time. When her chapped, purplish lips opened, I could see a set of brown teeth behind them, curiously worn down close to the gums. But otherwise, she appeared in very good shape for a century and a half. Her hair was gray but copious, and her feet bare but finely tended, with round, filed toenails.

"They all left in a hurry, last night," the interpreter finally reported. "She told them she was too old to run away, and went over there to lie down and die."

"Then she is fortunate we came when we did," pronounced Sullivan, more to me and to General Hand than to the old woman.

As our interview proceeded we learned she had closely witnessed the last hours of Catherine's Town. Through her account, we gained a detailed understanding of the events just prior to our arrival. After their defeat at the Chemung, the braves and Tories under Butler and Brant withdrew to the town. In their party were no more than two hundred of the white, red-coated "long knives" and five hundred braves, overwhelmingly Senecah. The latter were in a foul mood, because they had been led to believe that one of them was worth ten of the "Bostonians" who had just defeated them. Brant gathered the leaders, including the war captains and several sachems, and informed them that all the lands south of the lake were to be abandoned, and the battle against the rebels would resume when reinforcements from the English arrived from Canada.

At this, many of the clan mothers and two sachems objected, holding out hope for a peaceful accommodation with congress. Butler flew into a rage at the mere suggestion of a settlement, swearing that any "allies" in favor of suing for peace would be scalped on the spot for treason. There were moments of some anxiety between Butler's Tories and the Senecah, who moved to protect the clan mothers. Brant then interposed himself between the parties, playing the peacemaker. As the night waned and scouts returned with news of our approach, fear prevailed over prudence, and the savages began to stream north. The last braves, setting the last fires, had left only minutes before Parr's men entered the town.

Parr sent detachments out to seek these late departures, but returned the next day having caught no one. On balance, however, Sullivan was much pleased by what he had heard from the old woman. Butler and Brant had only a fraction of the force necessary to oppose him. They were awaiting reinforcements from the north, but it was unlikely that anyone in Canada would release significant numbers to march into the depths of a wilderness so late in the season.

"If we may trust this woman's word," he told us inside his marquee, "then the success of this expedition lies entirely in our hands. If we proceed properly, if we do not gift them with an opportunity, the conclusion is foregone. A mathematical certitude, like a siege designed by that French engineer, beginning with a 'V.' The name now escapes me . . ."

"Vauban," suggested Hand.

"Just the same," exclaimed Sullivan, affecting a fey and irritating enthusiasm. His complacence drew an unexpected reaction from deep within me. I broke my promise to myself to remain silent, asking "And may we take her word?"

Turning to me, Sullivan's eyes hardened to such a degree I believed I could see my own reflection in them.

"You suspect misinformation? Do you seriously believe they are capable of it?" And he cast his eyes around the table, looking for corresponding mirth from the others. But Clinton was already deep in his cups, and Hand's eyebrows had ascended his head in puzzlement.

"They appear to be capable of building fine towns," Hand said. "There is more window glass here than in many a farmer's village within cannon shot of Philadelphia. And the fields and orchards—"

"Are a matter of mere imitation," Sullivan interjected. "Envision, sir, that you might happen to see an ape in the street, dressed in a bricklayer's smock or farmer's sack. Or in a jerkin and shoes, or in any finery you might care to imagine. Would these things make that ape a bricklayer or a farmer? Or even a *man*? It is absurd."

"The Senecah are clearly men," I said, unable to conceal my weariness at this line of argument. "One might ask whether it was a nation of mere apes that turned the Huron beyond the lakes, or the Mahican."

"But is not one wild species always the scourge of another? Is there not always a hunter and a prey?"

Sullivan, at least, believed this point compelling. For my part, it was scarcely worth the effort to refute. Instead, faced with a long night, I poured myself another long glass of porter.

As at Chemung, the next day was spent "processing" what remained of the village. The orchards at Catherine's Town being more extensive, it was not practical to hack all the trees down. Instead, a corporal who grew apples at Canajoharie suggested the technique of stripping away the bark around the lateral base of the trunk. This introduced disease that killed the tree in a matter of months. Insofar as the Indians would return and witness the slow wasting of their livelihood, Sullivan believed this technique to be even more satisfactory than using an ax.

Our allies, the Oneidas, observed this activity from the edge of the forest. All of them were watching the sack of the village, albeit with varying degrees of attention. One old fellow, sitting back on his haunches and worrying the stem of an unlit clay pipe with his teeth, regarded the process in a manner that appeared almost philosophical. Another was apparently busy trying to stretch a pair of white man's pantaloons over his leather leggings, yet I could see he was also casting furtive glances in the direction of the village. A third was seated on a log, holding a peculiar contraption in his hands: a curved wooden stick about a yard long and ending in a loop filled with netting. He used the stick to cradle a small leather ball, rocking it back and forth absently. But when he saw that I was watching him, he quickly put the stick and the ball behind him, folded his arms, and frowned at me.

Our last act before resuming our march this morning was to dispose of the old crone. She seemed much troubled by the activity around her following her capture. Though she was offered a tent in which to refresh herself, she refused to use it, preferring instead to squat on the ground, rocking and faintly singing to herself. She was, no doubt, preparing for her death.

Nothing was better suited to bringing forth Sullivan's basic contrariness than such an expectation. Accordingly, she was presented with meals from the general's own table. And though she touched none of it, the mass of accumulating plates before her became powerful testimony to our commander's conditional humanity.

One cabin from the thirty was spared the torch and filled with provender from our own stores. A quantity of wood was chopped for the old woman's use and stacked neatly against the northern wall, and a small coop constructed and filled with cockerels, so that she might have meat. A small fire was lit in the hearth inside. And then, as a last act before the assembled troops, the crone was installed in her new home.

The woman had shown little emotion until that time, save possibly dread. At the sight of this cabin, however, tears unmistakably stood out on her face. The men saw these, which they took to be evidence of her joy, and cheered Sullivan. Because he had given up his mount, Sullivan could not ride before the ranks to absorb this exultation. Instead, he strode before them, inclining his fine head this way and that, raising his hands as if in benediction of his new foundation, a one-hut city.

The signalman sounded the drum to commence the day's march. As we departed, I took my place beside Clinton's rear-guard, and waited until the flat of the village was empty of troops to look back. The pristine cabin stood in a blackened field, the smoke from its hearth joining the rising fumes of the wastes around it. Beyond, fields of scorched stalks stood immobile in the wind as the boughs of the girdled trees bobbed, stripped of all fruit. The old woman was standing very still, her face turned away, as we entered the forest and I lost sight of her.

Yours ever in love,
JOHN

XI.

IN THE WINTER Rebeccah would shut herself up behind the oak panels of her bed. Inside, she was suspended inside a darkness as profound as the spaces between the stars, but bounded by a sensation that she felt at the roots of her scalp and the tips of her eyelashes. She heated this world with her own body, giving her the peculiar feeling of somehow lying steeped in her own fluids and essences. When she was younger, she would hide there and wonder if perhaps somebody might notice her absence. She would imagine she would be missed, searched for, and wistfully appreciated in retrospect. Her eyes would brim with the kind of exquisite self-pity that youth minted like the currency of hope.

She didn't imagine being missed anymore. More often, she wished the opposite—that the affairs of the house would run on while she lay safely inside. Lately, she hid even in summer, sauced in sweat, breathing her own exhalations over and over until the space seemed to pitch like a ship at sea, and she was forced to throw open the panels to discover not France or China or the Barbadoes, but the furniture of her personal desert.

Laudanum had ended her headaches, but not the nausea. Recently, she was plagued with the feeling that she was swelling up inside from some source she had never felt before. Thinking hard about it in her private universe, she came to suspect some conspiracy in her belly against her, and then, with a shuddering, wondered if somehow, in some unforeseen way, she was pregnant.

She was not ignorant of how that condition usually arose. Severence's fumblings, presumptuous as they were, never went beneath fabric; they amounted more to prestidigitation than to intercourse. Yet she couldn't rule out some more exotic transmission—bathing in soiled water, for instance. Or seating herself on a suspect privy. Was fabric, in fact, barrier enough? With time, her mind began to work on these possibilities. Pregnancies in unmarried girls, after all, were rarely attributed to sex when other vehicles presented themselves. It was a medical fact, or should have been, that fecundity could manifest its own motive in youthful bodies. Yet in the event she was pregnant, would her father pause, before he threw her out the door, to entertain these speculations?

So Rebeccah did a very dangerous thing. Risking a chill, risking immodesty, she stripped naked. Standing in front of her mirror in the open air of her bedroom, she examined her profile, splaying her feet and rounding her back to bring out the relief of the thing inside her. Twice, she heard footsteps in the hall outside and covered herself. Once, while kneading the mass below her midriff, she thought she could feel a new, lozenge-shaped mass under her belly—or was it always there? Her breasts suddenly seemed massive, pendulous, incriminating. Her heart sank as she understood that she simply was not acquainted enough with her body to know for sure.

Could mere forgetting be an antidote to this horror? She launched herself into her household duties with a new desperation, ordering the ornamental plantings in the yard torn out. Workmen with picks looked plaintively to her for guidance; a procession of farmer's wives came before her offering bulbs. But holding them in her hands, the prospect of the worm inside her forced itself forward. "Yes," she thought, holding a tulip bulb in her hand. "It would be about *this big* inside me right now."

"Miss?" asked the seller, startled.

"Nothing."

Rebeccah understood she could no longer distinguish thinking from speaking; she was becoming less visible to herself under each day's load of black dread. Only one person could help her now.

There was no question of the midwife conducting an examination in her father's house. Instead, Rebeccah trekked out to see her, going on foot to the western edge of the town. Mrs. Sparshot lived by a footpath some distance off the Boston road; the place was covered in faded whitewash, half-timbered, with wild roses growing unrestrained up to the shutters. Odd relics littered the ground—the rusted blade of a plow, the discarded suspension of an old cariole. Rebeccah, her head hidden under a hood, hands tucked into a fine set of chamois gloves, suddenly felt herself absurdly precious at that place at the edge of the woods. How the old woman would despise her, dressing so finely yet bringing such a common problem for her to diagnose—or to solve.

"The Lord strike me down," Mrs. Sparshot was saying, standing in the doorway. "If it isn't our little Becky."

The old woman's rawboned arms were exposed below rolled-up sleeves, as if she had been interrupted at housecleaning. A line of dried black droplets, of a substance Rebeccah could not identify, ran from under her lips and down the linen expanse of her chest.

"It is," Rebeccah replied as she turned away her eyes. "Come to take you up on your invitations."

"Among other matters, I suspect," said the other. "Might as well come in, then."

The tone of their conversation was nothing like their accidental meetings on shopping days. Sparshot offered none of the unctuous pleasantries Rebeccah had come to expect from her. Instead, the old woman was short, even cold; she didn't even offer her the seat closest to the fire.

"You should know I never see people here," she was saying. Her gaze flitted to the floor, where Rebeccah saw a milking bucket full of tobacco-stained spit. Black stains were scattered in the dust where she had missed this wide target. The curious thought occurred to Rebeccah that the bucket didn't smell. She would have expected spit to smell, in large quantities. How strange.

"I would have sent a messenger, except for the nature of the problem."

Sparshot shook her head. "No need to describe. There can be only one reason. But why so impatient, my dear? Time will tell in due course, no?"

"No. I must know now."

"I don't understand. Why?"

Rebeccah preferred to stare into the bucket of spat tobacco than to meet the old woman's eyes. "I don't know if I can explain it to you," she finally said, "Except I must know the nature of the . . . the *growth*. It exhausts me, the possibility. I am miserable with the loneliness of it, to carry another. Do you understand?"

"No. I think you're wrong to fear the possibility, though. Let's make ourselves sure—stand up."

With her head uncovered but her gloves still on, Rebeccah stood before her. She expected the other to touch her—even ask her to remove her clothes—but the old woman only stared at her face through half-lidded eyes.

"You know, I never understood why your father sent for me. He could have had a physic—not that a physic would have mattered to your mother. Unless it was the money, the lickpenny—did you know he still owes me for your sister?"

Rebeccah blushed. "No, I didn't."

"Have you missed your maidenlies this month?"

"The time hasn't come yet."

Their eyes met. Sparshot finally placed a hand on her abdomen, still staring as she laid her palm there with very little pressure.

"No," she finally said. "It is not in your face or down there. Not at all. Why would you think it?"

Rebeccah shrugged. At that moment, her reasons seemed inconsequential. Yet some part of her, some kernel of self-assurance, was disappointed by this easy dismissal. How could such profound dread be so deeply unjustified?

"Are you sure?" she asked.

The old woman laughed, spat, laughed some more.

"Young miss, I've delivered 53 children, including yourself! I should know my own business!"

"Yes, of course. But might you check again? To indulge me?"

Sparshot sighed. "I must inspect you directly, then. Undress."

At length, Rebeccah stood before her. This time Sparshot concentrated entirely on the area beneath her navel. She gathered Rebeccah's flesh between her hands like a seamstress gathering a bolt of material.

"That you seem so sure worries me," the old woman was saying. "For the green hand, it is sometimes hard to tell so early . . ."

Quickly, before Rebeccah could react, Sparshot seized her right breast in her hand. Rebeccah's spine stiffened, but she remained still.

"Tender?" the other asked her.

"Yes."

"Odd—the spot has not turned color."

The women remained this way for several moments, avoiding each other's eyes. Though the position should have humiliated her, Rebeccah was surprised to find she felt nothing at all.

Sparshot finally frowned. "No. It is impossible. I'm certain."

Rebeccah folded her arms around her breasts. Spasms began to shake her. The room seemed suddenly to fill with a kind of mist as her eyes poured with unaccountable tears. The other watched her with a practiced compassion. She draped a blanket around her shoulders.

"Yes, it is a relief, isn't it? Here, move closer to the fire. That's my girl. Would you like some tea?"

Rebeccah shook her head, sniffling, teardrops flicking off her lashes. Her hostess prattled on as she produced a cake of tea money and broke off a corner.

"Well, then, aren't we relieved by this news? Whoever did it to you—he didn't ruin you. No need to worry about seeming intact—there are ways to give that impression still. Men know more about far Cathay than the mount of Venus. I know a young lady, not much older than you, who was a virgin for no fewer than seven different men. All right, you forced it out of me—that girl was me. And she is much older than you!"

Rebeccah turned to the old woman, the expression on her face suddenly brighter than the flame in Sparshot's meager hearth.

"If it were true, if it were to come to pass . . . how would we . . . *process* it?"

"Process it? What an odd way to describe it, dearie. But there are ways it might be done. It is not my *speciality,* by any means. But there are methods."

"Tell me."

The other shifted on her stool. "We might be here for hours, counting the ways. Infusions of certain leaves and seeds. Or of a kind of seaweed. Introduction of certain liquids—vinegar, beer, bleach, dye, black powder, potassium salts. Those methods work when the growth is . . . not far along."

"And after?"

"Certain techniques of massage. Introduction of instruments—thin and sharp if the egress is not dilated, perhaps a rounder tool to clear the cavity if it is. A lady's domestic comforts have long had purposes busy gentlemen never dream of!" And she began to find this ironic, but realizing how macabre even doleful humor might appear, she pretended to cough.

"But these ways are likely to be risky," she continued. "There can be much blood, so matters must be carefully planned. A private place prepared, with water and cloths and so on. The best way, of course, is to make the body surrender up its issue on its own accord. It happens often enough naturally. If it is done early, the issue can be passed off as the normal flow. That is the oldest method—no advanced degrees required!"

"And how is that accomplished?"

"How do you think? One must crash the carriage, so to speak. Make allies of high places and gravity. I know of one good lady —a very elegant and creditable lady, in fact—who hired a young man to deliver her several sharp blows in the correct place. It wasn't difficult, she said."

"Wasn't it painful?"

Sparshot idly stirred her tea water as it came to a boil.

"Consider the alternative," she said.

"Yes, let's consider it. If one lets the child enter the world . . ."

"You try futures like some try bonnets, dearie! But if you wish to continue to hope, I'll amuse you. For the trials of birth, there is nothing for you to do—God provides. There is one matter you would need to arrange for, however."

"Then you must tell me what it is."

"You must nourish the child with the liquor that began it," Sparshot said as she strained their tea. "From a man. On a regular basis."

XII.

To press this matter further, let me ask you, whether there is not a
clear and distinct light, that enlightens all men; and which, the
moment they attend to it, makes them perceive those eternal
truths, which are the foundation of all our knowledge . . . this
light of nature, like that of the sun, is universal . . ."
　　　—Matthew Tindal, *Christianity as Old as the Creation:*
　　　or the Gospel, a Republication of the Religion of Nature, 1730

SEPTEMBER 8.

My dearest Rebeccah:

So here I am again, in this meager guise you hold in your
hands. Can it be, I wonder, that you understand the full measure
of the suffering this separation has caused me? Perhaps it will surprise you to hear that I dreamt of you at the spinet yesterday.
Though you think I have no musical sensibility, and barely listen
to your playing, I find I hear you very clearly and sweetly from
this extremity, the notes of your tune seeming to assemble from
the songs, half-heard in my sleep, of the birds, the insects, the
streams. I do not flatter myself as to the depth of my intellect, my
love; in rational matters I am a puddle, reflecting more than I con-
tain. But in matters such as the business between us, this business
of feeling, do not doubt my capacities.

The nature of my task here has changed in a way that I hesitate to describe. Please accept these words as a warning, and also
as assurance that the incident certainly means less to the health of
our concord than you might fear. And so, with fond faith in your
forbearance (my pen is shaking), I commence.

The morning after the departure from Catherine's Town was a wasted one. A number of the livestock had worked themselves loose and run off in the night; the main army was obliged to encircle the provisions while the pickets swept the woods to retrieve the scatterlings. Having grown more anxious to see the shape of this country away from the sights, sounds, and smells of other men, I joined the search. In light of the "accidents" that tended to befall individuals separated from our camp, all the parties, including mine, were commanded never to disperse themselves into groups fewer than three.

This is when Parr's men took another prisoner. This squaw is nearer twenty years old than a hundred and fifty. She was, in fact, seized from the crown of a tree. The vigor of her struggle to escape bolstered the prejudices of those officers who considered the Indian something closer to the animal than to the human. Having failed to entice her down from her perch by offers of biscuit and horse-jerky, the party of three riflemen—I will call them X, Y, and Z—took sport in throwing rocks at her. One of these missiles she caught in one hand and hurled back at her tormentors. I am assured that she missed, but her spirit caused the troops such amusement they conferred on how best to repay her. The following dialogue is entirely invented, but also entirely true to the spirit of the event:

Y: "Give me a lead to throw and I'll hit 'er."

Z: "That's too good. We can shake the tree."

X: "Even better! Let's cut the cunny down!"

Her refuge was a pine, something like half a yard around at its base. With three hands at the task, the trunk was soon reduced, causing the limbs above to quiver more and more with each blow. When the work was almost done, however, the men were astonished to see the squaw make her way out to an outlying branch and somehow gain her feet.

She ran and jumped, they said, with a monkey's vigor, though I must doubt that any of them have ever seen a monkey, and if so, ever seen one that wasn't on a sailor's shoulder. In any case, the maneuver worked: having traversed several feet of empty space and falling not far, she was now in another pine that was nearly twice as thick and three times as tall. The squaw climbed still higher and added the further insult of hurling pine cones at the astonished audience below.

Z: "That's enough. I'm gonna shoot 'er off . . ."

X: "Lay off. You know we can't fire for nothing."

Z: "Fuck yer orders."

X: "Lay off!"

At length these soldiers of liberty resolved to match the squaw's determination by cutting down the second tree.

My party reached them soon after. I found all three stripped to the skin and utterly lathered in sweat, lashing into the white core of the pine with all the ferocity of their wounded pride. It is no small thing, after all, to level one tree, let alone another in rapid succession.

"You men there!" I called to them. "What are you doing? Is there a shoat up in that tree?"

"No, sir," said X. "Begging the captain's pardon, it is something else . . ." And he was hit in mid sentence with a heavy pine cone on the crown of his head. Both his fellows and the men with me laughed; I then looked upward and saw the object of their exertions—or more exactly, her rear end—ascending away from me.

"Why did you not just send a man up after her?" I asked them.

"Again, begging the captain's pardon, but the orders from Major Parr say clearly, no parties of less than three. And we are just three down here, so if we send one up there . . ."

"Yes, yes," I said, waving aside this nicety. "We are now six, so you may apply that keen legal mind to fetching her down. Now."

This man's arms, weary of swinging his ax, shook as he pulled himself up into the first branches. The squaw's face was darkened and unreadable against the bright of the sky, but we could all see her looking down to regard her pursuer, then up and around again, as if to measure her options.

"Miss, if you please!" I called to her. "If you surrender, you have my assurance you will not be harmed. You have my word as an officer."

This offer inspired only the opposite response. She climbed still higher, then out onto a branch about as wide around as her arm at its base, but thinning rapidly.

"She's gonna jump," said Z.

Her only refuge was a nearby maple. As X drew closer, she gathered her feet under her and stood.

"I must recommend you remain where you are, Miss! Please don't be foolish!"

She moved to jump. But as she ran along the narrowing branch to gain speed, the bough snapped, ripping away her support. She fell short, grasping desperately at maple twigs on her way down, until she hit a thicker bough. This broke her downward momentum, but also (I later found) her leg. She landed on a cushion of old pine needles, unconscious.

"Don't see that every day," remarked Y as we gathered around.

"Is she alive?" asked Z.

Our prisoner was, I must tell you, of most surprising appearance. She wore a cotton dress not unlike the one on the old crone at Catherine's Town, except that the skirt appeared to be deliberately split up the sides and the remnants tied off in knots. This exposed her legs for purposes, one assumes, of running or climbing. The effect now, however, was to much titillate the men, who had not only failed to see the legs of many maidens after months of duty, but rarely ever one so smoothly and pleasingly shaped.

"Maybe she's Queen Esther," someone suggested.

"Yeah. Or maybe she's just Empress Maria Teresa of Prussia," came the response.

"Lot you know. Maria Teresa's of *Austria*."

I covered her legs with my uniform coat. But as she was still breathing, I could not conceal her face, which was white and beautiful and very unlike the moonfaced physiognomies one so often encounters among the savages. Rather, her cheekbones rose and arched like Gothic buttresses lofting her high, proud brow. Only later would I see her eyes, which were of such a light gray that they seemed to burn fiercely yellow when she bristled at me. Her cheeks were bruised and rouged with sap from the trees she had lately embraced.

"Orders, sir?" Z asked me, apparently for the second time. Interrupting my examination of her face, I noticed that the men had broken out in crooked, salacious smiles.

"Fetch a stretcher," I snapped at them. "and have the regimental surgeon come to my tent."

"To your tent, sir?" Y asked.

"Do you speak English, son?"

"Yes, sir!"

Unlike these apes, my dear, you can understand that my solicitude toward this squaw had nothing to do with petty lust, and everything to do with the substance of my commission. Until then, my charge to assist in the administration of prisoners had been entirely frustrated by the fact that there were none. This time, however, I had taken one of the Senecah myself. Insofar as possession is the better part of the law, I believe I may retain her, and perhaps, given the surety that she bears at least some white blood, to redeem her for education and civilization. Or so I hope.

"May they also fetch a ladder for me?" squeaked X to us from the pine tree above, his voice quavering. After the exploits of our squaw, this man's fear of heights appeared all the more contemptible.

"If he stays up there three minutes more," I told his companions, "you may try stones on him."

The squaw is installed in a small tent next to mine. As the surgeon confirmed her broken leg, then set it and fastened on a sizeable splint, there seems little chance she might contrive to escape. The multiple lines of lookouts and pickets Sullivan has placed around us, moreover, function as well to monitor those within as those without. As Frederick the Great informs us, such precautions are necessary in all modern armies—not even excepting ones consecrated to fine ideals.

When she woke up in the tent, I was watching. She showed no surprise at her captivity. Instead, the merest frown creased her face, as if she had not suffered capture but inconvenience.

"You're safe in my custody," I told her. I had no reason to suspect she spoke English, except perhaps that more of her people spoke our language than the reverse.

Her face a sheet of ice, she glanced at the confines of the canvas walls around her.

"You will not be harmed," I continued. "Our surgeon will care for you until you are healed, and then you will be released. For now, it is not safe for a young woman alone . . ."

Something about this squaw, something in the graveness that adhered to her, made my own voice sound tiny, childish to me. Having surveyed the dimensions of her prison, she turned her eyes on mine. Yes, I will own to you that she is beautiful. Yet this was not a quality that manifested itself in the usual form, in the platitudinous sense of something that pours forth, as in "the girl is *radiantly* beautiful." Instead, she seems to burn by rendering the air around her more cold, by consuming instead of radiating. The impulse seized me to fill the silence around her.

"Your exertions in the tree . . . ," I began, not knowing how to finish, ". . . do credit to your spirit. But they were unnecessary."

What she did next gives me no pleasure to describe to you, but

demonstrates with what regard she takes the word of a white officer. First, in a gesture of practiced casualness, she tucked a lock of
her hair behind her left ear. Then, with her gaze fixed on me, she
struggled to roll over onto her stomach with her splinted leg
splayed out rigidly. Pulling up the material of her skirt, she gathered it around her hips, exposing herself.

The girl was naked, yes, but hardly uncompromised as she
glared back at me from between her elbows. Her manner in that
delicate position somehow delivered me into a profound exposure
of my character. I will not insult you by claiming I did not look—
I did. I can say, however, that her presentation was at least
instructive in one matter of natural philosophy: she instantly dis-
abused me of that common ignorance that asserts a great difference
between the pudenda of white women and savages. I can now
assure you that no such difference exists.

"No, you will not be dishonored in that way. Please . . . talk to
me."

She made no reaction. Instead, she insisted on this prone position for some minutes.

"If it amuses you to converse with that face forward, I will
oblige."

This weak joke seemed to have some effect as she fell back onto
her side. Her manner, however, reflected neither surprise nor relief.
It reflected nothing.

"Tell me, was your mother white, or your father?"

She closed her eyes. With no answer forthcoming, I yawned,
then closed mine. We remained together that way for some time,
matching stubborn will for stubborn will, until the sounds of the
camp increased around us. It was near time for the evening mess.

"I must call you something," I finally told her. "I have no imagination for such things, so I will call you Polyxena, after the Trojan
maiden. But don't be alarmed: you shall end your days more happily than she did."

I then hazarded a peek at her face and saw, from the slow rhythm of her breathing, that she had fallen asleep.

Polyxena's arrival could scarcely fail to be reported to the general's staff, and thence to the general. Some official attention was inevitable, and it came just this morning in the miserable form of Unger, Sullivan's adjutant. He came upon me while I dressed for the day's march. With a smirk on his face, he made a show of checking my camp bed first.

"Are you lost, Lieutenant?" I asked him.

"Surely not, if this is the repository of pretty women prisoners."

"Then I believe you are lost, for this is no such place."

In an expert performance, his eyes swept over my uniform with an expression offensive enough to denote disgust, but just short of insubordination.

"The general understands you have taken custody of the squaw," he said. "And he *understands* your willingness to interrogate her. Has she been informative?"

I turned back to my mirror. "She refuses to speak to me yet. But I have reason to suspect she knows English."

"You need a translator, then. I will send one."

"That's not necessary."

"I will send one. But the general wishes to remind you that such prisoners must be sent back to Tioga at the earliest instance. The policy is flexible, of course, but the end must be the same for all of them. Do you understand?"

"The 'end'? What does that mean, Lieutenant?"

"I think the meaning is plain, sir."

"I see," I said, laying down the ribbon I had been struggling to place in my hair.

I then proceeded to seize Lieutenant Unger by the throat and push him against a sapling behind him. As he began to protest, I pinched his windpipe shut and leaned heavily against him.

"You may tell the general I understand very well, sir," I said. "I would also bid you to understand that disposition of prisoners figures in *my* orders."

Unger's face had grown so furiously red he had utterly lost all capacity for superciliousness. Attending an odd impulse, I then extended my tongue and licked him in the space between his cheekbone and his nose. The look in his eyes, in that moment of contact, instantly changed from defiant fury to impotent terror. In all honesty, I can't say what possessed me to do such a thing. It was like something Paul Jones would have done. I let him go.

"You may assure General Sullivan I will send her back at the earliest safe opportunity," I told him, returning to my toilet.

"That was *assault* . . . ," he choked, wiping away the trail of spit on his face. "You are insane. You will be *reported* . . . there will be *repercussions* . . ." And he went on like this as he walked away on his stiff, diffident little legs.

I continued to struggle with the ribbon, still puzzling over my own conduct. At that moment, however, I also became conscious that I was being watched. Turning, I saw Polyxena looking at me through the tent flap. There was an expression on her face that did communicate disdain and coiled hostility but, most of all, something like *mystification*. Her eyes lingered long enough for me to meet her gaze. Then she turned away into the darkness behind her.

The day's march was uneventful. Neither Parr's vanguard nor the rearguard reported significant enemy activity; all the structures we came across were already abandoned and carefully burned, with the orchards and fields untouched. We touched them, completing their ruination with the bags of salt Sullivan had brought up from Easton. The full absurdity of the latter task weighs on the men with each tedious, repetitive sack: after more than two weeks on half-rations, the men exhaust themselves to destroy such prodigious quantities of food as to satisfy all of them twenty times over. We are becoming, in short, an army that not only promises famine, but also realizes it, like the legions of marching, marauding skeletons in old paintings of Perdition.

I made frequent trips to the center of our formation, where I had installed Polyxena on a packhorse. At midday I was met there by an Oneida translator sent by Unger. He had no better luck conversing with her than I had. By the end of their interview he was shouting at her, his mouth inches from her ear as she gazed off serenely, down and to her right.

I intercepted him as he walked away from her in disgust.

"You there! Did you learn nothing from her?"

"Nothing from her words. By her clothes, she is not Senecah. She is Gweugwehono—Cayugah, you call them."

"Cayugah. I see. But what did you shout at her?"

"I said if she play stupid, she end up like the horse she sits on," came his answer.

"You were not instructed to make threats."

"Not a threat, fancy soldier," he replied. "A fact."

I found this remark insolent, but let the man go. I was, in fact, quite gratified that he had failed to exact a response.

Beyond this unfortunate exchange, I saw no one else attempt to talk to her. Indeed, there are some women who, through some quality of their person, invite the attentions of men. Very often these women are themselves puzzled over the source of the attraction, which may owe little any outward conduct but have much to do with an inherent receptivity that seems to glow from beneath all mere moods or appearances.

Polyxena is the opposite sort of woman. Though she sat very much on display above the troops, strikingly handsome and half-naked with her skirts gathered up over her splints, she inspired more the dread of a commander than the contempt of a captive.

The men whispered around her. There were jokes and shared, hushed remarks of predictable lewdness. No doubt many entertained themselves with particular thoughts about her. But no one dared disturb her.

At midafternoon we came upon a large, strikingly beautiful lake. It measured about a mile wide from east to west and stretched beyond the horizon to the north. Around it reared a bank of gentle hills daubed with the dusky yellow and orange of late summer blossoms. This, we were told, was the lake at the core of the territory of the Senecah.

As we strike north parallel to the east bank, I expect we will receive organized resistance at any moment. At intervals all along our route, gullies and chasms cut down through the hills, any one of which would make a suitable site to fortify and frustrate our progress. Enough delays will prolong the expedition deep into the autumn, obliging Sullivan to turn back before accomplishing all of his goals. At best, the skirmish on the Chemung could only have been a test of our strength; the real battle, I still believe, must lay ahead.

Yet, I must also confess that a score of perfect places for Butler and Brant to make their stand have proved deserted. As we penetrate farther into this territory, Sullivan grows more and more confirmed in his assurance that, south of Montreal, no army exists to stop us. With every town found burned and every field despoiled, the hour grows late for the Senecah to save any remnant of their kingdom.

I was blessed with an opportunity to view the general's confidence early this evening, when I received an invitation to his marquee for "diverse consultations." Ominously, the third party to our meeting would be Mr. Tindal's book, which I was reminded to bring with me. Having freshened my uniform and pried the mud and deer feces from my boots, I appeared at the specified time and found him much as I first saw him—hunched over his field desk, submerged in the flood of books and papers which seems to rise instantaneously wherever he settles for a night. There was, thankfully, no sign of Unger, so I announced my presence by clearing my throat.

"Ah, Severence," he turned, peering at me over the rims of his spectacles. "Come. Sit."

I took a stool near the tent pole as he turned his chair to face me, a sheaf of notes on his lap.

"At last we have a chance to discuss our mutual friend. Have you had the chance to examine his arguments . . . carefully?"

I had, in truth, read only the first two chapters of Tindal's book.

"Good," he said, without waiting for an answer. A glass of that indefinable red stuff he represented as wine was placed before me. "Be sure to check the rim before you drink," he warned. "The black flies like to settle in the residue."

"The flavor is not unknown to me."

"Nor to me!" he replied with that pub-room geniality that must be taught in law schools. "So that we may begin with some measure of agreement, what might you say is the crux of Mr. Tindal's deism?" Sullivan sat with his legs crossed, waiting for me to answer.

"Uh, in all earnestness, I say again that I would not mistake myself for one qualified to speak of these matters," I said.

"Ridiculous. A man like you, Severence, always has his *opinions.* I daresay you haven't stopped expressing them since the moment you joined us. Might you at least turn your acute judgment to my purposes, for just an evening? A man of your wide travels—to Europe, in fact! You have gone farther than me. So please don't affect modesty, sir. It does not become you."

I wiped the flies from my glass, bowed to the inevitable.

"As far as it is within my power to discern it," I began, "the author holds that the Lord's creation is, in fact, the best of all revelations. By the rational powers He has invested in Man, His subjects should be capable, with correct perception of the physical world, to apprehend all the wisdom that He requires of us. What we might apprehend in this way Tindal calls 'natural religion,' which is, by His design, perfect, because He is perfect."

"And what says he about the authenticity of Scripture?"

"Of authenticity, I believe nothing. Rather, he would regard it as superfluous, because all that needs be revealed of His plan is immanent in the world He created, and therefore attainable by reasoned reflection alone."

"Well said, Captain! You are good at this! But tell me, what do you think of these notions?"

"Think? As in whether I approve or not?" I was temporizing, for I had no idea exactly what flavor of denunciation Sullivan wanted to hear.

"Yes, true. The question is unfair. I should say that I myself have been seduced by these ideas. What is more—and I tell you this in confidence, Mr. Severence—I have found myself attracted to principles more radical still, such as those of atheism. Does that surprise you?"

It did not, because I hardly cared. "Yes, it does," I said.

"Yet through what you so properly call 'reasoned reflection,' I have come about entirely. Atheism, I would claim, is *prima facie* an absurdity, granted the design so evident in the world. Attending that design, as Tindal suggests, should indeed tell us much about His intentions for us. By this course of reasoning, we must conclude that all the trappings of our institutional faiths, all of our pomp and mummery, from the idolatry of the Roman Catholic to the cleaving to Scripture of the Protestant, must all be vanity. Instead, in the Deist's view, we may sit here in the woods and ourselves, cogitating unaided, by our own lights, attain all the Revelation we require without the aid of Providence."

"And indeed, not only we may accomplish this, but *anyone*," I added. "Including, in principle, the Senecah."

"But can you see the flaw in his argument?" he asked.

"I must confess, I do not."

"Of course you do. For we must inquire, is Tindal cognizant of the covenant between God and man?"

"Ostensibly not, as he would argue that the covenant is nothing explicit, but immanent in the arrangement of all things."

"Yes, yes, he would say something like that," Sullivan granted, impatient. "But is that view indeed correct? Might we imagine that the Freemasons are wrong—that the Lord is not an architect? Might we better conceive of Him as a *father*, and we His children?"

"Yes, we might imagine it so."

"The suggestion divides me, as I have been a free and accepted Mason myself for a number of years."

"How interesting."

"But if we accept this paternal conception," he leaned forward, seeking the advantage, "then might we say that there is indeed a role for revelation, insofar as no parent may educate his children all at once, but must reveal the truth gradually, at the fitting time for His wisdom to be received by them?"

I shrugged. "Perhaps."

"Thus, I posit that your suggestion, that the Senecah may possess a knowledge of so-called natural religion every bit as legitimate as civilized faith, must not be true, as it is most likely that the Lord has gifted His eldest children, *us*, with the greater measure of His grace."

"If I follow your argument," I replied, "then I would be tempted to conclude that this expedition itself is an instrument of His teaching."

He thoughtfully chewed the inside of his cheek. "Yes, it might be so concluded. In fact, it must be so. For why would the Creator surrender His children, if they all be coequal with each other, into destruction at the hands of his brothers? I ask you, if the Senecah Castle is the Jerusalem of this continent, why its defenders fly before us? Why do they not stand and fight and prevail on the strength of His grace? If Mr. Tindal is correct, how could such a thing as this conquest exist? Recall Exodus 23, of God's injunction to the Israelites to supplant the Canaanites: '. . . thou shalt utterly overthrow them, and quite break down their images. . . . By little and little I will drive them out from before thee, until thou be increased, and inherit the land.' It is clear to me that the Canaanites could possess no wisdom through Mr. Tindal's 'natural religion,' if they revere images and are scorned by God."

It would have been most easy for me to presume, at that point, that the general was haranguing me. Yet it would not have been true: there was no furor in his eyes. Instead, he seemed genuinely to be asking, and earnestly expecting an answer. I straightened myself on my stool.

"Yes, it may be as you say. Except . . . except Mr. Tindal might reply that He had invested His wisdom in the matter of his Creation *and* bestowed a rationality upon His children that allows them to discover the truth on their own, when they are ready. Nor would I be inclined to dispute the Lord's ingenuity in this regard."

Sullivan had taken to rearranging his papers beside him.

"But one might also quibble with the meaning of this, or any conquest," I went on. "Jerusalem herself, if I recall correctly, has suffered under the yoke of the infidel for much of her history. Indeed, Scripture attests that such conquest has been an essential element of His teaching—that His chosen people, the Hebrews, must suffer their transgressions. In this regard, the armies of Pharoah or Nebuchadnezzar were unwitting instruments of His wisdom. Look to Jeremiah 52, wherein God allows the Chaldeans to invest and ravage the city of David. Yet, by the argument you

advance, the chosen people would be the Chaldeans, and conquered Hebrews scorned by their own Father."

The general's head was shaking before I had even finished
speaking.

"Your history is flawed," he said, leaning back and addressing
the air above my head, "because you presume the Hebrews are still
chosen. If that were the case, Paul's mission to the Gentiles would
make no sense. The generations under the Caesars would make
no sense. And I must assume you are joking when you imply that
the Senecah are akin to the Hebrews."

"I presume no disrespect. I go where the principles of the argument take me. For the Senecah, this is their Jerusalem."

"Possibly. But I must act as if I lead the armies of David, not
of Nebuchadnezzar."

There seemed to be little point of continuing the dispute: in a
gesture I assumed to stem from annoyance, Sullivan was idly tapping the heel of his empty glass against the arm of his chair. But
he surprised me then by smiling.

"You are a remarkable man, Severence. I have yet to take the
measure of you."

"Thank you, sir."

"I'm not sure I mean it as a compliment, Captain. The way
you take up a dispute in which you profess not to take the slightest interest in suggests a subtle mind. May I tell you something
that might surprise you?"

"Am I free to decline?"

He laughed. "Frankly, no. You might as well know that Hand
and Proctor have collected information that confirm you are a spy
in the employ of Haldimand. What do you say to the charge?"

I shrugged. "I say, you are not very specific. What information,
exactly?"

"That is not your concern."

"In that case, there are parties who can vouch for me. I am not sure Hand and Proctor can say the same."

"Oh, I can vouch for them. But look here: there is a sentiment about that you are not wanted among us, and that you should either be given very dangerous duty or else sent down. Do you understand?"

How to respond to such a statement? For lack of a better—or civil—reply, I produced a somber nod.

"Your sense of superiority over your betters is more than implicit, sir," Sullivan continued. "It offends everyone you are in contact with."

"Indeed."

"The worst sort of prig, of course, is the one who dresses his pride in the robes of sanctimony. Were you aware of that?"

"I was not."

"A pity. But if you remain with us, it is solely at my pleasure. Clinton and Hand are so dull, after all! Like this business about the squaw you keep by your tent. I understand what you intend to convey perfectly, Captain: she is your Briseis, your spear-won property. I applaud the gesture, though you are no Achilles. I, however, am perfectly willing to play the part of Agamemnon."

I am not sure I am capable of translating into words the full absurdity of this dislocated interview. Sullivan appeared not the least bit ruffled, yet I felt I was being exposed to only the mere edges of his contempt for me. To claim that my protection of Polyxena from the "processing" meant for her stemmed from a lustful pride like Achilles' was cynically wrongheaded. His threat to take her away from me—to "play Agamemnon"—was plainly brutal.

I stood and handed Tindal to him. "Many thanks for a fascinating talk. If I may be excused, then?"

"Tell your masters your mission will fail, Severence. You will not disrupt this expedition. I leave it to you to decide whether you will return to Easton now, or see us through to Senecah Castle."

"Thank you, sir. May I wish you a pleasant evening?"

"You may," he replied jauntily, "Or you might go to the Devil. Again, I leave the choice to you. Let us talk again soon, shall we?"

I left the odious atmosphere inside the marquee feeling equal measures of anger, confusion, and despair. None of these vexations were relieved by my encounter with Unger sitting outside, his booted right foot up on a folding table. There was neither a salutation nor a curse between us. Instead, there was a look of ominous expectancy on his face that chilled me. The fear suddenly rose in me that Polyxena had already been seized.

I headed directly for her tent. I moved at first in a quick walk, then at a dead run. I picked my way through the horizontal ranks of men sleeping on the ground, through the park of idle cannon, past the damnable smirks of the sentries. Arriving, I ripped the flap open with the perfect assurance she would be gone.

My fumbling woke her. Leaning up on her elbow, she stared back at me, her eyes fluttering in the dying light of the campfires outside.

"I'm sorry," I said, embarrassed. "I thought . . . you might be in difficulty. Are you comfortable? Do you need water?"

She wearily began to roll onto her stomach, as if to repeat the presentation she had made earlier.

"No! Please, don't insult me."

She stopped. Instead, she rested her head on her elbow, showing me that expression of puzzlement I had glimpsed before.

"I think you find me funny," I told her. "Is that true?" Of course, she made no answer. "I am nearer the fool than the rapist," I said, "but would be better taken for neither. Until tomorrow, then."

With that, and without waiting for an answer that wouldn't come, I closed the flap on the day's drama.

With love,

JOHN

XIII.

I FELT no great calling to help the Yangeese win their war. Whether there was one less white man's ship on the water meant nothing to me. But face-to-face with the real dangers on board, rage and boredom, some action would have helped. The boredom wore on me like an ancient porcupine quill buried deep in the sole of my foot, aching with every step. The rage filled me with foul imaginings. In my daydreams, I slew phantom whites, phantom Huron, phantom Mahican. Once, I even killed the Memory of Fallen Leaf. She fell with her belly opened, this Memory, and I felt ashamed the very moment I pulled the boarding pike from her body. But the Memory of Fallen Leaf neither cried out nor cursed me, but instead made praise, saying, "Now do you see, brother? Now do you see?" I didn't understand what she said, what I was supposed to see.

"You see the heart of my sadness," she explained, "which is deeper than this river sailed by the whites. For that I am glad and forbid you to be troubled by this dream." And it was true—where a dream such as the murder of my sister should have driven me to shame and despair, I felt no burden. Perhaps the white men are False Faces after all. Or perhaps the burden would come later, as it often did.

So I chanced to see Jones on the quarterdeck one day, after the wind had driven us away from the port of the English. I called up to him, saying, "Hey, Captain. I did more fighting on that other ship. Maybe if I see them again, I'll swim back."

To which Lunt, the lieutenant, found himself a worming iron and came at me with a red face and his mouth running. I stood my ground, thinking at least the boredom would be finished when I made Lunt eat the thing. But Jones froze him at the ladder.

"Stand down, Mr. Lunt!"

"But begging the captain's leave, the Hindoo is clearly in want of respect . . ."

"It is our enemy that disrespects us, Lieutenant. I suggest you direct your energies thence."

"But Captain, I . . . ," and he went back to Jones to protest, which enraged the little captain still more. The end of their exchange was made in harsh whispers, with the end being that I went about my business, and Lieutenant Lunt paced the deck from rail to rail, fuming.

It wasn't the very end, though. Every time I would look in Lunt's direction that day, he made hostile gestures, like cutting his throat with his finger or thrusting his thumb up a bunghole formed by his closed left fist. I ignored this kind of threat, which just demeans the fool who makes it. Instead, I just went about my usual round of servant's tasks: coiling cordage, shining bright-work, holystoning and scrubbing gull shit from the decks, hauling and fetching whatever anybody wanted me to haul or fetch.

What I could not ignore, though, was a beating I received the next day. It happened in the dark, while I was collecting a cask of fresh water from the hold. They came on me while my back was turned and kept their faces shadowed from the single lantern near the companion-way. Once they had me, they held me for as long as it took to show me the range of their talents: kicking, knee-ing, raining down their elbows, blackjacking me about the neck and shoulders, banging my head against the bulkhead. They exhausted every resort except their fists on my face, which I sup-pose would have given away their identities by leaving tell tale bruises on their hands. Finally, the cobbly head of an old shoe knocked out four of my front teeth, upper and lower. The only words came when I was down on my hands and knees, looking for the lost teeth.

"Let that teach ye on account of complainin' to the Old Man.

That's a real man's business, understand? A Christian man's business. *Understand?*"

And they all gave me a farewell cuffing before they fled above decks.

I showed up in the galley with the cask of water ten minutes later.

"And where might you have been, you shiftless sack o' black piss!" the cook greeted me. "I might 'er gone down there myself if I knew you were going by way of yer father's arse! And why are you *bleeding,* might I ask?"

"Thell down on the way," I answered him, lisping now through the nice new hole in my teeth.

"Stupid, stupid fucker!"

In truth, my attention was not on the cook or on the beating, but on the collection of bloody-rooted teeth in my pocket. These could not be just thrown overboard or flushed with the bilge. They would have to be attended to with the proper procedures, like the burning of tobacco by a medicine man and burial with sprigs of maple. What spirit was in each tooth, however small, deserved nothing less. I would have to treat them all as his guests until I returned to Turtle Island.

I was no navigator, but I read my sun and stars well enough to know when we turned south-east. The smaller ships said to be under Jones's control did not behave like white soldiers under their commander. Instead, they seemed to come and go as they pleased, like braves out on a hunting party. The one they laughingly called *Alliance* had been gone for more than a week. *Pallas* went off just after the attack on the town was called off.

The more I saw of it, the more the whites' way of fighting by sea seemed absurd to me. As far I could make out, it depended too much on whatever the wind wanted to do. On our course that week, we pressed in toward the shore when the wind came from the west, since the pilots could always let it blow them out to sea if the coast nearby got rocky. When the wind blew onshore, though, the officers' moods grew dark and nervous, and the ship was turned out to deep water. There was so much zigging and zagging it seemed a miracle to me that we ever arrived anywhere. A better way would have been to outfit a ship with both oars and a sail, and a flat bottom, so the crew could come in close to the shore and land men on it. If the whites fought like that, and if Jones had had the good luck to have just a few dozen Gweugwehono braves with him, he could have raided up and down the length of that coast in a matter of days. The thought raised a smile on me: a good-sized war party, dressed only in their paint, set loose on that nation of fat tradesmen and milkwenches, like wolves in a sheep pen. They'd win Washington's war for him in a week.

Yes, using smaller, shallower craft would have forced the whites to give up their precious cannon. But as far as I could see, the cannon were only good for fighting other ships with cannon. And since Jones was already proving you could easily avoid the English navy, what was the point of that?

Two days later I finally got around to feeding my lost teeth. On Wednesdays they gave out knots of bread the color of the sea for rations. I could barely stomach the stuff, but I supposed it could be called food. When my watch was asleep, I slipped out of my hammock and went up on deck with a few of the husks of bread. Nobody on duty paid me much mind; unlike the day watches, the night ones didn't have to share the deck with idlers like cooks and carpenters at their busywork. Other than shadows, I could only see one man standing at the wheel, his face glowing from the lantern kept there so he could see the compass.

I went to the stern and fished the teeth out of my pocket. I kept them in an old handkerchief I'd found in the slops chest. Unfolding the cloth on the rail, I spread the teeth out and placed one bite of green bread in front of each one. Then I sat down and sang a song to the Great Spirit. I sang it softly but clearly, asking him to forgive me for not burning tobacco for him because open fires were forbidden on deck, and asking him to send the little spirits of the teeth to *Hawenneyugeh* and not to *Hanishaonogeh,* and not to let them hang around on earth to worry me. For there's nothing worse than having uneasy ghosts around.

I sang my song in a low voice, but not low enough to escape being heard. When I was done I felt like I was being watched and, turning, saw the Frenchwoman with the pencils, Mademoiselle Henriette, sitting cross-legged on the deck. I couldn't see much of her face by the light of the stars, but her eyes were definitely on me. I climbed to my feet.

"You ever thleep, lady?" I asked her. I flicked the pieces of bread into the water and began to wrap up the teeth in the handkerchief.

"No," she suddenly said. She had risen to her feet but that didn't seem to make much difference in her height." Don't use that filthy thing. They deserve better than that."

"What?"

"Those teeth. They are yours, no?"

"They are mine."

"Then accept this, as a gift."

She was holding out something in her little hand. Looking closer, I saw it was a velvet bag of some kind, its color hard to see, but with a gold drawstring that shone in the light from the helm. I looked from it to her.

"So what do you want?"

She took my hand and pressed the bag into it.

"I want us to be friends. No more."

"Why?"

"I see you are aristocracy. Not of our kind, based on flimsy pretexts to blood and wealth, but aristocracy of the original stamp, *au naturel.* I cannot help but admire you. In you, we may glimpse an older, finer sort of humanity. Like the ancient tale of the statue with a golden head, silver body, iron legs. Do you know it?"

"No."

"It is an allegory of the descent of mankind: the golden head represents the age of heroes, the silver and iron later periods, when the nature of men was more base. We in Europe are currently at the lowest stage, at the feet made of clay. But you! To my mind, you should be commanding this ship, not cleaning it. I think of Montaigne, Lahontan, Rousseau."

Hearing this, I couldn't help thinking: What women's nonsense!

"Lady, I'm not anybody. But if you think I'm tho highborn, why do you give me thuch a common gift?"

She stepped toward me. Closer up, I could make out her round white face, like a dish of cream, and her little nose the size of the end of a pinky. She was wearing a lace-fringed bonnet on her head and a cloak with a big bow tied beneath her chin. To me, she looked like an over-large, overdressed baby.

"I have nothing else here with me, unfortunately. My paints and my supplies—that is all. But of course, a man with your quality may take anything he wants. Anything at all."

And she said these last words in a way that made clear her meaning. So I reached up and pulled her bonnet off her head.

This by itself was maybe the most dangerous thing I'd done on the ship. If she'd wanted, she could have cried rape and had me tossed overboard before the echo died. I don't know why I took the chance, except maybe that I hadn't touched a woman in months.

But she didn't cry out. Instead, she started breathing hard through those tight, curvy little nostrils. I felt for the bun at the base of her skull. Her hair was fine but as unwashed as a sailor's. As I looked at her, she was pressing her head back against my hand, raising up her chin to me. I gathered her hair in my hand and squeezed.

"Ouch," she said, softly.

"Tho, aren't you afraid?" I asked her.

"Yes. But that is the lot of the artist, *mon cher,* to be in terror before all the works of God."

"Well, I'm more afraid of you. Go away."

"No. Not until we are friends."

I squeezed her harder, making her wince. Then I let her go. "You'll get me killed. You want my golden head to feed the fitheth, I mean, the ocean?" The lisp was making me sound so ridiculous to my own ears, I had begun avoiding words with the letter 's.'

"Don't be silly. I am an independent agency here—with whom I make acquaintance is no one else's business."

"Tell that to the guy with the whip."

She came closer—close enough for me to smell the old sweat hiding beneath her posey-scented perfume. Then she did something even more odd: she stuck out her foot in its pointed silk shoe and stepped on my foot. It was nothing more than that— she just stuck it out and leaned on me.

"My sweet savage," she said, "you may be assured that if you are *not* my friend, I will be unhappy. Do you understand what that means?"

I sighed. "Yeah, I thee."

"Then as my friend, you will come to my cabin and let me sketch you, yes?"

"Whatever you thay, lady. Now, pleath go."

She made a little fluttering gesture with her hands, as if to clap them excitedly, but the motion made no sound.

"Then it is a promise! Later this evening. After the first bell on the mid-watch." And with that she turned and scurried off, the fringe of her bonnet bouncing up and down as she made for the companion-way.

I went forward to the hammocks. Of course, there was no way I would keep my promise to her. A ship, I had learned, was not like some rich guy's mansion, where a man could toss a pretty maid in some closet. On a ship, there were eyes and ears everywhere; the walls between the cabins were thin enough to hear somebody scratching his privates, much less the racket of bending *mademoiselle's* timbers. And how was I supposed to slip past the marine guard in the mid-deck?

I knew I was taking a chance she'd be angry if I didn't go. But faced with two equally bad choices, I decided to get the four hours of sleep until I joined the morning watch. That way, I could at least face my execution well rested.

The next day they put me up in the shrouds with a brush and a bucket of hot tar. Some of the waterproofing had come off the rigging and I was given the privilege of painting it back on. The job was dirty because drops of tar kept flying off the brush and the rigging and landing in my face. But compared to, say, being down in the deep hold moving cobblestones around (for Jones seemed to have some idea that the rocks, if placed in the right order, would magically make the ship sail faster), my morning could have been worse.

I had a good view, it turned out, of the reaction to two strange sails sighted that morning. They weren't recognized at first. Dale was called up to the deck with his uniform half on, with Jones following behind. They stood below me with their glasses, staring.

"I feel I must see you half-naked more than your mother ever did, Lieutenant," Jones told Dale.

"My apologies, sir. Those are the *Alliance* and *La Pallas,* are they not?"

"Apparently. Now might you go below and endeavor to set a proper personal standard for young Mr. Mayrant here?"

Mayrant, a pretty, smooth-cheeked boy who had barely spoken aloud since I came on the ship, tried to make himself very small as he witnessed a superior officer criticized in front of him.

Dale went below, passing the surgeon Brooke and the lady Henriette as they came up for their morning turn on the decks. She was dressed this time in a dark blue suit edged with white and wore a queue covered with eel skin at the back of her head.

Her eyes found me up in the shrouds right away. She was studying me like a fish drying on a rack.

Brooke made right for the captain. "Might you settle a disagreement between myself and the good *mademoiselle*, Captain? It is my contention that we stand athwart the Wash, while she maintains that we here see the mouth of the Humber. Which would it be, then?"

Jones answered without taking his eyes off the approaching *Alliance*. "The news would not credit your geography, Brooke. We have not seen the Wash on this voyage yet, while that headland there is called the Spurn."

"Blast it, then," said the doctor. "I cannot hope to compete with the feminine intuition, can I?"

As they went on like this, Henriette drifted toward the rail beneath me. "I want to apologize to you," she said as she looked at the sea. "What I did, what I *suggested*, reflects shamefully on me. I cannot explain to you why I said it. I think perhaps that it is the air that fills a ship like this. It cheapens us. We no longer answer to our better instincts. Can you forgive me?"

"Yeah, sure," I told her quickly, wishing mostly that she would just shut up. The spectacle of her secretly whispering to me like some sweetheart was almost as dangerous as me touching her outright.

"I tell myself whatever danger I face here is bought with the currency of opportunity. It is dreadfully unfair, is it not, that this pursuit must entail compromises due entirely to my sex?"

Brooke was suddenly beside her, holding out his arm. "Perhaps all warships should therefore carry distaff navigators. What do you say, *mademoiselle?*"

He had surprised her, appearing there suddenly. But she recovered well, saying "If by that you mean to credit our intuition, I accept the compliment. But if you avail yourself of feminine *intellect,* you might be better served."

Brooke tossed back his cologned head and laughed.

It took most of the morning for the *Alliance* and *La Pallas* finally to reach us. When they did, *Alliance* just came around ahead of us without so much as a nod at the flagship. And Jones, I saw, had learned not to expect any acknowledgment from them. Instead, he just stayed at the rail, letting his lieutenants issue all the commands, taking out his spyglass now and again to check some detail on the water or in the sky.

The lookouts announced a ship to the north-east. She was travelling south along the coast, on a course parallel but opposite to ours. Jones ordered nothing at first, so as not to scare off the prize. But then, as the distance narrowed between us, he issued his first directions of the day, saying, "Inch us three points on the larboard, Mr. Carswell. But not quickly."

Carswell turned the wheel slowly. He didn't finish the turn until *Richard* had gone a good ten minutes farther on. For my part, the blacking of the shrouds had likewise slowed to a crawl, so fine was my view of the developing fight. I dabbed at something with the brush now and again to keep up the appearance of work.

"It's a brig. Probably a collier out of Newcastle," Dale pronounced. "We are certainly Royal Navy to her."

But Dale was wrong. The casualness of our approach seemed more to alert the brig's captain than to fool him. All at once, he turned into the wind and came around on a course to the north-west.

"Damn his eyes! Mr. Dale, signal general pursuit. Beat to quarters."

With that, the guy with the whistle blew it and the deck erupted. I had to give up my perch and help distribute boarding weapons to the stations where we were supposed to jump over the rail and onto the other ship. The older guys, the "ables," were stringing up nets above our heads to catch damaged rigging before it landed on the topdeck or down in the gun deck. Others were crossing in front of everyone with buckets of sand. They were spreading the sand around as if to soak up blood, but I learned on the privateer it more often served to absorb vomit when somebody's stomach turned on the eve of a fight. Whether we did it in training or for real, beating to quarters meant everybody getting in everybody else's way, but it all still seemed to get done quickly. I got in Lunt's way no less than three times, earning me a grumble the first time, a curse the second, and a shove the third.

"Thought you reds were supposed to be quick on your feet!" he mocked. This was, truthfully, one of the least insulting things he had ever said to me. But he had chosen a bad time to say it. All at once, Bad Mind was in me. I found myself leaning into him then and speaking in a very soft and calm voice, like Mademoiselle Henriette used with me the night before: "*If the enemy doesn't kill you today, I will.* Do you understand?"

Lunt kept his face still, but his eyes reacted. Ever so little, they widened at what must have been a frightening sight—a tall, scar-backed Indian, missing many teeth, a dozen sharp implements slung over his shoulder, leaning in close and bearing promises of murder on his foul breath. My mouth stank more at sea than in the woods, with that diet of sailor's biscuits soaked in coffee or "peas" with the softness of the stuff our mothers chew and spit into our baby mouths. I must have been the image of Tawiskaron as I bore down on him.

It took him a second to find his voice again, saying, "Threats to officers . . . buy you a date with the cat."

"I'll pay anything for the pleasure of seeing your insides," I told him as I backed away. He called after me a few times, but nothing more came of it just then. The truth of it was neither of us could do anything about our words at that moment, with the ship being prepared for fighting. He stared at me with a brave sneer on his face, but eyes trembling like a puddle in the rain.

"One shot through his rig should bring her to," Dale was saying. "She looks to be carrying little iron at all—six long-sixes, at most. To boot, she sails like a pig in a wallow. She will heave to long before Bridlington."

"Then *Alliance* will have the pleasure, not us," Jones said. And he was right: though our ship was reaching for the collier with long, loping strides of the hunting wolf, the *Alliance* was splitting the waves like a true creature of the water. In a minute she raced past us, followed on the other side by *La Pallas* and *Vengeance*. War captains at sea, I saw, sometimes couldn't help leading from behind. This was another reason not to depend so much on the wind.

"Sailing on the same tack at last," added Jones, so evidently bored by the promise of capturing another small merchantman. "A pity we lack a more worthy object at this rare moment."

"We thank Providence for all its rewards," answered Dale. "There is something to be said for sure captures."

"And what might that be?"

From my station amidships I could see Dale begin to open his mouth to answer, but he was prevented by another cry from the lookouts:

"Sail! One point fo'ward of the starboard beam!"

Out came the spyglasses again, pointed this time toward the tip of the headland reaching out to sea to the north.

"A Baltic merchantman," Dale said. "I'd bet my eyes on it."

This new sail seemed to put the officers in a more hungry mood. She was riding above the horizon at full spread, banners flying free in the wind, her proud little nose turned just slightly to landward. Her best feature, though, was that she was too far from any harbor to escape. *Alliance* and *La Pallas* were already abandoning the brig, heading instead for the easier prey.

"If they get there first, there may be more," the lieutenant was telling Jones. "And if Landais gets home first, there's no telling what stories will get afoot."

Jones looked from the brig to the new sail and back again. "Mr. Linthwaite!" he yelled.

One of the boy officers stepped around a gun truck and presented himself. "Here, sir."

"Take that pilot's boat and fifteen men. Secure that collier and put her in at Dunkirk. The prisoners are to be handled as we have discussed. Yes?"

"Understood."

His pimply face oozing self-importance, Linthwaite went down to the gun-deck to pick the men he'd take with him. He selected the biggest and meanest-looking French marines he could clap his hands on, and the ship's best coxswain and his mates. His good luck ran out, though, when Jones leaned over the railing again.

"And take that foul-tempered Indian, Mr. Joseph-to-you! Perhaps you can show him the action he's missing with us!"

"It'll be an education for him," Linthwaite agreed, but also tossed his head with annoyance. "C'mon, then, Chief!"

I took a boarding cutlass and laid it across my shoulder as I walked under Lunt's nose. For sure, he must have known that if I was off taking the brig and sailing it back to France, he wouldn't have to look forward to having me at his back in a fight.

"He just saved your life, nigger," he whispered to me.

"Okay, be killing you later," I answered.

Soon the sixteen of us were in the pilot boat and flying toward the collier. I could hear the waister's feet clomping on *Richard's* deck as they turned the sails around and pointed the ship north. Her wake hissed around us as she left us behind.

From near water level, our target, the collier, looked much farther away. She was about a mile off and turning her bow into the wind to maneuver her way into the anchorage to her south-west. But between her tacking and our rowing, the distance between us was narrowing fast.

"I'll be expecting every man to show me the kind of valor I know he is capable of," our boy captain was lecturing his trapped audience in the boat. He was probably the youngest of us all by half-a-dozen years, and half the war party were French marines who didn't speak English anyway. But neither of these things spared us his advice.

"For this commission I have received I take as the most solemn of covenants, to take the lives of men into my hands for the just prosecution of freedom's errands. When we fight, we fight like the angel beareth the sword into Eden. When we show mercy, we carry the shepherd's staff even amongst our enemies, who, though they be wayward—"

"*Sail!*" we could hear the lookout on the *Richard* call again. Mercifully interrupted, Linthwaite stood up in his seat and squinted north. Though we couldn't see much over the water from our seats, we could see the midshipman's mouth suddenly fall half-open, stupefied by what he saw.

"What? What is it?" somebody demanded. Before he answered, the lookout sounded again: "*More sail! Eight—ten—fifteen rig! Convoy ahead!*"

XIV.

My dearest Rebeccah:

Though I last wrote to you little more than a week ago, so much has happened I despair to catch you up on all of it. Since we have entered the core lands of the Senecah, and since Polyxena has come under my custody, each day presents an exhausting catalogue of incidents.

To the realm of diminishing consequence, I consign much of what this army has accomplished. Reduced to its essentials, it is the following: we wake, we march west to the next deserted town, we burn and girdle and mow under, we make camp, sleep, and then we march west again. Again and again, we stake victory against nothing more than armless phalanxes of corn. This routine has held with the exception of but a single extraordinary horror, which occurred upon our arrival at Senecah Castle, and which I will relate in due course below. But the greater part of this has, alas, become secondary to me.

Do you remember when I first told you of my purpose in this expedition that day on Ceres Street? Sullivan's campaign, I believed then, would be a capital opportunity to see and comprehend the Iroquois, who stand poised at the back door of New-York and must figure in any calculations of the future of the colony. It should be manifest to you by now, however, that there is little comprehension underway on this march. Though we have a score of Oneida scouts in our party, they and we stay resolutely separate, except perhaps to trade souvenirs and liquor. The battle at the Chemung River may be the closest approach I will make to a living Senecah. All that is left of my designs, in fact, is now invested

in my care for the squaw. It is my fervent hope that you understand this and are not tormenting yourself with vain jealousies, as
they must be vain indeed. Polyxena is not your rival, but no more
or less than a young woman *in extremis,* whom any reasonable
person must expect to be spared from the torments war too often
brings to your sex.

Though she said nothing to me for the first week of our
acquaintance, she was nothing less than an ideal prisoner in other
respects. She adopted the routines of camp existence easily. She
ate everything placed before her, was always ready to depart before
I was, and never seemed to tire from the rigors of the trail. Where
her presence attracted much attention at first, she rapidly became
nearly invisible. It was difficult to detect any expression on her
face at all, except for a concentrated contemplativeness she betrayed
when she did not know I was watching her. When she did know,
she gave only a faintly quizzical grimace, with one of her dark eyebrows arched at me. This face was commonly accompanied by the
familiar feminine gesture of gathering her hair behind her neck
in a queue. Such motions assure me, I must tell you, that despite
whatever is alien about Polyxena, she is in other respects much
like any civilized woman, pleasantly recognizable in her vanity.

"What do you think about on the march?" I would ask her
later, in her tent. Of course, she answered nothing, but met my
gaze bemusedly.

"Perhaps my greatest foolery is hoping one day you will converse with me," I told her. But this was inaccurate in at least one
regard: with each evening we spent together, the quality of her
silences had acquired much expressive power. Often, her silence
was hard, cold, and filled me with dread for her future. At other
times, her muteness was warm and alive with the many shifting
tones of her wordless breathing, as if heavy with the possibility of
its own end. For my part, the tenor of my questionings changed
with the variety of her quiet—keening and insistent when she gave

me no grounds for hope, and pressing less when she did. It was in this paradoxical sort of confidence that we passed the first seven days.

This week we have had a breakthrough, precipitated in an unexpected fashion. It began when I resolved to devote some part of our time together to improving her education. I began by reading aloud to her passages from the first two books of the Pentateuch: Genesis and Exodus. Indeed, this occupation served a double purpose, for as my voice carried through the tent walls and over the entire camp in these late summer evenings, it more or less laid the lie to all lascivious speculations on my conduct. After several nights of this piety, Chaplain Rogers deigned to greet me again when we met on the trail; the guards around the camp, alas, found less reason to smirk at my expense.

Polyxena took the readings less well. When I began, at Chapter 1, Verse 1 of Genesis, a very pronounced expression appeared on her face that I took to be one of reminiscence. Had some beloved missionary or parent already acquainted her with Scripture? There was no point in asking her outright. Instead, I read on through the stories of Cain and Abel, Noah, Jacob and Esau, and Joseph. At learning of the latter's career as an interpreter of dreams in Egypt, she seemed fired by a genuine curiosity. At the story of Rachel lending her handmaid, Bilhah, as receptacle for Jacob's seed, not once but twice, she showed a sneer. But her expression soured as she heard of the Nile soaked in blood, of Pharoah's army swallowed by the Almighty's vengeful tide, and the entrance into the land of milk and honey. She frowned as she learned of the Lord's command to Moses to send spies into Canaan, and of the names of the spies, and of the information the Lord wanted the spies to collect. As the story of the forty years in the wilderness unfolded, she grew progressively more agitated, sitting awkwardly upright, twisting her queue idly around her finger, clearly disturbed but too stubborn to break her silence. It was not until we reached Exodus 23, and the Lord told the Israelites He would send out swarms of hornets to drive the Canaanites from their homes, yet promised He would preserve their land so the invaders would not inherit a desert, and that the Israelites must utterly scorn and cast down the gods of the native people and drive all resistance before them, that she finally began to scratch her broken leg furiously and cried out, "This itching is driving me out of my mind! Please put down those fairy tales and help me!"

As you might imagine, I was taken aback at this outburst. It was remarkable that she decided to speak then, choosing such an odd pretext to excuse it.

"You'll get no help from me," I told her patiently, "if you blaspheme so."

"You call yourself a soldier, yet you are lost in childish illusions," she replied. "What good soldier is not a realist, and what realist believes in such *shit?*"

"We were good enough realists to defeat your warriors at the Chemung River."

"The sun will shine even on a dog's anus."

"You say your first words to me in more than a week, and you settle for feeble aphorisms?"

She clapped her hands over her ears and let out a wail of despair. In truth, this seemed as much an exercise of her long-dormant voice as a sign of genuine suffering. Then she resumed stratching at her splint.

"Please. It does itch."

I moved forward to oblige her, scratching under the canvas on her upper ankle. "There?" I asked.

"Around the back and higher—yes, that's it—keep going—yes, thank you."

I extended my right hand toward her. She hesitated, then laid her hand in mine with all the grace of an inveterate ball-goer accepting a dance.

"Perhaps it is time for proper introductions, then. I am Captain J—"

"Yes, I know your name, Severence. And you keep calling me something strange."

"Polyxena."

"Yes. It has an ugly sound."

"Then by what name do you prefer to be called?"

"You are not anyone I would tell my name," she said, pulling back her hand. I leaned back against the tent pole, still much pleased we were conversing at last. "And why should you care to know?" she continued. "I am a prisoner. You may call me what you wish. You may take me as your property. I would prefer that you kill me."

"That is a lie, I know . . . that you want to be killed."

"The ignorance of you whites is a constant wonder. You don't even know how to keep a prisoner. You don't know how to kill us without making apologies to yourselves, and it is plain you are too much a boy to use a woman properly."

"Among civilized peoples," I replied, taking a didactic tone, "women prisoners are not *used*. They are protected."

"And so you are back to flattering yourselves with legends!" she cried, laughing.

"Miss, it is not difficult to guess the cause of your fury. After a fashion, I can also understand the sense of injustice you must feel on behalf of your people. But I will thank you not to begin our acquaintance by presuming the worst about us. It is all too often that we find *your* braves' handiwork on our pickets. And the conduct of a gentleman should not be confused with that of a *boy*."

"Only a boy defends himself from the insults of weaklings," she parried quickly. "And please understand, I look forward to my death in this camp. I despise the cruelties of a gentleman."

With that paradoxical rant, she fell silent. I took a few moments before breaking this pause—I believed the time was more than ripe to introduce a more productive subject.

"How do you come to speak such good English?"

"Captivity is a tradition of our family," she answered. "My mother was taken from the settlements at Tioga."

"And where is she now? May we expect to rescue her?"

Her only reply to this was a smile containing equal measures of irony, pain, and resignation. Then she yawned, dropping her head to her blanket.

"I'm tired, Severence. Might you wring more information from me tomorrow?"

"Perhaps . . . if you are speaking tomorrow."

"Perhaps," she muttered, closing her eyes.

I have put Scripture aside in the last several days. In return, and with the notable exception of telling me her true name, she has been expansive on all matters. The Cayugah people, she has said, have lately been thrown into turmoil with their Senecah brethren. Though Sullivan has yet made no moves toward their lands, which lie some distance to the east, the Cayugah sachems commenced abandoning their towns and fields immediately upon Brant and Butler's defeat at Chemung River. As far as Polyxena was aware, there were few Cayugah braves operating with Butler, and none with the sanction of the elders. For this reason, there was some hope among her people that Sullivan would be convinced to bypass their lands.

And indeed, a delegation of Oneida intermediates did call upon the general as we neared the northern end of Senecah Lake. They argued that congress should not make war on the Cayugah, who were a relatively weak tribe and had no taste for meddling in white men's wars. Sullivan received the Oneida deputation, which included one of their sachems, and listened patiently. But his ultimate decision—a refusal to dismiss the Cayugah for their complicity in prior outrages—was foregone. Washington's orders in this matter could not be more clear.

Alas, my success in extracting intelligence from my prisoner derived me little credit amongst the general staff. Upon my report on the disposition of the Cayugah, Sullivan made lukewarm thanks, then rapidly changed the subject to our prospects among the lands beyond the Genesee River. In fact, and directly to the contrary of what I told him, he increased the afterguard under Clinton in strength by fifty Vermonters, as if he feared a strike from behind, from Cayugah-land.

Clinton, bless him, perceived my annoyance at this foolish dismissal. He approached me after the meeting to state openly, in his typically guileless manner, that any piece of intelligence from my quarter would never be accepted without grave suspicion. "They fear misinformation, yes?" he said. "That she was delivered to you and that you allow no other witnesses, they think curious."

"I would allow other witnesses," I replied, "if she would talk to them."

"The difference hardly obtains. You must force her."

"If you knew her, and therefore how absurd that sounds!" I cried.

The growing superfluousness of my presence here was underlined ever further by the capture of my second prisoner. Once again, my involvement was purely a matter of accident when I came upon a detachment of Parr's men as they brought in a messenger of the Senecah, complete with dispatches. There was patent distress on the faces of the corporal and his men as I appeared before them.

"Where did you find him?" I asked.

The corporal hesitated. A hard stare was enough to dislodge his tongue, however.

"He was found circling the north rim of the Canandaigua Lake. Lost, it seems."

"Yes, it does seem," said I, breaking the seal on the dispatches. This caused the party much anxiety, I could see, but I have decided that whether or not I express my inquisitiveness will hardly affect what appears to have hardened into a general prejudice against me. If they persist in baselessly viewing me as a spy, I will simply act in accord with my own judgment, their suspicions be damned.

"He wasn't lost. He just wasn't expecting the enemy to be so far to the west," I told them as I looked in the pouch.

He carried only one dispatch. I read it right there, and it astounded me. The message was written by one Mason Bolton, a lieutenant colonel of the King's Eighth Regiment, who was the current commander of British forces at Fort Niagara. In it, Butler and Brant were directed to return to the fort in preparation for its defense. Though Sullivan was then but forty leagues away from Niagara, with five thousand Continental regulars, Bolton had just four hundred men at his disposal. Reinforcements from across Lake Ontario were late in coming; there appeared to be some lingering concern amongst the leadership in Canada that, in the wake of Burgoyne's defeat at Saratoga nearly two seasons previous, another attempt would be made to strike at Montreal. Still more worrisome, Bolton complained, was the fact that two of the great guns covering the Gate of the Six Nations were in need of replacement due to a defect that caused them to explode. These pieces were at the moment untrucked and useless, gravely weakening the battery's effectiveness against a frontal assault from the land side. The last line of this dispatch I recall word for word. It read, "Without your assistance, I am in fear for the security of this post."

In fear for the security of this post. As yours is not a military mind, my dear, I will translate this as perhaps the most abject squeal for assistance that an arch, *haute* British garrison commander can make. Fort Niagara is, in short, plump and ripe on the vine for us to pluck. It is, moreover, the very nest from which the hornets go forth to ravage our frontiers. With Niagara in

American hands, the Senecah lose access to arms and powder from
Canada, and must seek a settlement with congress. A successful
assault on it would rank with Allen's seizure of Ticonderoga, and
garnish Sullivan with laurels. Rarely does the opportunity arise to
initiate an engagement with such a great prospect for success.

Yet of course, nothing will ever be done about it.

Allow me to explain. Modern armies are, in fact, not run on
strategical inspiration at all. Leadership of them is not the province
of temporizers, but of engineers, logisticians, and accountants.
Supplies, not glories, dictate the map of battle. This has been well
understood since before the days of Frederick the Great, who was
the master of logistical operations, and never moved an inch without knowing the disposition, exactly, of his soldiers' food, arms,
and latrines. That Sullivan would exploit Niagara's temporary
weakness by pulling up stakes, abandoning his stores, and making
a mad dash to Lake Ontario was inconceivable. I understood this
long before I handed the dispatch pouch to Unger, who handed
it to Sullivan, who read Bolton's plea and scowled.

"This is all very interesting, Mr. Severence," he finally said.
"And I suppose you would hold that this document bears some
relation to the truth of conditions at the fort?"

This question I anticipated and had my answer ready. "If it
pleases the general, the courier was secured under very plausible
circumstances. I understand he resisted creditably, and was captured by men under Major Parr, not by myself. To presume
disinformation is to presume a string of unlikelihoods that, in my
modest opinion, beggars belief."

"Your modest opinion, eh?" he replied ironically. "For my part,
I always think it wise to consider the source of such *apparently*
good news."

"Again, if it pleases the general, while skepticism has its uses,
it can blind us to the fact that opportunities do arise in this way."

He handed the dispatch back to Unger, who refolded it with great care, as if preparing it for deep and permanent storage.

"Yes," Sullivan went on, "you would think it wise, wouldn't you? For me to abandon our calculations, our supplies so painfully gathered? For me to order an attack on a distant target based on such evidence?" And he waved his hand contemptuously in the direction of the dispatch. "And so please tell me, Captain, how you anticipate we may *hold* Fort Niagara? Or are you willing to warrant for us that the enemy will repose happily on his side of the lake and let us keep it?"

And there followed the kind of laughter that greets authorities when, in the company of their lackeys, they beat down dissent with cheap ridicule. This, too, was not difficult to anticipate. Yet, I still felt my face burn with humiliation. Turning away, I saw Polyxena watching all of this from astride her horse. Her face bore little expression, except perhaps for a sympathetic softness in her eyes as she returned my glance. Or so I chose to believe.

"I don't presume to paint a strategical picture for the general," I replied. "Though I was given to understand that Colonel Brodhead is, at this moment, marching up the Allegheny River from Fort Pitt, and may be counted upon for at least one thousand reinforcements."

"I am glad you do not presume to paint a strategical picture. For if you did, you would understand that we have as little idea of Brodhead's situation as we do of the actual condition of Fort Niagara. And so we pass on to more practical matters."

That, then, was that. Sullivan turned to quiz Clinton, Poor, Maxwell, and Hand on their brigades' fitness to push on toward Senecah Castle, which was thought to be only a few leagues distant, that afternoon. The way the ring of conferees closed around the general had the effect of excluding me, leaving me to fidget with the handle of my sword as I stood beside them. There I stood for some moments—that is, until I noticed something unusual.

The Senecah courier Parr's men had captured was being led away into the woods. While I had already come to understand Sullivan's policy regarding the disposition of male prisoners, no mere execution squad attended this one. Instead, there were no less than six men in the escort, including two guards, two assistants to the quartermaster, and two cooks.

Curious, I followed them at some distance, pretending meanwhile to inspect the guards and tents along the way. The prisoner was then led some way into the woods, on a path beaten down by the tracks of heavy wagons threaded between magnificent stands of black walnut and oak. The entangled boughs of these trees formed the nave of a natural basilica, casting shadows that made it easy for me to follow the escort undetected. Their journey reached a clearing, no bigger in area than that of a modest house. The tract was pleasantly located along a stream, exposing it to fine breezes.

Within it were a number of accoutrements that seemed curiously situated so far from the rest of the camp. They included a great, cast-iron cooking pot, a pair of broad, planked tables, and a line of heavy storage casks. The wagon that had brought all that to this seclusion was parked nearby. Amongst the equipment moved one man, wearing a great canvas smock stained with some kind of dark liquor. The impression the scene made, in fact, was of a kind of mobile factory, albeit one dedicated to neither food, nor physick, nor ordnance.

Now it is not odd to see evidence of craft and industry in our camps. Unlike the lobsterbacks, we cannot depend on regular deliveries of manufactures. A Continental soldier, therefore, will regularly be seen at his mold making new musket balls, fashioning replacement buttons out of old bones, striking off new flints, or pulling at his own needle and thread. In my experience, however, I had never seen a rolling shop such as this one.

I clambered still closer, hoping better to see the tools scattered on the plank tables. I found cover behind a laurel bush just ten yards from the factory, and peering through the leaves could see an assortment of long, curved blades lying there. These did not resemble any sort of carpentry or butchering tools I had seen before. Curious, I watched as the craftsman chiseled open the lid of one of the smaller storage casks, withdrawing from it a section of fresh, pink animal skin. This he inspected for some moments and was apparently satisfied. He then laid the wet skin down on the table, taking care to assure it was stretched out flat. As it was no more than two feet by two in area, I judged the hide must be that of a smaller or younger animal, such as a calf or kid. Then the man, whom I perceived to be a tanner, took up one of his curved blades. Using long strokes of expert regularity, he scraped curls of flesh from the back of the skin.

"Captain?" someone asked suddenly from behind me.

I bolted upright from my hiding place. Though it would have been absurd for me to pretend I was not spying on the factory, I clung to my dignity by adopting a commander's tone.

"Yes, that is my rank. And why might you two be slinking around back there?"

The guards, two privates wearing the uniforms of the Massachusetts troop, looked at each other and then back to me.

"May we help you?" one of them asked.

"Yes . . . I thought I might inspect this shop, if that is what you profess to be guarding here."

"We do. This way, sir."

They showed me around to the tannery. Alas, I had by this time completely lost sight of my main concern—the prisoner escort. That had proceeded around the clearing and somewhere farther into the forest. But my problem then was much more immediate: in being discovered in such a position, I risked confirming the charges of espionage that wafted around me. My only

redemption, I decided, lay in showing a powerful curiosity not for
matters secret or military, but for the ancient and honorable craft
of leathermaking alone.

The tanner, at least, played his part for me. He was a tall, lank
man, with a great brush of a mustache. He towered over me in
his great white apron, the regular pleats lending him the impression of an ambulatory Greek column.

He welcomed the distraction from his work, gladly clasping my
hand and volunteering his name (Josiah Hopkins), his home (Easton, in Pennsylvania), and his apprentice (his son, Jeremiah Adkin
Hopkins, then off collecting more raw hides). The slightest hint
of interest was enough to inspire a detailed tour of his facilities,
beginning at the curing casks.

"It will surprise you how little most gentlemen know of this
craft," he was telling me. "They know leather is made from skins,
to be sure. But respecting the details, they're likely to know
little or nothing of the boots or gloves they wear on their very
own persons . . ."

He lifted the piece of hide from the table and gave it to me to
inspect. "As you may still see here, a skin is composed of three layers. The outside is the skin that we may see on the animal when
it lives, and may be seen as the foundation of the fur and the hair.
Can you see there are still hairs here, and here?"

He indicated several thick black tufts still rooted in the skin.
"This layer is removed first, using a hard solution of lime water.
That is what you may see under way in these pipes here," he continued, indicating the line of storage casks. "To remove the dermis
and the hair completely takes at least a week, but as we are required
to turn out boots at a particular rate here, we don't wait for the
chemical process but use a fleshing knife, like this one."

I was handed one of the curved blades. It was heavy, but well
balanced.

"We use the same instrument to strip the bottom layer, the layer mostly of fat. We lay the skin down flat, like this, and scrape in this direction, away from the body, like so. The residue is wiped off with the sharpening stone, here, which works also to keep the blade sharp. This part requires some care, because we must keep the knife keen, and one bad stroke can pierce and ruin the hide. It was years before I was trusted with the fleshing knife by my master. But I have still turned my share of fine boot hide into glove pieces! Jeremiah learns well, but I daren't trust him with these hides, rare as they are."

This was understandable, I thought, given that Sullivan had ordered no shooting or trapping during the expedition. Yet the tannery showed that at least some hides were being collected and worked into boots and leggings for the officers. A score of freshly sewn riding boots stood on a table nearby.

"So all this is buckskin? Or beaver?" I asked of the skin I held in my hands.

Hopkins regarded me quizzically, slightly shaking his head. "Nothing so fine. It is Senecah. And the ones in the far pipe, over there, are Cayugah."

I stared at him.

"You say 'Senecah' as in some sort of deer, correct?"

"I say 'Senecah' as in some sort of Indian," the man replied.

I put the skin back down on the fleshing table. All at once, the full extent of my ignorance was brutally impressed on me. For a moment my head swam, and I feared falling over at the feet of the tanner and the guards.

"They tell us to keep the tribes separate," he went on, "as if they retain some kind of distinctive quality after they are cured. The skin of the Senecah is requested among the cavalrymen, for leggings. The Cayugah and Mohawk are judged a softer material, best for ladies' gloves. But to me that is nonsense—I can make a serviceable pair of touring gloves from any of them. And no Indian is as good for that purpose as a fine kid chamois—kids as in *goat,* that is!"

I stood up straight, trying to attend to the tour once again. The tanner was opening an earthenware jar and showing me the contents within. It was a soft, grayish brown substance, with a semi-transparent skin shrouded over it.

"We can approximate chamois here by using brains, like these, applying them over the exterior of the corium and leaving them for a few days. This gives a better result than dog *excreta* or pigeon. But as with those, we must apply the infusion long enough to transfer the proper essences, but remove them before the substance of the hide itself begins to ferment. And the brains of the savages don't keep very long in this heat, unfortunately."

"Yes, unfortunately," said I, the mask of equanimity once again pasted to my face.

"Now, if you'll step over here, I can show you the tanning process itself, which in our case, for proper coloration, requires prodigious amounts of chopped maple bark."

In short, I endured the introduction to Hopkins' peculiar craft—all ninety minutes of it—and bore him sincere thanks for his trouble, even with my throat half-closed by vomit. For despite the manner in which I had learned it, I had achieved the purpose for which I had gone into the woods. I now knew the ultimate fate of the captured courier.

I drifted back to my tent by a route I can't recall. With every step, I sank deeper into a state of desperate distraction that must have resembled a fair drunk. Though my rational sensibility rebelled against it, I fixed a prosecutor's eye on every man who passed me wearing a new pair of leggings, grasping a pair of gloves, or bearing a leather pouch. One pair of suspiciously fresh footwear belonged to Clinton. I called to him as we crossed paths.

"Say there, James. How stands the glass around?"

"It stands full," he replied, missing the customary refrain, *two times full*. "And for you?"

"Tell me, where did you get that fine set o' boots?"

He stuck out one foot, regarding it.

"Boston. Where'd you get yours?"

"It doesn't matter. We are all accessories. We are all drenched in it. We are all infused with stolen brains and pigeon shit and beyond the pale of fermentation."

I brought up this disjointed *mea culpa* from the root of my soul, but it only moved Clinton to smile. He said, "I always thought you would stand to drink more, Severence! Bully for you!" And then he clapped me heartily on the back and went his own way, chortling.

I was in no state to sit in my tent, alone. Crossing over to Polyxena's tent, I found her sitting up with a lantern lit, the Bible on her lap. She closed it instantly, her expression sheepish.

"Back to check on me again, I see," she remarked.

"Yes. And I see you read as well as you speak English."

She put aside the Word of God with a contemptuous flip.

"You are arrogant to expect otherwise," she said.

"Nay, I am surprised, considering your stated aversion."

"Your library is small."

Indeed, she was right. Though I flatter myself that I am an educated man, I cannot recall that last occasion where I have read a book for the pleasure of it. Jones had always been pressing this or that work on me to read. And with the sole exception of Rousseau's *Discourses*, which I translated for Jones only so he could impress a woman with his knowledge of philosophy, I always declined.

"It is nothing to me," I sighed. "After what I have seen this day."

"What did you see?"

"It is not for a woman's ears. Or for that matter, for the civilized man's. . . ."

She made no answer as she stared at me. In truth, I could no more tolerate her quiet than the loneliness of my tent.

"Except that I might say, at risk of gratifying your arrogance, that I begin to hate them all as much as you do," I told her. Her eyes suddenly hardened at this, which moved me to conclude that she scorned my confessions. I turned to leave.

"Wait," she said. "Where are you going?"

"Would any particular answer matter to you?"

"No. But did I say I wanted you to leave?"

We regarded each other. She is, I must say, one of few members of her sex I have known who may stare at men without fear of the kind of misconstrual that can ruin her. I sat down again with my back against the tent pole.

"To have contempt for your own people . . . ," she began without finishing. Instead, her face completed the thought: her brow twisted with it, but her eyes were placid with familiarity. She was conversant with this species of loathing.

"Contempt—with what object?" I finally asked her.

"Their weakness," she whispered, staring at me but also through me.

"That is one word I would never have applied to your race."

"You know nothing," she said. "For if you did, you would know that it is not strength that has preserved us until now. It is all talk, diplomacy. You despise Sullivan, but he knows it. Tell me: do you truly want to learn about the Nundawaono, the people called the Keepers of the Western door, as we say?"

"Yes."

"There's only one thing for you to know: weakness. So now I have told you all."

"I know enough not to believe you."

Her gaze suddenly found its focus on my face. She laid her cheek down on the blanket.

"All right. It's a lie. So will you watch me go to sleep again?"
I laughed at her. "And why would I do that?"

She closed her eyes. And, in fact, I did watch her. I watched as her breathing passed into the long, shallow cadence of a slumbering child. I watched as creases furled themselves on her brow, and lines of intermittent cares chased themselves across the corners of her eyelids. I watched as the light through the eyelets of the tent drained to black, and the crickets rose, and the sounds of the camp slipped beneath the distant, bated muttering of the river. For a moment, as I watched, between the tents of the generals and the nests of the sparrows and the factories of the depraved, innocence and horror slept together beside the same fire. And so I, too, slept.

On the 13th day instant, the army moved toward the southern extremity of Conesus Lake. Lingering there to destroy a small town and to prepare lunch, we received disturbing news from Hand, who was among his vanguard two miles to our west. A large scouting party was overdue to return. The company, under the command of Lieutenant Thomas Boyd, had been sent forth by Sullivan with the object of reconnoitering the approaches to the biggest Senecah town of them all, which we called Genesee Castle.

That young Boyd had made a hash of his mission did not surprise me. From our days together on the trail, I knew him to be more than anxious to plant as many Tories and Indians in the ground as he could, and at the earliest opportunity. Though Sullivan had instructed him to take just a handful of men, Boyd beat about the camp for volunteers for a "fair frolick." The next morning he rode out at the head of a swollen mass of no less than 25 men—hardly the sort of party to slip unnoticed through the enemy's pickets.

The only report from Boyd's reconnaissance returned on the

14TH, when two men from the Fourth Pennsylvania found us as we moved out in the morning. Boyd, they reported, had discovered the location of a small, abandoned settlement some two leagues distant. Once there, the party spied four Senecah braves entering the village on horses. Taking cover, they attempted to bring down all four with rifle-fire. Alas, only one of Boyd's sharpshooters was sharp enough to find his mark, and three Senecah escaped. (At this point in the story, Sullivan groaned.) The party began to make its way back to the main force, but halted again when they saw Indians in the woods around them. These were almost certainly the sort of decoys the Senecah often dangled in front of their enemies, in order to provoke an intemperate charge.

Here, Boyd made a strikingly poor decision: after sending the two men back to Sullivan with news of the party's disposition, he rushed off with the rest of his company to ride down the Indians he'd spied on the trail. Of their fate, the two returnees could not say. All feared the worst, however, when they reported that the woods around Boyd's party was thick with Butler's rabble, and that in their own flight they had barely escaped capture.

Parr's riflemen were already sweeping forward to rescue their comrades. Marching at double-time, we covered two miles in forty minutes. The shape of the landscape turned ominous as we rounded the southern shore of the lake, which was girded by swamp and relieved at only a single point where the Indian path mounted an east-facing scarp. It was, it seemed, excellent country for an ambuscade.

The first hint of tragedy came when we encountered Hand's regulars idle on the trailside beneath the rise. Farther on, beyond the rim of the hill, Parr's company was drawn up in a field next to a copse of birch trees. My heart sank as I saw, at a distance, knots of riflemen milling around between the trees, looking balefully down at a scattering of pink objects in the grass.

More than a score of naked white bodies lay there. Most bore wounds from gunshots; a few others were worked by the tomahawk. I say "naked," because all of them were assiduously stripped, both of their clothes and of their scalps. Sullivan sneered at the Indians' lack of thoroughness in collecting the latter—only miniscule flaps of skin were taken from some heads, while whole bits of bone were ripped away in others. The Indians had clearly mutilated the men in a rushed fashion, fearing we would arrive soon.

"The action was close," Parr told us as he walked about, his rifle cradled in his arms. He pointed at one of the bodies. "See here, how the particles of powder are driven straight into the skin. Boyd took his position under these trees, hoping to be rescued. He was overwhelmed by waves of attackers—see the tracks. They came down from the lip of the hill, there."

"Barbarians," hissed Poor.

"Burning 'em out's too good for them," concurred Proctor, the artilleryman.

"This could not have been what Butler intended, then," Clinton volunteered. "The ambuscade would have been facing in the wrong direction."

Sullivan nodded. "Their object was the main army, not Boyd."

"Then our Mister Boyd did us a service, taking the fire in our stead."

Though I would always defend Clinton, and would insist that he surmised correctly, under the circumstances this was indeed a tactless remark.

"They removed all their casualties, I see," Hand interjected, "but where is the lieutenant?"

There were more than twenty bodies among the trees, making this action by far the most costly of the expedition. At the Chemung River, at our only set-piece battle, we lost just three men. But Boyd himself was missing from the pile.

Sullivan turned his back on the casualties. "Mister Parr, get your men in motion. The rest of us will apply ourselves to working the artillery up the hill and follow you directly."

"And the bodies, sir?"

"On the return, Major. We may still have time to find the lieutenant."

With that, I knew for certain that there would be no attempt on Fort Niagara. Sullivan had pledged to turn back in time to bury the bodies, which would preclude an advance much beyond Senecah Castle. Of the prospect of rescuing Boyd, even Sullivan must have known it was a fantasy only. Boyd was already dead, and given the traditions of the Senecah, his body likely no longer in its whole form. But as a device to motivate the rank and file, a rescue made a degree of sense.

Before we left, the remains of Boyd's men were hurriedly covered with lime and vegetation to discourage beasts from desecrating them. And then we were off, again in double-time. The exact location of Senecah Castle was unknown to us because the Oneida disagreed on it—some said it lay on the near side of the river, some insisted it was far beyond, halfway to Niagara. Considering the town's reported size and the breadth of Parr's vanguard, however, there seemed little chance we would miss it.

I walked back to check on Polyxena. She was below the hill with the artillery, astride her usual packhorse. Her attention was consumed with fashioning a nosegay out of late summer blossoms someone (not I) had collected for her. But when she felt my approach, she put aside the flowers much the same way she abandoned her reading when I had surprised her at her Bible.

"We move again presently. Are you comfortable?" I asked her.

"More than you, I would think. There are dead soldiers ahead, they say."

"There are."

"So you will be turning around and going home, then?"

This was her first joke. I ignored it.

"I will come back again later," I said. "When the next town is found."

"It is nothing to me," she replied, attending to her flowers again. "I don't know why you insist on checking on me."

"Nor do I, considering your most disagreeable nature."

She rewarded this complaint by freezing over entirely, and our interview was over.

Marching deep into the afternoon, we discovered the town around four. It lay on the other side of the river, some miles beyond the western bank. After fording the Genesee with the usual frantic wariness, the army drew up before a settlement that, in size, did the industry of the Indians much credit. More than a hundred buildings stretched away on the river plain before us. Around them was a virtual infinity of cornfields, bean fields, orchards, squash and cucumber and watermelon patches, all heavily laden with provender. The sheer amount of it made all the previous fields we had discovered seem as nothing; it was a puzzle, in fact, that the number of Indians we faced was so small, given the richness of their cultivations. There seemed enough food there to provision an army of one hundred thousand. The expressions on the farmer-soldiers around me, meanwhile, showed equal parts awe, for the fineness of these fields, and despair, for the necessity of their utter destruction.

Something similar attended the fate of the houses, which the Indians did not burn in advance of our arrival. These seemed uniformly new and well built. Many a white settler would have been pleased to take them over with little modification. The only difference between the homes of civilized folk and their savage imitations, it seemed, was that the Indians did not arrange their buildings in rows along surveyed lanes or streets. Instead, they built them scattered over the landscape with a logic none of us could discern.

I entered one of the Senecah houses as preparations were made
to fire the place. This was not a structure like those usually attributed to the Indians—some sort of longhouse with communal fires
and tiers of family bunks. Instead, this house was of a design
suited to an extended single family, with fine feather beds on the
ground floor and children's arrangements above, in the loft. In the
hearth, an iron cooking pot was on its stand over the glowing
remains of a fire. Corn soup was still warm inside, seasoned with
chunks of white fish and diced squash. Ears of corn twenty inches
long were scattered half-shucked at one end of the table. On the
other side lay a cob doll in a tiny cotton dress, her buttons fashioned out of polished seashells, her hair of fine corn silk. The
latter was half-tied in a queue with a single blue ribbon, a second
ribbon laid nearby, as if abandoned in mid-toilette.

It will perhaps not surprise you that such remains filled me
with acute despair for the criminal waste inherent in this sort of
war. Attacks on the lives of children, of mothers, are not the fit
occupations of armies, even in the guise of just retribution. I
understand full well that this is a minority view—the shape of
our contemporary politics cannot but foster such conduct. But I
also understand that we who live today, in the final quarter of the
eighteenth century, must lay at the very nadir of the moral evo-
lution of warfare. Future centuries must look back at our assaults
on innocent civilians and recoil at their savagery. From our current state of gross moral defect, there can be nothing but
improvement.

By sundown, the manifest temptations of the town—the food
ripe for the taking, the souvenirs—had bitten deeply into the
army's discipline. While half the men were preparing to burn the
place down, the other half was passing from house to house, arms
laden with fruits, vegetables, snowshoes, pelts, arrows and arrow
straighteners, saddles, ammunition, toys, leggings and dresses, jewelry, flints, combs, kettles, books. One private weighed a complete

buffalo skull on his shoulders. Some officers tried to curtail the looting, waving their swords and shouting, but the troops they retrieved just melted away into the general chaos as soon as their backs were turned. Other, less fastidious officers led the plundering themselves. For this reason, and the abundance of buildings and fields to be destroyed, the burning did not begin in earnest until the evening.

At that point, Parr's men discovered Boyd in a broad clearing at the center of the town. I suggest you skip the next paragraph if you don't wish to learn the condition of his body.

The wretch appeared to have been secured to the ground with ropes and stakes. Deprived of his clothing and boots, he was pierced in many places by hot sticks; the right half of his torso was then neatly skinned down to the ribs (which were whiter than one might expect) and the flap of skin turned aside like the leaf of a book. It was difficult to make out the precise order of events, but Boyd's tongue was cut out at some point, his fingernails pulled off, and right eyeball extracted. The left was left intact, no doubt, so the victim could watch with one eye as the other was mashed into paste on a grinding stone. At the very end, perhaps, his head was hacked off in an operation that seemed deliberately to require many hacks of the tomahawk. The head was found several yards away, face down in the blood-soaked dirt, surrounded by footprints, as if multiple feet had kicked it. A rippling haze of flies settled uncertainly over the spectacle, concentrating themselves over the wounds like living black bandages.

Even by the worst standards of frontier warfare, this was an exceptional degree of mutilation. To my mind, it clearly reflected the great amount of frustration the Senecah suffered due to our campaign. To Sullivan, however, it was a vindication.

"Let everyone see this horror," he said to those collected around the body. "Let those who speak of *accommodating* the savages, who wish to *negotiate* with them, see it. This is the work of our esteemed gentleman, Freemason Joseph Brant. It is the reason we are here, doing this work. This is why they cannot be left at the backs of our families, our industries."

"Industries, like our tannery?" I said aloud, before thinking. But it must have seemed a feeble protest, because I blushed as soon as I made it, and then could only look at Sullivan sideways.

He made no reply, announcing instead, "You all know what to do. You must leave nothing to them. You must break the hearts of this generation and the next. I'm counting on you, boys. Carry on." And then he turned his attention to logistical reports from Tioga.

I own now that I had no intention of applying myself to such vandalism. Instead, I made my way back to the house where I had seen the cob doll. The corn-and-fish porridge in the kettle was still warm; my spoon was in its usual place when I am on campaign, in my waistcoat pocket. Digging through the ashes in the hearth, I found hot cinders beneath, recovered the fire, and sat contentedly idle until the soup rose to a boil.

> *Yours in love,*
> JOHN

XV.

Sometimes in life situations develop that only the half-crazy can get out of.

—Francois, duc de La Rochefoucauld, *Maxim 310, 1678*

A TRANSFORMATION came over Jones late in the afternoon of September 23, 1779. He had endured much of the cruise in a deepening state of agitated weariness. Though his appearance and decorum had never betrayed him, his patience and his sense of humor were long gone. While his conversational voice remained strikingly small and genteel, it had lately fallen into a flat key. If any of those around him had been his friends, they would have noted that an unfamiliar aspect, a kind of gray, temperamental overcast, had settled on him. In fact, Jones had no friends aboard. But even Surgeon Brooke could perceive that he was either deeply sick of the captaincy, or not getting enough leafy greens to keep his color.

With the discovery of the Baltic convoy, Jones suddenly lost the appearance of a sleepwalker. The ends of his lips curled in fond expectation, like those of a man coming home to a fine meal. There was a real snap in his step as he crossed and recrossed the quarterdeck, ordering the hammocks spread more evenly in the rail netting *here,* a more effective arrangement of preventer chains *there,* as the crew prepared the *Richard* for action. In Henriette's eyes, he had not looked so magnificent since she had first seen him at Passy. She stood admiring him for some time—for so long, indeed, that when she finally moved again she found her fine sealskin boots half-buried in the dirty concoction of sand and ash the ship's boys were spreading on the deck.

"*Merde!*" she cried, shaking the gritty stuff out of her *castor* fur linings. To endure the discomfort of sand in one's boots for an afternoon, for an entire battle! But it was hopeless—those boys really were insolent, terrible.

"Miss Barlejou, if you please . . . ," Brooke was begging her. "For your safety, the captain requests you join me below, in the cockpit."

"But, my dear doctor, there is nothing to be seen down there! Might I find a quiet corner from which to observe, out of everyone's way?"

Dale was at her other shoulder and gently propelling her toward the companion-way. "I promise you, Miss, if there is action, you will see plenty to interest you in the surgery."

So many sails had pulled above the horizon that the lookouts stopped announcing them. Scattered all before Jones's little squadron, forty vessels were tacking their way against the south wind, working down to the Humber and to Hull. To Henriette, the flat sea was so crowded with canvas it became a ballroom floor. *Grande dames* of sail were gathered there, turning in their own circles, their wakes unfurling behind them like great trains of lace and jade velvet. The image would have to sustain her, in fact, because it was the last sight she saw before they extracted her from the rail and sank her below-decks.

"There she is," Jones nodded at the Royal Navy escort. Two vessels were protecting the convoy—a frigate and a sloop. The sloop was far behind and only then cracking on sail to catch up with her consort. The frigate was separating herself from the riot of fleeing merchantmen around her, dangling herself as a prize as she headed west toward Flamborough Head.

Her figure made Jones's heart ache with envy. She was sleek and sharp, with no poop-deck—a progressive design. The way she cut the water testified not only to the shapeliness of her young bottom, but that she was clad in copper. Her lean, black flanks were marked by a double line of yellow stripes. At that distance Jones could not count her guns, but with two decks she had to have at least forty, perhaps fifty. Against *Richard*'s cobbled-together battery, she was clearly more than a match.

"Mister Stacey, do you see that Red ensign?" he asked the sailing-master, indicating the symbol of British eminence blazing from the frigate's stern.

"I do, sir."

"Then you have your target. Lay us by her on the weather side. Mr. Dale, have the crews beat to starboard quarters. Load with double-shot, please."

"So the convoy—it is to be bypassed?" wondered Dale.

"They won't get far in this calm. But we must attend to first principles."

Dale understood what "first principles" meant. With a squadron supporting him, Jones could afford to eliminate the escort before picking apart the convoy. This decision would even be a popular one, since sailors in Continental Navy ships earned shares of the full sale price of captured warships, but only half from the sale of merchantmen. Prize-money aside, Jones also knew that capture of a Royal Navy frigate would be more valuable to the propaganda war than scattering the convoy.

Richard was cleared for action in just seven minutes. Dale was in command of the stern battery on the main gun-deck, Lunt the bow. The French marines, under their colonels de Varville and Wybert, were scattered all over the ship—a dozen each in the three fighting tops in the masts, two dozen more with muskets and buckets of grenades on the forecastle. It was midshipman Mayrant's turn to serve as captain's secretary that day. He stood behind Jones on the quarterdeck with the air of someone suddenly very uncomfortable with his own height. A head taller than Jones, he would make a splendid target.

In the light wind *Richard* sailed so poorly that the few miles of water between her and the waiting frigate seemed as wide as an ocean. As he waited, Jones fidgeted and fretted in a way he never had before a fight. He lifted and lowered his spyglass dozens of times, circuited the quarterdeck repeatedly, checked and rechecked the appearance of his shoes, his sword, his hat. He had himself observed, on that cruise, a new tendency to nervousness with each opportunity for battle. He felt like one of those veteran actors who found, despite an unbroken line of successful performances, despite triumph after triumph, that his stage fright was getting worse.

Small mistakes in the handling of equipment—a dropped reefearring, a miscoiled sheet—cast him into a vortex of rage. He found the idle chatter of officers and seamen around him deeply distracting. He sensed, and could not persuade himself otherwise, that there were precious few opportunities left in this war to make his mark. If too many slipped away, like the assault on Leith aborted by a turn of the wind, he might return to L'Orient with little to show for months of preparation and expense. The war might end at any moment.

With that, he would return to . . . what? In the blush of his innocence, he once imagined himself a gentleman farmer, a tobacco squire graced by property, the esteem of fashionable neighbors, and some prize flower of plantation womanhood. With the passage of years, the notion came to amuse him—he found he much preferred the pavements of Paris to the clods of Virginia. But his aspirations demanded the sort of renown that came only rarely to men. Without it, he was only a poor, ill-connected, somewhat well-mannered combat officer with an eternity of peace yawning before him.

"Shut your mouths down there!" he erupted at a pair of tars on the gun-deck. "Instead of wagging your tongues, you should be beseeching your Maker you live to see the sun tomorrow!"

Two sets of startled eyes turned up to him. "Aye, Cap'n," they said in unison.

"By God's good grace, did I demand you agree with me? I told you to keep your bleeding traps shut! Do you understand?"

The tars looked at each other in confusion. One began to speak again, but halted when Dale, the commander of that battery, shook his head. Conversation up and down the gun-deck faded; the only sounds audible were the ensign snapping in the wind, the *Richard*'s prow splitting the water, and the rustle of gulls' wings as they glided off the forepeak. Their errands temporarily finished, even the powder monkeys sat silent and cross-legged on the deck, their faces boyish but as grave as old men.

Mayrant, cursing his luck, discovered he had something to report. Turning his doe eyes to Jones, he dared open his mouth unheeded for the first time on the voyage.

"Er, the pilot boat, sir. It has left off chasing the brig."

Jones turned south. Linthwaite's boat was there, just visible where the traces of the *Richard*'s wake met the horizon. "Remind me never to give that boy anything to do again."

"Shall we lie to? We may need the sixteen men."

"Absolutely not! They may catch up as they may." Jones turned back to the frigate. They were close enough then to make out, against her yellow stripes, the faint outlines of her gun ports: he counted 25 on the larboard side, including 10 on the lower-deck. The latter were probably eighteen or twenty-four-pounders, in all likelihood as fine and freshly minted as the frigate herself.

"Signal line ahead."

A single blue flag was hoisted on the mizzen, and a single nine-pounder gun fired on the starboard side. At this signal *La Pallas,* which had been overtaking the flagship, immediately spilled her wind and fell in behind *Richard.* With *Alliance* ranged behind *La Pallas,* the line could sail up and deliver a series of broadsides amounting to twenty, sixteen, and eighteen guns vs. the frigate's single broadside of twenty-five. With those odds, the end would be foregone: the enemy must beg for quarters. After that, his squadron would move on to snap up the sloop and however much of the convoy he could man with prize-crews. With two Royal Navy warships and a half-dozen merchantmen in the bag, the life fortunes of every man in the squadron would be made. It was just a matter of pursuing matters to their reasonable, inevitable conclusion.

But *Alliance* did not choose reason. Instead of following Cottineau, Landais suddenly fell off on a starboard tack and headed in some vague direction away from the escort. There were no merchantmen where *Alliance* was going; the convoy, for its part, had collectively turned around for some port to the north.

"What's he doing? Where's he going?" Mayrant wondered.

"We may always safely assume that Captain Landais will sail by his own lights," Jones said.

"Captain, *La Pallas* is heaving to!" shouted Lunt.

And so, with Landais declining battle, Cottineau likewise fell out of line. This was a more ominous blow to their prospects—*Richard* and *La Pallas* still outgunned the escort, but now the flagship was approaching a 50-gun frigate alone. To his credit, Cottineau at least seemed to be heading in a productive direction, toward the other enemy vessel, the sloop.

"Shall we signal *line ahead* again?"

"No need, Mr. Mayrant. No need."

"Then this is traitorous . . . outrageous!" the younger man raged.

"Temper yourself, lad. For the sake of the men."

Mayrant's indignation lapsed into puzzlement. Such sudden philosophic calm—from a man who detonated at details like a misplaced bucket! What the boy could not have known, and what his captain would not tell him, was that Jones was glad Landais had run off. There would be no sharing of credit for this victory, no chance for Landais to enjoy reflected glory. If the latter's departure meant the odds were far worse for Jones, so much the better.

Even then, with the frigate still 200 yards away, Jones imagined telling the story of this day to the assembled ears at the Hôtel Valentinois. He was flinging the tale in the faces of Lafayette, Arthur Lee, Sartine. Somewhere in Paris, a married woman's heart was destined to flutter at his name.

The enemy frigate was sailing slowly west under reefed top-sails, her masts wagging indolently as she rolled on the gentle swells. Jones noted with appreciation that he was being welcomed by open gun ports on her larboard side, as if her captain fully expected Jones to take the initiating, windward position against her. More than likely, the misadventure at Leith had warned all the Royal Navy captains that the "pirate" Paul Jones was in the area. Jones had apparently gained a reputation for always attacking from the windward. He wouldn't disappoint them.

Stacey put the helm down and put the *Richard* on a parallel course. The frigate's sails were backed, allowing the Indiaman to catch up with her. At fifty yards, a voice sounded over the quiet strait between them.

"What ship is that?"

"It is the *Princess Royal.* What ship is that?" Jones replied through his speaking-trumpet.

"His Majesty's ship *Serapis.* From where do you hail, *Princess Royal?*"

In another moment the *Richard*'s bow would be abreast of *Serapis.* "Steady now, Mister Stacey," Jones whispered at the master, then raised his trumpet again, saying, "Er maygrath mis severan."

The frigate's officers were visible—and visibly puzzled—on the other deck. "Not understood, *Princess Royal.* Say again?"

"Certainly," replied Jones, and pronounced very carefully, "Mer-grain hanath gris."

"Sir, if you do not identify yourself, I shall be obliged to fire upon you!"

The frigate was now centered in *Richard*'s sights. Jones lowered his speaking-trumpet and said, in an intimate voice like one used in private dinner conversation, "Mister Mayrant, raise colors. All crews, *fire*."

The Indiaman spoke in tongues of smoke and wadding-sparks. A hollow rumble rolled through the deck and up Jones's feet and legs. With that, and in an instant, all his anxiety was swept away by an all-engrossing, diamond-hard concentration. He was, in that moment of time between *Richard*'s opening salvo and *Serapis*'s immediate reply, and for the first time in months, fully and finally himself again.

The frigate's flank was simultaneously lit by her own broadside and the cracking impact of incoming metal. The entry of *Serapis*'s fire staggered the Indiaman, sounding with hollow, drumlike blows up and down *Richard*'s side. Both crews apparently had been trained to fire into the hulls of their enemies. This alone, Jones hoped, must have told the enemy captain he was up against a different sort of antagonist. There would be no fine shot making today, no Gallic trimming of the opposition's masts and sails and then a quick retirement.

The race to reload and fire again was won by *Richard*—but barely. "Huzzahs" filtered up from the crews on the gun-deck, but as the frigate made her immediate reply, the cheers were abruptly cut off by an explosion so powerful it almost knocked Jones off his feet.

"The powder magazine is hit!" someone shouted from below, starting a wave of panic that swept palpably through the crew.

"Shut up, you shit!" Dale's voice followed.

The blast came from far aft, down near the waterline. Mayrant rushed to the rail to peer down and right, but Jones already knew that the magazine had not been hit. A torrent of black smoke was now pouring from his lower gun-deck, down where he had mounted the six ancient 18-pounders. The scatter of charred wood and human remains floating around the Indiaman clearly showed that the explosion had blown outward.

One of the carpenter's mates shot up from the companion-way, his face blackened. "Sir, the lower battery is gone. All of it."

Jones lips tightened. "Thank you, Mister Physic. Tell Mr. Gunnison to evacuate the survivors and seal the gunroom. Transfer all survivors to other stations."

"Begging the captain's pardon, but there aren't any survivors to transfer."

It had probably been only a small defect—a mere crack in the interior surface of the tube, invisible from the surface—that had split one of the old guns as she fired. But the result was disastrous: in that instant, *Richard* lost twenty percent of the metal she could throw at the frigate.

The enemy's guns were firing at will now, steadily hammering the Indiaman's hull, tearing off chunks of rail and rigging, opening man-sized holes in the netting. A strike by a small caliber ball on the aft quarter did not penetrate the strakes but, worse, propelled a shower of splinters into the top gun-deck. A shot rammer in the path of the splinters was eviscerated first, with many of the bloody projectiles continuing on to lodge in the face and chest of the boy behind him. Though many of the men had cotton wadding in their ears against the roar of the guns, the explosion below and the drizzle of blood and the boy's screams were powerful distractions. *Richard* was now firing only one gun for *Serapis's* three.

Within a minute of the opening of the engagement, Jones was staring at the likelihood of defeat. The frigate was flying along with the crippled Indiaman now, ministering punishment like a terrible, white-winged angel afflicting some demon's hulking hide. The beauty of her! Jones thought. The aesthetics of his own unfolding conquest were almost compensation enough.

Curious, the snarled sheets of Fate, he thought. The two ships were already cocooned in a cloud of smoke from the guns and the fires that swirled but did not disperse in the lazy breeze. Men and marines were running all around the deck below him, scrambling for cover, staunching wounds, bearing wads of powder, shot, plugs for repairing holes. Yet the chaos seemed to be so perfectly clear in its properties, so reparable with the precisely correct command. He gave it.

"Back the maintops and put the helm down, Mister Stacey. I believe we'll board her today."

"Aye, sir," Stacey replied, drinking deeply of Jones's serenity.

The master's mates transmitted the order and a gang of ables broke cover, scrambling over the ship's waist. British marines in the enemy's tops worried them with fire as they seized the braces. Angling the ends of the yardarms into the wind, they cut the Indiaman's forward momentum, allowing the frigate to surge past. Their counterparts on the other deck did the same, but they were too late—*Serapis* coasted well beyond *Richard*'s bow, leaving the Indiaman too far aft to fire upon.

"Now clap on those braces, boys! Give 'em some headway!" shouted Stacey.

With a turn, the topsail caught the wind and *Richard* gathered momentum again. On the other deck, British officers were looking with mild curiosity at *Richard*'s evolutions, until a barrage from the French marines in the Indiaman's tops forced them to scatter.

"Pass the word, Mr. Mayrant: our topmen must clear their sharpshooters first."

Mayrant's brows flew up. The manuals suggested that when the enemy was close enough, it was best to try to disrupt his maneuvers by playing musket fire on his decks. Jones preferred to use his sharpshooters to kill the enemy's sharpshooters.

"All their topmen, sir?"

"*All* of them."

Dubiousness still showing on his face, the boy went off to

instruct de Varville and Wybert that their men should not fire at the enemy's decks. Jones simmered silently as he noted a similarly dubious expression on the faces of the French officers as they absorbed the command.

Stacey, meanwhile, put the helm hard down, pivoting the ship to starboard.

The Indiaman was maneuvering as fast as he had ever seen her, Jones noted, but not nearly fast enough. The American's bow turned so ponderously it would take another minute to lay her close on the frigate's starboard side. *Serapis* swiveled smartly on her coppered bottom, presenting her rudder directly to *Richard*'s head. They were barely twenty yards apart now.

"Back 'er again!" cried Jones. "Hard to larboard, Mr. Stacey!"

But they ran out of water. With *Serapis* backed and *Richard* still accelerating, they struck nose-to-stern. For Jones, after the collision with *Alliance,* the sounds of tortured rigging, snapping woodwork, the crash of thousand-ton hulls striking each other, were all too familiar.

"Boarders away, sir?" Lunt suggested breathlessly.

"Not yet, idiot! Pull those men back!"

With more spirit than sense, half-a-dozen landsmen were scrambling over the bowsprit toward *Serapis*'s poop. Lofting pikes and cutlasses as they clambered, they made such slow progress that three times their number were waiting on the other deck to meet them. The parties swiped and poked at each other with their blades, lunging too awkwardly to hit anything, until one of *Richard*'s landsmen stretched too far and came away missing a forearm. Panicked, he then wrapped his legs and remaining arm around the bowsprit and refused to budge as he bled into the water beneath him.

Arcs of smoke flew in both directions as grenades were exchanged. Most of these were picked up and thrown back well before they exploded. Jones watched, appalled: all of his future crews would have to be instructed on the proper lighting and delivery of grenades.

Richard fell off into *Serapis*'s wake again. As the Indiaman lacked a bow-chaser and the frigate stern-mounted guns, the struggle became oddly quiescent. Only the crack of musket-fire from *Richard*'s tops broke the silence. The frigates' marines were either screened by their own sails or saving their fire for the next collision.

The dance resumed with *Serapis* leading, swinging her bow around to the north in a sudden bid to cross the "T" against the *Richard.* But Jones had already ordered his helm aweather, returning the Indiaman to the frigate's port side. Though he kept a look of placid semi-concern on his face, he felt his heart might burst as he saw that *Serapis*'s bid to rake him might instead leave her open to a raking by the stern.

"Hold your fire 'til she's framed pretty in your ports!" Dale was shouting to his crews. "Let's make the most of this, boys!"

The chance was gone before a gun was fired. With disheartening quickness, the frigate's master had perceived the danger and veered back to the south-west. Though Jones did well to keep the initiative, their weaving reel through the North Sea was assuming an inauspicious pattern. For every move Jones made, *Serapis* seemed to be making two.

They collided again, this time with *Richard*'s bow pointing over the frigate's port quarter. The armless man who had been hanging on the bowsprit was gone—had he fallen into the sea? Fortunately, no one was foolish enough to try to board this time. Instead, Jones saw through the frigate's stern gallery that some of her men were trundling up a twelve-pounder gun. In another minute she would be able to bring fire on the Indiaman's exposed stem.

"*Princess Royal,*" a sarcastic voice drifted over the distance between quarterdecks, "Have you had enough?"

Jones ignored the question and turned to Stacey. "Haul her off, helm. Then put us to windward."

He had tried, but probably failed, to keep the rising frustration from his voice. With his safe options cut off at each turn, there was nothing to do but risk an exchange of broadsides again. The frigate obliged, backing her topsails, allowing the tired *Richard* to lumber into her sights. The range was murderous—less than forty yards.

"*Fire!*"

Serapis's guns spoke for what seemed like an eternity. The punishment poured into the Indiaman with a rising intonation, thump—*thump*—*thump*—*THUMP*, as the British gunners successively found their targets. All around Jones, expressions were turning dejected, hopeless. Mayrant was holding onto the capstan with a look of determined misery. *Richard*'s broadside was weak and ragged in reply and inaccurate. Only one nine-pound shot struck *Serapis*'s side, and that one bounced off.

"Have you struck yet?" pressed the voice from the *Serapis*. "I implore you not to be foolish, sir."

"*Sir*, you must be joking! The affair has hardly begun!" Jones replied, then to the helm, "When we cover her, I will tell you when to cross her hawse. Understand?"

"Yes, sir," replied Stacey, staring at the captain with incredulity. For *Richard* had seemed so sluggish in the fight, it seemed she couldn't "cross the hawse" on Flamborough Head, much less the blonde, nimble frigate.

Though the close range was a tonic to *Serapis*'s gunners, it had one effect Jones was counting on. As *Richard* came up alongside, her sails stole the wind from the frigate, slowing her down. For the first time in the duel, the Indiaman had more headway than her opponent.

Keeping one eye on the frigate and one on the sea to larboard,

Jones froze in his shoes as the next rolling salvo from *Serapis* poured forth. This time she fired grapeshot, sending out a hail of tiny lead pellets that opened a thousand holes in sails, wood, skin. The hammock nets were particularly good for absorbing such damage, but Physic, the carpenter's mate, was caught, exposed at a rupture in the nets. Before everyone's eyes, his body dropped to pieces. Everyone's eyes, that is, except Jones's; he was watching for a telltale change in the color of the sea a half-mile to the south.

"Now, Mr. Stacey! Put us athwart her!"

Stacey spun the wheel just as a gust filled *Richard*'s suit. She turned sharply this time, faster than *Serapis*.

"Hooray!" cheered the gun-deck, their fists in the air.

"You have her in hand!" seconded Dale.

Richard was now in position to rake the frigate. Three guns fired from the stern battery, one shot cutting an anchor-cable, another penetrating her bows just under the sprit shrouds and disappearing inside to do untold damage. The third splintered the face of the frigate's figurehead, whom Jones could only guess was some sort of nude, bearded Greek deity—Serapis himself, he presumed.

But Jones was not congratulating himself. Instead, he was admiring the skill of the frigate's captain. Aware that with his wind stolen he couldn't match *Richard*'s speed, he had come about into the wind as the Indiaman broke to leeward. Turning in opposite directions would have minimized the length of time he was exposed to *Richard*'s raking fire. He had only failed to count on the Indiaman's slowness: with a following wind, *Richard* slowed to a crawl again. Jones found himself staring into the mangled wooden face of Serapis as the frigate ran upon the Indiaman's starboard side.

"Well done, boys! Now let's finish her!" Jones cried.

A half-dozen grappling lines arched from *Richard*'s rails toward

Serapis, hooking her in the shrouds, bulwarks, cleats. A throng of men instantly appeared on the other side with axes, hacking desperately to free the frigate. Though fierce, the struggle quickly reached equilibrium, with every severed hook replaced by a fresh one from the Indiaman.

Serapis's bows were now secured firmly to *Richard,* but the rest of her stretched away at an oblique angle. Her starboard gun ports were open, the muzzles of her heavy eighteen-pounders peeking through just before they fired. From point-blank range, they made small holes in the Indiaman's side and an enormous din as they tore through her vitals. *Richard* replied with the five or six 12-pounders she still had in operation, sending up great whale-spouts of spray as her shot split the water just above the frigate's hull.

Through the mist, Jones could finally see his antagonist on the other quarterdeck: a stiff-backed figure in blue, gesticulating, his great nose cutting the air like a hawk's beak. They faced each other across the space between them, and although Jones could not see his eyes, he felt them sweep contemptuously across him, without a pause.

"Well, we'll fix that," he resolved. "You'll have occasion to look at me yet."

The sun was gone now, sunk below the Yorkshire heather. On the other horizon, an enormous moon rose and blushed at the carnage that greeted her. As the gloom deepened, a shape appeared out of the north—a shadow with the sharp lines of a sloop.

"Cheers for Ricot!" Mayrant proclaimed. "*Vengeance* is here!"

"I fear you are mistaken, Mr. Mayrant," said Jones. "But let us do our duty as if she were."

Jones was right. It was not *Vengeance* after all, but *Serapis*'s little consort. Her gun ports were open as she ran on her larboard tack, and many curious faces regarded the Indiaman as she passed. But with every second the wind was spinning the conjoined *Serapis* and *Richard* clockwise and closer together. There was no way for her to fire on one without hitting the other. With relief, Jones watched the sloop recede without firing a gun.

But this hardly made up for the spectacle of half his own squadron standing well out to the south and east, spectators all. *La Pallas* was ranging up toward the British sloop, but doing nothing to assist the flagship. The dereliction galled him, but also confirmed the wisdom of his worst suspicions.

"It is enough to make one a misanthrope," Jones remarked to Mayrant.

"Sir?"

"Have boarding parties assemble forward, amidships and aft. Shirts off that they may know each other. And tell them not to move *until my order.*"

In the pilot boat, Two Fires found himself pushed far down on his haunches, out of the way of the boom. As soon as the full magnitude of the convoy showed itself, Linthwaite ordered a course back to the north, back to help with the greater prize. The men without a hand to the sheets or tiller were packed tight down the centerboard, so low that Two Fires could only see the action ahead when Linthwaite turned from the bows to shout encouragement.

"Now we go to the devil, fellows!" cried the young commander. "There's glory and perdition ahead, and I say let us claim our share of both!"

The old hands smiled at the boy's enthusiasm. But as *Richard* and the British frigate closed on each other, they came to see the talk of perdition had a disturbing ring of truth. Half a mile upwind, they could feel the concussions from the broadsides. From a distance, the two ships seemed to be stepping tentatively around each other, sailing in silent tandem, until the thunder suddenly rolled again and a sulphurous haze veiled them in shared obscurity. None of the other vessels—neither the Continental squadron nor the little British sloop—seemed anxious to join the action. Yet here was the plucky little midshipman taking a boat straight into the center of it.

"Likely be dark when we get there," Two Fires heard a man say behind him.

"Is that good or bad?" came the answer.

"Good . . . I think."

At 400 yards they heard the whiz of errant swivel balls flying over their heads. Closer still, a shot from a six-pounder hit the water just twenty feet from the boat's starboard side, dousing them in its spray. The murmuring all around Two Fires intensified— clearly, just one of those shots would easily snap their boat in half.

"Hey, Pimples, you tryin' to shink uth?" Two Fires called out to Linthwaite.

"Who said that?" the boy screeched, turning

"Perhaps . . . the better part of valor . . . *monsieur* . . . ," implored the corporal in charge of the French Marines. "We are no good to your captain if we founder. . ."

"At least let's wait until dark," Upham, the coxswain's mate, suggested from the tiller.

Linthwaite scowled, looked ahead again. The frigate's captain had ordered her anchor dropped in hope that the current would pry the Indiaman away. But that seemed unlikely now: the wind had blown the vessels cheek by jowl, *Richard*'s starboard side to *Serapis*'s larboard. They were lashed together in a thousand places.

They could see the orange muzzle-flashes from *Richard*'s tops, followed a second later by their reports. There were only a few flashes in response from *Serapis*—it looked as if the Continentals were gradually winning the battle for the topmasts. But the story seemed reversed below. *Richard*'s cannon were utterly silent, while the frigate was free to fire her eighteen-pounders into the India-man, point-blank. The men in the boat watched, incredulous, as a broadside passed straight through *Richard* and, with an eruption of flames, blew out her flanks on the other side.

"*Mon dieu,*" breathed a marine.

"Hmm," Linthwaite finally said, stroking his downy chin. "It appears we will not be able to approach safely on the larboard side, as I had hoped."

"So it appears," mocked Upham.

The midshipman fixed his eye on another vessel nearby. It was the corvette, *Vengeance.*

"Break out the oars. Let us find out what's detaining our ally, Mister Ricot."

They had to row into the wind as they approached *Vengeance.* She appeared as quiet as on a day of shore leave, her gun ports sealed. At fifty yards, Two Fires could see the eyes of her crew shining in the reflected light of the battle. They were ranged up on the rails and the tops like spectators at a fireworks display.

"Ahoy!" Linthwaite called.

"Who is that?" replied someone from the corvette's little quarterdeck.

"Linthwaite, from *Bon Homme Richard.* Is that Captain Ricot?"

No answer. But as the boat pulled closer, they could see Ricot looking down on them. Beside him was a battery of French marines with their guns leveled and ready to fire.

"*Détendez,*" the captain said to his men as the boat came in range of his lantern. The squad lowered its weapons and stood at attention.

"How might I help you, *monsieur?*" Ricot asked.

"Sir, I think I need not tell you our flag is under attack . . ."

Linthwaite paused as if further explanation was unnecessary. But Ricot was looking at him as if he had never heard a word of English in his life. Linthwaite continued, ". . . and so, might I hope you will bring your forces to bear, that we may secure an outcome favorable to our *alliance?*"

Ricot frowned at the word "alliance." "*Monsieur*, you must be assured that I would like nothing more than to help your captain, Jones, in his moment of trial. But as you see, it is impossible."

The occupants of the pilot boat looked up and down the hull, deck, and rigging of *Vengeance*, hoping to see the "impossible" factor Ricot referred to.

"I am sorry to say, Captain, that I don't understand you."

"It is impossible. Quite beyond my control. But might I suggest that you, *monsieur*, in my judgment, may still fly to the flagship and help to write a happy conclusion. So I wish you sincere good luck."

Linthwaite's expression was that of a young man discovering a particular form of human treachery he never imagined existed. In novels, perhaps—but not in actuality.

"Sir," he persisted, "I regret I must protest. To imagine there is anything this boat can accomplish that your vessel cannot . . ."

"As I say," Ricot interrupted, "it is beyond my control. Please do not be insulted—your plea is right and reasonable. I will commend you to your captain, should he survive. The regret is mine."

To this, Two Fires let loose a derisive snort. But there was nothing more to be done, except to follow Ricot's suggestion. Linthwaite turned his back to the Frenchman.

"Set the sail again, boys. We'll expect no help here."

With her rail laid on *Richard*'s, the enemy was in position to be boarded. Jones's dilemma, however, was that he couldn't be sure how many men *Serapis* had in reserve, waiting to cut down his boarding parties. On that score, it would be better to wait and see. Yet initiative was half the formula for victory. If he failed too long to seize his opportunity, the enemy commander inevitably would.

Casting his eyes down the length of *Richard*'s deck, he could only see a few bare-chested tars concealed behind anything they could find. They were clutching pikes, sabers, crow-bars, boat-hooks. Here and there, he could just see a leg, an elbow.

"Are the men ready?" he asked Mayrant.

"Fore, amidships, and aft."

"Then let's—"

His next order was preempted by a riot of screams from the other deck. A dozen of *Serapis*'s men, armed like Jones's own, were leaping, swinging, clambering across the short gap between the two rails. Jones's heart sank as most of them reached the Indiaman, whooping and swiping their weapons this way and that.

For a moment, Jones was sure he had waited too long to send his own parties. The enemy had now carried the battle to him. In that instant, he had no response to make, except to stand there, his heart sinking, and watch.

Richard's party met the invaders just aft of the main hatch. The battle was short and mute; in a peculiar show of reticence in combat, his men wasted no energy on spirited battle cries. Instead, there was only the clank of metal on metal, the scratch of sand under bare feet, the vegetable *thud* a skull makes when it is struck. Just as one side or another gained an advantage, both staggered in unison as *Serapis* rocked the Indiaman with another broadside. The struggle looked even—until a round of small arms fire crackled in the dusk above.

The well-aimed volley from the French marines in the maintop crumpled most of the enemy boarders. The rest, panicked, tried to retire to their deck and were cut down from behind. Two, wounded, fell into the cleft between the two hulls and were lodged there. Just one reached the frigate, scrambled desperately as musket balls peppered the deck around him, and slithered headfirst down the companion-way.

Jones found he could breathe again. *"Merci beaucoup,"* he muttered.

"Sir?" asked Mayrant.

The advantage had turned again: with all of *Serapis*'s top-men cleared out, *Richard*'s French sharpshooters had made the frigate's deck uninhabitable for her crew. Just the top of a head above the mouth of a hatch was enough to draw their fire.

"Her deck appears to be ours," observed Mayrant.

Yes, but for what purpose? Jones wondered. The bulk of the frigate's crew was still alive, just out of sight. If he boarded her deck, his parties would still be massacred. Meanwhile, the frigate's eighteen-pounders were freely operating, blowing holes in his hull. It was only a matter of time before they sank him, or they struck the powder magazine and exploded both ships. Of the two alternatives, Jones preferred incineration to failure.

"Begging the captain's pardon," said a voice at his shoulder. Jones turned, and was confronted not by Dale, but by his blackened husk. Black powder was blasted into his teeth, cheeks, even the corners of his eyes. His left ear lobe was tethered to his head only by a thin flap of skin.

"How goes it below?"

"Below . . . ," the lieutenant said, "no longer exists."

"We have no main battery?"

Dale smiled at the question. "You might say that. All the twelves are untrucked. The larboard side is completely open to the sea. I also understand that the hold is filling with water."

"I see. And what of Mr. Lunt?"

"Plugging holes with the carpenters, below."

They stumbled as another blast rolled the Indiaman momentarily to larboard.

"Very well, then. Find some men and take command of those forward nines, Mr. Dale. Apply yourself to that equipment there." Jones pointed at *Serapis*'s mainmast, shining with its new varnish in the moonlight. "See if you might bring it down."

Dale went off, shouting for men and for a handspike to lever the guns into position. Jones, meanwhile, resigned himself to the inevitable gamble.

"Now, Mr. Mayrant, let's see to those boarding parties."

"*Sail astern! Sail! Sail!*" a lookout shouted.

"Now what?" Jones grumbled as he turned to look over the taffrail. Out of the gloom, a long, dark shape was moving silently to his right. She had a single lantern hung on her starboard quarter, her maintopsail intermittently reflecting the flashes from *Serapis*'s guns. He recognized the rig.

"*Alliance,*" he said. Against political prudence, he was unable to keep a regretful edge from his voice.

"Three cheers for Landais!" someone cried. And there was one fairly enthusiastic cheer, then another halfhearted one, then a third that died. Landais had done little to make himself popular in the squadron so far.

"Then the battle is over! It's two against one!" Mayrant exulted.

"Steady, now," Jones replied. He wanted to tell the boy that he would be correct if Landais had a temperate—that is, a somewhat less treasonous—character. But he held his tongue; a midshipman's education need not include hearing captains disparage each other.

The boarding parties were poised to go. The final order seemed to hang over them in the smoke, tormenting them with suspense. Jones, however, would not give it. His eyes were fixed on *Alliance* as she slowly wheeled clockwise around the antagonists, to a position in their lee. He knew already, with a stab of dread, what Landais would do. With the frigate and the Indiaman lashed together, he would have to come into the wind to circle around to *Serapis*'s larboard side. Nobody ever fired their guns in the middle of tacking, when the concussion risked putting a vessel in irons. If Landais didn't fire immediately, he would have to bear away to the north and work his way back to—

Alliance's side erupted as she reached raking position. A punishing hail of round shot swept the decks of both *Richard* and *Serapis*, blowing down rails, yards, men. Half the bow boarding party was cut down where they had stood, cheering for the vessel that would kill them. One of the nine-pounders in Dale's battery was blown clean off its mount.

As Jones had supposed, Landais did not tack as he fired, but put his helm up and ran north before the wind. *Serapis*, meanwhile, suffered no more than a few chunks bitten from her woodwork and a few broken windows in her stern gallery. She had no men left alive on her deck for *Alliance* to kill.

"It appears you were right, Mr. Mayrant," Jones told the boy. "It is two against one!"

At the forward battery, Dale sighed in wonderment. "All right, then," he muttered. The whistle of twelve-pound shot was still in his ears. He had personally been saved only because he had bent over to retrieve a dropped handspike.

"Lieutenant . . . your head." One of his gunners pointed.

Dale felt himself, and only then realized that blood was streaming from a splinter wound at his temple. He'd felt nothing.

The surviving members of his gun crew were collectively cowering around him, stunned by what had just occurred. Their idleness brought Dale out of his reverie.

"No time to dally, lads! We still have iron to bear. Hands to the tackle, now!"

"Stand down, Mister Dale," commanded Jones as he crossed the ship's waist. "Report to the surgery, Lieutenant."

"Sir, if I might be permitted to stay on . . ."

"I've seen wounds, sir. You will not survive the loss of blood without the attention of Mister Brooke. Off with you now, before I have you arrested and carried away!"

Dale relented with a petulant scowl, took two wobbly steps toward the companion-way, and collapsed face first on the deck.

"You two, help him."

The shot-rammer and the powderer hauled the lieutenant down. This left Jones with a gun crew of just two men.

"Don't just stand there, Mister Mayrant! Give me that hand-spike. This gun needs warming."

Henriette was in an unladylike position at that moment, strad-dling the legs of a wounded marine. Brooke was kneeling beside his patient in his surgeon's smock, inserting the teneculum into the shattered stump of the man's arm. He rooted around with the hooked tool as he searched for the severed blood vessel. The patient's teeth were clenched over a wooden bit as he thrashed, his screams resonating so deeply through his legs that Henriette could feel the cries as much as she could hear them.

"Ligature," Brooke said as he finally pried out the pulsing artery. His assistant, a boy of twelve or thirteen, looked bored as he sat next to Brooke's array of needles, saws, retractors, and tourni-quets. By the boy's other arm were the disposable supplies, the styptics, tapes, threads, cotton swabs, linen. The whole arrange-ment struck Henriette as desperately makeshift: Brooke's surgery was just a floor of oak planks spread over tubs of supplies in the main hold. With the ranks of the bloodied and broken already crowded shoulder-to-shoulder, there was no room for a proper table or chest to elevate patients out of the common pool of bod-ily fluids. The only concession to hygiene, she observed, was some ventilation of the chamber through the ship's main hatch.

Deplorable as the conditions were, the surgery was an oasis of peace compared to the mayhem rising around it. Rumors flew about the sea pouring into the Indiaman. Men were converging from all corners of the ship to work the pumps. Smoke was ris-ing from indiscriminate blazes in every direction. The entire vessel shuddered as the enemy poured fire into her exhausted body. Now and again, Henriette could follow by ear the passage of cannon shots from one side of the ship to the other as they shivered bulk-heads and timbers on the decks above.

Over all this, she also had to endure the pleading cries of the British prisoners in the brig, begging to be let out before the ship went to the bottom. Some of them spoke to her in French through the airhole in the door, assuring her that her Captain Jones was insane, that any civilized commander would have asked for quarters by then, that he meant for them all to be sacrificed to his damnable vanity.

"Don't listen to it," Brooke told her as he knotted the artery. "These are not especially unusual conditions for battle."

The surgeon did not treat the wounds of his patients as much as abandon them at the least dangerous instant. Then it was off to the next lacerated soul, the next lopable limb. Henriette applied compresses when her body weight was not useful for holding the victims down. She was on a fruitless search for clean water when she caught sight of something small and white on the edge of the platform. Looking more closely, she was suddenly transfixed by what she saw.

It was just a severed nose. Yet, lying there on its side, it pre-sented a profile that filled her with aesthetic gratification. For this was the exact nose she had been searching for in all those years of travelling and sketching!

It was turning purple, and it was large. It was also gently hooked, as the nose of a Semite would have been. But there was a nobility to its curvature that was the undeniable signature of the most exalted Designer. The nostrils were wide and perfectly round, like those she imagined would suffer the dust of forty days in the desert. The candlelight rippled over the skin of this nose, she real-ized, like the light of the lamps at that final Passover.

But what could she do? Her sketchbooks were in her bunk, far away across an inferno of torment and disorder. There was no paper in the surgeon's cockpit.

"Alcohol! Alcohol and a jar!" she demanded, casting about desperately.

"What are you saying?" grumbled Brooke.

"There is no time! It must be preserved!"

Even as she spoke, the surgeon's mate upended a bucket of seawater on the deck. The water carried the strands of clotted blood, feces, and offal toward the scuppers. The nose went with them, disappearing over the edge of the platform.

"No!" Henriette cried. Leaping forward, she fell at the juncture of the deck and the hull. A stench rose up from the darkness there that made her feel faint with nausea. Flattening her hand, she slipped it between the boards and reached down as far as she could, down to her shoulder. But there was nothing to reach except bodies of storage casks, still wet with the passage of wastewater over them. She stayed that way, flailing in the unseen space, until Brooke pulled her up. His expression was furious as he tried to plant her back on her feet.

"Get hold of yourself, woman! Can you hear me?"

"You don't understand! It is a tragedy of art! A crime!"

Brooke took a flap of skin at her tiny neck and squeezed it hard between his thumb and forefinger. The pain surprised her, making her stand straight up. Her eyes stared at him in wounded indignation.

"These antics make you useless to me" he told her. "And there is nowhere else for you to go. So you will lay hold of yourself. Do you understand?"

Brooke didn't wait for an answer, and she didn't give one. The surgeon returned to his patient, a young man lying quietly with a six-inch oak spike lodged in his shoulder.

"Would you assist me here please, *madame?*"

She hesitated, chilled by a rising sense of unreality. It seemed as if she were enduring the delirium of some diseased imagination not her own. For the first time, she resented Jones. She had seen his face when the prospect of battle had first appeared. This was his element, his world. A place where beauty was washed out with the bilge.

"Hold his arm down, there. Don't grasp his hand—he might hurt you."

Mechanically, without compassion, she arranged herself with her knees on the patient's arm. As Brooke worked, she looked at the boy, and he looked at her, and both saw the other's tears, each running for their own reasons.

The pilot boat's second attempt to approach the battle went no better than the first. This time Linthwaite ordered them to come up on *Serapis's* larboard side, trusting that it would be safer with *Richard's* guns silenced. What he had not counted on was fire from the Indiaman's top-deck battery, which was keeping up a steady drumming on the mainmast of the frigate. Most of this fire hit nothing, however, until it arched through *Serapis's* rig, over the water, and into the sea close to the pilot boat.

It happened a dozen agonizing times as they inched closer: a *crack* as *Richard* fired, the unobstructed *whoosh*, the explosion of water and vapor ahead, behind, to either side.

"This is madness," Upham was sneering. "They can't see us."

"There is a moon," replied Linthwaite.

"There is a frigate screening us from them, the moon be damned."

"You will take a more appropriate tone, sir."

Upham fumed, spat in the water. The breeze was light but still steady out of the south, and the boat was within a hundred yards of the frigate. The danger came as fire from *Richard* struck *Serapis's* mainmast, striking off explosions of splinters and sending nine-pound balls in unpredictable directions. Even with little momentum behind it, an errant shot could easily hole the boat.

They were in luck, it seemed, that *Serapis* had lost all her topmen, so there was no danger of small arms fire from above. The problem was that the frigate's larboard side seemed shut up tight, with no obvious place to enter. Worse, it was not clear, either to Linthwaite or to the French marines nervously murmuring among themselves, what their small party could accomplish even if they managed to steal aboard. There were sure to be many more than enough defenders waiting for them.

There seemed just one chance: a preventer line had been cut from the rigging above and was now dangling over the frigate's side. They could scale it all the way to the top deck.

"Impossible," Upham groused. "We'd be shot by our own tops in this dark. That's not what I signed up for, to be shot by a frog."

"One such as you would be *honored* to fall to French guns," replied one of the "frogs" in the boat.

"Ah, hang on to yer baguettes, Frenchie. It's nothing personal."

"That's enough, Mr. Upham!" said Linthwaite. "In any case, one rope is too narrow a point of attack. We'll have to wait a bit longer for our chance."

Two Fires was over the side before anyone could react. Though he had some experience swimming at sea by now, the cold still surprised him. With such powerful motivation, it only took a half-dozen strokes for him to reach the end of the rope and pull himself up. Upham was shaking his head.

"That Indian . . . that crazy bugger!"

Planting his bare feet on the frigate and the blade of his cutlass in his mouth, he walked up the ship's side. At the level of the lower gun-deck he rooted around one of the ports with his toes. There was no purchase on it—it was shut tight. Looping the rope a few times around his left wrist, he freed his right hand and took hold of the cutlass. The sword was sharp; he had seen to this himself. To the puzzlement of the men below, he then hung there, cutlass poised over the small door.

"What's he waiting for? Someone to stick his head out?"

Just as *Serapis's* eighteens fired, Two Fires brought the blade down as hard as he could. The concussion of the guns almost perfectly covered the *thump* of his sword as it bit deep into the door.

"I believe I see his aim," admired Linthwaite. "For our part, we must retire for now. But let us all wish him good luck!"

The French and the colonials all muttered "good luck" in a desultory mass as they pulled away.

With his cutlass now planted in the gun port, Two Fires found he could coax the door open just enough to curl a finger behind it. He also found that the blade was too firmly seated in the wood for him to pull it out. He paused to consider his alternatives: to board the enemy, but unarmed; or to drop back into the water and try to swim after the pilot boat, which had already left him behind.

For a war party, the whites in the boat talked too much. Did the British have equally big mouths? He decided to find out.

His first view when he pulled open the gun port was the business end of a cannon. It was stopped up with a wooden plug, though, its body cradled in its protective tackle. Through the smoke, vaguely human shapes were moving across the frigate's deck, at the starboard battery. But no gun crew was there to greet him.

He slipped through the port and stood there. In the half-gloom, he slowly discerned that there were hundreds of men gathered in the narrow space. The ship's boarding parties were armed and idle, hunkered down in fat, chattering reefs of impatient activity. The masses seemed to ripple as fire from *Richard's* sharpshooters and long-nines rained on the deck above. In somewhat better order, red-coated British Marines were gathered in ranks at the ladders, their caps raked by moonlight. Ship's boys snaked through the throng in continuous relays, powder charges in their hands, as the boatswain worried them with flicks of his rattan, demanding more speed. It seemed eyes were everywhere passing over him, but none lingered. It was like he was on *Desdemona* again, present but unseen.

As on Continental ships, no one was wearing warpaint or a uniform or any other sign to tell friend from foe. Two Fires therefore strode confidently toward the ship's waist, making a show of his invisibility. A number of the British officers were gathered there, a circle of lieutenants around their captain. The latter was older than Jones, gray headed, his sword-hilt and decorations shining in the lanterns. Like many British officers Two Fires had seen, the man's spine was erect but his shoulders sloped—a strange combination indicating public arrogance and private anxiety, as the sachem Deawateho once observed. The British captain was nodding, his eyes closed, as his lieutenant reported to him.

"The question is when he must strike," the lieutenant was saying. "With a hold full of water and his gun-deck cleared, his situation is hopeless."

The captain kept his eyes closed as he answered, saying "A rational judgement, yes, Mr. Stanhope. But he shows no sign of striking now."

"He may still hope for help from his squadron."

"A possibility we may not discount . . ."

"Or he may just be mad," a second lieutenant suggested. The captain finally opened his eyes at this, his gaze fixed on the deck. The idea brought an abrupt end to the conference.

The British gun crews were exhausting themselves punishing the Indiaman. Their bodies streaked with a mixture of sweat and smoke that ran burning into their various wounds, they wormed, shotted, and powdered as if they were moving underwater. Now and again one of them jumped as he brushed against a red-hot cannon. Battles were supposed to be well over before the great guns were fired forty, fifty times. Many of the gun captains, Two Fires observed, were no longer even looking through their ports to see what damage their shots were doing. Steadily and mind-lessly, they all fired away at their own rates, like the turning mechanisms in the factories he had seen along the Susquehanna.

Yes, it was unpleasant. It was bloody and violent and demanded some degree of courage. But it was not the kind of warfare that was worthy of men. He could have picked up any of the weapons lying around him—sabers, grenades, lengths of chain—but he found he had no taste for it. Killing British seamen would have been like slaughtering things that were already dead.

And so, as transparently as he had invaded the frigate, he kicked open an unused port and stuck his head through it. There was not much of the Indiaman's gun-deck to escape to, he found; just a scatter of fractured gun-carriages, iron tubes loosed and rolled together like felled timber, a few broken bodies. A fat, contented moon was shining through from the opposite side of the vessel.

He climbed across the short gap between *Serapis* and *Richard.* Both to his right and left, the frigate's eighteens spat thunder and sparks as they fired, their shots making pretty moonlit splashes in the sea far to the east. He would have to time his escape below carefully, while the British crews were reloading. He would have to pick out a path to the nearest hatch in the dark, with the glare of the full moon in his eyes . . .

And then he saw Lunt. He was lying on his back ten yards away, breathing in gasps, his eyes open and staring at the deck above. Two Fires waited until the British gun just to Lunt's left fired, then strode casually to the lieutenant's side and lay down, his head planted on his cocked arm.

The lieutenant turned and winced at the other's face looking at him. A flash of recognition, fonder than either would have expected, lighted Lunt's features.

"So it's you," he said. "Of all the luck. Well, I'm guessing this is your chance to kill me, my boy. Make the best of it." Lunt grimaced as he blindly felt around with his right hand. "I've got some iron around here somewheres you can use. Just promise you don't make a hash of it, if you know what I mean . . ."

Two Fires listened and said nothing.

"Ye might have the decency not to let a body wait for it," Lunt continued. "Bad enough to suffer at the hands of a fuckin' savage. So, come on, then."

No answer.

"So you want me to beg for my life? Believe me, you'll get no such satisfaction. You may wait until this ship sinks and we meet in Hell!"

Two Fires smiled at this and reached for his sword. During a pause in the cannonading, he rose up to his knees, held the cutlass conspicuously over Lunt, and brought it down quickly with the flat side down. Then he delivered a "whoo-whoop" so loud that *Serapis*'s gunners looked through their gun ports in puzzlement.

"What in tarnation are you doing?" Lunt demanded.

Two Fires grabbed the lieutenant by his shirt and dragged him toward the companion-way—a task made more difficult by the need to keep himself flat on the deck.

"By the Lord's name, is this *torture*? Don't you know how to kill someone?"

"I have killed you. Now shut up."

The distance they needed to cross was only a few yards, but it was tripled by the tangle of scorched debris. Lunt began to help by propelling himself weakly with his arms, but his legs were inert. Nor could he stay silent for long.

"Well, if you're bound and determined, don't get yourself clipped on my account. Keep your head down."

At last, Two Fires tipped the other into the hatch and dragged him down to the surgery. He was by then slick with sweat and wheezing with exhaustion.

No one reacted at first to their sudden arrival. The surgeon was busy elsewhere, and Henriette had the look of a haunted soul. With a care that further mystified Lunt, Two Fires stayed by his side until Brooke worked his way to them.

"What a queer deliverer you've chosen, son," the surgeon remarked as he looked for the source of Lunt's bleeding. "I would have thought he'd as likely eat you."

"He may yet, Mister Brooke, he may yet. I can't figure him … he's as devious as a snake."

Two Fires governed his disgust of Lunt by turning his back on him. He was greeted in turn by the attentive gaze of Henriette, who was disheveled and covered with blood and vomit and yet somehow not unappealing. For the first time, he looked at her and seemed to appreciate her appearance—a development that caught her by surprise. But it was over before she had time to produce the appropriately demure blush.

There was yet another crash, only this time from below. It was followed by a riot of scuffling feet. Staring down to the bottom of the hatch, Two Fires could make out a small mob collecting there.

"They've loosed the prisoners," Brooke reported.

"The prisoners … give me some Marines," Dale muttered from his resting place near the aft bulkhead. But he was overtaken with dizziness when he pushed himself forward.

Another of Brooke's patients had no such trouble. Shooting to his feet and throwing his dressings aside, the man was scaling the ladder, crying, "The prisoners are escaped! Quarters! Quarters!" as he vanished above.

Having lost his cutlass, Two Fires cast about for a weapon to meet the new threat. All he could find was one of Brooke's discarded scalpels. The small party of French marines stationed at the hatch also seemed to acquire a new desperation, cocking their weapons.

But instead of rising up to take over the upper-decks of the

Indiaman, the pool of prisoners was draining away again into the
bowels of the ship. Over the firing above, Two Fires could hear the
faint sound of the boatswain's voice as he directed them aft.

"To the pumps, you limey bastards! Or are ye too pretty to save
yer own lives? Hands to it, now!"

Bar-shot, which was composed of two balls joined by an iron
arm, made a peculiar whistling noise as it flew. To Jones's ear it
was lower than a whistle—more like a moan. When his crew scored
a hit on *Serapis*'s mainmast, the noise was suddenly replaced by a
deep cracking sound, like the splitting of a thunderstruck tree.

Jones had not served as a battery commander since his lieutenant days. In all, he found it pleasant work, absorbing his entire
attention and rewarding him with immediate results. Somewhere
he lost his hat. His uniform was now stained with the residue of
powder and burnt wadding. His hair was freed from his queue
and dancing around his shoulders. The mess was unworthy of the
quarterdeck, but gratifying here. He could see the difference in the
way his men looked at him, with fear but also with complicity in
their well-earned disarray.

Serapis's mast was splitting and rocking now with every hit.
Very soon it would tumble, and her captain's situation would be
more complicated. At the very least, Jones thought, he must be
aware that without a mainmast he could not outrun *Alliance,* even
if he defeated *Richard.* Mad as he was, Landais could be counted
upon to claim a gift prize. His entire career was similarly gift
wrapped and presented to him by his benefactors, like those snakes
Silas Deane and Sam Adams, who had never, ever lifted a finger
on Jones's behalf, despite his successes. . . . His attention was drawn
to someone gesticulating on deck, half-dressed and shouting
incomprehensibly in the din.

"Hold," Jones told his crew, cocking his ear. That was when he
distinctly heard the man, a wounded gunner named Gardner,

say something like "Quarters! The prisoners are loose! We must strike, for God's sake!" He was directing this cowardice at *Serapis*.

Jones flew toward the man as if shot from a gun. "Shut that man up!" he screamed. "Shut him up! Shoot him!"

"Sir, do we strike?" a voice said from behind Jones's back.

"Strike, strike," said another.

"Don't kill us!" begged yet another.

"Captain, the hold is full of water. The ship is on fire. The prisoners have escaped. If you listen to reason . . ."

Jones spun around at this last speaker, his pistol drawn. He was looking at Gunnison, the carpenter.

"This ship will sink before she strikes!" he rumbled. Then he cocked the gun.

Terror flashing from his eyes, Gunnison dropped back down the companion-way. Gardner, meanwhile, had found a lantern and was waving it where the British could see it at their gun ports. "Mercy! Mercy, we beg you! In the name of humanity, the ship is lost!"

Jones took aim at him and fired. Nothing happened—he had forgotten to reload.

He turned the pistol around and threw it with all his strength at the coward. The gun spun through the air and kissed the back of the man's head while he was in mid-plea. Gardner pitched forward, bounced his jaw off the rail, and planted his nose in the sand-strewn deck.

"Lunt! Clap that man in irons!" Jones cried, turning this way and that. "Put those fires out! Keep fighting! Boarders stand by! Signal the *Alliance!* Lunt, put the prisoners to work on the pumps. Where is he? *WHERE IS LUNT?!*"

"Did someone call for quarters?" someone called from *Serapis*. Jones recognized it as the voice of the frigate's captain. His accent was redolent of fortune, some boy's academy, good tobacco, the petty frustrations of a conventional, inevitable rise. Every syllable enraged Jones.

"Are you going to strike?" his counterpart repeated.

Jones suddenly found his hat, lying under a fallen spar. As he smoothed it, a unidentifiable figure ran past him, his head and upper body a raging torch.

"I will not," Jones finally answered. "But before I am finished, I am sure to make *you* strike."

"As you wish," came the tart reply.

Two broadsides followed—the first from *Serapis,* knocking out more of the support beams for the top deck. With nothing left vertical below, there was now a discernible sagging of the deck at the ship's waist.

The second broadside was from *Alliance,* which had laboriously worked her way back against the light, contrary breeze to fire again.

"For God's sake, stop firing!" one of *Richard*'s tars called from the stern rail. "You're killing us!"

Jones retrieved his speaking-trumpet from Mayrant, raised it to his lips.

"*Alliance,* you will grapple and board *now!* Landais, you will answer to this flag! Do you understand?"

A faint word floated back—a peep that Jones heard as "understood."

"Mark it, he did acknowledge the order, did he not?" Jones asked Mayrant.

"He did."

But, in evolutions as inevitable as some blighted planet's, *Alliance* circled around *Richard*'s larboard side, came about into the wind, and served up her third broadside. This time Landais's gunners aimed higher, sending Jones and Mayrant sprawling to the deck with a shower of severed lines, singed leaves of canvas, and dead French marines down from the tops. The survivors above then leveled their muskets and, in a despairing response to out-rageous provocation, fired on a ship of their own navy.

Jones had to lean against the quarterdeck rail to steady himself. Though he prided himself on preparing for anything, he was not prepared for such brazen, bald-faced perfidy. One careless broad-side into the flagship, after all, might be put down to accident. Two might be excused by incompetence. But three? Three suggested betrayal mixed with stupidity and, perhaps, with desperation.

The Indiaman's forward nine-pounder resumed its assault on *Serapis*'s mainmast. Peering through the smoke, Jones spied Dale, turbaned under a wide, bloody bandage, commanding the gun crew.

"Mister Dale!" Jones called to him.

The lieutenant paused, looked.

"Are you bound to kill yourself tonight, lad?"

"Aye, but to kill a few of them first, begging the captain's par-don?"

"You have it," Jones bowed his head to the man, well pleased. Here, he believed, was a man who truly deserved one of those manly kisses Frenchmen gave each other.

"Captain, up there! It's Mr. Joseph-to-you!"

Following Mayrant's gaze, Jones could see Two Fires high above, shimmying along one of *Richard*'s topsail yards. Already more than three-quarters along its length, he was now directly above *Serapis*'s deserted deck. A bag of unknown contents was slung around his neck.

"What does he think he's doing?" Mayrant asked.

"His duty, I should say," answered Jones. "Pass the word to the sharpshooters, then—let us see to it that he succeeds!"

At that height, Two Fires was too high to hear any of the con-versation below. The decks of the two ships were bright with reddish moonlight which shifted and spun on the rising columns of smoke from hidden fires. Behind him and slightly above, he could make out the faint glow of the slow-matches *Richard*'s topmen used to touch off their swivel-guns. *Serapis*'s tops, in contrast, were shattered and silent.

In all his weeks at sea he had never been sent aloft. It would be a pity to waste such a view, he thought. So he lingered at the end of the yard, temporarily hanging his bag of grenades from the tip.

Behind him, to the west through the Indiaman's rigging, he could see a rocky promontory the shape of a ship's bow cutting into the sea. The sides of the eminence blazed under the moon, as if made of some glowing, milk-white stone. There was also a scattering of lanterns at the top of the headland. As his eyes adjusted, Two Fires began to make out more and more of these lights, until it seemed there was a village-full of people watching the battle. Did they bring food also? Did they bring their children to view the dying from a pleasant distance? It was like the battle he saw at Oneadalote, when he took the white soldier prisoner, except this time it was he who would be captured and, he supposed, killed if he swam ashore.

Ahead and to his left, he watched *Alliance* heading back out to sea. She was doing nothing to help *Pallas* in her running fight with the little English sloop. Musket and cannon-fire flashed steadily, like the commerce of fireflies, at the ships' broadsides, rails, rigging. It was hard to say who was going to win the fight there.

Two Fires rubbed his eyes. With the smoke rising up in his face, his eyes burned more up there than in the wasteland of *Richard*'s gun-deck. No sense in hanging around in that case— back to the battle!

He was looking down directly on *Serapis*'s deck. Specifically, he was looking into her open main hatch. The next move was obvious: picking out a promising grenade from his collection, he braced it on top of the yard with his chin, and used the other hand to fish out his flint and steel striker from his pocket. It was clumsy using both hands to raise a spark without falling to his death, but he soon had the fuse smoking. He held the grenade, regarding it pensively until it was mostly burned down. Then he dropped it into the hatch.

A fountain of flame immediately shot back out of the passage. The eruption reached so close to him it seared his eyebrows. In rapid succession, a series of explosions jerked *Serapis, Richard,* and his yardarm, almost flinging him loose from his perch. The frigate's gun-deck was now lit brightly by the flames. Two Fires could see a dozen bodies beneath him, some writhing, most still, as the stench of burnt flesh wafted skyward.

"Fire!" he heard Dale cry somewhere in the maelstrom below.

The nine-pounder spoke again and scored a direct hit on the frigate's mainmast. With that, the timber began to disintegrate under its own weight, popping and crackling. Two Fires had a good view as it finally snapped, about twenty feet from its base, and leaned lazily to rest against the Indiaman's rig, cradled in a snare of lines.

"Well done, Mister Joseph! Mr. Dale!" Jones cried. "Now let's keep pouring it into her, my brave lads!"

These twin blows—the grenade and the loss of her mast—staggered *Serapis.* An ominous silence came over her gun batteries below, though Jones was certain a single explosion could not have put them all out of service. Yet there was little he could do to take advantage of this halt.

Two Fires was suddenly signalling wildly at him, pointing into the frigate. The reason was quickly revealed: a great cry went up from a new wave of enemy boarders as they swarmed out of the hatches and over the side. There seemed an endless number of them, their faces ghastly black with smoke, their ears bleeding from explosions, some half-naked, some with clothes burnt entirely off. They comported themselves without a hint of spirited bucca-neering this time. Instead, it was like the last charge of some grim, besieged tribe.

❧

Richard's defenders rose to meet them at the Indiaman's rail. Their line held for a moment, then bent back as more and more boarders pressed them. The men from *Serapis* seemed to be winning purely by their numbers, piling in behind their fellows and pushing them forward into the blades and points of the defenders. Blood arced from the heads of the invaders as the French methodically found their targets from above.

More boarders swung over on hanging remnants of rigging, including two with the bad judgment to land on Jones's quarterdeck. The captain's sword was out of its scabbard and perforating one man's abdomen before Mayrant could even find his pistol on his belt. Then Jones was dueling with the other, his face cracked by a grin in the firelight, encouraging his shirtless, terrified opponent.

"A good fight, my boy! Keep your instrument up now! Lapses can tell the tale, like right there . . ."

And he extended his arm like a man poking an unlit log in a fire, steering the tip of his sword into the cleft just above the man's collarbone. The latter stopped fighting and looked down, surprised.

"Alas, I am done in!" he croaked. Then he pulled himself off Jones's blade and carefully sat down with his hands grasping his neck.

Jones laid his sword aside and searched himself for a handkerchief. "Mister Mayrant, a cloth, if you please?"

His hands shaking, Mayrant uncocked his pistol, put it back in his belt. By that time Jones had his coat off and was pressing it against the wounded man's neck.

"Curse your slowness, Mayrant! Keep the wound covered, here," he ordered the other. "And don't falter, as long as your strength holds."

With that, the battle for the quarterdeck was over. Meanwhile, as *Serapis* ran out of men to fling at her opponent, the defenders below and the muskets above wore down her numbers, until the struggle became even, then a rout. Turning, the boarders leapt back to the frigate *en masse* or tumbled between the hulls. *Richard*'s men stopped at their own rail and, showing good discipline at last, looked to Jones above for the order to pursue.

Jones was now clad now only in a white waistcoat streaked with ash and other men's blood. His hair loosed, eagerly surveying every detail of the carnage below him, he seemed no longer just a partisan in the struggle, but the caretaker of the battle. To Mayrant, he seemed to be admiring some precious thing, some memory of a moment that was not finished happening.

"Quarters! Quarters!" a voice called from the frigate's gun-deck.

"Hallo! Are you surrendering?" answered Jones.

"Yes, yes, damn your eyes!"

"I hear your words, sir, but see your ensign still flies," said Jones in a voice shaking with vindication. "If you do not strike, I will lay my men on board!"

They then heard the sound of violent cursing, distinct in its tone but too low to be understood. A handkerchief, ostensibly white but red as a scab from the glare of *Serapis*'s fires, ascended from the companion-way. As it rose, an arm clad in blue appeared, then a single epaulette, then the enemy captain's face. No one fired or spoke.

Captain Richard Pearson, commander of frigate *Serapis*, was the first man in many hours to stand unmolested on his ship's deck. Fixing his wide-set eyes on the small figure on the opposite quarterdeck, he saw a little man in filthy service whites. To him, this small fellow appeared crazed with blood lust. He had heard and scoffed at the stories of Paul Jones's pretentions to gentility, and now he had his proof. Anyone who would take a fight to such barbaric lengths, in the face of so many casualties, to the practical ruin of both sides, had to be little more than a corsair. He had seen it before, after all, fighting Algerian pirates in the Mediterranean. There was nothing remarkable about the tenacity of a man with nothing to lose. Nothing new at all to this particular action.

For surely, Paul Jones had been defeated. He had failed to capture a single ship in the merchant convoy. His ship was sinking. And it had been two Americans against one Briton, had it not?

Watching from above, Two Fires saw the Red ensign come down, and the cheers come up from *Richard*. It occurred to him, in fact, that he was not alone in that man-built forest of spars and lines, that grave scaffold for living men. His father was up there, too, in the memory of his last dream. For the beaver, small but determined, alone on the water, had indeed killed the bear. And Jones was no longer a machine, but a man, decorated finely in his own sweat and tears. Finally, fully, to Two Fires, he was War Captain.

XVI.

THE GARDENS behind her father's house marched in symmetrical rows toward a little pond at the far end. Rebeccah could measure her world's contraction using the parallel beds like ticks on a ruler. When she was a girl, she played along the far edges of the pond, fascinated by all the varieties of life that took their brief turns there. With her mother's death, her responsibilities increased, and her concerns retreated to the house and garden plantings. Having mastered domestic horticulture long before she'd mastered courtship, she had to watch her sister grow, bloom, and marry first.

By then, the old gardener understood Rebeccah's tastes, and she barely needed to go more than a few rows down the path to stop, look, and confirm all was in order. More recently, she rarely left the brick pavement near the house, or the wooden bench, ornamented with prancing, piping satyrs, that sat by the trunk of the dogwood tree under her bedroom window. When she worked, she worked impulsively, without satisfaction. When she sat, she sat impatiently, wishing she had the ambition to work. She looked with only a flicker of pleasure on the flowers near her slippers: marigold, hostas, Love-Lies-Bleeding. She wondered how a body could be so small, so inconsequential, and yet feel so much. It seemed like such an unkind joke, this occupation of living. Pregnancy wore heavily on her.

She understood very well that she was not carrying a child. Mrs. Sparshot had convinced her that was impossible. But this news was no relief to her, for her body was still a knot of unfamiliar feelings. This was a pregnancy, she suspected, that would deliver something far more disreputable than bastardy. Her belly seemed full of some emanation, some secretion, some perverse effluence that she could blame on no one but herself.

She brooded on the cause of it all. To begin with, she knew she was too full of opinions. She was a jealous, begrudging sister. She was indifferent to religion. She was unimpressed with empiricism. The skin across the bridge of her nose tended to be dry. She would never marry, because not even Severence moved her.

"Taking the airs, I see," her father said from behind her bench.

"Yes. And you as well," she replied, fidgeting with the edges of the unread book in her lap.

He sat next to her, staying silent for some minutes. He was usually given to neither activity.

"You have done well with the plantings," he finally said. "Remarkably well."

"Thank you."

His eyes were flitting around the garden in a way she had never quite seen before. Why is he here? She was pierced by a terrifying thought: that he had somehow learned of her visit to Mrs. Sparshot. Had the odious old woman sold her out in exchange for settling her father's unpaid account? Her heart was pounding with such force she could feel her eyeballs trembling in her skull.

"Any further word from our Mr. Severence?"

She closed her eyes. The answer to this question was yes. But the theft of his letters from her writing desk, even temporarily, had forced her to resort to deceptions of her own.

"I would think you would know already," she answered. "Or has your spy failed you?"

He hung his head and shook it ruefully from his neck.

"You really mustn't be so mistrustful. You know I act only in our best interest. This suspicion is . . . not acceptable."

She looked at him. "What are you accusing me of? Hiding his letters?"

"Never."

"If you wish it, you have only to demand them from me."

"Of course not."

They were interrupted by an imprudent bee, orbiting her father's head in nervous circles. Venting his annoyance on the insect, he hacked at it with the handle of his cane, muttering obscenities. Rebeccah, meanwhile, noticed that the head of a single drop of blood was peeking out at her from under her left sleeve. The wound she had inflicted on herself that morning, just below her elbow, had opened again. It was difficult to find the right balance: to cut herself deeply enough to let the corruption out, but not so deep that she bled inappropriately. She hid the bloody fabric with her other hand.

"I cannot expect you would understand the importance of complete candor between us in this matter," he resumed, "if we are to see profit in it."

"That is certain, if you can't explain your particular interest to me."

"An explanation . . . is not mine to give."

She could feel the bloodstain spreading under her hand. She needed to get away from him. Fortunately, he was driven to his feet by the bee, which had zigged out toward the columnal topiaries and zagged back at him.

"Damn the pests! I don't know how you stand them!"

He was short with both bug and daughter for a particularly personal reason. Despite his regimen, despite all his efforts to orchestrate the shape of his movements, his productions had recently gone appallingly small. Instead of large, coherent products, he delivered tiny, rodent-like things that gave him no sense of relief. Yet there was nothing he could do until his time to try again, hours away. His helplessness filled him with rage.

"You said I have but to ask," he told her. "Consider the request made . . . should you receive any more letters!"

And he retreated to his study without looking back at her. She made an obscene gesture at his back—a simple extension of the index and little finger, pointed toward him. She had learned it watching the workmen at the docks, and using it gave her a pleasing sense of power.

That evening, she began her first letter back to Severence. It was difficult, because she missed him only faintly, as she would a barely recalled friend. Yet she would not dare be so honest when he was far away, and in such danger. The matters he was writing about—horrors of battles and atrocities, theology, the politics of *petit* personalities—though not the stuff of love letters, seemed genuinely felt. She supposed she should exhibit some jealousy at his stewardship of Polyxena, but searched her heart and found none. After a number of false starts, she opted for a cautionary tone:

Dearest John:

I write without hope that you will receive this letter before the end of your campaign. But I feel I must write to you now, my love, for I am desperate . . .

She stopped, reread the last sentence, and tore up the draft. Then she began again:

Dearest John:

I write in hope that you will receive this letter before the end of your campaign. But I feel I must write now, dear one, for I am desperate with concern for you, and for the integrity of your trust in me. Though I have tried with all my ingenuity to preserve your correspondence from prying eyes (and to be, as you say, your "sweet soldier"), I must confess that my power in this regard is exhausted. It is more difficult than ever now, I despair to confess, to keep your confidences from finding their way inevitably to my father's desk . . .

XVII.

My dear Rebeccah:

I take pen in hand now with my spirit much improved since I last wrote. This can only be attributed to the fact that I am no longer in the company of Sullivan's army. Rather, I am sitting now many leagues from the main force, on a knoll richly carpeted with short-grass, overlooking the deep blue strait of Cayugah Lake. The sun is setting now beyond the opposite shore, into low hills innocent of agriculture. Behind me I have a force of two hundred men. They are also in a fine mood, as I have temporarily suspended Sullivan's restrictions and allowed them to hunt for their supper. The forest around us is so bountiful that the riflemen shot ten deer—including two fine stags—in three-quarters of an hour. The messes have thankfully put aside their cast-iron cooking pots and erected spits for roasting their quarters of venison.

How did I arrive at this fine position? As you might expect, Sullivan had long been wondering how best to neutralize my "espionage." The best to do so would have been to leave me behind. Yet there was no limit to the "damage" I could do behind his lines, unsupervised. A solution finally presented itself after Senecah Castle was destroyed and we turned back toward Pennsylvania. Now that all the Iroquois lands are aroused to our presence, and most of their villages already burnt, there is little I can do to compromise his situation. A packet of new orders was therefore delivered to my tent late in the evening after Boyd's men were buried.

In summary, I was given command of a single battalion of troops, including a platoon of riflemen, and assigned the task of proceeding down the east shore of Cayugah Lake. My aim would be to despoil the towns and fields of the local tribe in accordance with established procedures, and thence to march on, "processing" anything in my path, until I rejoined the main force in the vicinity of Catherine's Town.

To be sure, my reaction to this development was more than a little dubious. Two hundred men seemed scarcely adequate to the challenge of such an expedition. Disposed to my usual cynicism, I suspected Sullivan understood this danger very well, and was in fact counting on Butler and Brant to fall upon my little force. How convenient that would be, for the enemy to remove his problem for him!

Yet the more I thought upon it that night, the more determined I became to take up the challenge. The danger from enemy action, I decided, was minimal: Brant and Butler were certainly then retreating toward Fort Niagara, to salvage her defense. The Cayugahs themselves were few in numbers, and according to Polyxena, already scattered. The only conceivable danger would have been from enemy war parties arriving in Clinton's wake from the east. But a battalion of veteran troops would be more than enough to repel any party of a dozen or two dozen vengeful Mohawks, operating without the advantage of surprise.

Lying on my camp bed that night, I also began to glimpse the advantages of the assignment. It would amount, I believed, to a chance to demonstrate, to all who cared to notice, how a military expedition like Sullivan's should have been conducted. We might, for instance, take prisoners. Insofar as it is always more practicable to win over our savage neighbors than to exterminate them, I imagined my little foray as an episode of good sense in an otherwise dismal epic.

What to do about Polyxena? There was, alas, no question about taking her with me, despite her knowledge of the Cayugah lands. One simply does not remove a female prisoner from the battlefield only to escort her back into danger. On the other hand, under the circumstances in Sullivan's camp, her safety was hardly secured by leaving her behind. I took this matter most seriously; had it developed in a manner that would have placed her in jeopardy, I would have declined the assignment, exalted intentions notwithstanding.

General Clinton resolved the dilemma. Upon hearing my situation, he smiled and, with a sweep of his arm like some beneficent deity's, personally guaranteed Polyxena's safe passage to Easton. I exacted this promise in private, in his marquee, before he had procured the evening's liquid sustenance from the sutler. Then, like a leaf turning over in the wind, his expression turned solemn. Sobriety wore strangely on him.

"I would be pleased to help you, Severence, on account of your family's name alone."

"I'm sure my father would thank you, sir."

"That is what Sullivan does not understand," he continued as if I had not spoken. "If he had, you would not have been so ill-used on this march."

"I am not ill-used. I am fortunate."

"Spoken like a Severence!" he exclaimed, slapping my back. Under the force of this blow, it occurred to me that Clinton's good cheer had come closer to injuring me than any action of the enemy.

After preparations for departure and a dinner with Clinton, I didn't see Polyxena until late in the evening. She was sitting in front of her tent before a small fire, her splinted leg resting on a rock. Someone had provided her with an iron skillet, which she was holding over the flames. She protected her hand from the hot metal handle by gathering up the material of her skirt.

"There you are," she said, withdrawing the skillet and examining the gently hissing contents.

"What are you cooking?"

"They are ready. Have some."

She held out the pan. The bottom of it was lined with fat, crimped, cotton white kernels.

"What is it?"

"Poor child!" she laughed. "Don't they pop corn in New-York?"

I tasted it. The flavor was somewhat salty, but pleasantly filling, like roasted chestnuts. The consistency was surprisingly moist.

"I covered them with that miserable butter they give you," she said. "It makes the corn less dry and helps the salt go further."

"How ingenious."

I sat down. In truth, the warmth of her reception made it harder for me to tell her of my new orders. The tone of our conversation had been improving steadily since she began to speak, and especially since we began the return march. She only occasionally declared her belief that she would soon be murdered. I was no longer presumed to be a rapist—or so it seemed.

I told her. She listened quietly as I announced that I would set out the next morning and that she would be under the protection of Clinton. She gave no reaction when I said that my objective was the homelands of the Cayugah, and that I hoped to rejoin her just a few weeks hence, in Catherine's Town. Instead, she just held out the popped corn to me again.

"Why do you tell me this, Severence? I am your property. You need no leave from me."

"Not your leave. Your trust," I replied.

She gave that derisive grimace she often did when she was mute, adding, "Am I to trust someone who says at the same time he is going off? What sort of logic is this?"

"I am not 'going off.' And as I said, your protection has been arranged."

"I will tell you again, sir: your pledges are shit. They never meant anything to me, and they won't tomorrow."

We looked into the flames as they burned down. Though she

had a few sticks by her side, she didn't put them in the fire.

"And now I suppose you expect me to wish you luck, too?" she asked.

"Only if you wish."

In a practiced motion, she rose erect by balancing on her good leg and slowly reeling in the splinted one.

"You will find the fate you deserve," she said.

She turned and hobbled a few steps back toward her tent. I would have accepted this leave-taking, imperfect as it was, if not for a sudden spasm of indignation. I had sworn to her absolute safety. It would amount to a separation of only one, possibly two weeks. That would be all.

I raced around her, as she fell to her good knee again to enter her tent. That was the last time I saw her face that night—or shall I say, the faint impression of her face, lit by scant reflection of the fire on the bleached canvas.

"I will return," I whispered. "You must know I will."

Her expression, which had resumed the masklike implacability of her former self, softened a bit.

"If you come to a town above the east shore . . . one with peach orchards, that we call Chonodote . . ."

"Yes?" I pressed. I was suddenly, stupidly eager to please her. If she had asked me to spare the town, I would have agreed.

But her request died in her throat. Instead, her gaze fell from my face to the epaulette on my shoulder to my sword—the accoutrements of my commission. An iron door behind her eyes seemed to slam closed again.

"If you come to Chonodote," she said, "may you be afflicted by Bad Mind. Let the womb of the woman you love be filled with vomit. May an ax find your scalp and your balls shrivel with fear, and may you live with this curse and your shame. May your flesh end up in a dog's mouth. I say this aware of what I do. I know you no longer."

My company set out a day later, on the 20th. The expedition is cobbled together with platoons from every regiment in the army. I have backwoods Pennsylvanians in their hunting shirts and knives, themselves barely civilized. I have the sons of Yankee shop-keepers and farmers and preachers, looking askance at the foul language of the Pennsylvanians. I have elements of a private bat-talion organized by the scion of an Albany patroon family, each man in a complete and unique uniform designed by their bene-factor. Beside these splendidly frocked troops, I have a gang from New Jersey who had served Washington in his victory at Trenton but who, to a man, lack shirts and shoes.

My subaltern, is Lieutenant Nathan Francis Israel, a Vermonter who had arrived with Clinton. A severe, bookish-looking young man, he purchased his commission, I learned, after his education for the ministry had wrecked at the feet of a red-haired beauty from Brattleboro. So deep did his love run that the boy irrevoca-bly spurned his calling and declared his intent to marry. Unfortunately, the girl had by then lost interest, apparently find-ing an eligible lover far less intriguing than an ardent, unavailable one.

It was for the best, for a life of the cloth would not have suited a man of such spectacularly ill temper. His specialty, it seems, lies in taking desperate offense at the slightest personal provocation. As dueling with sword or gun is severely proscribed by the army, he has often applied bare knuckles to defend of his honor—or had bare knuckles applied to him, as the case may be. In Sullivan's camp, his face was a constantly shifting canvas of swellings, split-tings, mashed veins, and contusions. The many colors of his foul temperament made him no friends there, which may explain why he was banished to my service.

Our little force of rejects and cast-offs struck off first due east from the ruins of Kanadesaga village, at the northern head of Senecah Lake. We traveled along a wide, splendid Indian trail that seemed to span all the lakes of the area. The path wound between the low, long barrows that were particular to this country, so numerous that they might have marked the plow lines of titans. We noted that much of the forest around the trail was freshly burnt, but not by Sullivan's army. There was much speculation in the ranks over why the Iroquois would set such destructive fires on land they did not cultivate. The conventional judgment—that is, the one expressed most loudly—was that it was done out of simple, childish malice.

My experience of the woods has been very different on this march. After months on the deck of a ship, life on land has an expansive stolidity that can itself be unnerving. Yet this country, hundreds of leagues from the nearest shore, makes the clearest sense to the mariner. Its irregularities seem all but planed smooth by the hand of the Almighty. In aqueous rhythm, it rises and falls in slow, unhurried sweeps. As we reach the crest of one hill, we may look across a great wooded trough to the next hill rolling behind it, and another behind that one, until the swells dissolve in the extremity of the late summer haze.

To the eye, the forest is a still, green ocean. To the ear, it is a revelation. Though Sullivan holds that unnecessary noise is a liability, in practice it is impossible for an army to travel with anything less than a baleful riot of sounds. Over the great distances from van to afterguard, signal drums are essential for communication. In the ranks, knapsacks rattle with their effects, cooking pots clang against stocks, and lips flap with unsubtle complaints. At the center, packhorses neigh and stomp, and slip over slippery rocks, scattering their cargoes; at the margins, pickets and sweepers bushwack over dry leaves, break saplings, and keep up verbal contact with each other. I have already described the ordeal of moving the artillery, and only invite you to imagine the cacophony that must entail. An army in the woods is, in fact, an extended, mobile town spread over many miles.

The men in my little command still complain, of course, and carry knapsacks that rattle. But we have just a handful of pickets, no artillery, and move at a speed that (we hope) approximates that of the Indian brave himself. Into this profound quiet, the forest asserts itself. With the saplings regularly burnt away, most of the trees here are tall, holding aloft green suits of foliage that sigh in the wind. We can hear an incoming breeze, in fact, before we feel it, from the waves of trembling leaves rolling toward us from the hills. By night, of course, we sleep by the calls of insects, wolves, and coyotes. In the day, there are only the birds, which are here in some variety but do not fill the air with their cries as one might expect. We march, it seems, in the center of some great hush. It is as if the land itself were waiting to see the end of the present struggle and hence, perhaps, its own fate.

I was obliged to put my notions of constructive conquest into immediate practice near the outlet of Cayugah Lake. Just a few miles down the shoreline path lies the big village labeled "Cayugah Castle" on our chart, but whose Indian name no one could say. It was actually a complex of three adjoining villages, each of about fifty cabins, built along a streambed reduced to a mere trickle in late summer. Its fields were quite extensive, mounting up on the hills over the lake, all with handsome prospects of this rich country. The villages appeared to have been abandoned several days before we arrived.

The Cayugahs are not as populous a tribe as the Senecah, and their cultivations are not as wide as those at Senecah Castle. Still, torching all the cabins and fields was hard labor for our small force—more than enough work for a full day. This was true even without girdling the trees, which I have forbidden. The latter order raised many eyebrows around me. Yet while I understand the logic of chastening the tribes, it is an act of spite, not justice, to pauperize them by destroying their maples and fruit orchards. Nor have I countenanced the destruction of seed stores, which we often find in underground granaries that are hurriedly concealed with brush and green timber. To the men, I have explained that we may all profit from a race of healthy, compliant savages with the resources to trade with us, while a starving Indian is of no use whatever. To these lectures the troops listened politely, their ears unstopped a bit by the fresh meat I have allowed them. But I cannot discount that many of them do imagine one use for starving Indians: to die and get out of the way.

As I have never before taken direct part in the destruction of fields, I have only recently seen at close hand the nature of Iroquois cultivation. Lieutenant Israel showed me an unburnt field at Cayugah Castle, remarking on the pattern of small mounds extending over more than a hectare, with their three primary crops—corn, squash, and beans—grown all together with great efficiency.

"See how they use the corn stalk as a natural prop for the bean vine," he said as he crouched on one of the mounds. "The squash is grown at the foot of the corn plant, where its leaves shade the ground, discouraging evaporation. That is how they produce such great yields with dry methods. Remarkable."

"Yes, remarkable. And how do they burn?"

"Terribly. The crops are laden with water."

"I see. In that case, do your best, Mr. Israel."

"Yes, sir."

It took two days to complete our work on the three villages. Proceeding south, we were on the trail but two hours before we approached the outskirts of another settlement. This news provoked much grumbling in the ranks, as the thrill of revenge had long ago faded. The prospect of another destruction consigned us all to more long hours of exhausting drudgery.

We suddenly heard a voice calling to us.

"Are you the Americans?" it said.

The first rank cocked and shouldered their weapons as a dark figure appeared on the trail ahead. Two of my riflemen were escorting the man toward us. He was bareheaded, wearing a black working man's smock with knee-length breeches.

"I said, are you the Americans?" he repeated.

The man's accent was French, and he clutched a rosary in his right hand.

I ignored him at first, looking instead to the scouts for their report.

"Found him coming out of the village," I was told. "He's a missionary, I think."

"Thank you. I can damn well see that."

"I am Du Lac, of the Péres de la Merci. I minister to these people. You have been a long time in coming, I think."

Our visitor's face indeed did show the typical Gallic sneer. His hair was a striking red in color but cropped very short, in the peasant style. His face was scarred from years of shaves with very bad razors.

"But this is not the total of your army, is it?" he went on. "I think you are not so many!"

"Yes, thank you. And how might we help you this afternoon?"

"No, no! You may ask how might Du Lac help *you*. Please to show you, here . . ."

And he gestured for us to follow. We did, but observing our own procedures against ambush. Our slow progress frustrated the fellow. He was pacing frantically when we finally reached the center of the village, which was the typical collection of log-built cabins, pits for grinding meal, curing racks for game. He pointed at one of the storage mounds.

"They put their food in the ground here, yes?"

"Yes, we know that," Israel said.

"But do you know *this*? . . ."

Du Lac moved over a few yards, bent down, and with a deft

motion, pulled up a section of brown, sandy turf. Another storage pit lay underneath, filled to the top with fat, foot-long ears of
Indian corn.

"The devil take them!" exclaimed the lieutenant. "How many
of these have we missed?"

"Our Oneida allies have not been wholly informative," I said,
examining the turf covering. The plant material and soil were
somehow fastened to a mat woven from some kind of reed. The
whole thing was strong to support a man's weight, but flexible
enough to give like a soft patch of ground. Quite ingenious.

"You see, eh? And they have more—there, there, there—" Du
Lac was excited, pointing all over the compound. "There is much
food to destroy, enough for months. They think you too stupid to
find it all."

I stood, rubbing the dirt from my hands.

"If you please, tell us why you are doing this, Pére? Why are
you betraying the trust of your flock?"

The question did not have any sort of chastening effect on the
man. Instead, he appeared still more exhilarated, as if given the
chance to unburden himself at last.

"Betrayal? No! It is a blessing, the scourging of the proud. It is
the beginning of the salvation. Without humility, they laugh at
their damnation. I may tell you the blasphemy I see here! But this
winter, see the difference in them!"

"Do you mean, when they starve?"

"Some will starve, yes. It is sad. But we save the rest for a better purpose."

The rest of the battalion was in the village, their eyes devour-
ing the kitchen gardens. By long experience, they had learned they
might find potatoes in them, and carrots, as well as the usual
squash and pumpkins.

I looked at Israel, who finally tore his gaze from the concealed
corn to look back.

"Orders, sir?"

"Come, this will interest you . . . ," said the priest.

And he pulled me onward by the sleeve. One of the Indians' traditional longhouses stood in the center of the town. The door was open and I looked inside. The interior was lit through the smoke holes in the barrel-shaped roof, and I could see triple-tiered bunks lining the walls all the way to the other end. Only a few items remained inside: a pair of dried gourds hung from a rafter, a large iron kettle at one of the fire pits. It was impossible to tell whether the place was bereft due to a hasty evacuation, or because no one lived in longhouses anymore. The fires, at least, seemed quenched long ago.

"Yes, it is one of their pagan temples," Du Lac was saying in a low, doleful voice. "But it will not serve for a church. Better to worship *en plein air,* where they will not be distracted by old memories, I think."

It was indeed just the gathering place of savages. But the atmosphere there filled me with a consonant feeling of desolation. Did the Roman legionaries suffer the same languor when they sacked the Temple of Herod or when they invaded the sacred groves of the Druids?

"Let me bring you here, where the white woman lived," Du Lac went on.

"White woman?"

We stood before a windowless structure much meaner than the cabins. It was nothing more than a hovel, assembled from spare pieces of planking and short logs, leaning against a tree. The interior was partly excavated into the dirt and smelled strongly of urine.

"Yes, they keep a white woman here for many years."

"They keep her? Do you mean she is a captive?"

The father tossed his head, evidently pained by a compulsion to tell the truth. "Ah . . . no. She is adopted by them. She was given to one of their braves and had two bastard children by him."

Based on what little Polyxena had told me of her family, this must have been the house of her mother.

"Where is the old woman now?" I pressed.

"Who can say? Niagara, I think."

"And her children?"

"The son went off in the forest many months ago, and has not returned. As for the girl . . ." He paused to deposit a thick wad of sputum on the ground. "As for her, she is accursed. I hope the Devil has taken her."

"Why?"

"Because, *monsieur*, she is the Devil's daughter. Such arrogance! Pretty, yes, but what a foul temperament! And a prostitute, I'm afraid."

"A prostitute!"

"I assure you, yes. They teach their girls that way, you know . . . to give themselves for a mirror, a comb, or a ball of maple sugar."

"And how would you know this, sir, if you have not partaken yourself?"

He frowned, flicked his hand disdainfully. "It is commonly known. She is the property of all the men. I bring them the wisdom to stop degrading themselves, but she is the last to hear of it. I no longer try with her, if she returns. She may go to her reward. My hands are clean."

Israel had followed us. He cleared his throat at me.

"Yes, Mr. Israel?"

"Shall we give the men something to do, sir?"

"Yes, of course. Burn it. Burn it all."

"Yes, sir."

"First, kindly wait a moment, Lieutenant." I turned back to Du Lac. "This town. What do the Cayugahs call it?"

"Chonodote. In their tongue means 'peach fields.'"

"I see. Very good. Mr. Israel, you may also have the men strip this man of his clothes and beat him out of camp."

"Sir?"

"But, Monsieur Capitaine, this is outrageous!" Du Lac cried. "Have I not helped you today? Have I not shown you my confraternity? We go to my cabin now. I have cognac. Let us speak together now, like gentlemen . . ."

"And if he comes back," I told Israel, "you may shoot him."

Yours ever in love,
JOHN

XVIII.

He took the Serapis
Did he not? Did he not?
He took the Serapis, tho' the battle it was hot;
But a rogue and a vagabond,
Is he not?

—From a contemporary British folk ballad

JONES ACCEPTED Pearson's sword on *Richard*'s quarterdeck. The defeated captain grasped the blade and offered the hilt with exactly the formal obeisance required of him. Ever obliging in triumph, Jones reversed the sword and returned it, saying "Pray keep this, in our admiration for a stout defense."

With *Richard* still smoldering and her hull filling with water, only a few of her crew gathered to witness the surrender. Mayrant was there, with Linthwaite and the complement of marines from the pilot boat. Henriette was there, too, though with hair shot through with wood splinters and frock caked with blood. And Two Fires was there, studying from a bemused distance yet another strange custom of the whites: a competition between two pompous captains over displays of *faux* modesty.

Pearson stood a full head taller than Jones, and carried himself as if a shot rammer was permanently installed in his colon. To Jones's annoyance, he still did not meet his conqueror's eyes. Instead, he seemed to want to take Jones as invisible, focusing instead on some object in his middle distance.

"Your crew, sir . . . from what nation do they hail?"

"This is an American vessel," Jones replied. Pearson's question seemed innocent but had a galling effect. After all, the United

States ensign was flying prominently from the staff. It could not be denied, however, that there were a large number of red-coated French marines on deck, and British and Portuguese voices filtering up from below. From his vantage high atop his own nose, Pearson finally fixed an eye on Jones. He let it linger there for an instant—long enough to indicate his skepticism—before he looked away and answered, "Well then, we suffer in comparison only with our own countrymen. Not like that mob of Frenchmen and Spaniards dithering in the Channel, God help them. Only a diamond cuts a diamond."

"Just so," Jones said, only half-flattered. "By 'Spaniards and Frenchmen,' you refer to Admiral d'Orvillier's fleet, I expect."

"Yes, but the word 'fleet' hardly applies. 'Floating charnel house' would do better, I'd think."

"I see."

Though Pearson might easily have lied about the fate of d'Orvillier's invasion, its failure due to delay and disease had the sickening ring of truth.

"Will you join me for a glass of porter below?" Jones asked.

"I think not . . . but thank you."

"Very well. Mr. Mayrant, show the captain to his berth, if you please."

With that, Pearson took his sword below. Jones's work, however, was just beginning. *Richard* was clearly very grievously damaged from the main-deck down. *Serapis* was partly dismasted and badly cut-up above. With a jury-rig, the frigate would sail as if she were dragging an anchor. Now that the convoy was crowding into port and all those spectators had gathered ashore, the Royal Navy would soon know his position, if they didn't already. How many ships will they send after our little squadron? he wondered. The thought of all those ships of the line converging on Flamborough Head, all those thousands of men and guns, was not unpleasant to him. He found, instead, that the prospect focused his mind agreeably, firing him with a sense of exhilarating urgency.

He hardly had an opportunity to appreciate what his ship and his men had accomplished. In single combat, an old, foul-sailing, underarmed, converted mechantman had prevailed over one of the most modern frigates afloat. Moreover, it appeared that Cottineau had also taken *Serapis*'s little consort for himself. (What Ricot had been doing all along, Jones could not say.) The Royal Navy, he was sure, had not lost two warships to capture in a single action in four years of fighting with America and a generation against France. There was no question that the result would be highly favorable to his reputation in Paris and Philadelphia.

And yet, under other circumstances, fighting in the way he would have preferred, he could have accomplished more. The entire convoy could have been smashed. *Serapis* could have been induced to surrender more quickly, with less damage inflicted on her and on the Indiaman, and the cruise extended with her firepower added to his force. With some 150 total guns at his disposal, not even a ship of the line would have been safe from his combined squadron.

This was, he decided, a defeat wrapped inside a victory. Obliged to dance so long with a single partner, he had missed the rest of the ball. The thought stoked his frustration, which poured forth as impatience.

"Mr. Stacey!"

The sailing-master, just then supervising the disentangling of the two frigates' rigs, turned. "Sir?"

"I assume you understand we must be under way in the soonest instance."

"I do. But with a hold full o' water, we won't get far without a good spread o' sail. And *Serapis* needs a new main, and a course to bend on it."

"Yes, yes. But even a short distance from here is better than none."

"Aye."

"And please see that the message gets to the rest of the squadron: we make for Dunkirk or the nearest French port of any size."

He then swooped down to the orlop deck, hoping he might confirm that the leaks in the hull were finally under control. Instead, he was brought up short by a sobering scene. By the light of a few uncertain candles, he could see gangs of crewmen and prisoners working frantically at both of the eight-man chain pumps. The heat and choking lack of air made the place hardly bearable. Rats dislodged by the rising water in the hold were scratching and scrambling all around them, climbing casks, bulk-heads, pant legs. The orlop—just above the hold—was itself under six inches of water.

He saw a disembodied bandage float toward him out of the gloom. Closer, he could make out the smoke-blackened face of Dale beneath it.

"We've been at it four hours continuous," he said. "We're losing her."

"Dale, why are those prisoners not in the brig?"

"Begging the captain's pardon, but we'd all be chin-deep in brine by now if it weren't for those prisoners . . . begging the captain's pardon."

"I see, Mr. Dale. But you may now draw help from among our own crew. Understood?"

"Understood," he said, and added after a pause "So you wish us to continue?"

"Good Lord, of course! This ship shall not sink, sir. You will do what is necessary, yes?"

Dale frowned. "Yes."

His next stop was Surgeon Brooke's cockpit. The situation there was quieter than the one below, but hardly less grim. The sheeted dead were stacked against a bulkhead, heads pointing alternately left and right. Brooke, who seemed to have bathed in gore, had not put down his bone saw in two hours. A boy was standing beside him with a bucket of severed limbs; four more buckets like it were lined up under the companion-way.

"Do you have a count, Doctor?"

Brooke looked up, wiped the blood from his spectacles.

"Oh, it's you. A count? Who can say? Forty dead, so far. Fifty, seventy, one hundred in the end. It all depends!"

After a night of very possibly inflicting as much agony as he had eased, Brooke's voice had an edge of incipient frenzy in it. Jones withdrew, saying nothing more to distract him.

"Go over to the *Serapis*," he told Mayrant. "See whether their surgeon is likewise engaged. If not, ask him to assist Mister Brooke here."

After ten hours in the surgery, Henriette begged to be excused. She was still thinking about the profile of that perfect nose, cruelly flushed out with the bilge. Despondent, she pinned her hopes on sketching it from memory. But when she reached her quarters, she was confused to find they were no longer there. Instead, she was looking at a section of the berth deck that was completely blackened by fire. All the bulkheads had been removed, and all that remained of her personal things was a scatter of charred cloth, a melted mass of cosmetic wax, and scraps of singed paper. The sweet odor of burnt, wet wood hung in the air.

"The fire was only just put out," Linthwaite said behind her. "We all lost everything in your cabin, mine, Mr. Fanning's."

"Yes," she replied. She was simply too exhausted to fret or cry over the loss of all her work. "It is nothing now, after so many have died."

"Well, I won't say that! I had a new uniform coat just made . . . and a fine edition of Plutarch's *Lives!* But they saved this for you."

Her heart swelled as he offered her a sketchbook. Though the cover was singed, the pages appeared intact. However, as she leafed through it, she found it was one of her new, unused tablets. So all her previous sketches were, indeed, gone.

She gave a tired smile. "*Merci, mon ami.* It is a miracle."

"The carpenter will have the bulkheads back up by this evening, so at least we'll have our modesty!"

"Yes, at least we will have that."

After discovering her new penury, she couldn't bear to remain below. From the quarterdeck, she watched the survivors among *Richard*'s crew working furiously to restore the Indiaman to some sort of order. The able seamen were above, replacing damaged canvas and rigging. Sweepers were swirling around her, scraping up the blood-caked sand from the deck. Below her feet, she could hear the carpenters struggling to stabilize the drooping main-deck. There were sounds of heavy chopping, not unlike something one might hear in the forest, coming from *Serapis*. Wandering to the starboard rail, she saw men with axes trying to dislodge the cracked mainmast from its stump. All of the men seemed to work frightened, with one eye on their task and the other on the horizon.

Over on the port side, forward, she heard the sound of a large object hitting the water. Picking her way through the chaos, she got close enough to see Jones standing at a small ramp erected at the rail. More than a dozen tightly wrapped mummies were stacked around him, a single piece of bar-shot lashed to each pair of feet. The next corpse was loaded onto the ramp. Jones lowered his bare head, mouthed something inaudible, and replaced his hat. Two landsmen then tilted the ramp toward the water, slipping the body to its reward.

The morning had dawned overcast and hazy. The air was damp, but the flat light was good for Henriette's purpose. Finding a quiet corner for herself, she fished her last pencil from her pocket, opened her last sketchbook, and drew a line.

Except it wasn't a line. It was a thrashing, wiggling snake. She tried again, with the same result. She looked around her in confusion, wondering if the ship was somehow moving. But there was only a gentle, antiphonal rocking between *Richard* and *Serapis.*

Henriette tried a third time to draw a line and failed. It was then she noticed that her hands were shaking. She held them up and, with amazement, watched them vibrate like the wings on a bee. Laughing at herself, she summoned her will to quiet them. The shaking eased.

She took up the pencil again. But as soon as the point touched the paper, the trembling resumed, more violent than before. With that, her stoicism failed her. She felt the impulse building in her to do something. She wanted to do what all her humanity had demanded she do for the last eighteen hours, until she could resist no more.

She screamed.

On days like this, noted Jones, noon was much like the dawn. The wind had come around overnight, bringing down a blanket of North Sea mist. The thick weather was, in fact, an inordinate piece of good luck—it would make it all the more difficult for his inevitable pursuers to find him. Flamborough Head itself was the best indicator of his former position, and it was now out of sight due either to the fog, or the current, or both.

Serapis and *Richard* were now independent vehicles again. Despite her rump of a mainmast, the frigate looked far better than her conqueror, and would certainly sail better. The depth at which *Richard* sat in the water was worrisome, particularly since he had ordered the wreckage of all the eighteen-pounders dumped overboard. Ominously, the Indiaman failed to rebound with the shedding of more than 12 tons of weight.

"The scoops are barely clearing the waterline," Dale came up to report. After so many hours below, even the overcast daylight caused him a hard squint. "With respect, sir, we must expect she will not survive the day."

"This pessimism does not become you, Lieutenant. Have you measured the rise since we disposed of the eighteens?"

"Yes."

"And?"

"We have held our own."

"Well, then, perhaps we write the lady off too easily!"

Dale sighed. "I said, *we held our own*. If the guns had not been sunk, we would certainly have been even further behind. And I cannot vouch for the patience of the men."

"That is immaterial to the present crisis, sir. I expect you to govern that situation. Or if your wound prevents you, I can assign someone else in your place."

With a flash of persecution in his eyes, Dale gave a farcically stiff salute and climbed back into his hole.

The question of what to do about Landais had occupied Jones only intermittently thus far, but was growing more insistent as the hours passed. Obviously, the man could not be counted upon for aid should the enemy appear. Nor, for that matter, could Jones expect much help from Ricot. Both *Alliance* and *Le Cerf* were already far to the south, too distant to intervene should battle come. True, *La Pallas* was still close by, and her captain was made of better stuff. Cottineau had his own prize to protect, however, and would reasonably be expected to run from a superior force. Though Jones had survived many independent cruises in his career, he never before felt so alone as that day, surrounded by so many allies.

With a single topsail set on the foremast, *Richard* drifted in controlled fashion to the south-east. Staring idly down at the water, Jones traced a strand of foam as it materialized from the north and disappeared into the mist to the south. The first recourse, he thought, should have been a meeting of the captains on the flagship. But what would be the point? Landais would only further erode Jones's authority by refusing to recognize his summons. Ricot and Cottineau might easily decline to act against Landais, citing the independence insured by the damnable concordat. The conclusion was inescapable, then, that he could not move against Landais until he reached an allied port. Until then, he could do nothing but collect sufficient evidence of Landais's conduct for the happy day of his court martial.

"Mr. Mayrant?"

"Here, sir."

"Here, I have a task for you . . . a bit of research," Jones said as he pulled the boy aside.

By late in the afternoon the motley flotilla managed to make some headway east. Jones's first impulse had been to confound his pursuers by sailing not toward but away from the closest safe port, but *Richard* was too badly mauled for such a fine strategy. Pure good luck would have to suffice this time.

He stood an all-day vigil, watching the Indiaman subside into the water. With each passing hour, his perch on the quarterdeck seemed less lofty. At three bells on the first dog-watch, the jolly-boat from *La Pallas* came alongside. There was a four-man crew aboard, and their only purpose at first seemed to be to sail around the Indiaman, touring the devastation. This impertinence set Jones to simmering. When the boat finally came around to his starboard beam again, he hailed it. "Good day, friends! Alas, if you are here for the tea, I fear you are too late!"

As Frenchmen often do, the lieutenant in the bows pretended not to notice the sarcasm of others. "I come with the compliments of the Captaine de Brulôt Cottineau de Kerloguen, and to suggest, perhaps, that we redouble our pace toward a prize port," he said with a chipper air. But then he frowned. "But I am afraid to report, *contre-amiral,* that you are sinking!"

Jones's reply was civil, but taut. "You may tell le Captaine de Brulôt Cottineau that I welcome his compliments, but must confess I cannot at this moment improve our speed."

The lieutenant nodded to his boatswain, and the jolly-boat was on its way back to *La Pallas.* "In that case," he called as he departed, "le Captaine de Brulôt Cottineau de Kerloguen wishes you good luck, and safe passage to the Texel."

Jones started at this. "The Texel? Mister Stacey, beg remind me: did I ever give an order to proceed to the Texel?"

"No, sir," Stacey replied from the wheel.

"Did I in fact specify that our destination is Dunkirk?"

"You did."

"Then can someone explain to me why *La Pallas* is making for Holland?"

At this impossible question, Stacey looked like a man begging to be interrupted. His reply was indeed preempted as sixteen men, blackened by soot-stained perspiration, tumbled onto the deck. Dale was the last to appear, his face made even more ghastly by the blood seeping from his freshened head wound.

"What's the meaning of this, Mister Dale?" Jones thundered.

"The pumps are under water," came the answer. "The orlop is gone."

Jones paused as he governed his anger. Exhausted tars were scattered on the deck below, staring at him. The sun was beginning to peek under the overcast from the west, and the moment (damn the circumstance!) seemed to demand realism. He turned away, and as if reassuring himself of the ship's materiality, clapped a hand on the rail.

"I see. Very well, then," he said in a voice that suggested all was

proceeding according to plan. "Our flag will be moved to *Serapis.*
Alert all hands: we abandon ship."

Dutiful to the last, the Indiaman did not succumb for ten more
hours. Every minute was profitably used: first Brooke and his
wounded were brought off, then the prisoners, then whatever supplies worth saving. The transfer proceeded with an antic
determination, as the carpenters could not guarantee that *Richard*
would not take a sudden lunge for the bottom. The instruments
of Jones's office—his commission and orders and logbook—were
among the last items rescued, along with a kit of sailmaker's tools
and a pipe of sweet water. His copy of the damnable concordat,
he would later find, was also among the recovered treasures.

By first light the next morning, *Richard* was listing so heavily
Jones was loathe to let anyone return to her, though virtually all
of his personal property, including his wardrobe, his set of plate,
and his personal correspondence, were still aboard. All hands were
gathered on *Serapis* when the end finally came. Jones had *Serapis*
lie-to in the stiffening breeze four hundred yards to the east. From
there they watched the old, black hull turn over until she lingered
on her beam-ends; they all heard a sound very much like a great
sigh as the air rushed out of her. Then she resumed her roll and
vanished.

Stricken, Jones found himself bereft of even the conventional
pieties. Turning to Stacey to belabor some minor exception with
Serapis's rig, he emitted a croak, frowned, and remained silent.
Thirty-four corpses—the 34 he had not had time to lay properly
to rest—had gone down with the Indiaman. In the confusion of
her last hours, no one could compile a list of their names. And in
the near future, he thought, some mother or sister or sweetheart
would realize her beloved is overdue and suffer the particular grief
that comes with cruel, endless, uncertain absence.

Yet, only a few hundred feet beneath him, an unseen evacuation had already begun. The wreck of the Indiaman had righted itself on her keel at a depth of twenty fathoms, and was planing its way down to her rest at a gentle, stately angle. Churning seawater had flushed away every loose object from the exposed decks, surrounding the hull with a glittering halo of debris. Among the orbiting objects was a small velvet bag filled with human teeth and fastened with a gold drawstring. Joseph Two Fires had dropped that gift surreptitiously in the water as he witnessed the death of the great ship.

The cloud also included the draped bodies of the anonymous dead, which were issuing one by one from the body of the vessel like tiny white spawn. In time all the liberated corpses would break the surface again. *Serapis* and her consorts would be over the horizon, the spectators on Flamborough Head long since gone home. By then, current and tide would sweep the dead toward the shores to the west, where, along a front as wide as the breeze, they would at last begin the invasion of Britain.

XIX.

My dear one:

What is it like for you to love a murderer? For that is what they would call me, if certain facts were known of my conduct in the last few hours. I know it is foolish to send such damaging intelligence in this unsecured form, but as you can see, I am unconcerned. Your devotion sustains me. That these poor confessions will soon find their way beneath your compassionate gaze is a balm I scarce deserve. The price must be my complete forthrightness. And so I resume.

Our march down the eastern shores of Cayugah Lake proceeded with little further incident. In our eight days on the trail, we burned five towns with a total of 150 houses in them; we uprooted and burned 500 acres of cropland, 400 tons of fruit, 250 tons of stored nuts and meal, and 30 acres of wild grape. I was also proud to have preserved four pits of seed corn, despite the determination of Mr. Israel and a fair number of the men that the Indians never return. As they all see, this country is as fine as any in Pennsylvania or New England, and there is a covetousness in their eyes they lacked when their goal was merely to remain alive. Their conviction rose like the shafts of black smoke that stretched out behind us. The men were further emboldened, I think, by the plumes that answer ours on the west shore, from the vicinity of Colonel Dearborn's operations against the villages there. So many fires were burning on both shores that the odor of our heroism mingled over the middle of the lake, casting a pall that turned the water to an ashen gray.

The southern extremity of the lake is blighted by a swamp. With so little solid shore to build upon, the place will surely never fall under the improving hand of civilization. The eastern edge of the bog is marked by a chasm in gray stone ending in a wide and pleasing waterfall, beside which our party was delighted to camp for an evening. Fully seventy yards tall from top to bottom, the torrent exceeds anything I have seen in America or France. Even in late summer, a great volume of water flows over this precipice. It is curious to think, in fact, that its remoteness is the whole cause of its anonymity. If it were within a hundred miles of London or Paris, poets would have sung its praises for centuries. Here, not even our native scouts have a name for it. That night I slept on a flat shelf of dimpled stone beneath the torrent, my senses lulled by the percussion of water on rock.

We were ordered to rendezvous with the main army just before the Great Pine Swamp south of Catherine's Town. As we marched through the remains of the latter village, the fresh tracks of thousands of men and horses were still impressed in the mud from Sullivan's passage before us. I took special note of the fate of the cabin we had built for the old crone: it was still standing. Moreover, Sullivan had ordered the donation of further stores, which were piled up in a mass on the back wall of her cabin. I saw, however, no sign of the doleful beneficiary.

My pickets contacted the rearguard of Clinton's brigade in the afternoon of the 28th, instant. At that moment, my command effectively ended as the men were reunited with their home units and disappeared into the general mass. With the success of the expedition, spirits in the camp were as high I had ever seen them. On the way north, the men might well have been the Athenians somberly setting forth to face the Persians alone at Marathon. But as the army descended into Pennsylvania, the march became something of a moving fete, with jokes and laughter in the ranks and songs around the cooking fires at night. The general mood was directly contrary to mine, which was lightened by hope in the beginning but has now sunk into as abject a despair as I have ever known.

Without even a thought to wash the mud of the trail from my boots, I proceeded directly to Sullivan to present myself. I found him down at the bank of the Senecah River, reading his quartermaster's reports. At his feet and scattered thickly in the shallow bed of the river were hundreds of dead packhorses. They had been shot very recently, I judged, as the bodies had not yet begun to stink. Several of the creatures were still blowing their last breaths into the water.

"During the Crusades, the Normans would poison streams with rotting corpses," he said to me in lieu of a greeting. "We, of course, are not so barbarous as to use human flesh!"

"How fortunate for the enemy, that we are so civilized."

Sullivan smiled but still did not look at me.

"My commission is discharged," I continued. "The particulars are listed here. We had no losses."

He took the paper, ran his eyes over it. "Thank you, Captain. You have done yourself some much-needed credit."

This brief exchange represented the entirety of my welcome. I did not care, however, as I was anxious to confirm with my own eyes that Polyxena was safe.

Proceeding thence to the center of the camp, I failed to find her near the artillery park. Nor was she to be found among the tents of Clinton's brigade. Convinced, then, that she must have insisted on a spot down near the breezes from the river, I searched up and down the bank. The only party I found there, though, was Josiah Hopkins' mobile tannery, which seemed to be doing a fine business.

Finally, and with increasing alarm, I searched the prisoner's stockade. There was only one resident there—another captured Senecah scout, who was sitting with a distant look on his face, muttering to himself as he alternately clenched the toes on one bare foot, then the other. Conversation with him looked unpromising, but I was obliged to try.

"You there! Has there been another prisoner here? A woman—in a green dress? Have you seen her?"

The brave met my gaze. But instead of an answer, he gathered a smile on his face. The expression ended as a broad grin, his eyes blazing, and had the discomfiting quality of a threat about it. In truth, his expression could have equally betokened incomprehension or madness. But I took no time to learn which.

I found Clinton sitting on a folding chair outside his marquee. From the disarray of his uniform, I could see he was only just awake.

"Ah, Severence! How stands the glass around?"

Instead of the refrain, I gave a perfunctory salute and demanded to know where I might find the prisoner whose safety he guaranteed (but, alas, I asked not in so many words).

"She is in her tent, of course," he said.

"Unfortunately, there does not appear to be a tent."

"Curious. Are you sure?"

"Quite sure."

He blinked. "You must be mistaken, dear boy. Pray look again."

"Sir, I assure you I have scoured this camp."

It was impossible for me to keep an edge of impatience from my voice. Clinton did not object, however, adopting instead an expression of grave injury, as if some injustice were done upon him.

"Then there needs to be an investigation, I say! Inquiries must be made!"

Thereupon I turned and left him without another word. I suspected then that only one man would tell me where Polyxena was.

Sullivan was still where I had left him, by the river. Unger was seated beside him, taking notes at a field desk. This time Sullivan looked at me.

"Captain Severence, how fortunate for us to see you again so soon."

"With respect, sir, I must know what has become of Polyxena."

"Polyxena?" Sullivan frowned, looked to Unger.

"The name he has given his squaw," the secretary informed him.

"Ah, yes. She was shot trying to escape, I understand. Very soon after you left us."

I stood there, stunned, for some seconds. Sullivan resumed dictating a letter to Unger.

"General," I pressed, interrupting him. "Am I to understand that the prisoner is in the hospital?"

"You may understand that the prisoner is *dead*, Captain."

"I see. But begging the general's pardon, I think it singular that she attempted to escape at all, bearing in mind her broken leg . . ."

"Blast you, man, I didn't see her die! The report was made to me, and I accepted it, as you shall. Now if you please?" he said, inclining his head toward Unger.

"If I might know the name of the officer who reported such an implausible circumstance, I would stand in the general's debt."

"You are already in my debt, Captain, for suffering your damnable impertinence! Now get out of my sight!"

My alarm must have been all too evident on my face, as Unger seemed to enjoy this exchange very much. He sat with a cocksure expression, his quill stuck jauntily behind his ear, his legs stretched out beyond the end of his desk.

That was when I noticed he was wearing a pair of new leather boots. And it seemed to me that his pleasure only increased as he noticed me staring at them.

"Would it inconvenience the general if I requested to view the body?"

"It has been disposed of," Unger pronounced, shifting his feet, "in a manner deemed appropriate."

I took this as an admission of guilt on his part.

"I am obligated to inform the general that countenancing such a . . . a *crime* is unworthy of this cause," I said, biting off the words as I produced them. "I am astonished. There will be consequences, he may be assured."

"Captain, you are hereby ordered to gather your kit and report ahead to Tioga. Once there, you will confine yourself to your tent until such time as I call for you."

"Consequences!" I raged, and marched back up the bank. In truth, I had no understanding of what I was saying at that moment. I was leaving myself open for charges of insubordination and threatening a superior officer, but such distant eventualities seemed insignificant to me. Circuiting the camp, I began to feel the same visceral disgust I had felt upon first discovering the tannery. My face red with fury, stomping, gesticulating at an unseen Sullivan, Unger, George Washington, I must have seemed very much a madman.

After these hot perambulations, I wanted nothing more than to sit in my tent and pity my poor Polyxena. Instead, due to that trick of the mind that makes the dearest faces the most ephemeral, I found that her face had already faded in my memory. This inflicted on me fresh squalls of guilt. It was vanity alone that made me abandon her to her murderers. I had left with delusions of accomplishing something and had achieved nothing but a wan imitation of Sullivan's method. In my headlong rush to distinguish myself, I had proved myself no better than those I had so arrogantly despised.

Perhaps you feel I am hard on myself. Perhaps securing Clinton's assurances should have been enough to answer my responsibilities to my prisoner. Perhaps you think my self-loathing another manifestation of my vanity, and think me indulgent for expressing it here. I think, indeed, that I have no idea what you might believe—I fear I don't know you at all. But an awareness of my thoughts at the time is essential to understanding what I did next.

Indeed, I would obey Sullivan's orders and proceed ahead. I had my equipment packed on a horse that evening. What I did not plan to do, however, was to idle myself waiting for the army to arrive at Tioga; for in the Lord's sweet name, my days of serving at Sullivan's pleasure were finally and utterly at an end. My plan was to leave camp just before the dawn and to keep going, without rest, until Sullivan's face was as fully faded in my mind as Polyxena's.

There was only one task to perform before I escaped.

My errand took me to Unger's tent. Like mine, it was of the modest size typical of junior officers, just tall enough for a man to stand in. A lantern shone inside, confirming for me that his accursed person was within. The tent was at the riverbank, close to a thicket. There concealed, I waited for my opportunity.

Some minutes later he appeared at the flap with his uniform coat off and a wooden privy seat folded under his arm. Under the gibbous moon and clear sky, I could see, with a shudder of disgust, that he was wearing his fine new boots. Following him, I watched as he descended toward the water, erected his seat over the hole, and laid his toilet rag at his side.

My single concession to Unger's humanity was to allow him to complete his movement. But as he reached for his rag, I came up from behind and laid the butt of my pistol athwart his skull.

The latter precaution did not render him unconscious as much as cooperatively insensate. With little resistance and only a low murmur from his insufferable throat, I pulled up his breeches for him, tied his hands, and led him into the woods. As we walked, he regained his wits.

"What the devil? Se . . . Severence?"

I was not listening to him as much as for the telltale break of a twig, the whistle of some sleepless bird. Despite their defeats, the Senecah had never abandoned their vigil at our camps, never left it safe for a man to go out alone into the forest at night. Their predations only seemed to become more desperate, more wantonly savage, as we burned them out of their homelands. As recently as two nights before, a young private from Albany went off to relieve himself, despite blanket orders to the contrary. His remains were retrieved the next morning from three separate locations.

"What are you doing? What's the meaning of this?"

I led him to a place between our sentries. The only sounds at that moment were the steady carpentry of the insects and Unger's labored breathing.

"Severence, answer me, damn you! Tell me what I've done!"

"I'd hold my peace, if I were you," I answered.

"This is madness. If you and I have differences, let us discuss them rationally, like gentlemen."

"Let me understand—do you suggest I treat of our differences rationally, as you failed to do for Polyxena?"

Something shifted on the floor of dry leaves to the left. Unger heard it and turned to me with redoubled urgency.

"Severence, hear the truth: I had nothing to do with that. Sullivan does not involve me in all his affairs."

"Is it true she tried to escape?"

"I don't know! Sullivan knows."

We heard no more sounds, but something still more ominous: the crickets around us had stopped singing.

"In the name of God, man, you're going to kill us both!"

"Tell me then, where did you get those boots?"

Unger gaped at me.

"My boots? What of them?"

"You feign badly, Lieutenant."

"Feign at what? Are you insane?"

"Admit your crime and save your life."

"Very well, then! I admit my crime!"

"The crime of what?" I pressed.

"Of whatever you want! For the love of God, Severence!"

In a sudden eruption of shadows, man-shaped phantoms converged on us from right and left. I heard something whistle as it cut the air, and the muffled rending of what used to be Unger's collarbone. The lieutenant's body whipped to the ground like a snapped sapling, and then the shapes moved toward me. I fell backward and fired my pistol above one of the intruders. The shadows scattered.

With that small opening, I rolled to my feet and ran back to the camp. Though I was prepared to fall down or take cover at the slightest sound of firing or pursuit, no one followed me. I was back inside the pickets, among the ranks of tents, when I finally stopped running.

And so, that quickly, it was done. The only sounds of the struggle were the whistle of a tomahawk, which was barely audible, and the report of my pistol, which was ignored. There was such common occasion, after all, for our sentries to fire into the woods when their challenges went unanswered. The men had learned to sleep through random discharges in the forest.

I left at first light. My conscience, at first, was clear: Unger had only found the fate he fairly deserved, so tainted was he with the odor of atrocity. To murder, to mutilate, to render one's adversaries into the products of animals—these were irredeemable acts. My only regret, at first, was that justice had to be taken by stealth, in a manner that could be mistaken for an accident.

But the trail south was long, and in that time other regrets were born. I had taken the task of vengeance upon myself, after all, rather than leave it to Providence. This was my vanity, to presume to set a world right that did not wish to be corrected, to arrogate to myself the wisdom to teach such lessons. Was it not possible that Unger's disappearance would only allow the rise of someone still more odious? Would not the death of an officer excuse the murder of still more prisoners?

With each step of my horse, my righteous surety died. The forest, too, was recoiling, dying. The leaves were touched with yellow and red, and stirred by a breeze that hinted of the cold to come. Red squirrels dashed nervously across my path and on the boughs over me. A vixen walked the trail far ahead for some minutes, bathing me in the musk of her scent, until she cast back a wary glance and vanished into the brush.

Chilled by the mere idea of autumn, I turned up the collar of my coat and sank more deeply into my saddle. For the next few miles, I determined to think only of your face. In that image, I aspired at last to a joy that was unbounded and unmixed. Though I return a different man, with something subtracted from me, I live in hope that you will accept me, despite the ugliness I have revealed to you. Are my hopes in vain, my love?

There is a phrase the churchmen use: *Vox clamatis in deserto,* which means "a voice crying in the desert." It is supposed to inspire advocates of moral wisdom in lonely places. But I have now been to the wilderness, unlike the churchmen. You may tell them from me, when next you see one: the desert is silent.

JOHN

XX.

BY THE SPRING of 1780, Portsmouth had been under blockade for more than five years. First, the Royal Navy sloop *Scarborough*, 20 guns, stood a solitary vigil off the mouth of the Piscataqua. She was later joined by others—aloof, opportunistic British privateers; the occasional frigate; itinerant ships of the line on their way to more significant postings south. Their sails had become fixtures in the picture windows of rich Portsmouthians, many of whom were familiar enough with the sea-trade to know that blockade duty was miserable duty. To watch the warships' pointless evolutions, their endless beating up and running down before the wind, offered some consolation for the damage they did to legitimate American commerce.

Illegitimate commerce was another matter. As the merchants too fainthearted to challenge the blockade were finally bankrupted or bought out, a healthy industry rose in smuggling and privateering. The docks were busier in 1779 than they had been in 1778; there was every expectation that 1780 would be better still. By then, only the most unenterprising of patriots still cursed the sails flitting on the horizon. Some in the better houses in town had good reason to toast them.

Rebeccah, too, was on a kind of blockade duty, running a course of errands that covered a lot of ground but achieved little. She was often seen at the shops, seldom buying anything other than medicine. She was so often unescorted on the streets above the harbor that the wives of Portsmouth—properly engaged in constructive pursuits like embroidering napkins and taking tea— would remark on her. The remarks matured into full-blown gossip when she became a common sight by the dockyards, impeccably attired of course, but still unattended.

Is she waiting for someone to return by sea? they wondered. Inquiries were made. There was a sweetheart, a captain in the Continental Army, who had gone on campaign in the West and had still not returned. Yet wouldn't he more likely arrive by post-carriage from Boston rather than by sea?

Was she compromised, then? Did she somehow ruin herself with some casual laborer, some broken-nosed Portuguese? Again, inquiries were made, but not a shred of corroboration ever appeared.

Perhaps she was insane. As the winter came and she was seen trudging through snow, this theory finally became the consensus. For not only was she visiting the docks, but walking on them, exposing herself to all the grime and stenches particular to the trade. Was it not known on good authority that a panicked goat once soiled her as it was lifted into the hold of a smuggler? Shat upon on her shoulder and—pray, sit down for this—*in her hat?*

Even Rebeccah pondered the motive for her wanderings. The gossips assumed she was looking for something, when, in fact, she was motivated most by the need to get away. Though she had not thought of Severence in months, she had absorbed from him an attachment to the sea and ships. Somehow, though she had never spent a single night afloat, she had in her own mind crossed the threshold from lubberdom to seasoned mariner. The change was at the same time both trivial and profound: it was nothing more than an understanding, deep in the bones, that water is not the barrier it seems. The same drop of water that washes the road-stead of Kittery may—in fact, *must*—wash the shores of Penzance or Cape Verde or the roads of Jamaica. And if a mindless drop of inanimacy may accomplish this feat, why not her? Why not her?

She got as close to the vessels as she dared. Courting danger, she passed in arm's reach of men who smacked their lips at a hint of female odor She heard them whisper terms for parts of her anatomy she had not known she had. She saw the unfamiliar tools of manual work around her and tubs set to boiling with viscous stuff. There were winches and coiled ropes and wicker cages full of chickens. Above her head, there were bowsprits and cargoes swinging on slender ropes, and below her, shit and dead fish. All around, she saw a wealth of dangers that could, all of them, injure her body or her dignity or her precarious repute. She was afraid, and she was attracted to the prospect of her useless existence finally erased by these forces. She never felt more at home.

In a dark corner, in full view of her, a boy stood relieving himself against the hull of a privateer. Transfixed with disgust, she met his eyes, staring back at her with an air of brazen abjectness. Such a spasm of lust in a beardless boy! she thought. If he only knew the execrable substance of the body he so desired! Her gaze then dropped impulsively to the reddish bulb between his fingers. The arc of his urine straightened and sputtered as he hardened before her eyes.

Distracted, she didn't see the heavy meat cask as it swung in its blocks. Both moving with little guidance, the two objects—the cask and Rebeccah's body—met corner-to-shoulder. The cask went on its way undeflected, but she was propelled off her feet and planted nose-first into the dock. Someone shouted a warning after the fact. Rebeccah felt the bump and the world tumbling around her and then nothing.

Or more exactly, less than nothing. At what seemed like the very next moment, she was propped up against a locker, an oily rag shoved tightly against her nose. She became conscious of a concert of squinting mugs above and around her. The oily rag was saturated with her blood. And she heard a voice, very soft and slightly musical in its inflection, talking to her:

"There, now. You had quite the tumble. Take this and hold it tight, there. There's a lass. . . ."

Her eyes slowly focused on the face of the figure kneeling in front of her. It was a pleasing face, both handsome and worn rugged by wind-driven salt. The cheeks were broad and angular, the eyes green and set wide apart, the brow cut by a furrow of permanent disquiet. He was wearing an impeccable navy uniform with shining epaulettes on both shoulders. The workmen around her, she saw, were as fascinated with his virile resplendence as with her feminine dishevelment.

"Never saw a woman o' such quality touring the yards!" the officer told her. "But I think she shall be righted at last!"

That voice! The softness of it was a pleasant shock, coming from a face of such intensity, from jaws so precisely operated. It was the voice of some dew-flecked lover set in the throat of a predator. Rebeccah felt her head swim for reasons that had nothing to do with her collision with the cask.

His manners befitting his wardrobe, the officer bent to lift her to her feet. That was when she saw, with a smile, that she was a good two inches taller than her hero. He almost certainly perceived her amusement, for his expression grew very serious. Striking a very straight posture, he offered his arm. "May I show you home?" he asked.

His name was Paul Jones. He was indeed in the navy, where he held the rank of commodore. He had just arrived in Portsmouth after consultations with congress in Philadelphia. He made perfunctory mention of achievements at sea she knew nothing about, causing her the particular embarrassment that comes from meeting someone who is famous to everyone else in the world.

They arrived in front of her father's house. He turned to face her with his eyes narrowed, saying, "If I might survey the damage one last time?"

"Of course," she said, cocking her head up for him to examine the underside of her nose.

"The bleeding has stopped."

"I am in your debt," was all she could say. The blood that had been flowing from her nostrils was now supplying the blush that had broken over her face.

"If I might advise," he said, eyes twinkling, "the waterfront is no place for . . . a civilian. If the lady wishes to tour the roads, however, I would be pleased to escort her."

She cast her eyes down modestly. A stock gesture, to be sure, but it gave a lady the opportunity to examine a gentleman's stockings and shoes, which were as good a clue as any to his true nature. Jones's hosiery was white like a virgin snowdrift; his shoes were polished, but very slightly roughed. Not seriously, like someone down-at-heels, but with a light scuffing, like the shoes of a man of action.

"That would be satisfactory," she said.

"Very well then," he replied with a very definite air of expectation. "I shall call on you."

She ascended the front walk in discrete, genteel steps, and did not look back. Once inside the door, she rushed to the day parlor window and, moving the curtains as little she could, peeped outside. He was still standing there, drawn up to the full extent of his modest height, looking around at the world with an expression of philosophic contentment on his face. A typical Lothario, she thought. How remarkable, the power over their happiness some men grant to women. To women! A species that is, at best, ornamental, companionable, useful—but never grand, never consequential, like a man. Was this God's sense of humor? she mused. Or the Devil's?

Watching him turn and walk away, it occurred to her that his name sounded familiar. It was almost laughably common—she knew of two other Paul Joneses in Portsmouth alone. But somewhere before she had heard of a sea captain by that name. Was it Severence who had mentioned him?

Her courtship with the latter seemed so long ago that she could barely conjure an image of him in her mind. Despite the fine-sounding declarations in his letters, he had not rushed to New England to see her. The newspapers, in fact, had reported the successful end of the Sullivan expedition six months before. There was no indication that he had been killed in action or taken prisoner. There was no excuse at all for his absence.

Rebeccah found, for her part, that she was only slightly curious about what had become of him. She felt no lover's torment, no transformation of eager love to jilted fury. Indeed, the party who seemed to take his disappearance the hardest was—of all people—her father. He would still ask her every morning if a letter had come through, until she tired of answering in the negative and seeing the skepticism on his face. But this was no lie: his last letter was seven months old. Her father would look away, his face contorted in nervous distraction, and they would not speak until he asked again the next morning.

Now there was this Paul Jones. Would he call on her? She looked at his receding back, the lift in his step, and thought, yes, certainly, he will call. Would she allow their acquaintance to become anything beyond the merely congenial, then? Now there's a question, she thought, idly twisting the tassel of the curtain. For while she was not formally betrothed to Severence, there had been no formal break in their courtship. And yet. . . . This Commodore Jones was very pretty and, by all indication, prided himself on his conquests. Some of these, she supposed, were French sophisticates. She found herself imagining a salon full of powdery duchesses, comtesses, marquesses, all pretty, all glittering, all far exceeding her in their charms. What could he want from her, except the kind of trivial amusement sophisticated men must find when they are stuck in small towns? When the inevitable came, then, what would she do?

Rebeccah went to her room without thinking of an answer. Though it was only midafternoon she undressed for the day and brushed her hair and, after an hour staring at a book, found she scarcely recognized the story and characters. Even then, she had no answer—except, perhaps, that it was not "nothing." She still felt full of something she could not describe, except to say that it was awful and was entirely her fault. She felt something that needed to be let out, if only she could find a receptacle strong enough. She could pour herself out upon this Jones, she thought, and he would take it all away.

So silly, she thought, to think such thoughts. She had just met the man. Let him be. He would not call.

Jones imagined a dalliance with Rebeccah Shays might bring a welcome dose of Yankee simplicity to his relations with women. He had been too long in Europe, enjoying a few successes and one hard disappointment in his campaigns. *Bon mots* and admiring glances from beneath painted lids were, he feared, not sustenance enough. To be thought of as a prize himself, competed over by wealthy *mesdames* and their winking husbands, repulsed him. He had strayed too far from the dream he'd had for his America: a storied career, a fair manor, a bit of respect, and a fecund and age-less wife. What simple needs, for a man who once had Europe at his feet!

After *Richard* was gone, his squadron rushed headlong to Hol-land. The French captains were determined to fulfill the provisions of Chaumont's concordat, which stipulated the Dutch island-port of the Texel as their final destination. Accordingly, neither Landais nor Cottineau nor Ricot answered his signals to follow him to Dunkirk. As much as the fact pained him, there was no possibil-ity at all of Jones conducting the damaged *Serapis* safely to an allied port without the protection of the French guns. The leader's only option, then, was to follow glumly. For not the first time in his career, the world refused to listen to him, and the result was disaster.

Their arrival touched off a diplomatic imbroglio that lasted for months. The Dutch, as neutrals in the current war, were non-plussed at the sudden arrival of an American squadron with a British prize. The British, hoping to win with official suasion what they had lost at sea, blockaded the port and laid diplomatic siege to the Dutch government. Their suit against the "pirate" Jones made headway among the Orangists in Amsterdam, who demanded he sail away immediately—presumably into the gracious arms of the Royal Navy. The liberals just as vociferously demanded that the freedom fighter Paul Jones be given every opportunity to settle the disposition of his prize, quarter his prisoners, and rest his men. Neither side had the power to prevail over the other.

Minister Sartine, with his usual tin ear for American sensitivities, sought to break the deadlock by resurrecting the old idea of declaring Jones to be a French contractor. Jones refused, citing his solemn vow to wage a war for liberty, no matter what the personal inconvenience, et cetera, et cetera, et cetera. Jones, attempting to be gallant, offered Pearson leave to return to England on parole. Pearson refused, fearing his crew would turn rebel in his absence. From Passy, Benjamin Franklin implored the Dutch liberals to insure three months' refuge for Jones at the Texel; the party leadership was sympathetic but denied such a pledge was in their power. At the behest of the British ambassador, the Dutch Orangists arranged to have Jones arrested; the authorities in Amsterdam refused. Jones applied to house his 500 English prisoners ashore; the Dutch authorities refused, citing vague British concerns. Jones begged the Dutch workmen to work faster on *Serapis;* they refused. The Dutch brought up a warship, insisting Jones leave; Jones refused. And as the refusals and counter refusals mounted up, weeks and months dragged by, until Jones believed he would go mad with idleness and frustration.

Nor was the misery of his situation eased by the usual amusements ashore. The Texel was not so much a port as an offshore factory, with no scenery or women to relieve the eye and suffused at ebb tide with the stench of exposed muck. The men were irritated by the unaccountable delay in getting to a decent waterfront and looked upon Jones with disdain on those occasions when, doing ship's business, he lit out on the channel to Amsterdam. There goes Paul Jones, some said, off to rock a pretty miss in the capital, while we rot in this mud hole. There goes Paul Jones, off to spend borrowed money, while we have seen nothing from our prizes, said others.

Here comes Paul Jones! the good citizens of Amsterdam would shout, gathering around him as he landed. For the other side of the Zee was a different world, where his achievements were storied, his name toasted. Walking down the street earned him spontaneous ovations; shopkeepers ran out of their stores to shove gifts at him. Dutch soldiers wanted to shake his hand. How intoxicating was the acclaim, Jones thought, and how useless. And how he craved more, though none of it would mean his ship would be repaired any faster or his men paid.

He would have wished, at least, that this alternation of useless acclaim and bitter inactivity had a happy end. His reward was the simple fact that it did, at last, end. Thanks to an imponderable series of negotiations between Chaumont and the other parties, *Serapis* and *Count of Scarborough* were finally sold. The terms were an outrage. Jones got the minor fortune of 500 *louis d'or*, scarcely enough for a down payment on a modest farmhouse in Virginia. For his contribution to the battle, and according to the standard fleet formula, Landais was awarded 435 *louis*.

Prize shares for each ordinary seaman amounted to seven *louis d'or*, or about five months' shipboard salary. This only just covered the 25 dollar advance the men were paid for enlisting, which most had already spent in France. This was their reward for risking their lives in the name of congress. They were fortunate, in fact, that *Richard*'s crew suffered forty percent casualties in the battle: had more of their comrades survived, they would have suffered even smaller shares. Sickened, Jones wrote letters of protest. It was no use.

The final indignity came at the end of the year, when *Countess of Scarborough* sailed to Plymouth under a neutral flag to exchange prisoners. Jones was in the city at the time, attending a series of balls where the music would stop and the collected devotees of liberty would pause to clap their gloved hands in his honor. When he returned to the Texel, he found that the British prisoners, including Pearson, were exchanged not for the Americans starving and dying in Mill Prison, but for French officers and men captured from d'Orvillier's farcical exercise in the Channel.

Jones was sick again; he wrote letters. It was no use—except this time they gave him a medal, the *Ordre du Mérite Militaire*. Such baubles should not have consoled him, but like the cheers of the Dutch and French crowds, they did. He wore his decoration at every official function and had it chiseled onto the bust he commissioned of himself. And when his thoughts turned to the Americans still incarcerated, still suffering, he took out the *Ordre* and gazed at it, and found he could still sleep.

By this time Jones had had enough of "victory" in Europe. If he was to be misused in this way, he decided, it was better to be misused at home, by one's own countrymen. *Alliance*'s hold might still do the cause some good if it were filled with gunpowder, uniforms, and other supplies for Washington. This, at last, was surely the kind of simple project everyone must support.

Alliance's captain had made defiant noises throughout the voyage from L'Orient to Holland. But when there was some possibility of meeting Jones at the Texel, Landais fled to Amsterdam, and then Paris. Fortunately, Jones posted his pre-written letter to Franklin the moment he landed, detailing all the events at Flamborough Head, with particular emphasis on Landais's treachery.

He included testimonials from Dale, Lunt, and Mayrant. The packet beat Landais to Passy, forcing him to face Franklin when the latter was armed with the facts. The minister's report several weeks later gave a rare bit of good news: Landais had been convinced to give up command of *Alliance.*

Despite Jones's determination never to think of Landais again, he heard scraps of news about him in the following months. Landais had gone to Franklin's nemesis on the American Commission, Arthur Lee, seeking redress. Lee was at first sympathetic, it was said. But then, at a dinner aboard a sloop Lee had procured as a consolation for him, Landais pulled a steak knife on Lee for daring to cut his own pork before the captain was served. From that point, even Lee would have nothing to do with him.

The mystery of Landais perplexed everyone else, but was transparent to Jones. There was a particularly weak cast of mind, he understood, that was unhinged by command of a ship. To a character short of security, the captaincy demanded an impossible combination of omniscience and blindness. To know the limits of one's men, the captain has to read the signs, including the thousand little insubordinations that arise but mean so little. To make every visible act, every skeptical arch of eyebrow, every unbelayed sheet a test of personal authority was to court madness. Landais had courted madness, married her, and consummated the union.

Jones did not understand Landais's acts, but he understood the man. Henriette learned as much on her last day at the Texel, as she waited for the skiff to take her through the channel to Amsterdam.

"You let him go, and I was sure you would kill him, fight a duel, or some such thing," she told Jones as they stood on his quarterdeck rail looking south-east. The city seemed to her like a distant ship, its tallest spires like masts on the very farthest horizon.

"That kind of act would have no use."

"You did not fight a duel with a man named Simpson some years ago?" she pressed.

He grimaced. "Simpson was insubordinate and devious, but he was not mad. His acts were those of a rational man, and he behaved as such in our . . . meeting."

"I see," she said. Her crew had finished loading their cargo into the skiff's flat bottom. Though Henriette had first boarded the Indiaman with a full carriage-load of impedimenta, the fire had left her with nothing but the bloody, threadbare suit and beaver-lined boots she wore on the day of the battle. For the trip across the North Sea, Jones had lent her some rags from the ship's slops chest: a pair of grease-streaked pantaloons, a smock, a tarred cap. Quite a miserable ensemble, yes, but it had the fortunate side effect of helping the crew to accept her at last. Where they would barely look at her before, her service in the cockpit and the deplorable state of her wardrobe combined to earn her a degree of sympathy. This acceptance almost, but not quite, made up for the total loss of all her sketches.

Jones took her hand and placed a farewell kiss in the cleft between the second and third knuckle. He could feel the hand tremble slightly under his lips.

"I trust you will recoup your losses?" he asked.

"Of course, *mon ami!* The work is replaceable. This cruise . . . has shown me so very much. I regret nothing!"

"Then I am pleased."

They looked into each other's faces for a last time. Jones hoped the fact that he regretted inviting her did not show on his face. Henriette, for her part, hoped that he would not perceive the feeling that had preoccupied her since September 23: the horrible fear, as her hands continued to shake, that she would never draw again.

"Until next time, in Paris!" she called to him from the skiff.

He waved, smiled, but didn't reply as she receded down the channel.

Jones did encounter Landais again, months later, though he did not know it at the time. It was in Philadelphia, where Jones was presenting an account of his expenses in Europe to congress and Landais was being court-martialed. The latter was a happy event Jones did not choose to attend personally, sending affidavits instead. He was standing in front of the hall, sharing pleasantries with Robert Morris, when his attention was drawn to a commotion behind him. Turning, he saw a vaguely familiar pair of rounded shoulders moving quickly away from him. He then returned to his conversation with Morris.

Later, Jones learned what he had missed. A rumor was circulating, very certainly at Landais's instigation, that Landais had confronted the great John Paul Jones on Chestnut Street in Philadelphia, and in full view of all present, had challenged him to *une affaire d'honneur!* Jones learned that he himself had cravenly refused to answer this call, and that Landais, in contempt, spat directly into the commodore's face.

Though Jones had no memory of these events, they were very good material for a rumor. As the story seemed to spread and become embellished with even more fictions-upon-fictions (Jones had made apologies to Landais; Jones had pissed himself with fear), he was forced to publish an advertisement in the *Freeman's Journal.* It read, in part:

BE IT HERE ACKNOWLEDGED, on this fourteenth day of May, seventeen-hundred-and-eighty, that the Commodore John Paul Jones, of the Navy of the United States, herein and upon his personal Honor, does DENY any and all lies perpetrated upon the publick by certain disreputable Parties. Be it known also that the Commodore John Paul Jones does deplore and condemn the barbarous practice of DUELLING, and if any of the aforesaid DEFAMERS would desire to dispute the QUALITY of these statements, the commodore would be pleased to take the field against such Parties at a time and place of mutual agreement . . .

Thereafter, he heard no new rumors. The decision of the court martial, unfortunately, was not rendered before Jones was forced to leave Philadelphia for his new command in Portsmouth.

While all of Jones's friends in congress and some of his enemies agreed that his victory over *Serapis* merited some reward, there were precious few plums available for naval officers in 1780. The Continental Navy was too depleted of ships, and there were too many rival claimants with Congressional patronage, for a suitable command to be found for him. Jones offered a Solomonic solution by volunteering to take command of an unfinished vessel: *America*, a 74-gun ship of the line, then under construction in Portsmouth. *America*'s keel had been laid, Jones understood, back in '77, so he imagined she must be close to completion. Once launched, she would throw twice the metal of any ship he had commanded before. Provided he could light a fire under Colonel Langdon, the local navy agent, he might be able to get back into the fight before the war was over, in a vessel (at last!) big enough to make a difference.

To his relief, congress unanimously agreed. As secretary of the Marine, Robert Morris was pleased to draft his new commission and present it to the commodore at a small gathering of his well-wishers—principally, Morris's wife and staff. Jones took the commission, had a drink, but did not stay long. *America* was waiting for him.

The trip to Portsmouth would take nearly three weeks. He looked forward to only one stop along the way: a visit to Washington at his headquarters in Morristown, New Jersey.

The commander in chief had kept winter quarters there, keeping a wary eye on the British army in New-York. The conceit was that he was "blockading" the British, when in fact, with control of the water, the British commandant Sir Henry Clinton could and did come out to strike anywhere he pleased—the Hudson highlands, Connecticut, North Carolina. At the least, Washington would make the enemy pay some price for moving along the roads to Philadelphia.

Washington met Jones in the modest townhouse where he had spent the winter. Jones was shown into the parlor and asked to wait for the general. The commodore had worked hard at his appearance that day. His uniform was newly laundered, his hair lightened with the best powder, his shoes shining like mirrors, his new *Ordre du Mérite* prominent in his buttonhole. But when Washington finally entered, Jones found it was impossible to feel anything but diminished in his presence.

The general had an advantage of at least ten inches on him, as Jones expected. Yet it was more than an issue of height or rank or fame. From the first second he set eyes on Washington, he was conscious of a physical prowess he could not precisely explain. The way the man crossed a room and extended a hand reminded him of the lope of a fine stallion. The way he stared Jones in the face, with an expression that seemed more to invite inspection than to perform it, seemed to evoke casual excellence. He was too broad-faced to be conventionally handsome, with an overlarge jaw, protruding brows, and weariness showing around his eyes. Nevertheless, he seemed to present the very essence of what the ancients—not those sallow, hollow-chested descendants, the Christians—called *virtus.*

"Commodore Jones, I've heard so much about you," the general said, taking Jones's comparatively tiny hand between his fingers and shaking it. The general honored him by using the flag rank Jones assumed in France, though congress had, in fact, refused to confirm him in it. Curiously, the pitch of Washington's voice was higher than his stature suggested. Jones made a deferential reply and followed the general's lead as he fell, somewhat heavily, into a chair.

Their conversation skipped lightly over diverse subjects—the political situation in France, the weather in Philadelphia, Jones's prospects in Portsmouth, the expense of his victory at Flamborough Head. Jones hoped the supplies he brought over in *Alliance* would prove useful; the general assured him they would. Washington was appropriately empathetic over the loss of *Bon Homme Richard* and the heavy toll—108 killed, 47 wounded. Have letters been sent to the families? he asked. Yes, in my own hand, replied Jones. Good, came the response, the army needs more commanders like yourself. Have you ever considered the land service? No, Jones demurred, the sea vexes me, but it runs in my veins. Like any proper spouse, Washington joked, somewhat cryptically.

Of course, the sum total of all the men Jones had lost in all his battles were as nothing compared to the devastation bearing down on Washington. Twelve hundred were killed or wounded at Brandywine, eleven hundred at Germantown, two thousand at Long Island. Jones could suffer the total loss of three or four vessels the class of *America* without matching these disasters.

But these facts did not buoy Jones's mood. What they meant, in fact, was that for all of Jones's success and talent and effort, what he did or did not accomplish at sea was not very important, compared to the momentous events on land. What they also meant was that a man such as Washington, whose qualities made him universally respected and beloved by most, could go on this way, losing battles and losing men, and still be regarded as indispensable. Though he was a confident man, and to some degree proud of his successes, Jones knew that many people would gladly dispose of him if he gave them the excuse of defeat. These were simply the facts.

Washington invited him for a walk in the gardens behind the house. Again, Jones saw that fine rocking gait, that splendid energy in motion. He feared that, in comparison, he looked like a terrier scurrying beside the general. And he imagined further that Washington, in his respect for all things of quality, would look down upon him the same way, with that same look of wan paternal pleasure, whether the commodore was a decorated hero or a prize show dog.

Jones gave no hint of any of these thoughts. He made his one mistake, however, when he complained of the endless delays he had seen in Passy, at the Texel, and at L'Orient, when he was waiting for *Alliance* to load. At this, the general disagreed with him for the first time.

"But you must know, sir, that it has always been the soldier's job to wait. It is his particular curse, but it may also have its own virtues."

"Well, yes, but . . ."

"To use that time for contemplation is no vanity," he went on without noting Jones's interjection, "for there is no shortcut to victory over the forces against us. Better leave impatience to them. It is their weakness."

At that, Jones surrendered the point. There was no arguing with him about this strategy, because it was Washington's particular genius to win by not losing too often. That his army had more or less survived for five years was testament enough.

They parted at the garden gate. For the first time, Washington looked down at Jones's *Ordre du Mérite Militaire*, hanging there by its little blue ribbon. "We are all most proud of what you have done," he said, laying his finger lightly on one of the medal's eight golden points. "Am I correct to assume a title comes with this?"

"Chevalier, merely," Jones said with a dismissive toss. "Such personal honors are the least dear to me."

"Well, then, Chevalier John Paul Jones, I thank you for your visit, and for the sake of our cause, bid you good luck."

And Washington, pulling himself up to his full height, saluted Jones formally, stiffly, like a private. The gesture so surprised the chevalier and touched him so deeply that he blushed with embarrassment and retreated with relief to his carriage.

As the team got under way, he gained a last look, peeping out at the oceanic expanse of the general's back as a secretary brought dispatches to him. He was sure then that he would gladly risk death for Washington's approval. He would risk it, if the idiots around him gave him the chance. It was too late for him to accept patience as a virtue. There was still too much to do.

Tight, pretty little Portsmouth was much as he remembered it three years earlier, when he assumed command of the sloop *Ranger*. It was the same, except the young women he had known then were now all married, and their younger sisters had now come of age. As his stay would likely be longer this time, he found rooms for himself in the second floor of Mrs. Purcell's boardinghouse. This was a little out of town, in the woods, but had a bedroom with a window overlooking the garden.

Within a few days he refined his routine to shipboard precision. He was up at half past six and had a light breakfast (Europe had made him stout) by seven. He was down the front stairs by half past seven, and after a last look at himself in the mirror to the left of the door, he was on the Piscataqua for the quarter-mile trip to Rising Castle island (to *America*'s stocks) by eight. After a day of cajoling and hand-holding among the temperamental carpenters, plankers, dubbers, trunnelers, and painters, he would board his boat by half past three, and be back in town well in time for the evening's round of social events.

These made up the same program of dinners, balls, races, and recitals he had attended three years earlier. They seemed more provincial now and a bit more precious, after he had seen Paris

and Amsterdam. And while Portsmouth had shrunk in the inter-
vening time, his international profile had grown, so that his
presence and his movements were matters of fascination to everyone. The season was a fine antidote to his despair after meeting
Washington.

The day ended after nine, when he would plunge into the
wooded lane leading to Mrs. Purcell's. Twice a week a hot bath
would be waiting for him in the great mahogany bathtub, where
he would sit up and read the papers from Boston, Philadelphia,
and New-York. Standing out prominently against the background
of bad news were reports of a successful end to General John Sullivan's expedition to Iroquioia. Among the corps of officers on
that campaign, he was interested to learn, was a Captain John
Wickes Severence of New-York—certainly the very same who had
served with him on *Ranger*. He felt a definite pleasure at learning
something of Severence's fate. But this was quickly replaced by a
frisson of despair: Severence, after all, represented another lost
connection, another bridge burned in his wake.

Jones's first hint that the construction of *America* was in trouble was when John Langdon declined his invitation to meet him
on Rising Castle. Apparently, the colonel was ignorant of Jones's
appointment until the commodore was actually in town, demanding to see a ship he erroneously believed to be all but ready
for launch. Jones was educated on that score on his first trip to
the stocks: not only was *America* not ready for launch after three
full years of construction, she was just a half-clad skeleton. Moreover, Langdon's men were cannibalizing her materials to construct the privateers that were making him and his fellow
Portsmouthians rich.

Jones, furious, wrote to the colonel for an explanation.
Langdon, freezingly, saw no need for one. They were all contending with scarcity, he noted. The demands of the project were

staggering, Congress was broke, and the price of wood had quin-
tupled. Had the commodore heard, asked the colonel, that there
was a war on?

The tone of this exchange was about where it had been left,
three years before. That was when Jones first proposed what he
thought quite reasonable (but to Langdon, fantastic) specifications
for *Ranger:* a new suit of sails and cordage, new guns, a copper
bottom, the mainmast shortened and restepped. When none of
these wishes came to anything, Jones made very public complaints
to the Marine Committee. And why not, since he would soon be
leaving Langdon and his pinchpenny, Yankee ilk far behind on his
way to glory and renown in Europe?

His *cursus honorum* had taken some unexpected twists.
America would not sail until Jones repaired his relationship with
the colonel. A good sailor knows when to seize the braces and back
his sails. It was long past time, then, for a campaign of a different
kind.

So he staked out a place in Pitt's taproom. In civilian clothes,
nursing a bowl of rum, he was in a good position to see everyone
coming through the door. Or if the colonel somehow slipped past
that way, he could intercept him before he mounted the stairs to
the Freemasons' lodge meeting on the third floor.

Jones was not a man given to ruminating. But lately, time had
a way of weighing heavily on his hands. Sitting there, he was looking at the dirt streets of Portsmouth, but he was thinking about
Paris, about Severence, and about that woman, La Vendahl, whose
skirts he gallantly lifted when he helped her into her carriage. He
could hear her voice, that *"merci"* that sounded like a plucked
harpstring, and about his fruitless schemes to bring her and her
tastes to Virginia. And he thought of *America* with a steady wind
over her quarter, weathering the Gris Nez as a Baltic convoy scattered before her, and the sight of Red ensigns falling from staffs

all around him, and La Vendahl smiling from the shore and clap-
ping shut her fan into her open right hand as she did at the end
of a concerto.

Langdon was there, in the street. Jones had noticed him belatedly, just as he paused to pop the top from his hollow cane and
drink from it. He was, as one might expect, a little shrunken, his
eyes a little more deeply ensconced in their cadaverous hollows.
But the cut of his jib, the gabardine suit from his tailor in Boston,
the yellow-gray tendrils of hair glued against his speckled pate,
were the same.

Jones waited until the colonel came in the door before he rose,
his best diplomat's smile on his face, hand ungloved and extended.
"Colonel! What an unexpected pleasure for us to meet again at
last!"

He honored his pledge to call on Miss Rebeccah Shays. As custom
demanded, he made the acquaintance of her father first. Like Langdon, the man was a shipowner with one foot in the black market
and the other in the legitimate trades. He seemed begrudging of
his time at first, but upon formal introduction, the commodore's
reputation worked its effect on him. Permission to acquaint himself with his daughter was freely extended, with no reservations
and the usual condition that a chaperone accompany them under
"reasonable circumstances" (said Shays, with a half-wink).

The following Friday, Jones broke his routine to stroll with her
by a millpond south of town. And although the view was very fine
from there, with a clear vista to Kittery in the north, the girl was
more intent on plying him with questions.

"Is it very beautiful in France?"

"Very often. But no more than here."

"Have you met the king?"

"I was honored to be decorated by His Most Christian Majesty."

"What does he look like?"

"He is kind of aspect, serene of temperament, assiduous in his care for his people."

"What is Lafayette like?"

"His nails are very clean."

"Will we win the war?"

"I have resolved to consecrate my life to that end, regardless of the cost or any temptation to sway me toward some less perfect one."

"What are you doing here?"

"That, my dear friend, is one of the most prized secrets of our navy."

"Does it have to do with that big ship across the harbor?"

Rebeccah watched Jones flush at this innocent suggestion. The commodore had a lot to learn about keeping secrets! Of course, it was the obvious guess: every morning, everyone in town watched Jones board the four-oared pinnace and run out to Rising Castle. What else in the world could he be doing?

To his credit, Jones didn't persist in a useless evasion. Instead, he transformed it into a holiday, taking her out for a look at *America* late one July afternoon.

For all her experience down by the docks, Miss Shays had never so much as taken a rowboat across the river. For the occasion, she wore a good white linen frock with a vaguely naval blue stripe around her waist. Amie, her Bajan chaperone, wore a dress the color of a yellow tea rose and sleeves so long they trailed in the water. Rebeccah laid a searing frown on her, but Jones seemed pleased to be in a rowboat with two such well-kitted young women.

"Miss Amie, you look the image of my friend, the gentle poetess Phillis Wheatley," waxed Jones. "You have the same delicate carriage, the warmth of soul from the beating heart of your mysterious continent!"

"But my continent is here, sir," replied the girl.

"Amie! You will not contradict your betters!" Rebeccah scolded her.

"No, she is certainly correct!" said Jones, ever gallant. "She has better sense than my poor poesy."

"But look—Pompey is so small," said the girl, pointing. Rebeccah put a hand over Amie's mouth, looked apologetically at Jones.

"'Pompey' is her idiom for our town, which we more appropriately call *Portsmouth*."

"I think I took her meaning," said the commodore.

The day was perfect, with the sun arcing to the west in a cloudless sky, the river breezes tempering the heat. Conditions were so perfect that it seemed odd for just a handful of men to be working on the great vessel.

But it was true. As the women walked around the hull, which was still only half-planked, they marveled at the scale of the work. It was the largest soon-to-be-moving object Rebeccah had ever seen. Yet only three workmen were standing on a scaffold on her port side. They seemed to be making slight hewing motions along the ribs. Each glanced at the women over their shoulders, shared a smile, and resumed their jobs with something less than wartime urgency.

Jones escorted them around the stocks, pointing out to Rebeccah details of structure and armament that all seemed to merge into a single indistinct buzz of jargon in her mind. Her attention was captured by a flight of larks above the ship, dipping their wings and crying *tee-hee, tee-hee*. Watching them, she kept smiling and nodding as the commodore went on about his vessel's comparatively shallow "draught" (whatever that meant) and how that feature would permit *America* to chase her prey into shallows where most "first- or second-rates" (whatever those were) could not go.

"Her draught will help her make captures, but she will be a

poor sailor in the line," he said. "That is a good trade, I think, because this country will never build a fleet of first-rates for her to sail among!"

"Mister Jones?" Amie asked.

"You might think of her, then, as a kind of 74-gun frigate, the likes of which the enemy has never seen!"

"Mister Jones?"

"Amie, you must not interrupt!" flared Rebeccah.

"It is quite all right," granted Jones. "What is it, child?"

"I thought you should know. Mister Shays cleans out those nests when he sees 'em on the house."

She was using her chin to indicate a cleft in the planks. Looking closer, they saw what she was talking about: hanging from one of the great ribs was an enormous cone of crude, gray paper. Wasps reposed in the hole in the bottom before flying in or out. It was the kind of nest that one saw under inaccessible eaves or in the rafters of little-visited barns.

"If you will excuse me, ladies . . . ," the commodore said, unsheathing his sword.

Based on her experience with these nests in the garden, Rebeccah would have warned him against a frontal attack. But the commodore had already impaled the flimsy object on the tip of his sword, extracting it from where it was attached. The result was predictable. Before Jones could dispose of the thing, he was surrounded by a thickening cloud of angry avengers.

"Just a minute," he told the ladies as he pried the ruptured nest off his sword with his shoe. "To retire for a moment, if I may attend to this . . ."

But he didn't wait for their permission to run off down the beach, stop short, then run further on. He was soon a tiny blue figure a long distance away, flailing with his sword at his invisible adversaries, as Rebeccah and Amie sat down for what they took to be a long wait.

XXI.

Our wise men are called Fathers, and they truly sustain that
character. Do you call yourselves Christians? Does the religion of
Him who you call your Savior inspire your spirit, and guide your
practices? Surely not. . . . It is recorded of Him that a bruised reed
He never broke. Cease then to call yourselves Christians, lest you
declare to the world your hypocrisy. Cease too to call other
nations savage, when you are tenfold more the children of cruelty
than they.

—Joseph Brant to King George III, 1785

I TOOK MYSELF off the ship *Alliance* a free man in the city of
Philadelphia. After my time in the white man's navy, I had one
pair of pantaloons, one linen shirt without sleeves, and twenty-
five dollars in Continental money. I also had one gold sovereign
which the war captain Paul Jones gave me as reward for what I
did in the battle.

He called me to his cabin to give this to me, getting up on his
feet and giving me a salute. He said, You are an honorable man,
and I told him, Did I not tell you I would fight, if you would lead?
And he laughed, slapping me on the back like my brother. Go
forth a free man, but come to me again if you want to fight, he
said. I told him I would never fight on the water again, because a
man should not fight in a place where he can't stand. So he saluted
me again, and shook my hand. And that was the last I saw of him.

One of the strange things about coming home from the sea is
the way the land feels. On the ocean, my blood got used to moving back and forth, like the waves. But when I came back to Turtle
Island, the stillness felt wrong, like I expected the ground to swell

under my feet. This made me worried, and I was happy when the feeling faded away. From that day, I hoped never to go on the water again—even on a canoe, if I could help it.

Philadelphia is a bigger white town than Quebec, and even more ugly. There are tall painted churches, yes, and clean brick houses, but they are surrounded by mud and rotting trash and horse droppings. Any people with sense would have moved their settlement to a new place a long time ago, but I think the whites are too lazy to move. I stayed in that town long enough to go to a shop where I could trade my twenty-five dollars for a rifle or a musket. When I went in, though, the shopkeeper looked at my Continental money and told me it was worthless. But I needed arms, so I traded my gold sovereign for an old British carbine, .65 caliber, along with an old powder horn and a cartridge case with its shoulder strap missing.

After that I went out and camped north of town. The next morning I was able to make a new shoulder strap out of the material of an old canvas tarpaulin left in the woods. I also learned the shopkeeper was wrong about my Continental dollars. They were not worthless, because they made very good kindling for a fire.

In that time I had only one thought in my mind. I wanted to get back to Chonodote, to the grave of my father, and to Fallen Leaf. At the Texel, I had seen what Europe was: a muddy island in the sea, with another dirty city spreading in the distance. There were no trees, no game, no fruits to eat, no mountains. The spirit of the bear and the wolf and the beaver were dead; the people were miserable and smelled bad. I had been curious as a young man, wondering if maybe Europe held some secret that we might want to know. But now I know that our fathers were right after all. There is no place as blessed as Turtle Island, no knowledge worth knowing but our knowledge.

I had been away a full year. I had missed the Berry festival and the Green Corn festival and the Sacrifice of the White Dog. I had missed a full winter and the plantings in the spring. There had been babies named and dreams I might have understood, had I been there to hear them.

So I rushed north, though my legs and my lungs were weak from all that time on ships. I should have reached the Susquehanna in four days, but it took me a week. Hunting was bad on the way: the settlers had shot out all the elk, the beaver, the deer. The only targets were small ones, like opossum and turkey. I didn't have time to wait for traps to work, so I had to make due with the carbine, which was less accurate than a hunting rifle because it was shorter. By the time I was near Tioga, I was out of cartridges. I was lucky, though, that I was approaching the lands of the Gweungwehono, and being close to home made me so happy I didn't need much to eat anymore.

The great southern path went close to a few white farms and villages of the Shawnees and Munsees. These places all seemed very quiet when I passed them. The only gun I heard in the forest was my own; nobody came up or down the path while I was on it. Such a lonely journey would have been typical for the winter, but this was the spring. Everybody, Indian or white, seemed to have gone off somewhere else. This, I thought, was a good sign, because our braves must have made such attacks on Pennsylvania that all the settlers had left.

Tioga was deserted too, except for a stockade with a few Yankee soldiers in it. It seemed foolish for them to be there, guarding a valley with nothing in it but burnt farms. The soldiers even seemed afraid to go out of their fort, sneaking outside the walls just to pick out supplies. What a good war my people must have had, I thought, for the soldiers to be so scared!

I saw the reason the next day, as I went up the path beyond the Chemung. Coming around a bend, I was face to face with a Mohawk brave going the other way. He was dressed for war, with his face painted black, musket slung across his back, and an officer's pistol stuck in his pants. He was looking at my sailor's clothes like they amused him.

"Hey there, brother!" I greeted him in my own language, which wasn't exactly like Mohawk but close enough for small talk.

"Where are you going, friend? The war's that way," he answered.

There was a noise behind me, and I turned to see three of his friends coming out of the brush. They had their tomahawks out and were looking at the first brave. He gave a little flick of his head. They put their weapons away.

"I know where the war ith, friend," I said. "I haven't been home in a year."

"Where's home? Ganogeh? Gayagaanha?"

"Chonodote."

One of the warriors behind me had three white scalps hanging from his belt. One of these included an intact set of little girl's pigtails, with blue silk ribbons. He started to say—"Then you got a big surpr—" but the first brave cut him off.

"What? What ith it?" I asked.

"Nothing, friend. Go home. Maybe we see you again here . . . after."

"Maybe. Good luck, friend."

"And to you," replied the Mohawk, looking suddenly very thoughtful under his war paint. His was acting odd, but I didn't think to make much out of it. Our brothers at the Eastern Door were known to be moody.

So I went on. At the foot of Gweugweh Lake I saw the foundations of a bunch of burned buildings where the villages of Neodakheat and Coreorgonel used to be. I didn't think this meant anything—our people sometimes burned their own towns when the land was worn out and it was time to move someplace else. A burning could do some good, especially in places like Philadelphia. But it made me wonder.

It was when I saw the condition of the fields and orchards up and down the lake that I was sure something had gone wrong. Everything was ripped up, torn apart, planted back in the ground in a crazy man's mockery of our ways. It looked as if the giant Shagodyoweh had drummed on the skin of the world, scattering everything.

That a white army had come was clear from the many boot-prints, all the same size. The tracks were strewn everywhere, wandering, not organized the way a Mahican or Shawnee war party might travel to hide its numbers. So many whites must have come, I thought, that they didn't care to conceal their strength. Their feet and artillery tore up the ground so deep that their tracks were still plain after the winter.

I kept going, my heart growing sicker. I saw more charred fields, invaded then by a green stubble of spring weeds. I saw grain stores pried open, still smoldering from the fires working through the corn deep inside. Houses stood blackened, turned inside out, open to the sky. To add insult, the soldiers left the hard remains of their feces in the hearths, where our families once cooked food for their children. A lone dog stood watch at the door of the slouching husk of a house. I greeted it, happy to see some small reminder of the life of the village. But it bared its teeth and growled. I backed away and left it alone. It circled twice and settled back in the dirt of the threshold, as if still waiting for its master to return.

What saddened me most was not the destruction, but the solitude. This was not the first time a white army had come into these lands, after all. The French did it, generations before; the British came too, before we smoked the pipe of peace. What made this different was that the Gweugwehono had never retreated far and had always come back right away. This last attack had been months before, and no one had returned to rebuild or replant. I was deep in the heart of the country of my people, and I had yet to see a soul. The whites had burned out the grain supplies, so unless the season's crops were growing someplace else, there would be famine again next winter.

The sourness of despair filled my throat. Not only the present, but the future was laid waste. A thought occurred to me—a dark thought. Maybe this time we didn't return because we were different. Maybe we had all been too changed, with our taste for fancy muskets and pewter buttons and cotton dresses and pet kitty-cats. Maybe this was how our ancestors decided to punish us, not only for a wrecked present and hopeless future, but for our failure to defend the past. For the whites, you see, had sacked the graveyards this time. The burial mounds were cut by spades, the bones scattered. Scaffolds had been chopped down, the bodies looted for souvenirs. Later, animals came and chewed the remains of our mothers and fathers. All around me, ghosts must have been wandering, hungry to avenge themselves on the children who had abandoned them. No wonder nobody came back.

This was a worse disaster than losing the buildings or the corn. And it would affect us in ways that go beyond what the whites call "religion." I will not try to explain it, because people would read my explanation and roll their eyes and pity our simple idolatry. But understand it this way: while houses come and go, and fields return to forest, the bones of our mothers and fathers are the same as the ground. Not conveniently "kept" in the ground," not peacefully "resting" in the ground," but *the same* as the ground. To separate them, to make them and the land lonely for each other, is as foul an act as ripping an unborn child from a mother's body. Think of it that way.

I went on, thinking maybe the whites had only gone so far before they were defeated. But the story was the same at the remains of every village. And when I finally reached Chonodote, I was empty of hopes. I expected to see the orchards on the hills stripped bare, and they were; I expected to see the longhouse where I had been born reduced to a bed of cinders, and it was.

Only my mother's house was left standing, though it had been ransacked. No one was left—my mother, Fallen Leaf, Deawateho, even Father Du Lac—all gone. They would have gone among the Nundawaono, I thought, unless the same had happened to the Keepers of the Western Door. If so, they would have fled to Fort Niagara, to the British.

I was too tired to go and see just then—too tired and too sick. For this was the kind of thing we had seen before, happening to people to the north, east, and south of the Great Longhouse. First, their farms were destroyed, and they were reduced to poverty. Then, they were removed from the land because they had no farms and were poor. Or first, their graves were opened; then, the lack of graves was taken to mean they had no claim to the land.

It was a hard argument to beat, for there was evidence. Was the earth not empty and bleeding? Were not the Indians hanging around the forts as if they had never known how to feed themselves? Did they not prefer to worship the Cross than to be killed or starved? How simple! How fortunate for us that these things could be explained!

So I got angry. And when I got to the place of my father, I found the wolves had ground his bones to splinters, and I got more angry. I came on a burlap sack by a stream, with a litter of drowned puppies inside, their tongues sticking from their jaws, their throats pouring foam, and thought, what brave soldiers! How I would have liked to meet one of them, one of those brave puppy killers! I was sorry then I just counted coup against the miserable officer, Lunt, during the battle with the British ship. Why did I not kill him? Yangeese must always be killed when the chance comes. Even the whites think there are too many of themselves walking around. Do the world a favor—kill a Yangeese.

I saw the army officer sitting on a log just outside the village. He had his boots off and his legs spread out. His feet were in the stream where our women used to go for water in the summer evenings. He was wearing a blue uniform with a cape and lazily tapping the ground between his knees with the end of his riding crop. I looked at his face: he was young, like me, with a long scar up his cheek. His expression was not what I would have expected. Looking at both of us, you would have had trouble telling whose army had conquered and whose people were defeated and scattered.

I was too surprised at first to do anything. It was the kind of thing that never happened, like when you find your fish traps picked by somebody and look around hoping the thief will still be nearby. He never is. But you still stand up straight, an injured look on your face, staring stupidly up and down the empty shore for the guilty one.

Well, here was the guilty one, waiting for me. Looking at him there, with his sword sheathed by his side and his horse a long way off, grazing, it occurred to me that this must be a trap. Fifty Continental muskets must be waiting in the trees, all loaded, all taking a bead on me. So I went around, scouting for his regiment. I did a whole circle, in fact, and found nobody at all. So unless they were watching over him from far away, he really was alone.

I powdered and shotted my carbine, fumbling a little because I kept one eye on him. It seemed to me that he must disappear any second, like a dream. But he didn't.

When I came out, I stepped on some dry leaves and he looked up. He was surprised too—I saw his hand jerk right away toward his sword, as if he did it without thinking. But he stopped himself for some reason, putting his hand back on his knee.

"Hello," he said in a pleasant voice you might hear from a passing neighbor.

I came closer. I had my carbine cradled in my arms but did not point it at him yet.

"I might have expected you'd come," he went on. "Couldn't trust you would just give up. Speak English?"

I stopped about ten yards from him. Aside from when he first saw me, he hadn't moved.

"Did you . . . do all thith?" I asked him, pointing all around with my chin.

"I did my part."

"What are you doing here, then?"

He frowned, looked at the ground.

"I came back to find someone. Or shall I say, to see what is left of her."

"And did you thictheed?"

"Your accent is strange, friend. But if you ask if I succeeded—no."

There was an explosion of feathers from the tree line to my right—a crow chased by a pair of screeching jays. If I were a wiser man, if I had listened to my elders as I should have, I might have read the significance of this event at that time.

"So I assume you'll want to make a trophy of my scalp," the officer said.

"I would make my peace with your Jethuth, if I were you."

"I see. It's to be retribution, then."

"I think your people would call it *juthtice.*"

"Touché, my friend. I suppose it would not matter if I deny that anyone is 'my people.'"

"You may deny what you want. It doesn't matter to me. Are you ready?"

There was a hint of fear in his eye, as if he was finally understanding that I was serious. But it was only that—a hint—and it was gone right away. This was a relief; after all I had seen and felt that day, I was in no condition to tolerate the womanish pleas of white soldiers when they face death. I pointed the carbine at him.

"Is there a possibility you might let me put my boots on?" he asked.

"Not much point. I'm gonna take them anyway."

"As a last request, then?"

I shrugged. "Okay."

So I waited there as he pulled on his boots. He did it slowly, taking deep breaths like a man who knew there was no hope, and wanting to enjoy his last chestfulls of air. I was watching him closely, making sure there was no funny business, and there wasn't. He stood up slowly, taking a long look around the woods, and faced me.

"Ready?" I asked him.

"All right," he answered, his voice shaky.

There was no sense in prolonging the job. I came a few paces closer, just so there would be no chance of missing, and cocked the firelock.

"I'm sorry," the officer said, staring into my face.

I pulled the trigger.

XXII.

THERE BEGAN a peculiar period in Severence's life. He traveled constantly, riding up and down the roads and paths of eastern Pennsylvania. Through the fall and winter, he saw the frontiers of the colony in a way only tax collectors and surveyors might. But he arrived nowhere. He never stayed anywhere more than a night or two, and had no stomach to talk much to anyone of the things he had seen and done.

It was not the discharge from Sullivan's army he had anticipated. In his imaginings, he would have left the Continental service after the expedition ended, his body of business contacts enriched by scores of Senecah, Cayugah, Mohawks. While the war itself seemed far from over, he began to think himself out of the uniform he had worn for more than four years. The prospect had filled him with anxiety, but also with the sweet excitement of first endeavor. For in a real sense, it would have been the beginning of his independent life. At last, he would break away from the institution that had nourished him in the first, tentative flowering of his adulthood.

My dear Rebeccah:

Free at last! I interrupt my return to you only to write this letter, which you may take as proof of my health, my happiness, and my steadfast love for . . .

His dismissal from camp and the circumstances of his last hours there made this optimism seem absurd. At Easton, he took a room above a tavern and began to compose his first letter to Rebeccah. There was no use in upsetting her from such a great distance, so he intended to emphasize his happy journey homeward, to her arms. But as he wrote, he came to feel the weight of the lie on his conscience. Something else had gone up in the smoke above those first villages of Chemung. His home now seemed as lost to him as to any of the savages he had helped dislocate.

He scrapped the first line and started again.

My dear Rebeccah:

> Disaster! I write to you now, a refugee from my own folly, in as deep a hatred of myself as I can stand without taking my own . . .

But again, what good would come of spreading his despair ahead of him, to Portsmouth? And what presumption, to think he could encompass the magnitude of the tragedy with his amateur's prose! When in his life had he ever written anything more important than mildly colorful, amiable letters to "friends" he barely knew? Letters that concealed as much as they told? That, he decided, was his most characteristic talent: to hide, to conceal. Rebeccah would hardly know him otherwise.

By the turn of spring he had settled on a kind of plan. True, his time with Sullivan had afforded him no chance to make contact with the Indians. But there was nothing to stop him from trying again, on his own. It was then months after the army's withdrawal; most likely the Senecah and the Cayugah had begun to return, just as they had after every other invasion. He resolved to ride north again, and if they didn't kill him, to salvage what he could of a commercial relationship.

That was the reason he gave outwardly, to suppliers and the anonymous diners who shared his table at fifty dreary meals at fifty forgettable inns and taverns. But there was another, better reason for the trip. Through a long winter of bad nights he had been disturbed by vague imaginings of Polyxena's body abandoned in the woods, unburied. Leaving the bodies of the savages to scavengers was indeed the established procedure in Sullivan's corps, though after six months there could hardly be much left of her. But as his memory of Polyxena became fuzzier and more sanctified, the insult to her body rankled him. It was something he should have remedied before he left. He resolved to return and bury her properly. And if, after a diligent search, he couldn't find her, he would content himself with the attempt and finally move on to Portsmouth.

A guide, of course, was unnecessary. He bought a good trail horse, packed the saddlebags with dried pork, two five-pound sacks of flour, and a canteen of spruce beer. He was offered a hunting rifle at a good price, but opted to enter the forest with just his pistol and a small cartridge case. This left him at a severe disadvantage in firepower against anyone he was likely to meet in the heart of Indian country. Nor would he have means to hunt anything larger than a rabbit or a raccoon. Yet he hardly cared. He preferred to call this decision fatalistic; most of his dining companions just called it suicidal.

He stuck to the trails Sullivan had cut through Easton and Tioga. Riding hard, stopping little, he crossed the Chemung and reached the site of the first battle within a week. But although winter was well over and a few corn seedlings were coming up on their own in the weedy fields, the village nearby was empty. He rode on to the place near the stream where the packhorses were shot. Their bones were still there, scattered and draped with gray skin. Dismounting, his heart heavy, he searched there for Polyxena's remains. It took him two days to satisfy himself he had covered every square inch of the area around the old camp. There were ample signs of human presence—an iron hatchet, a broken bayonet, dozens of old buttons that were carved, in the penurious style of the Continental Army, out of hard cheese. But there was nothing that might have resembled Polyxena, even after a winter's sleep under the snow.

So he pressed on to the only place that bore any connection to her. It was the little town on the east shore of Cayugah Lake, with the peach orchards. Along the way, he passed four more sites of ruins. After two days, heartsick and saddlesore, he entered the shattered precincts of Chonodote. It was not a very populous place in its time, he observed, but it spread out far on the landscape. He would need many days to search it thoroughly.

At last he heard movement in one of the cabins. Coming closer, he glimpsed a dim figure rising from the smashed bed frame inside. Standing on two legs, it kept rising, to his height and beyond, until it sprang forward at him. It hurtled through the doorway and would have run him down before he could raise his pistol to fire. The blur resolved itself into the blunt rear end of a bear as it veered off. The animal vanished so quickly into the brush he couldn't tell if it was black or brown. He was startled again when a smaller blur bounded from the cabin, grunting with a humanlike plaint as it followed its mother into the woods.

Severence was shaken by the encounter. He went down to the brook beside the village, then swollen with spring runoff, and wet his face. It occurred to him that he hadn't removed his boots in 48 hours. Settling himself on a log beside the stream, he pulled the boots off and rested with his feet in the water. The sensation was a balm after his scare. He became strangely content in this position; in retrospect, he was tired of riding out ahead of his fate and resigned to let it find him there.

And so it did, in the form of a young Indian brave. Though his features marked him as a savage, he was wearing the kind of loose breeches and tar-smeared smock Severence had seen before, at sea. His weapon was similarly incongruous—an old cavalry piece with rusty iron furniture. The brave put on a defiant face, but was clearly confused by Severence's presence.

There followed a brief interrogation, during which the newcomer displayed a pronounced lisp through the broad window of his missing front teeth. The fellow then informed Severence that he would be shot. And so it appeared. Severence's pistol was out of reach, buckled in its holster, and the savage had him squarely in his sights. For the second time in an hour, Severence found himself staring at the prospect of imminent death. Only this time it was not a surprise, and he had the luxury to think about it. And this is what he thought: *It's no great loss if I die. The war will go on, and the same side will win. There are a few people who will mourn me, but not too many and not very much. And is there not a sort of justice in dying here, in Polyxena's village? Why don't I just sit here, facing eternity in this pleasant calm? It is the kind of end many would have reason to envy.*

So that was that. But then the boy allowed him to put his boots on, giving him time to think again: *Yet what a waste it would be to die now. Not a waste of personal quality or excellence, but of potential to repair my mistakes. And why should I, particularly, pay the price for what others had done? Real justice would have been for Sullivan to be sitting on this log, not me! Or a thousand other men in the campaign who had robbed a corpse, burned a house, or starved a family.* And at that moment, staring into the rusty aperture of the carbine, Severence realized that he probably should live. Not because he really wanted to, but for the abstract, principled reason that decent men should always try to outlive fiends.

"Ready?" the Indian asked him.

"I'm sorry," Severence said, though he was not quite sure what he was sorry for.

The next events occurred at almost the same speed as his meeting with the bear. The carbine fired, but instead of receiving a ball in the chest, Severence watched the old weapon hang fire. The burning powder in the pan stung his captor's hands, forcing him to drop the gun. Severence used this opening to pull out his pistol. The other stood there, glaring at him.

"An unlucky turn for you," he told the boy, "but it need not be fatal. Go now."

"It'th my village," came the reply. "You go."

"Don't be foolish. I have the advantage, sir."

The boy's gaze fell on the carbine, still hissing and sparking at his feet. "I'm going to pick up that gun," he said. "And then I'm going to kill you."

"Do you speakee? Understand that you will *die?*"

"I'm not afraid. But if you thoot me, know that you killed Jotheph Two Fireth, thon of Mantinoah of the Bear clan of the Gweugwehono people, thon of Mantinoah and Tharah Whitcombe, brother of Fallen Leaf. Remember to leave the bundle, and that the maple ith the tree with the thtrongest medicine," the brave said. "Are you ready?"

"Wait . . . no . . ."

"Okay," he said, and reached for the carbine.

Severence fired. The ball entered just above the youth's collarbone and split into two halves. One half lodged in his neck, severing his carotid. The other spun through his left lung, ripping the soft tissue until it stopped in his diaphragm. Clutching his neck, a look of faint annoyance on his face, Two Fires fell and lay still.

And this was how Severence, who came back to Iroquoia to meet live Indians, ended up shooting one. It came to seem to him, as he buried his face in his hands, that he could do nothing but inflict pain on these people. It was mystifying—had he not given all the warning he could? What was it about them all? What had he done that everything should end in disaster?

It was the least he could do to bury the poor wretch. He did it the way he'd seen bodies left in the Cayugah graveyards: propped upright in scaffolds, facing east, with their weapons in their hands. A group of these scaffolds were a short distance from the village, built into a stand of birch trees. They were all desecrated, empty, their occupants dumped onto the ground below. Severence chose one for Two Fires. He rigged up a crude lift by throwing a rope around a high branch and hauled the body up. He then did his best to arrange the corpse's limbs the way he'd seen before. And when he was done, he stood on the ground below, wondering what the young brave had meant about the maple, but having no idea. He thought maybe he should say something or pray, but mainly he felt guilty and foolish. So he left.

He made his way listlessly south-east, along the Delaware trail. As he crossed the highlands above New-York, he heard that General Washington was in residence at White Plains. An idea occurred to him that revived his spirit. Arriving at the camp, he requested a meeting with the general, promising "surprising intelligence" with respect to Sullivan's errand to the north country. Unfortunately, he was fobbed off instead on an underling, an artilleryman-*cum*-secretary named Hamilton.

This adjutant was dressed like a field marshal, with a uniform coat so finely piped and combed Severence felt rumpled by comparison. Hamilton's saving grace, however, was that he was a good listener. He attended patiently at first to his visitor's account of Sullivan's cruelty, his egoism, his petulant refusal to press his advantage against Fort Niagara. But as he spoke, Severence became more and more aware that Hamilton already knew the whole story. No doubt Sullivan's written account had preceded him by many weeks. By the end of the interview, it was clear the secretary preferred to pass his time with anything but the sound of Severence's voice.

"Thank you for your report, Captain," Hamilton finally said. "The general will find much of interest in it."

Severence nodded, well aware that the general would probably hear very little of his report, if anything at all. But as he watched Hamilton leave, he was compelled to shout after him.

"They call him the Destroyer of Towns."

Hamilton came about, stared at him.

"They call the general *that?*"

"Yes."

The secretary looked thoughtfully at the wall. "Curious," he said. And then he was gone.

Severence never received an invitation to speak with Washington. Instead, he got his only glimpse of the commander in chief the next morning, when the great man walked from his private quarters to mount his horse. He was surrounded by a half-dozen young men in a hurry, all contending for that ear that hung so tantalizingly close above them. This animate curtain parted once, if only for a few seconds, as Washington ascended the mounting block and swept that great white pillar of a leg over his horse's back. But Severence saw enough. Washington was indeed tall, and indeed hale and genteel and severe, but no more impressive than dozens of stockinged suits Severence had seen in the men's clubs and counting houses of New-York. No more impressive, in fact, than the down-at-heels merchants who used to come to beg Severence's father for loans. Worse, the general's movements seemed calculated for effect, as if he expected the cant of his head or the way his wide rump filled his saddle to alter the course of empires. This made him seem more like an actor hired to portray the part of a commander than a real soldier.

Yet, incredibly, that appeared to be enough to hold his blasted army together. The conundrum preoccupied Severence on the long journey to Portsmouth—the way men valued the appearance of ability over the substance of it. What a powerful force was the mere illusion of leadership. Still, Severence could not find the cynicism within him to accept the complete irrelevance of true, personal quality. Sooner or later, talent must find its reward. And nations that place their destinies in the hands of actors cannot endure.

A week later he was sitting in the front parlor of the Shays house, looking at Elijah Shays's varicose pate. The older man was bent over copies of Severence's letters, reviewing them with an appreciative grunt here, an incredulous snort there. The moment felt like one of the pregnant silences in any job interview, where the employer turns to the written references. Every one of his meetings with Elijah Shays, in fact, felt like a job interview.

"Yes, your communications . . ." he began, trailing off for a moment to concentrate on a particular passage, then continued, " . . . have been everything we may have hoped for. Most well done."

Severence shifted on his seat, said nothing.

"A damn peculiar trick, concealing your intelligence in this kind of . . . tender correspondence. Sullivan's people could never have suspected you."

"They did suspect me."

"But only by association. They had no evidence. Meanwhile, you have done the congress a measurable service. Mr. Jay is pleased."

Severence frowned as he stared at the traffic beyond Shays's gate. Compliments from execrable men unnerved him.

"But I never did anything to make a difference," he said. "I might as well not have been there."

"That is a useful attribute in a spy. And you are wrong to say you won't make a difference! Sullivan's patrons are already making a great victory out of his vandalism. Your work will stand to remind everyone of what was not accomplished and of the parties to be blamed. You have assured that no one's star will rise on account of these events."

"My only hope is that Rebeccah understands."

Shays's face suddenly and unaccountably darkened. He put the letters aside and leaned back in his chair, fixing a heavy-lidded eye on Severence.

"*That,*" Severence began, "is a matter I hope we may discuss at a later time."

"Indeed we may."

"But if I might inquire if she is at home . . ."

"Miss Shays is not at home."

The tone of Shays' denial had the ring of a slamming door.

"Then I may call on her at a later time?"

The older man's eyes dropped to his lap, the sternness draining from his face. It was only a tolerable imitation of compassion.

"My dear boy, I hardly know what to say to you. That your feelings persist in that regard has puzzled us all, and makes my position most difficult."

"If you speak of my delay in coming here, I can offer no explanation. Except that it is a matter of personal pain to me, one that I hope you may forgive."

"Your delay did not help your suit, I agree," said Shays. "But it is not the first concern."

"Then if you object to your daughter's marriage to a mere spy, I would remind you of your own estimates of my worth to the cause."

"That is not at issue, sir."

"Then, sir, I must plead ignorance of any grounds for concern."

Shays pursed his lips as he poked desultorily through the pile of letters. Finding the one he sought, he hooked his spectacles around his ears, raised the paper to his eyes, and read aloud. As he did so, he occasionally glanced at Severence, measuring his reaction.

"'All that is left of my designs, in fact, is now invested in my care of my squaw. It is my fervent hope that you understand this and are not tormenting yourself with vain jealousies, as they must be vain indeed. Polyxena is not your rival, but no more or less than a young woman *in extremis* . . .'"

Severence could only stare at Shays in growing astonishment. The old man continued, "'There are some women who through some quality of their character invite the attentions of men, noxious and otherwise. . . . She sat very much on display above the troops, strikingly handsome and half-naked with her skirts gathered up over her splints . . .'"

"I see no purpose to this recitation!" erupted Severence. "If you mean to insinuate that something untoward occurred between myself and Polyxena, I would prefer you charged me outright!"

"You misunderstand me. Whether you consorted with such persons is a matter upon which I prefer to remain agnostic. What I charge you with, instead, is hypocrisy."

"Hypocrisy? How?"

"To protest your innocence, when you could only have known the cost of appearances. To dishonor my daughter so, with this conduct! And then to write to her of the smallest details! What possible effect could you have expected of this . . . salacious account!"

"I resent that characterization, sir."

"You have only yourself to blame for it, young man."

Roiling with anger, Severence rose from his chair. He was squeezing his kidskin gloves so tightly in his hand he was rolling them into a ball.

"You bewilder me with this . . . to praise my conduct and then indict me for a few intemperate words in a letter!"

"For your service to your country, you have my admiration. But I would not commend my daughter to a man such as you."

"And what does Rebeccah say of this?"

"Rebeccah trusts my judgment. But if you seek evidence of her feelings on this score, you should know that she has sought my consent to take company with another gentleman."

Whether this bit of news was true or not, Severence could not say. The intent of it was baldly obvious—to pierce him to the quick, to inflict despair. But as much as he understood Shays's purpose, his words found their mark on his heart.

"Who?" he whispered.

"Does it matter? An officer."

Severence unrolled his gloves and pulled them on. In his haste, he skipped a finger, and was forced to pull the left one off. He slapped the glove to the floor and strode to the doorway with only one hand clad. He turned to Shays again.

"I only hope, sir, that you may one day understand the depth of the injustice you do me."

The other didn't answer, but made a neat pile of his copies of Severence's letters. The whole episode had so thoroughly thrown Shays off his rhythm, he hadn't relieved himself in days. As the sound of Severence's boots died in his hallway and the front door slammed, his thoughts turned to the chamber pot under his bed, with the face of King George, and the little Latin inscription. Such wit, so little honored! He had a pleasant fantasy of filling that worthy receptacle, fully logging over that detestable face, adding a garnish of urine for good measure. *Pro iustitia sedeo.* And he smiled.

Severence withdrew to the Marquis of Rockingham tavern. He stayed behind the closed door of his room, taking no food, until nine in the evening, when he came out again and retraced his steps to the Shays house. No self-respecting lover, of course, would accept such an arbitrary decision. If Rebeccah no longer wanted him, she would have to tell him herself. Indeed, she would have to insist. If he saw even a hint of her continued affection, he was prepared to take her away from Portsmouth that very night. His bag was packed, a horse prearranged for a night ride to Newburyport. These preparations, in fact, made him feel far more like a spy than anything he had done on the trail with Sullivan's army.

He was standing under Rebeccah's window at 10 PM. There did not seem to be a candle burning inside. In case she had retired early, he found a few pebbles on the road and tossed them discreetly against the windowpanes. No answer. Did she sleep so soundly that she couldn't hear them? He found a slightly bigger pebble and threw it with somewhat more force. This one hit with an appalling cracking noise that sent him diving for cover.

But again, no answer. Could she be out . . . possibly with her so-called "gentleman?" He crossed the street and positioned himself behind an elm where he could see anyone come or go through the front door of the house. Again, he was skulking in a way he never had as a spy. The whole affair filled him with embarrassment; as he acted the jealous buffoon, he could feel himself becoming one. To be so foully treated for exercising his basic humanity, by a man like Shays! He would marry Rebeccah and give her a fortune and a family just to prove the man wrong.

Three figures appeared down the street. One he recognized as the thin silhouette of Amie, the servant. The other was Rebeccah, walking in her usual way—her head slightly bent, her shoulders swinging as if on opposite ends of a weather vane. The third figure was a man carrying a lantern. He also seemed familiar, but in a way Severence couldn't quite place.

The evening was quiet, with no wind. As they came closer, he could hear the gentleman holding forth, though he couldn't make out the words. The voice also seemed familiar, the precious cadence, the rolling of pearly consonants from his tongue. Severence strained to hear, closing his eyes, until recognition washed over him in an appalling wave.

"I hope I may trust you with the secret of what you have seen today," Jones was telling the women. "There are many parties who would be glad to learn what you now know."

"To have seen the commodore's battle with the wasps! Yes, what pluck! What strategy! What credit to American arms!" Rebeccah teased him. But when she saw the commodore glower, she hastened to reassure him, adding, "But of course we treasure the trust you place in us. Don't we, Amie?" And she shot the girl an admonishing glance.

"Yes, we do—" said Amie, who clearly wished to say more, but was prevented when Rebeccah cut her off.

"So we may flatter ourselves to expect further adventures with you?"

Jones took her gloved hand and planted a kiss above the knuckles. "You may," he said. Then he did the same for Amie, though his lips lingered a bit longer on her bare skin, and his eyes deliberately and suggestively met hers as he did so. This had a good effect, as he could see her mistress's face flush in the lantern light.

"Good night," Rebeccah told him, tartly.

"Good night," he replied, amused.

Jones saw the women to their door and watched them go inside. And as he had the last time, he waited for the curtain of the front window to move slightly as someone observed him from inside. As if on cue, the curtain did sway. Satisfied, he went on his way to Mrs. Purcell's. Considering how the afternoon had gone, the evening had an auspicious ending. The girls had been impressed with *America*, to be sure, but all too amused by the state of the ship's undress. It was the peculiar weakness of women to be moved more by frivolous kisses than by mighty works of man. Or was it their particular wisdom?

Severence watched the commodore pass within four feet of him. He stood against his tree, but made no strenuous effort to conceal himself. If Jones had turned around at that moment and discovered him, Severence would not have retreated. He could equally imagine embracing Jones or slapping him across the face. He was lashed by warring emotions: jealousy, at first, and cynical resentment. But there was also curiosity, a sense of amused irony, and simple pleasure at seeing an old friend. Since their time in Passy together, there had been no direct communication; Severence had only heard that Jones had accepted another command sometime in the summer before he joined Sullivan. He hadn't thought to ask for news of Jones when he visited Washington's camp at White Plains. To see that he was there, in Portsmouth, was really a startling coincidence. What was it Rebeccah had called him? Commodore? Clearly he must have done something to earn a flag rank. But what? What captures had he made? Had he heard what his old friend Severence had been up to?

These were not the questions asked by a man lost in romantic paroxysms. The thought was unexpected, and a comfort—it was not fair, after all, for a man of 24 to suffer such mixed feelings. Young men deserve simplicity. Complexity would always certainly come later, in its own time.

When he thought again of losing Rebeccah, her smooth face so cleanly untouched by cares, and her flaxen curls dangling doll-like, and her intellect so bright and brittle, like a vase, he felt not jealousy, but relief. What was this woman to him, if she could read his letters, could read of the special hell he had seen, and somehow callously and lightly turn to flirtation with the most shallow man in the service? She and her commodore had to be a matched pair. And Jones—had he not always been, between them, the more impressed by baubles? Let him have her—and her damnable father! It was really the best possible resolution, he thought, turning the corner to the Marquis of Rockingham's. If his rival had been some nincompoop, some Boston fop with a purchased commission and honeyed *bon mots* for the ladies, he would have been obliged to smash his face. There would have been blood and recriminations and watchmen and consequences. But Jones! That was all too amusing. Hadn't he washed his hands of that man long ago? Hadn't he warned him about the equivocal charms of certain ladies before, such as those of Madame de Lowendahl? Where was his precious Madame now, after all?

Severence smiled to himself as he lay in bed. The man was fated to make a fool of himself, he decided. He wanted to lose himself in eyes like Rebeccah's, eyes of such perfect reflective properties, like fine mirrors, so perfect and perfectly cold blue—or were they some kind of indigo? But he realized he was thinking of Polyxena's eyes, for he had forgotten Rebeccah's.

When he woke the next morning, his plan was already in his head, as if it had hatched overnight. This business of spying, he found, had its own momentum. And with compatriots like Shays and Sullivan and Jones, it was less and less clear he was working for the right side. Perhaps—yes—he would try the British service for a while. The prospect had a certain spiteful appeal. His mind settled on the question at hand: when a spy comes in from the cold, where does he go? First to breakfast, obviously. But then what?

XXIII.

THAT SUMMER, the naval maneuvers most significant to Paul Jones's career occurred nowhere near him. In August a fine fleet of sixteen French vessels were riding near the approaches to Boston harbor. As the channel through the outlying islands was narrow, the Lieutenant-Général le Marquis de Vaudreuil properly requested the services of a pilot. His request was fulfilled in the person of an accomplished but profoundly hung-over harbor salt, who was still recuperating from his brother's wedding in Nahant. Though the pilot had steered uncounted merchantmen and sloops around the islands, he had never seen, much less simultaneously directed, a fleet of thirteen ships of the line and three frigates. Nor did he speak French.

The fleet began its passage to the inner harbor at the height of the morning flood. Within twenty minutes three 74-gun vessels ran aground. Vaudreuil and his officers screamed at the pilot in French. The pilot sent a stream of curses back at them in Yankee English, which Vaudreuil's aide-de-camp promptly mistranslated. As this discussion went on, a series of swells lifted and smashed His Christian Majesty's ship *La Magnifique* pitilessly against the New England granite. The old ship, a veteran of Ushant in '78, split open and began to fill with water.

The other 74's would later be hauled off the rocks, but *La Magnifique* was foundering and helpless. With the rest of the fleet out of danger, boats were sent back to rescue the crew and begin to salvage the guns and equipment. It was the first significant loss for Congress's new French allies in American waters.

The disaster presented Philadelphia with an unexpected opportunity. News of it reached Robert Morris just as he considered a packet of bills from Colonel Langdon in Portsmouth, demanding repayment for expenses incurred in the construction of *America*. Commodore Jones, Langdon complained, was insistent on such extravagant changes that the vessel would likely cost twice what had been estimated. Langdon himself was in favor of stripping the unfinished hull to outfit privateers. Arthur Lee, seeing his chance to strike a blow against Benjamin Franklin and his minion Paul Jones, had an inspired idea. Why not simply give *America* to His Majesty, to compensate him for the loss of *La Magnifique?* The magnanimity of this gift instantly appealed to those who worried about French commitment to the cause. Getting rid of the perpetually unfinished *America* appealed to everyone else.

To everyone, that is, except the little commodore. Congress's decision reached Jones at his breakfast table at Mrs. Purcell's, in a letter from Robert Morris. As he read of *La Magnifique*'s demise, he sympathetically eyed the half-cracked shell of the egg in his dish. But as he read on, his eyes inevitably began to flare under clenched brows. Mrs. Purcell paused at the half-closed door of her pantry, watching. She had heard him erupt before, cursing Langdon and his contractors from behind his bedroom door. She expected an eruption now—but was surprised. With shaking hands but otherwise cool, Jones merely folded the letter back into its envelope. Then he looked up at her, somewhat doleful but quite calm.

"I don't think I care for a breakfast today, ma'am. Thank you," he told her, in a voice more soft than usual.

In the letter, Morris asked Jones, as a great personal favor, not to resign but to midwife *America* to her new fate. Not implausibly, he argued that satisfying the French navy would bring more net benefit to the American cause than anything Jones could accomplish with just one 74. Arthur Lee and his partisans, moreover, appeared to be fully expecting Jones to burn his bridges with Congress over the matter. Don't give them the satisfaction, Morris begged. If the commodore showed due patience, there existed a very good chance that Congress would find him some suitable reward in the near future.

The future! Jones reflected on Morris's appeal as he was rowed to Rising Castle later that morning. Not only did Arthur Lee expect him to run his career aground, it seemed, but his friends feared it too. And indeed, was there any way for him to deny he'd given ample reason for such fear over the years? Lately, he'd become acquainted with the unfamiliar sentiment of regret. After so many idle months, so many letters unanswered, so little meaningful company, it was inevitable for anyone, no matter how self-possessed, to develop misgivings.

Of course, he would not give Arthur Lee the satisfaction. But nor would he give Robert Morris the satisfaction of convincing him to do the obvious. For once, he would not immediately respond to a letter. Instead, Lee and Morris and the rest would have his answer soon enough, in a form far more eloquent than he would manage in prose.

It took eighteen months for Jones to fashion his reply. It came one mild afternoon in late October, when *America* finally slipped out of her cradle and into the Piscataqua. The good people of Portsmouth—all of them—lined the mainland shore. Dignitaries from New Hampshire, Philadelphia, and Paris watched from the tented, tasseled gallery Jones had constructed for the occasion. The ship was gladly turned out for her debut, trimmed with banners of the two allies dancing prettily on a jackstaff. She had no masts and no guns, but by God she had music and bunting and ladies dressed as if for a ball. Entering the water by her stern, *America* plowed up a wave that rolled across the river and broke at the feet of the delighted citizenry. As she floated free, she was greeted with a 21-gun salute from the fort on Pierce's Island, seconded by another 21 guns from a French warship in the harbor. The crew aboard hauled on cables attached to three anchors set in the river bottom to the south and east, kedging *America* off to deeper water. Then her own anchor, salvaged from the wreck of *La Magnifique,* was let out. The people cheered again as the first and last voyage of U.S.S. *America,* all of fifty yards' distance, was complete.

The spectators checked their programs, which were printed at the personal expense of "the Commodore Chevalier J^N. Paul Jones, USN, OMM, Esq." The next event was scheduled for sunset, when the attributes of command would be officially turned over to *La Magnifique*'s captain, the Mon. Macarty-Macteigne. For this occasion the unvarnished, unfurnished deck of *America* was covered with distinguished eminences. These included Colonel Langdon, who looked exhausted and relieved to have the ship off his ledger, but who spoke not a word to his host, Commodore Jones. They also included Mr. Elijah Shays, distinguished local shipowner and merchant, and his daughter Miss Rebeccah Shays.

Rebeccah had ordered her dress from Boston. In honor of her lover, she chose a tartan-patterned cotton material, with green velvet reverses, and added a sunshade with a handle fashioned of rustic cherrywood. Her pregnancy, which began several weeks after her father retired Amie as their chaperone, was then a certainty, attested by Mrs. Sparshot herself. It was early, however, and would not show for months. By that time she would have been long since married to her dashing commodore. And he looked so handsome at that moment, a bundle of concentrated charm in his blue-and-white uniform, his French medal newly buffed and sparkling in the dying light. She would have preferred a more explicit proposal from him, to be sure. It would have been very easy for her to upset herself with frightening eventualities. The special agony of limbo was behind her, at least: she no longer thought of Severence, who had never showed up nor written, and whom she decided she had never truly loved. Now, for the first time in years, she had the components of a conceivable future before her, all ready to be assembled.

But for the moment, she would just mingle with the important people around her, and smile, and allow herself to be witty. It was as if she, too, were afloat for the first time; she dared imagine it was she, and not just the ship, who was on her way to France.

As the sun bowed to the horizon, the chevalier faced Macarty-Macteigne on the quarterdeck. It was the largest, most splendid quarterdeck Jones had ever commanded. The Frenchman, however, had examined *America* with an amiable but slightly bemused grin on his face, as if he were examining a child's sandcastle. Indirectly, Jones had heard the unflattering evaluations made by Vaudreuil's officers of the construction, and particularly of the "degeneracy" of American wood. He had also heard misgivings about the design of her hull, which was broader at the beam than the French standard. To Jones, this criticism confirmed that the French had no notion of the fundamental truth about *America:* because the colonies would never afford a fleet of capital ships, she was essentially a 74-gun frigate. Where her draft assured she would fare badly in the line, she would outsail and outgun any of her more likely, solitary adversaries. After his fight with *Serapis,* Jones would have demanded nothing less.

In the interest of diplomatic amity, Jones did not inform his allies that they were stupid. Instead, he played the role Morris begged of him. When the time came he handed over to Macarty-Macteigne a ceremonial sword of command, a sealed letter to the French admiral, and a logbook clad in morocco. As Jones had decided to overlook making any official entries, the logbook was empty. The letter to Vaudreuil was the result of a compulsion— an inability, after so many months of work on the ship, to resist advising the French on how to arm, equip, sail, fight, and repair her. As for giving up the sword, it was the first time in his career he had been obliged to do any such thing. The gesture, in fact, made his stomach turn; he imagined he felt worse than Pearson did when he lost *Serapis.* The British captain, after all, lost his command after a long and satisfying fight. Jones lost his at the stroke of a pen.

Two weeks earlier, word had arrived that a British army under Cornwallis had surrendered to the French and Americans at Yorktown. With everyone else, Jones rejoiced at the news. But in another sense, the victory could not have come at a worse time. After *America*, it would take at least many months to wheedle a worthy command out of Congress. With so few ships available on the left side of the Atlantic, he might well have to return to Europe. Would the war last another year?

He would have preferred to be sick, but instead grinned genially, like the father of the bride. He let the smile lapse only later, when it was dark enough for the fireworks. As the rockets trailed sparks across the river and the flares erupted on the banks, he felt that insistent reflectiveness rise in him again. For although the surrender of *America* was a national calamity, did the people not gasp and clap at the flaming pinwheels? Was there not a universal convulsion of good will when the French warships saluted again, and the battery at Fort Pierce replied, and then toasts all around? Was not every uniformed shoulder whooped and pounded by civilian admirers? For all this, Jones's name was on everyone's lips. For this surrender, a victory celebration. Win a ship, lose a ship—did anyone know the difference?

Rebeccah appeared beside him, her face glowing intermittently under cascades of sparks. She did not touch him, but instead stood very close. Jones took her arm and, for a moment, allowed himself to see his spectacle through her eyes. This was no victory to him. But whatever it was, it happened before the grand audience he had so persistently imagined. With that, he glimpsed the possibility of his happiness, and allowed himself to celebrate.

AUTHOR'S AFTERWORD

BETWEEN TWO FIRES is in same mode of highly embroidered fact as its predecessor, *The Eighteenth Captain*. Those interested in learning about my primary sources and about the historicity of my hero, John Severence, are encouraged to consult the latter book—and better yet, to buy it.

This novel reflects the very real coincidence in time of Jones's battle with *Serapis* and General Sullivan's march against the Iroquois. I have taken some liberties with the timing of other events in the book. Jones actually remained in Europe, soaking up popular adulation for his victory, until February of 1781. *America* was not launched until late in 1782. It was actually in these years, and not in the time of *The Eighteenth Captain*, that Jones wooed Madame de Lowendahl. While Rebeccah Shays did not exist, Jones had a number of similar admirers in Portsmouth and elsewhere.

Henriette d'Barlejou is pure fiction. She is, however, just the sort of distaff artiste Jones would have admired. Her goal—to reconstruct the face of Christ—is based on my vague recollections of similar material in the library of the Benedictine monastery at Melk, Austria. For me, such a project perfectly exemplifies the rationalization of faith and art so typical of eighteenth-century thought.

Joseph Two Fires himself is an invention, but my portrayals of him and his people are based on ethnographic accounts. Certain aspects of his character were further inspired by Senecah people I have known. His most dramatic act in the story—turning the tide of the battle between *Bon Homme Richard* and *Serapis* by dropping a grenade through an open hatch—did happen. The name of the man who actually did it is William Hamilton, a Scotsman. He deserves to be remembered.

Severence's account of Sullivan's march is an amalgam of information from the campaign dairies of the soldiers who participated. According to Whittemore's biography, John Sullivan's feelings about deism were so strong that he once wrote a thirty-page tract against it "in less than a day." Sadly, that officers and men of Sullivan's army flayed Indian bodies and used their skin for boot leather is not fiction. In his diary, Lieutenant William Barton of the New Jersey Brigade reports that, on Monday, August 30, 1779, "At the request of Major Platt, [we] sent out a small party to look for some of the dead Indians—returned without finding them. Toward noon they found them and skinned two of them from their hips down for boot legs; one pair for the Major the other for myself." Sergeant Thomas Roberts, also of the New Jersey contingent, writes that "[T]his morning Our trupes found 2 Indians and Skin thear Legs & Drest them for Leggins this morning."

By the same token, it is well attested that the Iroquois engaged in ritual mutilation of prisoners. Warriors necessarily had to make their peace with this possibility before they went off to fight. My fictionalized account adds to or embellishes a number of details, but I had no need to invent the most sensational of the atrocities committed by both sides.

An etymological note: there is good reason to believe that the word "okay" (or "OK") did not yet exist in late eighteenth-century American speech. It is conventionally held to be an acronym for a jokey variant of the phrase "all correct" ("ol korrect"), supposedly first used in a Boston newspaper in 1839. Corresponding as it did to Martin Van Buren's popular nickname Old Kinderhook, it became widely used in the Presidential reelection campaign of the following year.

It should be noted, however, that the white characters in the novel do not use the word. Rather, I put it in the mouths of the Indians, and that primarily for colloquial effect. Only later, on a visit to the famed OK Corral in Tombstone, Arizona, did I happily learn that the Choctaw tribe did have a word very much like our "okay," meaning something very similar to what we mean by it. Historians may argue over whether American English "okay" is somehow traceable to the Choctaw version. For my purposes here, though, it is entirely conceivable that Two Fires' people could have encountered the word either directly or indirectly.

Finally, I want to acknowledge my debt to a number of friends and collaborators. Sandy List's talents, both as a writer and an editor, greatly improved the manuscripts for both this book and *The Eighteenth Captain*. Bill Benson, who executed the cover painting for the latter, also did a magnificent job on Henriette's sketchbook drawings here. I am also looking forward to further work with the talented people at McBooks Press, who have obstinately continued to believe in these stories. My deepest thanks to all.

EPILOGUE

THE WHITE OFFICER didn't do a bad job putting me up here, and giving me the things I'd need in the dwelling place of Hawenneyu. But he forgot to tell the Great Spirit I was coming, forgot to bundle the maple twigs and burn tobacco at my grave. Just like you don't come to your neighbor's house without an invitation, you don't want to show up in heaven unannounced.

The white officer also forgot to come back and bury my body. This was an even worse oversight, because it encouraged the spirit to hang around the village making trouble, instead of taking the road west. In my case, it wasn't quite so bad, since there was no place left to haunt. But it isn't easy finding your way without even a door to start from.

When I was young I was taught what to expect of heaven. It was a green valley, with snow-capped mountains all around and streams running through it. There were no storms there, and no winter. The leaves were always tender, like they were new in the spring, but all the fruits of every season were always ready, the maple syrup and the raspberry and the grape, all together. We were told that heaven was full of game, with fawns that always kept their starry coats and never grew up. The bear was there, sticking his great snout into hives where the honey is always restored overnight. And Brother Wolf was there, with his belly never empty and the night always full of his songs. And here are more things I heard about heaven: the air there was warm, but never hot. Everyone who had ever lived was there, but it wasn't crowded. When you walked toward the mountains, they got closer, but you never seemed to reach them. Instead, you see villages filled with people from all the Six Nations. Every village had a great fire burning in the longhouse, but there were no piles of firewood.

And there were baskets of fish that never spoiled, and pots of grain that never emptied, and a deerskin stretched on every rack.

This sounded pleasant. So after a few long, dull years up in the scaffold, I decided to go up to heaven anyway, even if they didn't expect me.

At first I just went west—the direction where they always said the Great Spirit lived. But this only brought me to the Ohio country, and to a place that wasn't heaven but instead called "Cleveland." Being a spirit, I could stop and watch them building this town. I could see it swelling out along staves of metal that ran all over Turtle Island, and towers like the cliffs of mountains heaving up from the center, and a blanket of blue air settling down over the towers. This was interesting, but it wasn't the dwelling place of Hawenneyu.

Then I saw great, straight ribbons of vapor crossing the sky for miles, put up there by white metal birds who laid smoke instead of eggs. And I thought, maybe these are the roads to heaven our elders keep talking about. So I followed one of the birds, going west and also up, higher and higher into the sky.

Time and again I flew inside banks of clouds, and came out hoping to see my destination. And though I traveled for what seemed like forever, I never arrived. Being dead, it was not as if I needed food, of course. But spirits can still get bored. After a while I learned to curse those metal birds, who cut up the sky with their noise and their smoke and led souls no place.

So I gave up and came back to my scaffold. Sitting there through more years, with not much to do, I had a lot of time to listen. I heard a lot of different sounds. First, there was the tooting and clanking of a strange kind of animal. By their sound you could follow them through the hills, making their way through the valleys, their voices echoing off the hills. After that, I heard them as a buzzing, like something insects made, only much louder. Then they became like a herd of buffalo, moving back and forth, thundering like great phlegmy giants clearing their throats. The roar of them all started to mix together, like the rushing of water, until they drowned out the sounds of the real creeks and the waterfalls. Between the tooting and the buzzing down here and the thundering of the metal birds above, it seemed like the forest lost its voice. Even a ghost couldn't hear itself think.

The forest changed too. The trees all disappeared one day, in the blink of an eye, and then grew up again, except they were spindly and sick, and nobody burned the forest floor anymore to clear the brush. All the good game disappeared, leaving only the vermin, and one kind of deer that bred itself out of control, like the Yangeese. The blue air I saw over Cleveland was everywhere, drunk thirstily by the weeds and the vines, which then strangled the trees. Night was lonelier because the fireflies were gone.

Of my people, the Gweugwehono, I saw nothing. They went away as Sullivan came and must have taken up someplace else. And seeing what happened to the land of our fathers, so humbled and so reduced, I must say I don't blame them. Sitting there, I felt my dried, moth-eaten heart beating angrily, and the bones of my fist closing, and yelled, "See what they've done to the land! Let the whites have it, then. The joke's on them!"

The joke's on you. But here's another joke, white man, as you sit in your suffocating town with your little hard white clothes and your bland white mush food: someone else is coming. Someone else from across the ocean is coming to take what's left of Turtle Island from you. He will make you a memory. He will take it all, and leave your lives to the museum cases.

You, too, will end up a ghost, sitting right here beside me. And you know what? I can't wait.